Immortals:
The Redeeming

Other books in the Immortals series:

THE CALLING by Jennifer Ashley
THE DARKENING by Robin T. Popp
THE AWAKENING by Joy Nash
THE GATHERING by Jennifer Ashley

Other books by Jennifer Ashley:

HIGHLANDER EVER AFTER
THE MAD, BAD DUKE
JUST ONE SIP (Anthology)
PENELOPE & PRINCE CHARMING
CHRISTMAS CARDS FROM THE EDGE (Anthology)
CONFESSIONS OF A LINGERIE ADDICT
THE CARE & FEEDING OF PIRATES
THE PIRATE HUNTER
THE PIRATE NEXT DOOR
PERILS OF THE HEART

JENNIFER ASHLEY

IMMORTALS:
THE REDEEMING

LOVE SPELL   LOVE SPELL   NEW YORK CITY

LOVE SPELL®

September 2008

Published by

Dorchester Publishing Co., Inc.
200 Madison Avenue
New York, NY 10016

ISBN-13: 978-0-7394-9868-2

Printed in the United States of America.

ACKNOWLEDGMENTS

Special thanks go to my editor, Leah Hultenschmidt, for her patience, encouragement, and support on this project, and for allowing me the time to make it the best it could be. Thanks also go to the other two Immortals authors, Joy Nash and Robin Popp, for their talent, support, and creative brainstorming. We make a great team!

I'd like to dedicate this book to Trudy, an extraordinary woman who was a true lover of romance, and who passed away while I was writing this novel. Thank you, Trudy, for all your support and love, and for being so proud of me....

Immortals:
The Redeeming

CHAPTER ONE

Los Angeles, September

Samantha hated being demon bait.

She sat at a high table near the bar in Merrick's demon club, wearing a form-hugging, short black dress, black thigh-high stockings, and four-inch heels she'd had to practice walking in. It had been her job for the last two weeks to perch on a high stool, cross her long legs, and wait for Merrick or one of his demons to offer her the illegal drug Mindglow. So far no one had pushed her to do anything more than order a second martini.

Tonight was typical for Merrick's. Every table was full, the Venice beach clientele waiting eagerly for the demons to come in and choose their marks for the night. A few people sat alone at the bar, one of them a man with hunched shoulders who stared down at the line of empty shot glasses in front of him.

At eleven o'clock, the demons strolled out of the back rooms. They were beautiful and sensual, greeting guests with smiles filled with promise. Samantha felt their auras like dark purple smoke as they touched their victims, those whose life essences they would taste that night.

Laws in all states said that demons had to have humans' permission to feed on their life essence—that elusive substance that made a being alive rather than a collection of biological parts. Like the laws that kept vampires from draining their victims dry, likewise demons could not siphon off all life essence and leave a person dead. Demons constantly sought ways around the "permission" clause, and the black market for life essence was huge and profitable. Hence Mindglow, the demon date-rape drug, and Samantha's LAPD assignment.

Merrick, the owner, glided to her table, dressed as usual in a pristine gray Armani suit. "Ah, Sam, I knew you couldn't resist coming back to Merrick's. Is tonight the night I convince you to partake in the glory of me?"

Her nostrils curled at the unmistakable scent of the netherworld, something normal humans couldn't smell. It was the tiniest bit of sulfur and dry air, the scent of power and arrogance.

Modern demons didn't consider themselves evil, unlike the Old Ones, powerful demons who'd walked the earth in centuries past. Samantha had once fought an Old One—not by herself, but with a group of witches and Immortal warriors—and she could attest to the evilness of the ancient ones. The whole experience still gave her nightmares.

The demons at Merrick's were lesser demons who'd learned to adapt to living in the human world. If they stepped out of line, they could be arrested, carted off to special jail cells, and tried for crimes like taking too much life essence or coercing their marks to use Mindglow.

Samantha pasted on a vacant smile as she looked up at Merrick. "Maybe."

He had dark eyes, like most demons, all the better to suck in his victims with. *Not victims,* Merrick would insist. *Clients.*

He traced her cheek. "I live in hope."

"I'm still not sure. I mean—you're hot." She let her gaze rove over his body. "But I'm so nervous."

"You never have to worry with me, Sam, my dear."

Merrick's touch became softer, trailing down her bare shoulder. "I can make it as pleasurable as you like, or if you like it to hurt . . ." He broke off suggestively as his finger moved to her cleavage.

"No," she said quickly. "I'm not into that."

"No, you're obviously a sweet, gentle soul." His pupils were wide, eyes black all the way across, hungry. "I can tell by the way you dress."

As she seethed at his arrogance, Samantha's half-demon senses picked up the pheromones he sent her way. He was trying to relax her, arouse her, make her pliant. She kept cool by remembering the young woman her partner Logan had found in the alley not far from here, her body drained of life, helped along with Mindglow.

"I'm scared," Samantha said. "I know it's supposed to be the best experience ever, but I just don't know."

Merrick moved behind her to massage the nape of her neck. "You know, my pet, I've let you sit at my best table two weeks running while you make up your mind. Most would have taken the plunge by now. What must I do to convince you?"

Offer me the Mindglow, already, damn it.

"It's not like I don't *pay*."

"Yes, but, sweetheart, there are so many others clamoring to get in. I have to make them wait while you sit here night after night. It's bad for business, my darling."

She pretended to pout. "Fine, I'll sit at the bar then."

"If you want. My bartender likes you—I'll have him give you a couple of drinks on the house."

She made what she hoped was an inane giggle. "Are you trying to get me drunk so I'll go upstairs with you?"

"Of course not," Merrick purred. "It's not as good when you drink too much—for either of us."

"What about drugs? Is it better when you're high?"

"No." Merrick's voice was firm. "It's much better when you're aware and alert and feel everything."

"I could have sworn I heard it was better when you have a buzz on."

"You heard wrong." Merrick breathed in her ear. "But there is something that enhances the experience, makes you feel less afraid. It's not a drug, more like an herbal tea."

Oh, frigging finally.

"What's that?" she asked.

"Come upstairs, and I'll show you."

Not really the best scenario. Upstairs, Samantha might get herself trapped before Logan could get to her. She was strong, and she had a gun in her large beaded purse, but even so she couldn't take on a dozen demons by herself.

"I still don't know . . ." She found her face pinched in a viselike grip, Merrick forcing her to look him in the eye.

"What are you trying to pull, Samantha?"

Her first instinct was to roll away from him, giving him a kick in the balls along the way, but she held back. "Nothing. Can't I wait until I feel better?"

She felt his pheromones drifting over her, trying to sway her to him. She resisted, and knew he felt it.

"All right, damn you," he growled. "But only because I like you so much."

He snapped his fingers and one of the demon waiters came over. "One dose," Merrick said to him.

Samantha tried to keep triumph from her eyes. She'd have to sit still until the waiter actually came down with the stuff. Then Logan and his backup could raid the club, and Samantha could go home and slip into more sensible shoes.

Merrick smiled his most charming smile, but she sensed his arousal, his growing hunger. "You won't regret it, you know. Because you're so special to me, I'll make it extra sweet—"

At a table near the door, a woman screamed.

Merrick jerked his head around as two well-dressed

male demons near the club's entrance suddenly burst out of their human forms. Their clothes ripped as their muscles bulged and their bodies elongated into leathery skinned monstrosities. Everyone was screaming and scrambling to get away from them.

"What the . . ." Merrick gaped as the two demons knocked over tables and grabbed his clients with powerful swiftness.

At the same time the hunched-over deadbeat at the bar came to life. A deadbeat no more, he unfolded himself into seven feet of warrior in a brown leather duster, a bronze sword in each hand. His granite-hard face bore a pentacle tattoo high on his cheekbone, and his hair was flame red. He glanced at Samantha with eyes like patches of blue sky, and her mouth went dry as dust. *Tain.*

Merrick didn't notice in the confusion. He yanked Samantha out of the chair and pushed her toward the back of the club. "You get upstairs and stay there. I'll take care of this."

Samantha tottered on her too-high heels, the surprise of the demons' attack overridden by the shock she'd just gotten. Tain couldn't be here, he was off wandering the world trying to find himself or else in that magical realm they called Ravenscroft, wasn't he?

She hadn't seen him in a year and a half, not after he walked off after the battle in Seattle without even saying good-bye. Samantha had been sure he'd forgotten all about her. Now he turned up here, out of the blue, in a club she just happened to be staking out.

"Go on," Merrick snapped, still trying to push her in front of him. "Get upstairs and stay safe. I'd hate to see your cute little ass reduced to little tiny pieces."

The club employees were trying to herd their clients in the same direction, while the demons proceeded to wreak havoc. Samantha shoved her hand into her purse and pulled out her gun.

Merrick stared at it in amazement. "What the hell are you doing with that?"

"It's your lucky night, Merrick," Samantha said.

He gaped a second longer, and then rage mottled his face. "I don't believe it. You're a cop. You double-crossing little bitch, you're too edible to be a cop. I even *liked* you."

Logan and his men burst through the front door, weapons drawn. She saw Logan toss aside his weapon and morph into his wolf form, snarling as the demons leapt at him and the room filled with gunfire.

Tain lifted his swords as people screamed and dove for cover. Samantha watched in a daze as he crossed them above his head. Then white lightning streaked from the swords across the room and straight into the snarling demons. The demons flew high into the air, slammed against the ceiling, and fell to the floor, stone dead.

For a moment the club went quiet. Logan stood over the dead demons, his lupine nose wrinkling in distaste, his clothes scattered where he'd ripped out of them. Samantha looked up at Tain, but his gaze was remote, blank, like he didn't see the bar or Samantha, or the demons he'd just killed. The rest of the clientele huddled in little clumps, trying to decide what had just happened.

Merrick was the first to recover. He swung around, his eyes blazing red, and tried to kick the pistol out of Samantha's hand. She dodged him at the last second, keeping hold of the gun, and he punched her full in the face.

Samantha's head snapped back, but she kept her weapon on him and fired.

Merrick tumbled across a table with the force of the shot, but demons were hard to kill. Merrick righted himself, blood all over his Armani suit, and went for her again. Samantha leveled her gun at him, but Tain shoved himself between them. Merrick looked down at the crossed swords pinning his throat.

Merrick snarled and shifted to his demon form, completing the ruin of his two-thousand-dollar suit. He lunged, but Tain almost negligently slammed his swords into Merrick's neck, and the demon gurgled and slid to the floor in a pool of blood.

Samantha's face throbbed. Blood streamed from her nose and a deep cut in her cheek where Merrick had punched her, but she barely noticed. Tain stepped back, lowering swords that were stained black with demon blood, as though he knew the danger was over and he no longer needed to be on alert. Watching him change from vicious warrior to bystander again was unnerving. On the other side of the room, Logan had resumed his human form, unworriedly dressing again.

"Samantha."

It was Merrick, still on the floor. He'd returned to his human form, his beautiful suit in shreds, his dark hair matted with blood. Blood streamed from the gash on his neck, but he was still alive. Demons were *damn* hard to kill.

Samantha limped to Merrick, trying not to slip in his blood. She pulled out her handcuffs with shaking fingers and snapped them around Merrick's wrists. "Merrick, I'm arresting you for possession of Mindglow. You have the right to remain silent . . ." Anger flared in Merrick's eyes, but he was in no condition to argue.

Samantha felt a warmth behind her and turned to look up at the man she hadn't seen in more than a year. *One year, four months, and one week.*

The last time had been in the battle with the Old One, a vicious butt-kicker of a demon who'd wanted to watch all of humankind suffer just for fun. Tain had been the demon's follower—maddened, powerful, tortured. Samantha had helped set him free and restore his sanity, but she wondered if he would ever be healed.

"Tain," she whispered.

He placed his fingers on her face. She felt a sharp pain,

then a pull that was almost sensual. Warmth pooled in her belly, and her nipples pearled against her skintight dress.

She recognized the feeling—she'd had it last year when Tain had healed her broken arm. He'd done it dispassionately, while she'd been bathed in a glow of his power that was nearly orgasmic.

He lifted his hand away, and she touched her face, finding it whole and uncut, the blood dry. He said nothing but flicked his blue gaze over her skin as though looking for more wounds.

"Do you remember me?" she asked him.

His unruly red hair reached his collar, strands brushing his impossibly handsome face. She'd met his four brothers, all of them breathtaking, but Tain had appealed to her the most, with his fine-sculpted face and lake-blue eyes.

He also had a presence that could knock her off her feet. Her knees wanted to bend, not so she could worship him, but so she could press her face to the fly of his jeans and feel what lay beneath. . . .

He pinched her chin between his fingers. Merrick had done the same, but while Merrick's presumption had angered her, Tain only stunned her to silence.

Tain leaned down and growled into her ear, with the faint Welsh lilt she remembered, "Stay away from me."

He released her, turned on his heel, and strode out of the club.

CHAPTER TWO

"Exactly what the hell happened in there?" Logan asked Samantha hours later.

They sat in Lieutenant McKay's office at the paranormal division headquarters downtown, Logan lounging in his chair, long legs stretched out in front of him. Logan had sand-colored hair, a tall, lean body, a hard face, and golden-brown eyes.

"Merrick's rivals decided to stage a hit tonight of all nights," Samantha said.

Demon gangs regularly fought among themselves and expected the police to keep out of it. Vampires did the same, although these days a vamp called Septimus kept most things under control in this part of the world.

"No, I meant the other guy," Logan said, twining his hands behind his head. "I saw the other demons slide into the place, which was why we came tearing up."

"Bad timing," Lieutenant McKay agreed. She'd been a cop for fifteen years, and was one-quarter Sidhe but hadn't inherited their height or much of their powerful magic. She had a small, wiry body, black skin, and close-cropped, tightly curled hair that she liked to dye orange red. "But Samantha had the presence of mind not to let Merrick get away in the fuss. We have him on possession of Mindglow at least."

"But not dealing, unfortunately." Samantha sighed. "He can claim his rivals planted anything we find in the club."

"True, but he'll be cagey about it even if we can't get a conviction. Merrick will be out of the Mindglow picture for a while."

"Can we get back to the other guy?" Logan interrupted. He sat forward, bringing the heels of his motorcycle boots to the floor. "I've never seen magic like that. Plus he nearly sliced Merrick's head off like it was butter, and demons have damn thick necks."

"He's an Immortal," Samantha said, not looking at him.

Logan blinked. "He's a what?"

"An Immortal warrior. There are five of them, half brothers. Tain is the youngest."

Both Logan and McKay stared at her in surprise. "And you know this, how?" Logan asked.

"I've met him before."

Logan's sandy brows climbed up his forehead. "Oh, really? Is that why he jumped in front of you and tried to cut Merrick in half?"

"He doesn't like demons. One tortured him for hundreds of years and drove him a little insane." *The understatement of the year.* "It had nothing to do with me."

"So he just happened to be in the right place at the right time? Sure, Samantha."

Samantha shrugged. "Maybe he got a tip-off that Merrick's would be attacked tonight."

"He not only killed the demons but got Merrick, too. I'd say he had some kind of agenda."

Samantha tried to keep her expression neutral. "Why don't you bring him in and question him, then?"

"Why don't you?" Logan countered. "He knows you, and I'd be interested in what he has to say."

"So would I," Lieutenant McKay said. "By law, killing demons is murder, though we can make a case that he did it in defense of innocent humans. If he knows something about Merrick or his rivals, I want to hear it."

Samantha thought back to Tain's hot touch on her skin, his voice grating, *Stay away from me.*

"I think you're both optimistic," Samantha said. "We're not exactly friends."

"Try anyway," were the lieutenant's encouraging words. "I'd like to see him within the week. Tonight didn't go exactly as we hoped, but it could have been worse. Go home and sleep, both of you. We'll clean up the mess in the morning."

Dismissed, Logan and Samantha went to their lockers, collected their things, and walked out together. The Los Angeles night was cool, September finally taking the edge off the shimmering summer heat.

Logan peered at her as they made for the parking lot. "Are you all right? You took a good punch in there."

Samantha put her hand to her face where Merrick's rings had torn it. Tain's magic had completely healed the flesh. "I'm fine. I just need some rest."

"We could go for pizza, maybe a movie? Some mindless, fake violence to help us forget about the mindless, real violence?"

She managed a grin. "Sounds tempting. Thanks, Logan, but I'm ready for a hot shower and a soft bed."

"Fair enough. I suppose I can order in pizza and find mindless violence by myself on TV. See you tomorrow."

"See you."

They'd reached Samantha's car by then, a used Toyota pickup. No glamour cars for detectives in the LAPD paranormal division. Logan rode a Harley that he lovingly tinkered with in his spare time. Days off saw him on his Harley flying through mountains and the open desert far to the west of L.A.

Samantha's apartment was in a fairly decent complex in west L.A. with a pool and cherry trees that bloomed in the spring. Her mother had invited her to live at home in

Pasadena, but her demon father had just returned after years of being estranged from her mother, and Samantha wanted to give them their privacy. She was still coming to grips with getting to know her father and finding she didn't hate him.

Her apartment welcomed her with art posters that gave the generic walls some color, comfortable furniture, and a short-haired black-and-white cat called Pickles. As she closed the door Pickles leapt from the back of the sofa to the kitchen counter, purring like crazy.

"Cupboard love," Samantha said as she scratched him under the chin. *"I love you—so feed me."*

Pickles shamelessly butted his head against her hand until she picked him up and cuddled him. She set him down again, and he raced expectantly to his food bowl, which she filled with dry cat food.

"I slave, you master," she quipped, but her heart wasn't in it.

While Pickles ate, Samantha showered, letting the hot water and steam in the glass-walled stall relax her. The aroma of soap and lavender permeated the bathroom, and for a time, she leaned her head on the glass and breathed it in.

She knew that when she went to bed she'd see him in her mind—the tall man she'd been dreaming of for a year. She also knew that seeing him tonight hadn't been such a big coincidence—Tain's brother Adrian owned a house in Malibu where his other brother Hunter and his wife were currently living, and Tain visited them from time to time. It was more surprising that she hadn't run across him before this.

Tain and his four brothers had been created eons ago, she'd been told, each born of a goddess and a human man. Their purpose had been to keep the world safe from the most dangerous creatures—the Old Ones—ancient demons and vampires. But seven hundred years ago, Tain had been captured, hidden, and endlessly tortured by an

Old One called Kekhsut, and his brothers and the witches they'd fallen in love with had battled the demon and gotten Tain free.

Tain had been so maddened by the demon's torture—flaying him, waiting for his Immortal body to heal, then doing it again—that by that time he hadn't wanted to be free. Tain had tried to destroy the world to end his own torment instead, and only the combined effort of his brothers, and somehow Samantha, had restored him to freedom and sanity.

Now her boss wanted to interview Tain. Perfect. Samantha supposed she could call Leda, Tain's brother's wife, find out whether Tain was staying with them, and get Leda or Hunter to take him down to the police station. She wouldn't even have to attend the interview—Logan and McKay could ask him about his knowledge of the demon underworld by themselves.

Samantha shut off the water determinedly but stood dripping for a moment, unable to think about anything but Tain's blue eyes and the warmth in her body when he'd healed her face. *Damn.*

She started shivering, grabbed her towels, and dried off. She turbaned her hair in one towel and wrapped another around her torso and walked out to the kitchen, craving lots of hot coffee and all the microwave food she could handle.

Tain was sitting at her kitchen table.

Samantha stifled a scream and jumped back, the towel tumbling from her head. Tain had folded his big body into her kitchen chair, his unruly red hair rolling back from his forehead. He rubbed Pickles under the chin with a broad forefinger, and her traitorous cat purred up a storm.

"What are you doing in here?" she demanded.

Tain's blue gaze took in every inch of her towel-clad body. The gaze unnerved her, and not only because she was all but naked. She saw darkness behind the blue, a hint of the madness that maybe had been too engraved on him to be easily erased. She'd sensed that at the club, and it was stronger here, alone with him.

"I wanted to talk to you," he said. His voice held the note of Celtic peoples, slightly musical with faintly rolled *r*'s.

"You know, most people knock on the front door," she said, her nervousness making her voice sharp. "Or are the rules different for Immortals?"

"I did knock."

"I couldn't hear you. I was in . . ."

"The shower." He raked his gaze over her again, and she tightened her hold on the towel. "You left the door unlocked."

"No, I . . ." He might be right; she'd been so tired she'd slammed the door, thrown down her stuff, and started in with the cat-feeding ritual without thinking. "Even so, that doesn't mean you get to walk right in."

"I came because I need help, and you were the only one I could think of to ask."

She stopped in surprise. "What, your four Immortal brothers and their kick-ass witch wives aren't good enough anymore?"

"Not that kind of help. I need police help."

"I see." Water trickled down her face from her wet hair, and she impatiently wiped it away. "Stay there," she said, then hurried back to the bedroom and slammed the door.

When she emerged, dressed again, Tain was feeding Pickles tidbits from a can of cat treats. Pickles purred hard, his Geiger-counter buzz filling the room.

Last year during the battle Tain had lifted Samantha twenty feet off the ground with his magic, a drop that could have killed her. He'd set her down again only because she'd talked fast and hard at him, and he'd become intrigued by their banter. It unnerved her now to see the man who'd so terrified her sitting in her kitchen playing gently with her cat.

"His name's Pickles," she said, her voice strained. "Because he likes to chew on them."

"That's not what he thinks his name is," Tain answered.

"What does he think it is?"

"Master of All He Sees."

Biting back a hysterical laugh, Samantha drew out the chair across from him and sank into it. "I thought your brother Hunter had the affinity with animals."

"Don't all cats think that's what they should be called?"

He sounded perfectly sane, and except for that spark buried deep in his eyes he looked sane. He'd tossed a long leather coat on her couch and sat in a black short-sleeved T-shirt. His forearms were mottled with scars, though they didn't look as bad as Samantha feared they would. Silky, red-gold hair had grown in across his skin, disguising many of the marks of torture.

"Why were you at Merrick's tonight?" she asked abruptly.

"Two reasons. One of them to see you."

Tain's eyes were steady when he said it, no lying. So much for Logan's theory that he'd been there because he'd known in advance about the demon attack.

Pickles put his paw on Tain's hand, and Tain resumed rubbing the demanding cat's jaw. "I saw you go into Merrick's last night. That surprised me—I hadn't put you down as a woman who'd seek demon sex, until I noticed your partner lingering down the street. I got there early tonight and planned to follow you when you left."

"How did a demon club even let you in? What, they didn't notice you were an Immortal warrior with two very long swords?"

He didn't rise to her banter. "I can hide my aura well if

I want to. My swords, too, which are short swords, not long. Late Roman bronze."

"I'm sure you have a fascinating collection of weapons."

He ignored that, too. "You aren't very good at pretending to be a demonwhore. You smiled at Merrick but with loathing in your eyes."

"Yes, well, I'm not fond of that part of the job. I don't think Merrick noticed, though. He was too busy staring at my cleavage."

"I didn't like him doing that, but I can't much blame him."

He really shouldn't look at her like that, and she really shouldn't respond so easily to him, either.

"It was just to entice Merrick," Samantha said. "It almost worked."

"He never would have touched you. I'd have stopped him even if those demons hadn't attacked."

Her heart gave a strange flip. "And ruined a perfectly good undercover investigation? I was going to arrest him as soon as he brought me the Mindglow. I was *this* close." She held up her forefinger and thumb.

"Merrick is dangerous. Leave him alone."

The flutter turned to irritation. "I arrested him, in case you didn't notice. He's in custody at a hospital, although he has the best lawyer in Los Angeles, so I'm sure he'll go home as soon as he's healed. Demons make terrific lawyers."

Tain watched her with hard eyes. "You should stay away from him."

"That assignment is over for now, so it's a moot point. You said you wanted my help. With what?"

Tain dug out a few more treats for her greedy cat and watched while Pickles ate them. "You've been staking out the demon clubs in Venice and Santa Monica, and so have I. That's the second reason I went to Merrick's tonight."

Samantha rubbed her damp hair. "Wait, wait, wait. I'm

confused. Before you left the club, you distinctly told me to leave you alone. But what you really meant to say was, 'Samantha, can you help me out?'"

He wouldn't look at her. He studied his hands, the white scars on the backs of his fingers stark against his brown skin. "I don't want to need your help. I never wanted to see you again after Seattle."

"After I saved your butt in Seattle, you mean."

To her surprise he gave her a hint of a smile, one that made his eyes warm like a summer sunrise. If she'd thought him handsome before, the smile made him devastating.

He exuded power and sensuality, all of it contained as he sat at her table teasing her cat. What would it be like to make love to a man like him, that heady power tempered for her? He'd warm her in the dark while she waited for the flash of smile that made him absolutely beautiful. She didn't want to admit it to herself, but she was demon enough that the hint of darkness she sensed inside him would make it all the more exciting.

"My Immortal brothers had something to do with defeating the Old One," he said. "And the goddesses."

"So they helped me out a little. You left, you know, before I was able to thank you for healing my arm."

The smile faded. "Nothing I didn't do for anyone else."

"Adrian told me your innate talent was healing. I'm surprised you're not running through the world curing AIDS and cancer and everything else."

"It doesn't work quite like that. If it did, I would."

They studied each other for a moment in silence, as though a barrier stretched between them that neither wanted to cross first.

"Let's get back to the question at hand," Samantha said. "What was it that you wanted my help with?"

His eyes flickered in relief at the change of subject. "In the last couple of months several demon prostitutes have gone missing in the area around Merrick's club. These are very young women, freelance, not associated with the clubs as far as I know. But they're disappearing, and I want to know why."

Samantha's surprise returned. She got up and started the coffee, definitely needing a caffeine fix.

"What has you interested?" she asked over her shoulder. "I'd think you were the last person worried about the well-being of demon prostitutes."

"Because I was tortured mercilessly by Kehksut, now I should hate all demonkind?" he asked in a deceptively mild voice.

"The thought occurred."

She waited for the machine to finish and took two mugs of steaming coffee to the table. "I have sweetener if you want it."

Tain shook his head and took a sip.

"You *must* be all powerful," Samantha said as she watched the swallow move down his throat. "You didn't even have to blow on it."

She'd hoped to prod another smile from him, but his look turned grim. "If I wanted to destroy all demonkind in revenge I would have destroyed every demon in that club—the attackers, the defender, Merrick . . ."

He left it hanging and Samantha wondered whether, if he weren't sitting in her kitchen, he'd have added, "You."

"Good thing you needed my help, then," Samantha said. "And I looked good in that dress."

His eyes flickered over her again, although she'd put on a fairly shapeless T-shirt and loose jeans. "You did, yes."

Her body heated. She had no business thinking about sex with him, although she reasoned that as long as she kept it a fantasy, she was safe. Who wouldn't fantasize about a hard-bodied male with intense blue eyes and hair she longed to run her fingers through? A man who'd made her feel so incredible when he healed her she'd almost jumped his bones right there in the club?

"So why *are* you worried about these prostitutes?" she asked hastily. "They usually solicit for the clubs, for bosses like Merrick, although some go out on their own. As long as there's no actual sex involved, just people giving them money for the 'demon experience,' it's legal."

"Four girls have gone missing in the last two weeks," Tain said.

"That many? I haven't heard any disappearances reported, not that I necessarily would. L.A. is a big city, and the western division handles what goes on in Venice. I'd only be called in if a definite crime had been committed by or against a paranormal."

"I don't think the disappearances have been reported. If the young women are freelance, they won't have bosses to notice them gone."

"True, but it might not be such a mystery. They might have decided to move to a different part of the city, one or two might be lying low because they're pregnant or sick. It happens."

"Maybe, but it feels wrong. I can't explain more than that."

Samantha sighed and sat back. "If you were anyone else, I'd say you were worried for nothing, but since you're a big, bad Immortal, I won't. I learned the hard way what happens when I don't pay attention to an Immortal's 'feelings.' It won't hurt for me to look into it."

"Thank you."

His lips were stiff when he said it. She wondered how long Tain had debated with himself before he'd decided to find her and ask for help.

"Why come to me?" she asked. "Why not go to the police yourself? There are a couple dozen detectives in the paranormal division you could report to." Not only was Samantha a half demon, but she'd seen him when he was crazy and she'd been part of the force that saved him. Three strikes to keep him from wanting to ever see her again.

He met her gaze with his piercing one. "Because I knew you'd believe me."

Damn, his eyes were beautiful. They were like pieces of the sky, so blue you wanted to stare into them forever. She could picture his eyes up close, while she slanted her head to kiss him . . .

She made herself put aside the tantalizing idea. "Did you wait outside the police station and follow me home? You could have come inside and asked for me, you know."

"I didn't follow you."

That relieved her a little bit. She'd hadn't had the prickly feeling of someone behind her, although Tain could probably track like a panther. "How did you find me then? Magic?"

He actually chuckled as he lifted the coffee to his lips. "I just called Leda, and she gave me your address."

CHAPTER THREE

Tain leaned his head against the wall of his tiny shower and let the water beat on his body.

He hadn't wanted to go to Samantha. He'd never wanted to see her again, with her dark soul-searching eyes and beautiful face that floated in his dreams.

After I saved your butt in Seattle, she'd said, and he'd wanted to laugh and laugh.

She'd never know how well she'd saved him—that her voice and her words and her *presence* had begun to pull him out of the darkness in which he'd lived for centuries. She'd wrenched his focus away from the demon who'd held him captive, allowing his brothers to band together to save him.

At the end, everyone expected him to sweep Samantha into his arms and run away with her.

He'd barely been able to touch her. When he'd healed the arm she'd broken in the battle, their connection had been powerful. She'd melded to him in a way he hadn't felt in eons, their essences connecting while his magic knit her bones.

He'd sensed the tug of joy that surged through her body, and the temptation to make love to her there and then had overwhelmed him. He hadn't been able to get away from her fast enough.

A year and more had passed since that day in late May

when he'd finally gained his freedom. He'd thought the memories of the battle and Samantha would pass, but fifteen months later, they were as fresh as ever.

The water started to cool, his hot water reserve gone, but Tain remained in the shower, letting the needle-sharp spray batter his flesh. Samantha was a half demon, and he felt the siren call of that species pull at him. Never again, he'd vowed. He'd survived his captivity by retreating into madness, by grabbing on to the pain and twisting it into something that he could take.

Never again.

He shut off the faucet and stood with his forehead pressed against the wall, his naked body covered with beads of water. He wanted so much to feel her body, to press his mouth to her skin, to run his hands up the curves of her, to feel her nipples bead on his palms.

He indulged himself in the pleasure of these thoughts, but it wasn't long before the usual black memories of madness and pain seeped through to brush them away. He'd managed, with the help of his brothers, to heal somewhat over the past year. He'd learned to sleep sometimes without nightmares, to go still when the blackness punched at his gut like it had fighting the demons tonight, to breathe deeply until it left him.

But there were the times he didn't tell his brothers about, when he couldn't stop himself from folding into a ball, screaming with pain that threatened to squeeze the life out of him. He drifted to the bottom of his shower now, wrapping his arms around himself, not feeling the chill that crept over his wet skin. He watched the last of the water trickle down the drain, mesmerized by the liquid swirl.

You are mine, Kehksut had told him over and over. *You belong to me, body and soul. I will use you as I please, and you will love me for it.*

Tain's cheek burned, the pentagram tattoo that had been etched there when he came of age singeing him like a badge of fire. The tingle of the mark had saved him from being lost forever, had made him keep a tiny part of himself safe that Kehksut could never reach.

Samantha had reached that piece of him with her voice and her defiance. Then his brothers had torn him open the rest of the way and dragged him kicking and screaming into the light.

At the same time he savored his freedom, it brought pain and a weight of guilt. His brothers, damn the four of them, still loved him and watched over him. They wanted him to be all better, and it hurt him that he couldn't be back to "normal" for them.

About an hour later the blackness began to recede, and Tain climbed painfully to his feet. After episodes like this he was always surprised to find no blood on his body, that his scarred skin remained unbroken. He reached for a towel with a shaking hand and mopped water from his face.

The missing prostitutes had caught his attention because the situation was unusual, and he needed something unusual to focus on. Demons were not chaotic people; they were precise and methodic and rarely did anything without calculation. Four girls missing for no apparent reason showed a flaw in the system, and an anomaly could mean trouble to more than just the demons.

Tain regarded himself in the misted mirror as he plied the towel. Every inch of his body was scored with scars. His face had been spared, partly because of Tain's power-infused tattoo and partly because the demon wanted Tain's handsomeness to remain unmarred.

Because Tain had Immortal flesh, ever renewed, the scars had started fading into faint white lines. His seven-foot body rippled with muscle, unbroken. He was still a warrior.

He held the towel around his neck, staring at himself, remembering how Samantha had looked emerging from her bedroom in only a towel. Lush, long-legged, slim arms, compact breasts. Beautiful black eyes staring at him in startled amazement from under slick, wet, black hair.

He'd hardened then, and he was hardening now, his stem rising quickly from a thatch of dark red hair. His penis bore no scars, either—the other part of him the demon had never cut.

He'd wanted Samantha in Seattle, and he still wanted her. But the thought of sex was overlaid with so much pain he wasn't certain he'd ever be able to make love to a woman again. If he was with Samantha, would the pain make him crazy, and what would he do to her then?

Best to never find out. He'd thank her for her help and walk away. It was the only way he'd survive the contact with her.

Tain finished drying himself, dressed, and went out into the cool dawn streets of Los Angeles, but it took a long time for his erection to fade.

"Whatcha working on?" Logan asked. He turned a plastic chair around and straddled it backward, gazing at the profusion of files on Samantha's desk. "That's not the Mindglow case."

"No."

Samantha had been sifting through reports of missing demon girls, then looking up computer records to see if any of them had been arrested for soliciting. Tain's inquiry piqued her curiosity, and she thought it would do no harm to check into it.

She felt Logan's stare.

"How long have we been partners, Sam, my friend?"

"Almost a year."

"That's a long time in this job. I now know you better than I know my own sister. Something's happened, so spill it."

Samantha hesitated. During the terrible happenings

last year the police department had basically shut down and let the vampire and demon gangs fight each other on the L.A. streets without interference. Laws keeping vampire and demon activity under control went to hell, and people had died.

When Samantha had returned home from Seattle, the city had been busy trying to get back to normal—as normal as Los Angeles ever got—and Lieutenant McKay had begged Samantha to come back to work. They needed every detective they could get their hands on, she said. Samantha decided that diving back into what she was good at would help her recover, and besides, she needed the paycheck.

McKay had paired her up with Logan, who'd moved to L.A. from Minnesota at about the same time. Logan was long-legged, narrow-hipped, laid-back, and just the person Samantha needed to spend her ten-hour shifts with. He never pried and never asked nosy questions; he just worked on cases or drove them around the city with the quiet enjoyment of someone who liked being on the road.

Logan was a werewolf, from a pack in Minnesota that he never talked about. Werewolves weren't Samantha's specialty, so she didn't know very much about them, but she did know that they didn't move so far from their pack without good reason. It was difficult emotionally for a werewolf to leave the close-knit confines of his family, and yet here was Logan, whistling tunes and driving Samantha around L.A.

Samantha had found herself easily making friends with Logan, not telling him all her secrets but gradually getting through the fears that had swirled through her since Seattle. But she'd never been able to mention Tain.

"So this Immortal guy," Logan said as Samantha started closing the folders. "Do you know where to start looking for him?"

"No." Tain had left her apartment that night without disclosing where he was staying, saying she could leave a message with Leda if she needed to. "But I talked to him."

Logan's brows rose. "When was this?"

"Last night after I got home."

"And you've kept this little piece of info to yourself, why?"

She busied herself putting the folders into a neat stack. "I don't think he knows anything about Merrick's gang wars, or cares very much. He'll gladly let demons kill other demons."

"Shouldn't you let McKay question him before you decide that?"

Samantha slammed the last folders to the pile. "If he knew about Merrick and his Mindglow, he would have told me, I know that much. Or he'd have killed Merrick all the way without batting an eye. If you'll stop second-guessing me and buy me a pizza, I'll give you what he *did* tell me."

Samantha knew it would take her too much time to find the needle in the haystack Tain was looking for, and she trusted Logan enough to ask for his help. Plus, Logan had a curiosity that made him a good investigator, a willingness to do what it took to get the job done.

Logan bought her lunch at a pizza place across the street, and over the pepperoni and sausage, Samantha told him about Tain's request.

Logan listened with interest. "We should ask Merrick if he's seen anything."

"He's still in the hospital, but the D.A.'s office already dismissed the case, because they said they don't have anything that will stick. McKay and I had time to ask Merrick only one question before his lawyer got there, and he didn't even answer that."

"We don't have to make it an official inquiry," Logan suggested. "Just a friendly chat. What hospital?"

"You're saying *we*."

"Doing Mindglow stakeouts for months on end is getting on my nerves. I need a hobby. Besides, if the girls worked the streets near Merrick's, what's to say it's not connected?"

"To tell you the truth, I'd welcome the help."

"That's settled then." He held out his hand for her to shake. "Partners in crime solving."

"I thought we already were."

"Partners in crime solving for cases we aren't assigned to. We'll get suspended together."

"You're all heart, Logan."

He grinned. "That's why the girls love me."

They reached the hospital specializing in demon care only to discover that Merrick had already been released. Demons healed quickly, but Samantha didn't think they healed *that* quickly. Merrick's neck had nearly been severed.

Logan didn't comment when she suggested they drive back to Merrick's club. Merrick lived in the penthouse above it, and he'd likely be home convalescing.

Venice during the day was a different place than the middle of the night when the vamp and demon clubs did their business. Tourists and locals in T-shirts and shorts streamed down the colorful streets to the beach, blue sky arched overhead, and the September sun was warm.

Merrick's club was closed, the smoked glass doors shut and locked. Samantha banged on them, Logan standing just a little behind her left shoulder.

"We're closed," the bartender said as he pulled open the door. "But you know that."

"I want to talk to Merrick," Samantha said.

"He's busy. Talk to his lawyer."

"It's not about what happened last night—this is unofficial. By the way, you don't happen to know who those demons were who busted the place up, do you?"

"No."

"Or whose clan they belonged to? We could go have a talk with them, if you want."

The bartender's eyes narrowed. Like all demons, he had a handsomeness that went deeper than physical attraction, one that compelled a person to look into his eyes and to crave what he had to give.

"Merrick really is busy talking to someone else," the bartender said. "He's pretty pissed at you anyway."

"Because I arrested him? I'm surprised he didn't see it coming."

"Yeah, well." He turned as someone called something to him from the darkened interior. "What do you know?" he said to Samantha. "Merrick says to let you in."

Logan looked uncomfortable as they ducked inside, uneasy in a place made by demons for demons. Werewolves were creatures of intense life magic, and Logan always said the death magic of demons made his fur itch.

He looked like his fur was itching bad as they followed the bartender through a private door and into an elevator that took them up four floors above the club. The bartender ushered them into a sunny penthouse with a wall of windows that revealed a panorama of dark blue ocean.

Merrick was indeed talking to someone in his lush living room—Tain. Samantha stopped in the doorway, and Logan almost ran into her.

"That's him," Logan hissed in her ear. "That's the guy from last night."

"No kidding."

Samantha moved numbly into the apartment. Tain stood when he saw her, like an old-fashioned gentleman, and so did Merrick. Tain looked uneasy, with that dark glint in his eyes again—probably being in a place permeated with death magic made him even jumpier than Logan.

He flicked his gaze over Samantha, his eyes as blue as

the ocean behind him. She reminded herself that he possessed powerful magic and incredible strength and could do anything to her, to Merrick, or to Logan without them being able to stop him. She should be afraid of him—and she was—but at the same time he commanded her attention, her fascination, and wouldn't let it go.

He moved his penetrating stare to Logan. "You're a werewolf."

"I have that pleasure," Logan answered. "I'm Logan Wright, Samantha's partner."

"I saw you last night."

"When you all so thoughtfully busted up my club," Merrick interrupted. "So good for business, fried demons."

"When your rivals busted up your club, you mean," Logan corrected him. "We pretty much saved your ass."

Merrick gave him a cold look and gestured for Samantha to sit down. "Tell me what you're doing here and why my lawyer shouldn't start a suit for police harassment."

"I wanted to talk to you about something completely different," Samantha said. "Maybe if you help me on this, I'll forget about the Mindglow."

"And what Mindglow would that be?" Merrick asked smoothly.

Samantha restrained herself from rolling her eyes. "Never mind. Maybe you could help out of the goodness of your heart."

"My evil demon heart?" Merrick smiled.

"That's the one."

"I already asked him," Tain broke in. "He says he might be able to help."

Samantha bit back a retort. "I see."

"Why don't we sit down and discuss it?" Logan asked. He kept looking at the ceiling for some reason, as though it would come crashing in on them, but she knew it was just a reaction to being in a demon's lair. She alone didn't cringe at the press of death magic, though she could still feel it. Usually, Logan was a master at diffusing a tense situation with his drawling voice and slow smile, which made her again wonder what event had wound him up enough to leave his pack.

Merrick lounged back on his sofa, pretending to be perfectly at ease. He wore a casual but finely tailored suit, the scarf around his neck hiding his injury from last night. The living room was fairly decadent, with satin-soft leather chairs and shelves filled with crystal sculptures. The Hockney over the sofa appeared to be genuine. Tain remained standing, turning to look out the floor-to-ceiling windows to the vast Pacific beyond.

"Your *friend* here says the missing prostitutes were freelance," Merrick said. "And they might have been. But I knew one of them, a little sweetheart called Alice. She was Lamiah clan, but she was out on her own."

Samantha jumped, and at the same time Tain asked, "Where can I find someone from this Lamiah clan?"

Merrick started to laugh. "There's one sitting right here. Dear Samantha is Lamiah."

Tain shot her a sharp look, and Samantha grew suddenly more uneasy. "How did you know I was Lamiah?" she asked Merrick. "My father is, I mean."

"You are, too, Samantha my dear. There's no getting away from your roots. When I learned to my horror last night that you were a cop, I had my lawyer do a little research on you, you half-demon vixen. How exciting to find you come from my own clan."

Logan's eyes narrowed. "Wait a minute, you mean you two are related?"

"No," Samantha said hastily. "Clans are made up of many different families. The families that formed clans in the distant past weren't necessarily related. They came together for protection or for strength, according to what my father's been trying to teach me."

"But we still have a connection." Merrick smirked at Samantha.

"And a matriarch," Tain broke in, his gaze hard. "All clans have matriarchs, don't they? She might know something about the missing girls."

Merrick laughed again. "You're kidding, right? No demon matriarch is going to talk to *you*, Immortal one. You stink of life magic."

"What are they going to do?" Tain asked. "Kill me?"

"Such wit. Is everyone at home like you?"

Merrick didn't know the half of it, Samantha thought. "Why did you let him in here if he stinks of life magic?" she asked. "Which I agree, he does."

Magic sparkled just under Tain's skin, power so strong he could take out the building. Samantha had learned in her job that life magic didn't necessarily mean "good." It meant that a life-magic creature was sustained by life and light, unlike vampires and demons, who lived by death. Samantha had been in Los Angeles long enough to know that good and evil didn't always fall into neat categories, and that shades of gray existed everywhere.

"Tain healed you, didn't he?" she asked Merrick after a moment of thought. "That's why you were released from the hospital so fast."

"Correct," Merrick said. "*Some* people are willing to pay for answers."

"You are such a bastard," Samantha said under her breath.

"And I am disappointed in you, Sam, for tricking me into thinking you liked me. I'd almost decided to make you one of my own."

Samantha bit back revulsion. When a demon took a human as "his own," it basically meant he became her dom. He took care of her and gave her everything she wanted—cars, jewelry, a job—and in turn she gave the demon her life essence whenever he needed a fix. Samantha had seen demons subs, glassy-eyed women and men who would do anything for their masters or mistresses.

"No, thank you," she said.

"Well, I'm not about to ask you now, two-faced bitch."

Tain sent an almost casual trickle of white magic from his fingers to wrap around Merrick's throat. Merrick jumped, face whitening, and then he looked enlightened. "Oh, is *that* how it is?"

"Returning to the point," Logan broke in firmly. He sat forward on his chair, leaning his elbows on his thighs. "Tain, why do you think talking to the clan will help?"

Tain closed his fingers, and the light around Merrick's throat vanished. Merrick rubbed his neck, looking thoughtfully from Tain to Samantha and back again.

"Because it might have been an honor killing," Tain said.

"The clan objecting to the girl deserting and taking to the streets on her own?" Samantha asked.

"The Immortal one is possibly right," Merrick agreed. "He has brawn *and* brains. They wouldn't so much object to her selling her services as not doing it for the benefit of the clan. Also some of the families can be very conservative, especially about their women. Or a gang boss might have grown angry at her for striking out on her own."

"And their boss is not you?" Logan asked.

"Any young woman who works for me or in my clubs is treated well. They never desert me."

"But the women who work for you come from different clans?"

"I welcome people from all clans, and we manage to be close, despite familial differences. I like to say Merrick's is a little clan away from clan." He chuckled.

"Very funny," Samantha said.

"Are you this diplomatic interviewing all your witnesses?" Merrick asked her. "You could take a few pointers from your werewolf friend. See, he's not even breaking into fur and claws."

"I see no need to be hostile," Logan said mildly. "Yet."

"Set up the meeting," Tain broke in. Samantha sensed his impatience, could almost see it rippling on his skin. "Contact Samantha at the police department when everything is in place. This interview is over."

Merrick contemplated Tain a moment, his eyes speaking volumes. "Not quite yet, my friend," he said. "There's something else."

CHAPTER FOUR

Tain had to get out of the room. How Logan and Merrick could sit so calmly with Samantha between them he didn't know. Her black-hued aura enclosed her like silk, and her coffee-colored eyes did their best to draw him in. She suppressed her demon side on purpose, obviously uncomfortable with it, but he could see it in her, darkness wanting any excuse to get out.

He knew Merrick could see it, too, the demon looking at her as though he wanted to devour her. Merrick had wanted her at the club last night, had smarmed all over her. Tain had derived great satisfaction from attacking the man. Merrick remained alive only because Tain needed to question him.

"What is it?" he asked Merrick impatiently.

Merrick rose and strolled to a desk on the other side of the room, shuffled through some papers, and brought a couple of sheets back to Samantha.

"I've been getting these for the past couple weeks. I'm used to volatile letters from demon haters, which I dutifully turn over to the police. But these are different."

Samantha perused each sheet, her eyes widening. She passed them to Logan, who looked them over and handed them up to Tain without Tain having to ask.

The messages were simple. On each sheet letters cut from newspaper headlines spelled out YOUR DOOM IS COMING.

"When did you get the first one?" Samantha asked.

"Two weeks ago. On the twenty-third of August, to be precise. The other two arrived about five days apart."

Tain looked for any magic clinging to the papers but found none. He felt the hatred of whoever had cut and pasted the letters, but many people hated and feared demons. The aura didn't seem especially strong and definitely not magical.

"Why warn you?" Logan asked. "If they want to come after you, why put you on guard?"

"I imagine they're trying to frighten me," Merrick replied. "A pathetic attempt, though. I'm not frightened by cutouts from newspapers. Take them if you want—test for fingerprints or whatever it is you do."

"Do you have the envelopes?"

Merrick fetched them—postmarked in Los Angeles, though Tain wasn't familiar enough with the city to recognize the zip code.

Logan took the papers and envelopes and tucked them into his pocket. They turned to leave, but Merrick said, "Samantha," and beckoned her aside.

Tain was not about to walk out of the room without her, and he saw that Logan wouldn't, either. Both men waited tensely in the open doorway while Merrick murmured something in Samantha's ear.

She reddened but otherwise didn't look distressed as she squeezed past Tain and Logan to walk out the door.

"What did he say?" Logan asked her as they emerged into the sunshine.

It was warm in the September air, and Samantha's face soon took on a sheen of perspiration. She impatiently wiped at it, but Tain wanted to still her hands, lean over, and lick the moisture from her upper lip.

"Nothing helpful." Her black hair shimmered as she unlocked the door of their car.

"What did he say that was *un*-helpful then?" Logan asked.

She looked at Logan and Tain, and then started to laugh. "Can the pair of you possibly exude any more testosterone? It was about my father, and no, I'm not going to tell you what."

Logan let it go and opened the driver's-side door. "Can we drop you anywhere?" he asked Tain.

Tain looked at the vehicle, at Samantha's hair shining in the sunlight, at the way her eyes creased in the corners with her amusement. He imagined sitting behind her in the car, breathing in her scent, watching her turn to say something to Logan, feeling her dark aura brush him like it had in her apartment. He'd tangle in it and never want to stop.

"No," he said abruptly, then turned and walked away.

The young demon woman called herself Nadia, because the humans she met in the clubs liked the name. She stood with her hands cuffed behind her back and gazed with disdain on her captors as they discussed what to do with her. Her long black hair had been cut off and thrown away, her clothes disposed of.

At first they'd taken away her ability to resume demon form, and she was too weak and sick to do anything but glare. Now they wanted her to change, and because they wanted her to, she refused.

Demons were difficult to kill, but not impossible, and the methods they outlined showed they'd done their homework—burning her, beheading, tearing out her heart. Nadia stood with her head held high, though her body was cold with fear. These people knew how to kill.

Her captors wore masks, and the room was dark, but she knew there were two women and a man. Outside the room, more men lurked, and they had guns. She'd be mown down if she tried to run, and though the bullets might not kill her, they'd injure her enough that she'd not be able to get away.

"We could send her back as a warning," one of the women suggested.

"We could send her *head* back as a warning," the man growled.

"There have been too many warnings," the second woman broke in. Nadia didn't like her—her voice was far too chill and dangerous. "We need to stop warning them and start moving."

"Are we ready for that?" the man said doubtfully.

"We're ready enough."

"Hurry up and kill me," Nadia snapped. "I'm getting bored."

The man, who'd already forced himself between her legs, grabbed her by what was left of her hair. "We'll do what we want, demon bitch."

She spat in his face. He threw her on the floor and kicked her. "Change," he snarled. "Show us what you really are."

She knew they wanted her to change because they wanted to slice off her head while she was in demon form and display it like a trophy.

She refused. If they killed her, the human police would find her like this, beaten and raped, and be appalled. Sympathy would be with her, not her captors. But if they displayed a slain demon carcass, people might rejoice, or at the very least say she had it coming.

"Stop," the woman said sternly. "We'll do it tonight, in front of her sister."

Nadia's rage surged. "You leave her out of this, you stupid fucks."

The man stopped kicking her. He backed away, leaving

her bruised and hurting on the floor. "Yes," he said almost reverently. "She will be witness."

Nadia lay curled in on herself, a cold fear in her heart that had nothing to do with the certainty of her own death.

Tain prowled the streets as the sun went down, preferring the warm darkness of the city to the alternative of returning to his tiny apartment. Leda and Hunter had invited him to live with them in Adrian's Malibu house, but he'd declined.

Spending an evening with Leda and Hunter and their infant son could soothe him somewhat, especially holding his energetic and fearless nephew between his large hands, marveling at the child's innocence and innate strength. He sensed in small Ryan a power that would eclipse his parents' one day. But though he could banter with Hunter and enjoy Leda's warm friendliness, there was still some part of him they never could touch.

Worse than that, Tain didn't trust himself around them. What would happen if he succumbed to the dark madness that still lurked in a corner of his mind? He was stronger than Hunter—he'd emerged from Kehksut's torture stronger than all the Immortals put together. Hunter and Leda wouldn't be able to stop him, and there was baby Ryan, so small and vulnerable. If Tain succumbed to darkness, his family would suffer for it. Best he stayed as far from them as possible.

The haunting streets of Los Angeles better suited his moods. Los Angeles held many different spectrums all merging on each other—opulent neighborhoods for billionaires blocks away from gang-controlled slums.

People from every human race found a home here, and magical races also converged, especially those that preferred nighttime existence. Vampires and demons were most prevalent—werewolves preferred open country as did Sidhe and other magical creatures more tied to nature. Why Samantha's werewolf partner, Logan, was in Los Angeles was anyone's guess, and how he tolerated working with a half demon was another puzzle.

People, human and otherwise, left Tain alone, whether he sat by himself on the bus or wandered while city lights began to gleam out in the dark. They knew danger when they saw it, and a tall man in a duster, jeans, and motorcycle boots radiated danger with a capital *D*.

Tain's wandering took him up Wilshire Boulevard to MacArthur Park, a place where vampire and demon territory overlapped. If trouble happened at night, it would be here or nearby.

He could dampen his glow of life magic if he wanted to—something he'd learned during his years as Kehksut's prisoner. He'd learned many things as Kehksut created his monster, until the most dangerous thing in MacArthur Park tonight was Tain. In fact, last year, if he had chosen, he could have imprisoned his brothers forever and let the world go to hell.

He'd never told them that. He let them believe that they'd saved baby brother with their collective power. He let them believe he was all right, that he just needed a little time to readjust.

He smiled grimly. His brothers could never understand the torment, both physical and mental, he'd endured. Even the physical pain was nothing compared to the madness that he'd used to cover the pain, a madness that hadn't quite released its grip. Recovering from being endlessly tortured wasn't like getting over a bout of flu.

He spotted a vampire crossing a narrow street, the creature's dark aura like a smudge around his body. The vamp ducked into an alley, and then Tain sensed his gloating.

Vampires paid a stiff penalty for accosting humans

outside the vamp clubs and for drinking a human's blood without consent. But the law didn't forbid the undead from preying on each other, and in the back streets there was little enforcement of the "consent" rule.

Tain jogged across the street into the alley the vamp had taken. The vamp had his hand around a woman's throat, holding her up against the alley wall. She was naked, struggling, and Tain smelled a hint of brimstone. Demon.

The demon woman fought pathetically, surprisingly not changing to her demon form to try to rip the vamp's head off. The vampire had his fangs out, but he was no longer just interested in her blood—he likely planned to rape or kill her or both.

Tain drew his short swords from their crossed sheaths beneath his duster.

"You have three seconds to run," he said.

The vamp whipped his head around. His lips drew back from his fangs, his eyes bottomless pits of blackness. "What the hell are you?"

"One Mississippi . . ." Tain began as he advanced. "Two Mississippi . . ."

The demon girl hung limply in the vampire's grasp, wretched and terrified.

"Three Mississ . . ." Tain let his power glow, white snakes of it twining around the sword blades.

The vampire's eyes widened. He dropped the demon girl and assumed a fighting stance.

"No, I really meant run." Tain pointed one of his swords at the vamp, blue-white light shooting from the tip to send the vampire tumbling backward. The next burst turned the vampire around and gave him a shove.

The vampire finally took the hint and sprinted down the alley, the sound of his footsteps quickly swallowed by city noise. The demon girl tried to slink into the shadows.

"Not you." Tain wrapped white magic around her and gently held her in place. "Let's have a look at you."

She shrank back against the wall, trying to cover herself. She was naked except for a pair of panties that looked like they'd seen better days, and someone had cut off her hair. Her dark eyes were haunted, the hands that cupped her shoulders were brown with dried blood.

"I left it," she said, tears trickling down her cheeks. "I left it. I didn't know what to do."

Tain sheathed his swords. He removed his duster and wrapped it around her shivering body, letting his healing touch close the small abrasions on her face.

"What are you doing?" she sobbed, pulling away. "You're life magic."

"I don't pick and choose who I heal." He touched her hair, but stopped himself from sliding his magic into her demon aura. Some things he still could not bear to touch. "What's your name, and what happened to you?"

"My sister . . . I can't leave it."

"Leave what?" Tain gentled his voice, his lilt pronounced, and traced his finger over the bruises the vampire had left.

"They killed her," she choked. "They were supposed to kill me. I couldn't stop them."

"Couldn't stop who? Who did this?"

She tried to wipe her tears away, but her hand shook too much. "You don't care. You're life magic."

"I do care," Tain said.

She fell silent, sobbing in quiet hiccups.

Samantha, I need you.

The thought came out of nowhere, as though someone else had put it into his mind. With it came an image of her face—sharp cheekbones, dark eyes, red mouth laughing.

But he did need her, at least in her capacity as a detective in LAPD's paranormal division. This was the kind of problem she could solve.

"I'm going to summon someone who can help you," he said.

Or whatever the jargon was for bringing Samantha here. In the seven hundred years since Tain had been taken prisoner, the world had changed. Gone were buildings of stone heated by burning peat or wood, rooms that were warm only near the fire. This city had houses of brick and thin wood and stucco, yet the buildings were cool against the summer heat and flooded with artificial light. People now cooked without fire and washed away the remains of their meals in a complicated mass of pipes.

Seven hundred years ago, he might summon a half demon with his magic—now he pulled out a cell phone and flipped it open. Leda, who'd given it to him, had programmed Samantha's number in it.

When Leda had handed him the phone, she'd smiled and said, "I'm going to teach one of you Immortals to use a cell phone if it's the last thing I do. Keep it on your belt and stay in touch."

Tain didn't like the annoying little devices, but he humored his new sister-in-law. It took him two or three tries to figure out which buttons to push, but soon he heard Samantha's breathless voice. "Hello?"

"Samantha," he said, one hand lightly on the weeping girl's shoulder. "I need you."

Samantha angled her car across the end of the alley and got out, letting its headlights flood the narrow passage.

She'd been driving home when her cell phone had rung, and she'd pulled into a 7-Eleven parking lot and answered. When she'd heard Tain say *I need you* her heart had flip-flopped, and she'd imagined him saying that in the dark, his hand on her hair as he lay against her.

I'm crazy, she told herself as she drove to the alley Tain directed her to. *He hates demons. He touched me with his healing power, and I'm reacting to that. Nothing more.*

She kept her hand on the butt of her gun as she hurried down the darkened alley to where Tain crouched on the filthy pavement facing a young woman huddled in his duster coat. Samantha felt a brief stab of envy. She'd love to be the one wrapped in a coat that held Tain's warmth while he gazed at her so intently.

The feeling evaporated when she got a good look at the young woman. She was a demon, but her demon-beautiful face was covered with scabbed-over cuts, her hair crudely chopped off above her ears.

Samantha knelt next to Tain, gentling her voice to not startle her. "What happened to you?"

"Her name is Nadia," Tain said. "That's what she tells me, anyway."

Nadia had been crying, tears streaking the dirt on her face. "I don't know who they were."

Tain related in a few brief sentences how he'd followed a vamp and found her. "She won't talk to me."

Samantha found that surprising. If Tain had draped his coat over *her* shoulders and given her comfort, she'd be pouring her heart out to him.

She took out her ID and badge and held them so the girl could see. "I'm paranormal police. You need to tell me what happened here."

"Not here," Nadia said, her voice hoarse. "They took me, and Bev. They killed Bev and sent me back to take it home."

"It?" Samantha glanced at Tain, but he shook his head. "Take what home, Nadia?"

"I left it over there." She pointed with a grimy finger farther down the alley.

Samantha started to rise, but Tain said, "No, let me."

He strode swiftly through the trash-strewn alley until

he stopped a few yards away. He stared at the ground a moment, then leaned down and picked up a bundle.

He brought it back, holding it out from his body, as though it might explode. Samantha caught a stink of death and terror from it.

Nadia moaned and covered her face. "I couldn't stop them. I should have stopped them."

Tain unwrapped the bundle. Samantha gasped and took a step back, bile rising in her throat. A heart lay on the bloodstained cloths in Tain's hands, black and horrible.

"It's Bev's," the girl cried. "My sister. They killed her."

"This is going to keep us up all night," Lieutenant McKay said in her office. Samantha had brought Nadia and the grisly evidence back downtown, where Nadia was given medical attention, food, and clothes.

Samantha half expected Tain to leave as soon as they reached the paranormal division headquarters, but he'd accompanied her to McKay's office. He'd said nothing, simply followed Samantha upstairs as though he had every right to be there.

"Forensics has the heart," the lieutenant said. "But there isn't much doubt that it came from a demon. Killing like that must have made a mess, difficult to clean up. We'll search the buildings around there. She's from the Lamiah clan, she says, so we'll have to question the rival clans." McKay sighed, looking tired. Demons clans were notorious for closing ranks and being uncooperative.

Tain shook his head. "Nadia's sister was probably killed far from there. Perhaps they teleported Nadia to the alley, choosing one at random."

McKay focused on him, her dark eyes no-nonsense. "And who are you exactly, again? You were in Merrick's club in time to stop an all-out gang war, and then you just happened to find this girl in an alley?"

Tain's gaze flicked up and down the small Sidhe woman with black skin and red-orange hair, and Samantha saw a flash of dark irritation in his eyes. His look was one of a being far stronger and more dangerous than McKay could ever understand, one who could wipe out the entire room with the flick of his pinky. Samantha watched him tamp down the darkness deliberately, perhaps reminding himself that he'd chosen to be one of the good guys.

"I'm a demon hunter," he said.

"Demon hunting is illegal," McKay shot back.

"Demons follow your rules because it's to their benefit," Tain said in clipped tones. "The rules let them drink the life essences of fools, and live in comfort among you. But they are death magic, and when the balance shifts, they become the masters. Never forget that."

"Samantha is half demon," McKay pointed out.

"I know. Even she has the potential to turn, and she's more powerful than she understands."

He rested his full gaze on Samantha, the one that made her feel the weight of his power. Why was it harder to face him here in her boss's office than last year when he'd wrapped magic around her that could have sliced her in two?

"Excuse me," she broke in. "Could we make this not about me? Demon girl found with heart in alley. That's a little more serious than my heritage."

McKay shrugged and let it drop. "You were right about the demon prostitutes who went missing from around Merrick's. Nadia admitted she was a streetwalker with her sister, but she can't tell us who captured her or where they held her. She says her captors wore masks and black clothes, and she couldn't tell if they were vampire or demon or human. Their true natures were cloaked, probably with a spell."

"So are we looking for demon hunters?" Samantha asked.

McKay gave Tain a pointed look. "It seems so."

Tain returned the look. "Not the same kind of demon hunter as me. These young women were tortured, and neither my brothers nor I would do that."

McKay's expression was carefully blank. "Maybe I should talk to your brothers."

"They don't live here," Samantha said. "Except for Hunter and his wife. But they're not responsible, I already know that."

"But they might be a good resource. Samantha, I'd like you and Logan to ask Tain's brother about what he knows about demon hunters in L.A. that we might not. I'm going to try to set up an interview with someone in the Lamiah clan—find out if there is a clan war brewing, which we do *not* need. We're still recovering from the gangs getting out of hand last year." She sighed. "The clan matriarchs are damn touchy, though. It's anyone's guess whether they'll let anyone talk to me or tell me the truth." She fixed Samantha with an inquiring look. "Samantha, you're Lamiah clan. Perhaps you could put in a good word for me?"

Samantha lifted her hands in protest. "I have no contact with the demon side of my family—they don't exactly like half bloods. I've never met any of them except my father."

Even that was tricky. Her father, a demon called Fulton, turned out to be not so bad for a demon, but she still walked on eggshells around him. She and her mother and Fulton had made good progress this year at finally becoming a family, but it was slow going.

McKay rubbed her hand over her close-cropped hair. "It could be a good resource, Sam. We don't want this getting out of hand. If your father could ask around in his family if anyone knows anything about these kidnappings, or whatever they are, I'd be grateful. Young girls disappearing from the streets is not good."

Samantha nodded. "Got it. Ask Tain's brother about demon hunters, my father about happenings in the Lamiah clan."

McKay merely gave her a curt nod and told her to go home and get some sleep. Tain walked out with Samantha all the way to her pickup, then opened the door once she unlocked it and got into her passenger seat without invitation.

Samantha put her key in the ignition with force. "Somewhere I can drop you off?"

"I want to make sure you get home all right."

"I usually do. I'm careful, I'm a cop, and I'm armed."

"But someone is cutting out demon hearts," he said. "And you happen to have one."

He had a point. She'd had to leave squeamishness behind long ago in this job, but what had been done to Nadia and her sister would stay with her for a long time.

"All right, then, buckle up." She put the car in gear and pulled out of the lot.

CHAPTER FIVE

Samantha sighed as they hit freeway traffic, still thick even in this late hour. "I only have half a demon heart," she said. *The half you're never going to let me forget.*

"Not your fault you were born demon," Tain said absently. He looked out the window, his blue eyes flickering as he took in what they rapidly passed.

"So generous of you." Samantha swerved around a car that had come to a complete halt.

Tain didn't answer. Her demon self cringed from his overwhelming life magic barely contained in her small vehicle, while the human side of her was drawn to his tall, broad-shouldered body so close on her little pickup's bench seat. He rested his arm on the seat between them, which ensured that she kept both hands firmly on the wheel.

"Where do you live?" Samantha asked. "Or are you staying with Leda and Hunter?"

"I have my own place."

She waited for him to tell her where it was, but he fell silent again. "Thanks," she said. "I always did like cryptic men."

"You should like me, then."

She looked sideways at him. "Was that a joke? Tain, the brooding Immortal warrior, made a joke?"

"You expect me to darkly reflect on my tragic, tortured

past all the time? What's the expression Leda likes to use—twenty-four, seven?"

"No. I mean . . ." She tried again. "I guess I'm just wondering if you're all right."

"I'm not." He looked away again.

Cryptic, right. "So why did you come to Los Angeles? To be near Hunter?"

He shrugged. "Here's as good a place as any to find out what I'm supposed to be."

"You know who you're supposed to be. You're a big, bad Immortal warrior people call on when there's trouble."

"No, that's what I *used* to be." His voice grated, like it had broken along with the rest of him. "What I am now?"

The quiet question worried her, so she kept her tone light. "In other words, you've come here to find yourself?"

"Maybe."

"Some people find themselves by going to Tibet and climbing mountains and meditating with a guru."

"Seems like a lot of work."

"I was joking."

"I know." His rare smile flashed out for an instant, then was gone. "No one has to go very far to find themselves. The hard part is what you do once you've looked in the mirror and accepted the scars."

She wondered if he meant the literal scars she'd seen on his hands and arms or something much deeper. "So, helping figure out what's going on with these girls is kind of a pit stop on your road of life?"

He looked at her without expression, and she realized that a man who'd been hidden away for seven hundred years might not understand the reference. "I mean . . ."

"I know what you meant." He shrugged again. "It's something to keep me busy."

"Bull. When you were at the club last night, you could have taken down every demon in the place—Merrick, his rivals, the bartender—everyone. If you wanted to keep busy, you could enjoy yourself destroying demons and demon clubs. You didn't even kill Merrick when you could have in a heartbeat. Why not?"

"I needed to talk to him."

"Bull again. You could have questioned him, then killed him, but again, you didn't."

"Not worth the bother," he said mildly.

She drew a breath and asked what she really wanted to know. "Last year, you could have killed *me*. I was at your mercy, and I couldn't have escaped you. Why didn't you?"

His tone never changed. "You were innocent in that struggle. My brothers were using you, and so was my mother."

Samantha shivered. During the battle the goddess Cerridwen, Tain's mother, had briefly infused Samantha with incredible power that helped defeat the Old One. Samantha still had nightmares about it. "I was happy to help. I was ready to take you down, whatever the cost."

Tain chuckled, a harsh sound. "You couldn't have taken me down."

"I was willing to die trying."

She felt his gaze touch her though she couldn't take her eyes off the traffic to look at him. "Why?" he asked. "All you had to do was run away and save yourself."

"I had nothing to lose. If your brothers couldn't stop you, what was left for me?"

"You have a home and family. I'd say that was something to lose."

"What are you trying to get me to say? That stopping you was in my own self-interest? Well, it was. It was my butt on the line, too. Besides, Amber and the others were compelling."

"Yes, my brothers' wives," he said in a resigned tone. "Very compelling women."

"I like them."

"So do I. They've made my brooding, arrogant brothers extremely happy. They're changed men."

"They're not lonely anymore." Samantha pulled into her apartment's parking lot and stopped. "Being alone is a hard thing, believe me. But I guess you'd know all about that."

"Oh, I was lonely, Samantha," Tain said, opening the car door. "But never alone."

He was out of the car and walking around to her side before she could ask what he meant. She slid out while he held the door, another gentlemanly gesture.

"Well, here we are," she said. "How are you going to get home?"

"I'll walk you upstairs first."

"It's a gated complex. Only those who live here or their guests can get in."

"Someone out there knows an effective way to make sure a demon stays dead. I'll walk you upstairs."

Samantha wasn't used to being protected. Logan watched her back, but that was different—he wouldn't stop her doing her job, and he assumed she'd watch his back at the same time. Samantha had always taken care of herself, and since joining the police force she had the physical training and expertise to do so. Tain hovering on guard at her shoulder as they went up the stairs was a new sensation.

"There are thousands of demon women in this city," she said. "Are you going to walk them all home, too?"

"I would if I could."

He waited until she unlocked the door, then pushed in ahead of her. Pickles jumped down from the counter and ran at him, meowing pathetically.

"I obviously never feed him or pet him." Samantha dropped her briefcase on the sofa and shut the door. "He probably hasn't eaten in at least ten minutes."

Tain took the bag of food from its place on the counter and topped off the cat's bowl, while Pickles pranced around him, tail high.

"You'll spoil him rotten." Samantha dropped her keys on the counter and kicked off her shoes, determined to not show Tain how much he unnerved her. "By the way, I'm home now."

Tain straightened up and put the food away. He started for the door, and she thought he was leaving without saying good-bye, but he swung back to her, his face hard. "The glamour," he said. "It's very good."

"Glamour?"

His eyes darkened and he stepped to her, making her back up into the counter. This close, his impossibly tall body made her feel small, his life magic brushing her like a crackling net. His face was too damned handsome, the pentacle tattoo on his cheek almost glowing with his power.

"The one you keep up to hide your demon self."

"I don't . . ."

She stopped, not knowing how to answer. Half-blood demons chose their physical appearance in childhood, instinctively mimicking whatever parent was closest to them. Half demons without strong magical skill also lost their ability to change to one form or the other, she'd learned, so Samantha would look human the rest of her life—no morphing into claws and scales, like Merrick did.

"It's very, very good." Tain brushed his fingers over her chin, his hand hot, like he had a fever. "It's difficult to say what you truly look like."

"I look like this, as far as I know. I don't use a glam."

"Of course you do. It's what demons do—draw in the unwary to give up their life essence to you."

"I don't feed off life essences. I prefer cheeseburgers."

Tain didn't laugh. "I have such an overwhelming life essence, it must be difficult for you to resist it."

"More like an overwhelming ego." She tried to keep her voice steady, but she was shaking. Tain's eyes darkened, his fingers biting down.

"I don't know what *ego* means," he said as he leaned closer. "Everything is new to me, including your language. But I know what I'm drawn to."

"You think *I'm* enticing *you*?"

"Aren't you, Samantha? Ever since I saw you, I've been struck by the need to kiss you."

"That's not my fault . . ."

She trailed off as the blue of his eyes was swallowed by black, and his hot breath touched her lips. A fraction of an inch separated their mouths and her body began to respond like it did when he healed her—a rush of heat, the need to meld to him, the stirring of intoxicating desire.

He closed his eyes as his lips touched hers, the lightest featherlike brush. His hand went to the nape of her neck, his large palm cradling her.

The kiss was slow, his lips learning hers, the pad of his thumb brushing her chin. He opened his eyes, the blue of them intense.

If she had any sense, she'd pull away, tell him to go lose himself, and slam the door behind him. But kissing him was incredible. It was like stroking a wild animal that let none approach but her.

He slid his tongue between her lips, one tingling stroke. She chased it with her own tongue, her fingers locking behind his neck. The ends of his hair tickled her fingers, and she indulged herself rubbing the rough silk of it.

"Stay," she whispered. She suddenly wanted him with everything she had. She wanted to make love with this amazing man who was strong enough to end the world. She wanted his body on top of hers, his strong arms cradling her. What couldn't she face with a man like Tain to hold her at the end of the day?

"No." He kissed her again, harder this time, his teeth

scraping her lower lip. She was suddenly hot and wet between her legs, her hips rising toward him of their own accord. She wanted to rub herself on him, to feel his hard body against hers, to lick his skin and love the taste.

She turned her head to kiss the tattoo on his cheek, and he broke the contact and pressed her away from him.

She gasped. "Tain . . ."

He stood still, breathing heavily, his mouth in a rigid line. "I told you to stay away from me."

"You called *me*." Samantha's body heat remained high, her cleft squeezing and driving her crazy. "And you insisted on coming up here."

"And now I'm going."

"Good." Her needy body heated with frustrated rage. "Don't let the door hit your ass on the way out."

He just looked at her, his eyes like flint, his face unmoving. She wanted to scream and rage; she wanted to burst into tears of relief. There would never be anything between them, never mind how he made her feel when he healed her, or how many times Leda expressed the wish that Samantha and Tain had gotten together after the battle.

He hated demons, and the only reason he'd helped Nadia tonight was that he felt sorry for her, because he was, somewhere down inside, a healer. But a demon had destroyed him, and he had no room in his messed-up life for a half demon who was eating her heart out over him.

Damn Immortals.

"Go on, then," she said, folding her arms tight across her chest. She could feel her heart pounding, her nipples hard as little pebbles. "I'm not stopping you."

He gave her one more look, then opened the door. Cool night air drifted over her as he strode out, his duster swirling around him. The door slammed, and he was gone.

Pickles jumped up on the windowsill with a disconsolate meow, staring out over the dark parking lot.

"Let him go, Pickles," Samantha said, tears pricking her eyes. "He's not worth it." Her words ended on a groan, and she hid her face in her hands. "Damn it, why do I want him so much?"

Pickles didn't answer. Samantha turned to draw the blind and saw Tain with his distinctive stride moving from the parking lot to the street beyond.

"Damn," she said again, and let the blind rattle close.

Tain returned to the alley where he'd found Nadia, too pent up from his encounter with Samantha to return tamely home. His body throbbed from the kiss, his arousal still hard as a rock.

He never should have touched her, never should have told her he was in danger of succumbing to her. She might be only half demon, but all demons learned early that they were irresistible and spent their life honing their talent for luring victims. Samantha seemed surprised that she had the siren's pull, but that didn't negate the fact that he couldn't stay away from her.

When he'd started looking into the problem of the missing prostitutes, he'd told himself that it would be logical to ask for Samantha's help—she knew the city, and as a police detective, she handled things like this for her job. Now he realized he'd simply wanted to see her again. She was right; he could have just gone to the police and reported his concerns. He hadn't needed to seek her out specifically.

But he had, and he was paying for it. He'd been thinking about her since Seattle and pretending not to, pretending he had no use for a half demon he owed his life to. And yet as soon as he'd come to Los Angeles he'd found a way to see her again.

When she'd come into Merrick's last night, in that skintight black dress that bared her shoulders and made her legs look a mile long, he'd known that he'd made a grave mistake. No more pushing the gorgeous woman out of his head—she was there to stay.

He tried to distract himself, looking around the alley, but found nothing he hadn't seen before. He sensed the tiniest taint of magic from the teleportation but couldn't tell where it had originated from.

Tain gave up on finding anything further, flagged down a taxi, and gave the driver Hunter's address in Malibu. He didn't have any money with him, but Hunter would be good for the cab fare, and Tain would pay him back the next time Hunter dragged him to a bank to explain how ATMs worked again. Adrian had set up an account for Tain and deposited a substantial sum into it, saying he deserved it after all he'd been through. Tain thanked him but rarely used it, partly because their damn machines regularly ate his card, partly because he'd never in his life had much use for money. Easy enough to get along without it, and he didn't have the need for decadence.

A black limousine stood in the driveway of the long, low house on the Malibu hill. Tain told the cabby to wait and went to the front door, smelling the taint of vampire. The driver in the limo was certainly vampire and clutched the steering wheel defiantly when Tain stared in at him.

"Tain." Leda Stowe greeted him in delight with a one-armed hug. The other arm cradled baby Ryan, who was blowing bubbles with his own spit.

Leda twined her hand through Tain's and dragged him inside, handing off Ryan to him. "Look who's here," she said brightly to the two men in the living room.

One of them was Tain's brother Hunter. Hunter had tawny, flyaway hair and intense green eyes. He was no stranger to tragedy—his first wife and his two children had been brutally murdered by demons long ago. He'd found peace now with Leda, but Tain observed that Hunter watched his wife and new son with a fierce protectiveness.

The other man in the living room was a vampire—an Old One, which meant he was ancient and strong. He had dark hair and bottomless blue eyes and a death magic aura that made Tain nauseated. Tain never understood why Hunter let such a being into his house, but Hunter and the vampire had become friends of a sort.

"Aha," Hunter said. "Mystery solved."

"What mystery?" Tain hefted the baby in his arm and leaned against the back of a sofa.

"Septimus here came banging at the door at midnight," Hunter said. "He wanted to know why I was harassing one of his vamps earlier tonight in a downtown alley, but I haven't been out all day."

Septimus broke in smoothly. "The vampire from my jurisdiction complained that he was accosted in an alley by a tall man with an incredible life-magic aura and a sword."

Hunter grinned. "So Septimus naturally thought of me. But it was you, wasn't it?"

"Yes."

"Any particular reason why?" Septimus asked.

"He was bothering a demon girl," Tain said.

Septimus arched dark brows. "A demon?"

"Who'd been tortured and nearly killed, and forced to watch her sister be brutally murdered. I didn't think she deserved to be sucked dry by a vampire on top of it."

Leda, Hunter, and Septimus stared at him in shock. Ryan made contented noises, enjoying lying in the curve of Tain's arm.

"She isn't sure who did it to her," Tain went on, with a pointed look at Septimus.

Septimus shook his head. "None of *my* vampires are responsible."

"Are you certain?"

"I will be." Septimus's mouth flattened to a grim line. "When vampires get out of hand, I'm usually the first to hear about it, but I've heard nothing."

Tain knew that the reason Los Angeles was relatively quiet these days regarding vampire and demon battles was that Septimus controlled the entire vampire population. As an Old One, he wielded great power and used it to dominate all other vampire lords and their underlings. In addition, he'd taken advantage of the chaos the year before to start power bases in other cities.

Septimus had made a deal with Adrian, the oldest of the Immortal brothers, to keep the Los Angeles vampires contained. In return Septimus was allowed to continue his long and sin-dark life, and Adrian left him alone.

"Demons do fight among themselves," Septimus reminded him. "Clans battle for domination."

"But those are simple, straightforward fights," Hunter said. "They either gather weapons and do battle, or they sneer at each other at luncheons."

"I agree," Septimus said. "They have an honor, of sorts. I've not heard of them torturing and killing women of a rival clan, at least not these days."

"Civilized demons?" Leda mused. "Samantha is civilized, and her father's not bad, but . . ."

"Welcome to the twenty-first century," Septimus said with a cold smile. "Demons have discovered the comfort of the modern city—why dwell in a death realm when you can live in a mansion in Beverly Hills?"

Tain broke in. "If you make sure it's not the vampires, I'll take your word for it. Hunter, there's a cab outside waiting to be paid. Would you mind?"

Hunter gave him an exasperated look. "You lost the check card again, didn't you?"

"It's somewhere."

Hunter heaved a sigh and stalked past him. "I'm going to have to explain it all again, in words of one syllable."

"Time was, an Immortal didn't pay for anything," Tain said, handing Ryan back to Leda and following his brother. "People were happy to give us a drink or a ride in gratitude."

"Yes, well, this is Los Angeles, and nothing's free anymore. The world forgot about us while you were away."

The chink of darkness that always lurked in Tain's mind suddenly rose and swallowed him. Sometimes all it took was for one of his brothers to say something that made Tain realize how much he'd lost, how long he'd been imprisoned. He should have been with them all those years, fighting, drinking, chasing women, having stupid one-upmanship rivalries. He should have been with his family that loved him, no matter what. All that had been stripped from him until he couldn't even lie back and bask in the joy that filled Leda and Hunter's home.

"Tain? You all right?"

He found Hunter's green eyes right in front of him, a worried frown on his brother's face. They were standing out in the driveway, the cab pulling away, taillights flashing in the night.

"Fine." Tain heard himself distantly, as though he watched the scene from afar. "You were supposed to tell the cab to wait for me. I only came to see if you knew anything about demon hunters."

"Leda said to send it away, because you're staying for dinner. Didn't you hear her?"

"No."

Hunter's frown deepened, and Tain saw the frustration of a strong man who knew he couldn't fix everything. "It still gets to you."

"It always will. I've accepted that."

"I don't accept it, damn it," Hunter growled. "I didn't

bust my ass pulling you out of that demon's power to lose you again."

"But you pulled me out, and now I'm free. My brain will catch up after a while."

Hunter lowered his voice, glancing inside at Leda, who was smiling at a glowering Septimus. "When we formed the circle, when we joined, I felt some of what had happened to you. I took it inside me. I know what you went through."

What Hunter's and Tain's other brothers had experienced when they'd pulled his pain into themselves had only been a fraction of what Tain had endured. Tain himself had latched on to that chink of light and kicked his way out.

"You hurt yourself to get me free, and for that, I'll always be grateful. Don't beat yourself up for what you didn't do."

"But I can't stand to see you go all blank like that. Like I've still lost my baby brother."

Tain shook his head and managed a tight smile. "Believe me, anything I suffer now is only a millionth of what I suffered before. I'll get over it."

Hunter gave him a skeptical look, but he had learned when to drop the subject. "Fine. Leda will come looking for us if we don't get our butts in there."

"Why are we having dinner?" Tain asked as they went back into the warm, bright house. "It's the middle of the night."

"Because Leda decided to fix it, and don't even think about refusing."

"That's right," Leda told them. "Septimus will join us and give you a ride home."

Septimus looked pained. "I hardly need food."

"You drink wine—I've seen you. You can always wait in the limo if it upsets you that much."

A little amusement trickled through Tain's darkness as Septimus, the supreme vampire lord of one of the largest cities in the world, deflated before Leda's insistent look and obeyed.

Tain learned the reason for Leda's insistence that he stay when he volunteered to help her with the dishes, mostly to get away from the uneasy looks Hunter kept giving him. Septimus, too, watched him closely, in a way Tain didn't like.

"So," Leda began brightly. "You've talked to Samantha. How is she?"

Tain studied the water slicking his scarred forearms and hands as he held one of Leda's good plates. All through the meal Tain had tried unsuccessfully to shut Samantha out of his mind, and now the sensation of kissing her slammed him in the gut. Samantha had tasted too damn good, her hands strong as she'd laced them around her neck. He'd thought even a half demon would taste like death, but her spice was heady.

"She's in good health," he managed to say.

Leda impatiently handed him a scrub brush. "No, I mean *how is she?*"

Beautiful. Dangerous.

Tain knew Samantha was not Kehksut, who'd flayed him and then turned into a beautiful, seductive woman and forced him into sex. Kehksut was dead, the ancient being's evil magic gone. Kehksut had been death magic incarnate—Samantha was alive, warm, a woman.

Tain saw now that he'd made a mistake avoiding sex in the last year. Kehksut had so warped sex for him that Tain feared he wouldn't be able to stand the erotic touch of a woman. He had no way of knowing what he would do, whether he would hurt her. He realized that he should have eased back into it, found a woman who was so much the opposite of Kehksut that she could remind him how gentle and pleasurable sex could be.

Now he came to Samantha like a starving man, and he

knew he wouldn't be able to hold back. He felt himself drawn to her and her dark beauty, something in him crying out for her.

Hunter, hearing the conversation, came and leaned his elbows on the breakfast bar. "She's not going to be happy until she's got you paired off."

"Don't be a smart-ass," Leda said. "I just think the two of them were made for each other. I always have."

Because Leda was happy, she naturally wanted everyone in her world to be happy. Tain understood that. Leda and Hunter were to have gone to Ravenscroft after Ryan was born, but Leda had put it off, saying she wanted to wait until Ryan was a little older.

But Tain knew damn well the real reason was that she didn't want to leave while Tain was in Los Angeles. He could be rude and tell her he didn't need a babysitter, but he kept his silence. Hunter and Leda were trying to be good to him, and the least he could do was let them.

Leda persisted for a while, but after a few more evasive answers from Tain, Hunter persuaded Leda to let the topic drop.

Tain rode back downtown in the smoke-glass-windowed limousine with Septimus, both of them eyeing each other uncomfortably. Tain's skin crawled with Septimus's death magic, but he felt better knowing that his life magic bothered the vamp the same way.

Septimus insisted on dropping Tain off at his apartment building and waiting until he went inside. Tain knew this was half to satisfy Leda about getting Tain home safely, the other half so Septimus would know where Tain lived, especially because the converted motel was in Septimus's territory.

The quiet of Tain's one-room apartment welcomed him, the darkness soothing. Tain liked the dark; this century's artificial lights grated on his nerves.

He'd bought candles, dozens of cheap votives, and tea lights, and strewn them about the room. He drew the shade, lit the candles, then stripped off his clothes and sat in the middle of the floor in meditation.

As he feared, the mind-quieting of the meditation didn't come easily to him. Instead he kept seeing Samantha, her lips red with his kisses, her dark eyes betraying hurt when he told her *no* and walked away.

"I know it's not easy for you," Logan said to the demon girl Nadia. "But can we go over it again? I want to find something—anything—that will help us figure out who did this to you and your sister. And possibly other girls out there."

Nadia reclined in a hospital bed in the clinic, the sheets pulled up over her hospital gown. A nurse had kindly trimmed away the hanks of her shorn hair to even it up, but she couldn't cover the bald patches on the girl's scalp.

Nadia was twenty-three, the file in Logan's lap told him. No parents, left her family and clan three years ago to work in a club in Santa Monica. Tiring of answering to the club owner, she took to the streets to sell the pleasure that came with life-essence draining.

Normally, Logan left dealing with demons to Samantha, because the wolf in him hated all death magic creatures, and he had a hard time not ripping demon criminals to pieces. But something in him had grown angry when he'd looked over Samantha's notes this morning, and he decided he wanted to find the person—demon, human, werewolf, or otherwise—who had done this.

Nadia's eyes were bruised in her white face, but she was pretty—probably mostly demon glam, Logan reasoned, but right now she simply looked pathetic and exhausted.

"I told you," she snapped. "I barely saw them. Mostly I was tied up in a closet."

"An ordinary closet? Not a cell?"

"There were brooms and pipes in the walls," she said in a hard voice. "Like something in a maintenance room. I tried to use a broom handle to break open the door, but it didn't work. Hard to do it with my hands and feet tied."

Logan closed the file. He'd been told he'd develop calluses on his feelings, especially in Los Angeles, a city that drew those who wanted to prey on others, although he'd seen nothing here so far to what werewolves could do when one turned against the pack. But so far his calluses hadn't grown, so he spent a lot of time with his heart squeezing in compassion for people like Nadia, even if they didn't appreciate it.

"I want to get these bastards, Nadia."

"Why would you want to help a demon?" she demanded. "Why would that other guy want to—who the hell was he, by the way?"

"I'm not even sure myself."

"So why do you care so much?"

Logan stretched out his long legs and folded his arms. "This is my town," he said, drawling like an old-West sheriff. "I want to keep it clean."

"Bullshit, werewolf."

The wolf in him snarled, but that was only his life magic with its hackles up.

"No, I really do want to find out who did this to you and your sister," he said in calmer tones. "There's a difference between a good fight and—this."

Nadia deflated, her eyes moistening. "I'm sorry, all right?"

Logan shrugged, telling the beast in him to shut up and sit down. "What happened to you was terrible. You're allowed to be pissed."

"I wish I could help." Nadia sank back to her pillows, her face fine-boned and vulnerable. "They gave me something that took away my strength. When I was in the closet, I couldn't change into my demon form, and then later they wanted me to change. They wanted to kill a demon, not something that looked human."

"Probably. Which means they weren't after you in particular but demons in general."

"Yes, but it was my sister *in particular* who was killed."

Her face crumpled, and she looked nothing more than a young woman who had stumbled into tragedy. Logan couldn't stop himself reaching out to brush back the shorn ends of her hair. She gave him a startled look, tears streaming down her face.

He was glad now that Samantha had roped him into this case, because he would do anything to get the bastards that had made this helpless young woman grieve.

CHAPTER SIX

Tain lay stretched full length on the floor, his eyes wide open, anything but calm. Meditation usually soothed him, but peace of mind had eluded him tonight.

As dawn light seeped through the window, silence descended and time seemed to slow and stop. The presence of a goddess began to fill every space, like a perfume permeating a close room.

Cerridwen didn't manifest all the way but became a white light hovering above him. "Tain." He felt her love and her warmth flow around him, her healing magic seeking out the hurts within him.

She'd helped him heal little by little over the past year, giving him enough magic to boost his own Immortal life magic and complete the healing of his flesh. Sometimes, like tonight, Tain's body cringed from the healing, somehow needing to hurt. Something inside him believed that if he hurt enough he'd make up for what he'd done, and he didn't always want comfort from that.

"Why?" he asked, willing her light from his body. "Why did you let it happen? You're a goddess. I understand why my brothers didn't come for me—they tried and couldn't find me. But why did you stand by and not help me?"

He'd asked the question often enough since his escape from Kehksut, and Cerridwen had never answered. Now her sorrow heightened until he could barely stand the crush of it. "I let it happen so that you would be strong enough to defeat the ancient one. Your imprisonment and pain gave you strength, and now you are greater than all your brothers put together. It had to be thus."

He stared at her, trying to understand. "You let me be tortured on purpose?"

"It had to be, or your brothers would not have come together to save you, and the world would have been lost. One of you had to have the strength to kill the Old One—even all of you together wouldn't have been able to defeat him, the most ancient and powerful of his kind."

"One of us? Why was *I* chosen? What made me special?"

Thinking about his life before his capture and imprisonment, Tain knew he hadn't been special at all, at least as far as being an Immortal went. He'd been raised by a Roman soldier in Britain who taught him about fighting and honor and strength. When Tain joined his brothers, he'd battled demons and other death magic creatures with them and celebrated afterward in the traditional warrior way—wine, women, and song.

He'd always known that Adrian and Kalen were far more powerful than he was. He and Hunter and Darius had been closer in strength, and the three of them had time and again awakened together after a long revelry with little memory of it.

Tain had never thought of himself as special—just a warrior whose magical talent was healing. He couldn't even heal Immortals, so he and Hunter and Darius always had to suffer through the hangovers.

"We drew lots," Cerridwen whispered. "It was to my great sorrow that I won."

Tain sat up. "You drew *lots?*"

"It was the only way, the goddesses and I, to decide

which of you would gain the strength. We didn't have the fortitude to make such a decision, so we left it to fate."

Tain got to his feet, power crackling from him in his rage. "Do you mean I suffered for seven hundred years because *you drew the short straw?*"

"Yes."

The one word. Tain roared in anger, light exploding from him. While he wouldn't have wished what he'd suffered on his brothers, the full betrayal of it struck him. He and his brothers, the indestructible warriors, had been mere pawns in a game of the goddesses.

"You should have asked us," he raged. "You should have told us and let us decide who would go."

"We didn't have the strength. We couldn't bear to stand by and watch you choose who should make the sacrifice. The decision of who would go to Kehksut was made before any of you were even born."

If she told the truth, that meant that everything he and his brothers had ever done and ever endured, from their birth to the time of Kehksut's death, had been part of a long, elaborate scheme. He'd suffered torture, Hunter had lost his wife and children, Kalen had endured a terrible punishment. Darius had been kept a prisoner by the goddess Sekhmet, and Adrian still blamed himself for Tain's capture and imprisonment. But all along it had been the goddesses who planned every move and watched their sons suffer one after the other.

"Do my brothers know?"

"No. Please never tell them."

Another wave of power boomed from him. "Get out of my head. Get out of my house."

"Tain—"

"I said get *out*."

He slapped his magic at her, a whiplike tendril wrapping her and shoving her away.

Cerridwen stilled in shock, her grief pressing at him like a dark wave. Then she dissipated and was gone.

Tain rampaged through his apartment, knocking over everything in sight, blasting pieces out of the brick walls with white-hot magic. He stopped, shaking in rage, then pulled on his clothes and slammed out, unable to stay any longer.

His neighbor poked his head out of the next door, eyes round. "Hey, man, you all right?"

"Fine," Tain snarled. He snaked a gentle tendril of magic at him. "Sleep and forget."

The man shook his head, started to yawn, and said, "Take it easy," before he went back inside.

Tain walked out into the dawn, creatures both mortal and magical melting from his path.

"Good morning," Logan said cheerfully as Samantha hopped into the car Logan stopped outside her apartment complex gate. "Glad to see you this bright and early. Me, I never went to bed."

Samantha pushed her damp hair out of her eyes as Logan slid into Los Angeles traffic. Logan had called her as she was getting out of bed to tell her they'd been summoned to a disturbance near Union Station and that he'd pick her up on his way in.

"Why do they need detectives?" she asked. "Uniforms are supposed to handle stuff like this. What's different about this one?"

"This one involves our friend Tain."

Samantha came all the way awake. "Oh no, what's he done?"

"Remember those demons that attacked Merrick's place? Turns out they were from the Djowlan clan—I think I'm saying that right. Tain walked into one of their clubs, kicked out all the human customers, and is holding the demons, including the one who ordered the raid on Merrick's, hostage."

"You've got to be kidding me."

"He says he's not letting them go until one of them tells him what happened to Nadia. And that he's only *thinking* about letting them go. There's been fighting, but he's got them cornered and scared shitless."

"He said he thought demon hunters did it, not demons."

Logan shrugged. "Guess he changed his mind."

"And McKay wants me to—what? Talk him out of there?"

"That's her idea."

"What makes her think he'll listen to me?"

"Lieutenant McKay says you have to make him listen, and that everyone's counting on you."

"Gee, thanks," she said, and Logan chuckled.

"I'll be right here with you, partner."

Samantha's gut ached as they dodged through traffic. She thought of calling Hunter to see if he could help, but Hunter was no friend of demons and might see nothing wrong with Tain taking his revenge. Two Immortals would only double her problem.

The club was typical of the downtown demon clubs, very businesslike on the outside with a modest logo above the door. Samantha recognized it as one run by a demon named Kemmerer from the Djowlan clan. He'd kept things fairly quiet and clean in the last year, not because he was a moral citizen, but because he couldn't afford to have the paranormal police shut him down.

The club looked quiet now except for the circle of police cars in front and along the side alley. Most were uniforms from the paranormal division with some backup from the regular division.

Samantha got out of the car and approached the officer

in charge, showing him her credentials. "Did the guy inside say he'll negotiate with me?"

"He hasn't said anything at all," the officer answered, scrubbing his close-cropped hair. "Your lieutenant says you can talk him down, so I'm to let you in."

"I'm going with her," Logan said.

"I wish you wouldn't," Samantha returned. "At least not until I know what's going on. If he hasn't slipped back into insanity, I might be able to reason with him."

"*If* he hasn't slipped back into insanity?" Logan repeated, an incredulous look on his face. "That's it. I'm coming with you." He slid his gun from his holster and flicked off the safety.

"Don't shoot him. You'll just piss him off."

Logan's jaw tightened. "But it might distract him while you get away. Sorry, sweetie, I have a wolf's protective instinct. Doesn't matter that you're not pack or mate, you're my friend and partner. He even looks like he's going to hurt you, he's going down."

"I outrank you. If I tell you to stay put, will you?"

"No."

Samantha conceded that it was smart to let Logan come in with her, even if the two of them together were no match for an Immortal. If Tain *had* retreated into madness, they were screwed. She'd seen what he was capable of, and she never wanted to see that again.

Her heart hurt. Last night he'd bent to kiss her like he couldn't stop himself. She'd wanted him then, and she still did.

But she wanted whatever she had with him to be—normal. Friends if they couldn't be lovers. But Samantha was half demon and Tain was a rampaging Immortal demigod, and they were probably always meant to be star-crossed.

Logan kept his weapon drawn, and Samantha drew

hers. The guns might not work on Tain, but there were demons in there, too.

The first thing Samantha noted when they went inside was the smell. Demon musk, overpowering and awful. When demons wanted to seduce, they could send out sweet pheromones to trap the unwary, but these odors had to do with defense and terror.

Several demons lay in the doorway. "Not dead," Logan murmured as he checked. "Just out." They walked into the main club, which looked strange and a bit seedy with all the lights on.

Tain was in the middle of the club, sitting tilted back on a chair, arms folded, his duster brushing the floor.

This part of the club was a vast open space three stories high, and demons hung on the walls all the way up, pressed there by Tain's magic. About half of the demons had reverted to their monster-from-hell forms; the others retained their seductive human forms and expensive clothes from Rodeo Drive. The one thing they all had in common was fear. One of the female demons saw Samantha and shouted down at her.

"Help us!"

Samantha started forward, but was forced to a halt six feet from Tain's chair. Whether he'd erected a magic barrier or simply spelled her feet not to move, she didn't know, but she had to stop in her tracks, and Logan halted beside her.

"Tain," Samantha said quietly.

Tain flicked a gaze to her and she gasped. The darkness in his eyes was vast, nearly drowning out the blue. She couldn't tell if he sparked with insanity or rage, but either one wasn't good.

"Go back outside, Samantha," he said. "Tell them I wouldn't negotiate."

"I can't." She wished her voice sounded stronger, but it rasped. "My lieutenant expects me to bring you out and save the day. I have the feeling future promotion will be riding on this, so how about you do me a favor and come outside with me?"

"Don't try to cajole me." Dark magic flashed out of him, and then he gestured to the demons pressed against the walls. "Do you want to know what they told me?"

"Tell me outside. McKay will want to hear it, too."

"I don't work for law enforcement. Your procedure is too slow, and I like to be direct."

"Barging into a club and threatening everyone is certainly direct."

He gave her a flint-hard stare. "Put away your guns. This isn't a TV show, and someone might get hurt."

That was true—flying bullets were never good, and cops had to justify every shot. She could concede that much to him, because her gun would have no effect on him anyway.

"All right." She made a show of clicking on the safety and stowing her gun back in her holster. She nodded at Logan to do the same. He did, but kept his hand near the butt of the gun.

"There, gun gone." Samantha showed him her empty hands.

"Don't patronize me. This one . . ." He shoved a demon in a black business suit farther up the wall than the others. He was Kemmerer, the demon who owned the club. "He sent the demons against Merrick's club. He is trying to expand and wants the beach towns, and he considers Merrick fair game."

She wanted to say, *oh shit*. If Merrick found out, he'd go on the warpath, and the clan battles would begin.

"I also questioned him about Nadia," Tain went on. "He admitted to picking up Nadia and her sister off the street, but he claims he had nothing to do with the torture and murder. What he did was sell the two girls to the people who did it."

Samantha looked up at the defiant demon with loathing. "Slavery is illegal, by demon law as well as human," she told him.

"Are you sure you still want me to let him go and walk outside quietly with you?" Tain asked her.

Samantha itched to ask Tain to knock Kemmerer's head against the wall a few times for what happened to Nadia and her sister, but she sighed. "We have to do it by the book, or we can't make the charges stick."

"It would be faster if I ripped off his head. I can do it for you." Tain held up his finger and thumb as though the demon's neck were between his grip. Kemmerer made strangled noises.

"I wish I could let you," Samantha said.

"I'm strong enough to kill everyone in this room," Tain said in a calm voice that was more frightening than a rage. "They made me strong like that on purpose, and here I am, so powerful that they don't know what to do with me. What would they do if I became uncontrollable?"

Samantha had no idea what he was talking about and wasn't sure she'd like it if she did.

"Should I test it?" Tain asked softly, half to himself. Kemmerer rose higher and gasped at Samantha to help him.

Samantha looked at Tain's eyes, so blue they could be pieces of the ocean under a summer sky. The surface looked quiet, even calm, but she sensed that beneath it lurked a roiling, wild churning, pain more vast than she could imagine. He was trying to relay to her what he was going through, to show her a glimpse of his anguish that surpassed all the anguish in the world.

It was the most frightening thing Samantha had ever seen, and she could think of only one thing to do. She pulled out her cell phone and flipped it open.

"Who are you summoning?" Tain asked without much interest. "Your SWAT team?"

"No," Samantha said, thumb hovering over the button that would complete the call. "I'm calling Leda. All I have to do is push this."

Tain looked at her for a long moment. "Oh, Samantha. You play dirty."

"Against Immortals? I've learned to."

The wild magic subsided just a little bit, his eyes clearing. "Put away your phone, and I'll leave with you. Just you," he added as Logan straightened up. "You take me to see your father so I can set up a meeting with the Lamiah clan matriarch, and I'll walk out with you."

"A meeting? That sounds very civilized. You mean you won't simply burst in like you did here?"

Tain glanced dismissively at the demons. "These are thugs who live by manipulating humans with their magic. The clans are somewhat more civilized. The matriarch will hear me if nothing else."

"I'll see what I can do," Samantha said with caution.

"I will take your word. I'll walk out with you now, and you take me beyond your circle of police and let me go."

"They won't let you go—they'll follow you and arrest you."

"Don't tell him that," Logan hissed. "No way am I letting him take you hostage."

"They won't follow me," Tain said. "They'll forget all about me. What your partner and your lieutenant decide to do with the demons is their own business."

Samantha flipped her cell phone closed, still wary. "Fine."

Tain got up from the chair and came to her, then turned her around and put his hand on her shoulder. The demons remained where they were, hovering in midair, and she had no way of knowing whether he'd simply let them fall or turn around and strike them dead as he'd killed the demons in Merrick's club. She felt tension shimmering through him, towering rage that he held back with Herculean effort.

"What happened?" she whispered to him.

"Walk."

Samantha led him past Logan, out through the dark bowels of the club toward the main door. "What about the demons?"

"They're fine where they are. Logan can enjoy himself arresting them—the wolf in him wants to tear apart the club owner for what happened to Nadia."

"You can read Logan's thoughts?" Samantha asked, still walking.

"I don't need to."

Samantha wasn't sure what to make of that. She stepped over the demons sprawled in the doorway and out into the balmy night.

"Don't shoot," she said to the waiting uniforms, her hands spread. "I'm bringing him out."

The uniforms didn't lower their weapons, and as Samantha walked by, their eyes glazed over slightly, and they kept their guns trained on the open door.

"Keep walking," Tain said to Samantha. "They won't notice us."

"What did you do?"

"Very simple magic. They'll remember coming here to arrest the demon leader, and Logan will take—as you say—the kudos for it."

"And what will we be doing?"

"Talking to your father."

They'd walked beyond the circle of police vehicles without any of the uniforms or the officer in charge noticing. The area was relatively quiet beyond that, people either focused on watching what the police were up to or taking themselves well out of the way.

"What did you have in mind for transportation?" Samantha asked, keeping her jaw clenched so her teeth wouldn't chatter. "My truck is at home, and I can't take Logan's car and leave him stranded."

"That's all right," Tain said, his hand warm on her shoulder. "I don't mind taking the bus."

They took a taxi. Samantha found it surreal to be sitting next to Tain in the dark backseat while the driver sped up the Pasadena freeway.

Like he had in her truck last night he sat close enough that she could feel his warmth, smell the scents of the night that clung to his duster coat. His intense life magic could knock her out of the taxi if she let it, and she marveled that the driver didn't seem to notice.

"Why did you let me take you out of there?" she asked in a low voice.

"I was finished."

"What made you go there in the first place?"

Tain looked out the window, passing lights flicking yellow-white bands across his face. "It was the club closest to the alley where I found Nadia. I wondered why whoever had captured her had chosen to release her there, and reasoned that it was probably where they'd snatched her in the first place."

"Not bad," Samantha conceded. "I'm sure Logan will be happy to interrogate the club owner. What happened to Nadia truly pissed him off."

"And me."

That's the trouble with being paranormal police, Samantha reflected silently. *Sometimes our true natures want swift and final justice, but we have to work within the law while people like Tain are outside it.*

The taxi dropped them at the end of the driveway of her parents' house in Pasadena, a quiet neighborhood that showed no sign that last year it had been overrun by demon gangs. Her mother's flowers grew undisturbed in the front garden in the early morning light, and the stucco and tile-roofed house with its small windows was calm and welcoming.

Her father lived here with her mother now. For a long time Samantha had hated Fulton, believing him to have coerced and abducted her mother in the way of demons.

But she'd come to understand that he'd fallen in love with Samantha's mother, Joanne, and had returned to her when they'd both thought Samantha ready to accept him as her father. Samantha had been skeptical and angry, but when her mother had disappeared the previous year, she'd seen exactly how much Fulton loved his wife. They'd worked together to find her, and Samantha had stood back and watched her parents embrace with the frantic clasp of those who'd believed they'd never see each other again.

The past year had been difficult, but Samantha had gradually come to know the man who was her father, and he to understand her. Joanne had never been so happy, and for her sake, Samantha was willing to try.

Fulton answered her knock and greeted her with delighted surprise. He was a demon male who'd made himself look about thirty-five, but Samantha knew he was more than a hundred years old. He was dark haired, brown eyed, well built, handsome.

"Your mother is running errands while I cook breakfast," he said over his shoulder as they came in. He picked up a spatula he'd left on the hall table and headed back to the kitchen. "I'm mastering banana pancakes."

"My favorite," Samantha said.

"I know. Your mother told me. I wanted to practice."

That her estranged father would try to make her favorite childhood food made her eyes sting. She and Tain followed him into the kitchen, where Fulton frowned at a griddle as it heated on top of the stove.

"This one's different." He glanced up at Tain, making it clear he wasn't talking about the griddle.

"This is Tain, Hunter's brother," Samantha said.

"I thought he might be. I've never felt life magic that concentrated. Gives me the willies."

"He'll behave himself." Samantha gave Tain a look, which he ignored.

She told Fulton about Nadia and the purpose of their errand, while Tain wandered about the kitchen, studying everything from the clock on the wall to the stove-top griddle. Fulton flipped pancakes, scowling when Samantha told him how Nadia's sister had been killed.

"That was done by someone who knew precisely how to kill demons," he said grimly. "A demon can't recover from a heart being torn out."

"Not many people can," Samantha said.

"Vampires can. They die when a stake is driven through their rotted hearts, but that's more symbolic than biological. They're the only race that can be killed by a metaphor."

"It's part of my job to know how to kill a demon if necessary," Samantha said. "But the average person on the street doesn't have that knowledge or ability."

"We're not looking for the average person on the street," Tain said. He abandoned the griddle and moved to the French doors that led to the small backyard, hands in his pockets. "Demons know how to kill other demons."

"So do vamps," Fulton said. "I'd bank on vampires doing this."

"Vampire activity has been subdued since Septimus took over," Tain said, turning back. "But demons are still fighting for domination throughout the city."

Fulton looked stubborn. "From what Samantha just told me, Nadia's death isn't the result of a downtown demon gang trying to muscle out another demon gang. This was a deliberate act of murder, and sending the girl's heart back was a signal of some sort. A message to other demons."

"That doesn't rule out the possibility that one demon clan wants to declare war on another," Tain said. "That is why I wish to speak to your matriarch."

"I think you should let him," Samantha said to Fulton. "I'd like to hear what she has to say, too."

Fulton sighed. "Child, you know so very little. What's been done is an abomination. If our matriarch thought another demon clan had committed an atrocity deliberately against the Lamiah, she would declare war, and you do not want to be in the middle of a demon war. What happened last year was a schoolyard scuffle compared to what an all-out war would do. There hasn't been one in centuries."

"But if we can talk to her, she might know what's going on," Samantha said. "She might already know who is doing this and point me in the right direction. Then I make an arrest and stop this before it starts."

Fulton shook his head. "That is the other thing you don't understand. I can't simply take you to the matriarch. You have to be accepted into the clan before you're allowed to even get near the matriarch."

"But I'm your daughter. Doesn't that make me of the clan Lamiah?"

Fulton slid another finished pancake onto the stack warming on the back of the stove. "You're not of full blood."

Samantha's anger rose, and she felt Tain's gaze focus on her. "And that's bad, I take it?"

"Demons are highly conservative," Tain said. "Trust me on this. I was taught about demons by a master."

He looked off into the distance, somewhat like he'd done at Merrick's club after he killed the demons.

Fulton nodded agreement. "It is difficult for demons to accept that we now sometimes mate with nondemons. Only a hundred years ago a demon could be slain if he married outside the clan, along with his mate and any offspring. Times have changed, but still it is difficult for demons to accept intermarriage."

"If you weren't allowed to marry outside the clan, didn't that lead to inbreeding?" Samantha asked. "Receding chins, genetic diseases, that kind of thing?

"Demon clans are huge," Fulton said. "So it was possible to marry someone not too closely related. But yes, learning about genetics was one reason for lifting the ban on intermarriage. That is, it's acceptable for demons to mate with humans, but marrying across clans is still frowned on and carries a terrible stigma for the mated couple and their children."

"What happens if the Lamiah clan decides not to accept me?"

Fulton looked away. "That's up to the matriarch."

The way he carefully avoided her eyes as he finished the pancakes told her he knew things could get bad for the rejected half-blood demon.

"Nothing will happen," Tain said, his deep, lilting voice breaking the silence. "I won't let it."

"You won't be there," Fulton said. "The clan matriarch will never allow someone as full of life magic as you near her."

"That's what Merrick said," Samantha added.

"Merrick." Fulton scowled. "He's scum of the earth. Stay away from him."

"I know he is—that's why I arrested him. It's kind of my job, Dad."

Fulton turned away quickly. Tain watched both of them as he had the entire conversation, his eyes revealing nothing. "The matriarch will see me—the easiest way is for you to bring me in with Samantha. I'll follow the matriarch's rules, but she'll see me."

Tain was going to insist, and Samantha decided to stop arguing. The idea of having Tain at her back when Fulton presented her to a matriarch who could accept her or throw her out or try to kill her—whatever was the penalty for rejection—appealed to her.

"She might decide to take it out on me," Fulton said without turning around. "Maybe forbid me to see my wife and Sam."

"She won't," Tain repeated.

Fulton finally turned, his eyes moist. "I take it you've never met a clan matriarch—you couldn't have, or you wouldn't be so cocky."

"Perhaps not," Tain said.

"He killed an Old One," Samantha pointed out. "One of the most ancient and powerful demons that walked the earth. Perhaps it's the matriarch who shouldn't be cocky."

"I heard about that," Fulton said. He looked sharply at Tain. "But when you meet the matriarch, you might wish you were back doing battle with that Old One."

Samantha's mother returned not long after that, happy to see Samantha and intrigued to meet Tain. Tain even agreed to a breakfast of pancakes and bacon, and ate heartily—maybe tearing up a demon club first thing in the morning gave him an appetite. Fulton finally agreed to try to set up the appointment with the matriarch and told them what they'd be expected to wear and do if the matriarch accepted.

Another taxi took Samantha back home, Tain insisting on accompanying her.

"I think my father started crying while we were talking about what the matriarch might do," she said as the taxi rolled away from Pasadena. "He must be very worried about this meeting."

Tain's harsh gaze softened suddenly. "He wasn't crying because of that."

Samantha gave him a puzzled look. "What, then?"

His blue eyes became as gentle as she'd ever seen them. "He was crying because you called him *Dad*."

CHAPTER SEVEN

Before Samantha and Tain could meet with the clan Lamiah matriarch, Merrick's club burned to the ground.

It happened at midmorning, when anyone who worked at the club, which closed at five A.M., would be asleep. Samantha and Logan went to the call, watching from the perimeter while firemen directed their hoses on the club and the buildings around it in an attempt to keep the fire contained.

The demon employees who lived in the building—the bartender and several of the female demons—huddled in blankets outside the ring of police barricades. The girls were crying, the bartender watching the fire with a stunned look on his face.

"Where's Merrick?" Samantha asked him.

The bartender shrugged as though he couldn't manage enough energy to answer.

"He didn't get out," one of the women sobbed. "He pushed me down the stairs, but he didn't come after me."

"Shit." Samantha shoved her way to one of the firemen who'd stepped back to drink some water. "Did Merrick make it out?" she shouted at him. "The owner? One of the girls thinks he's still in there."

The fireman shook his head, looking grim. "We tried to get to him, but we couldn't. The middle floors are completely gone, and the ladder trucks had to back off."

Samantha gnawed her lip. She didn't like Merrick, but

she didn't necessarily want to watch him burn to death, either. If he'd reverted to his demon form, he might make it—demons were tough—but smoke inhalation could take down any form of life.

"Hey!" one of the firemen bellowed. He backed up to where Samantha stood with the other fireman. "Someone just ran in there. Asshole. It's a death sentence—for us, too, because now we have to try to get him out."

"No." Samantha stopped him. "You don't need to go after him. He won't die in there."

The two firemen stared at her in shock, but she'd seen the sunshine on flame-red hair and knew exactly who'd run into the fire.

Tain found Merrick sitting in his living room, sipping from a glass of brandy. Flames and smoke rampaged in the rooms surrounding it, but the living room was an oasis of relative calm. Merrick had employed some kind of magic to seal it off, but the magic would not be strong enough to keep the fire back for long.

"Now I know I'm in hell," Merrick said when he saw Tain. "And not the good kind of hell."

Tain didn't answer. Smoke began to seep under the doors on the other side of the room, the fire starting to break through Merrick's spell.

"Are you here to save me?" Merrick asked. "Or to make sure the fire does its job?"

"Samantha wants you out."

"Sweet girl, our Sam. What do we do? Run out through it? That's fine for you. You can survive having a burning building fall on you."

"I don't particularly want to live through the pain of that. Whenever you're done with your drink . . ."

The magic shield cracked like breaking glass and fire roared through the open door. Merrick threw aside his brandy and leapt from the chair.

"What now?" he shouted.

The window was already broken, and Tain kicked away melting, jagged shards.

"You've got to be kidding me," Merrick said behind him. "We're fifty feet up."

Flame roared through the room engulfing the opulent leather chair Merrick had just been sitting in. Tain slung Merrick over his shoulder, balanced on the precarious windowsill, and jumped.

Merrick screamed obscenities. Tain threw a handful of white-hot magic at the ground to slow the fall, but they still landed hard. Tain rolled with the fall as the building's bricks began popping outward with the heat.

Paramedics dragged both of them up and out of the way. Tain tossed off his ruined coat and scrubbed his hand across his grimy, cut face. Merrick lay on the ground and groaned.

Samantha hurried to them, her dark eyes round. She reached for Tain, her cool hand contacting his hot skin, an impulsive gesture of worry and caring.

"Are you all right?" she gasped. "I saw you jump."

Tain waved off the paramedic who was trying to get him to sit down and be examined. "Merrick will live, though I think he wet himself on the way down."

"I would, too, if you jumped out of the window with me. You damn near gave me a heart attack." Her eyes were watering, probably from all the smoke. She blinked them clear, then looked at him in horror. "Tain, your hair."

Tain put his hand up and came away with a handful of brittle, charred lumps. "Doesn't matter. I'll cut it off."

"I like your hair." She sounded wistful, as though his hair burning was the worst thing that had happened that night.

He held out the clumps to her. "You can have it if you like it so much."

She put her hand over her mouth, and tears leaked from her eyes. "You're such a shit. I know you can't be hurt, but . . ."

"I can be hurt. I heal, but it takes time."

Again, the cool hand on his wrist. "I hate seeing you hurt."

Tain looked down into dark eyes that seemed to drag him into her. He hadn't seen her since she'd left the taxi they'd shared down from Pasadena several days ago. His basic urges had wanted him to go into the apartment with her and stay there, but once she was safely indoors, he'd made himself turn away.

He'd wanted to call her sometimes in the night when he lay on his bed and stared at the city lights playing across his ceiling. He wanted her to be with him, her head snuggled on his shoulder, his fingers threading her silk hair while his neighbor's music thumped through the wall.

He craved it like a starving man. He feared it, too, feared what he felt for her. He didn't want the emotions that had begun to stream through him when he'd first seen Samantha in Seattle to continue, nor did he want what was growing within him to be destroyed.

He remembered how her voice had cut through the nightmare of his mind that night of the final battle. *I prefer to go out kicking and screaming,* she'd said when he'd demanded her surrender. And then she'd given him an all-over assessment and told him she liked what she saw.

It had been the first time in centuries that a spark of interest had crept into his dark, tormented world. A half-demon woman, of all people, had finally snapped the bond.

Tain touched the corner of her mouth, wiping away a smudge of soot. "We should talk to Merrick."

She swallowed and nodded, turning her burning black eyes away from him.

They picked their way over to the ambulance where Merrick lay on a stretcher, an oxygen mask over his mouth and nose. His hair had burned, too, leaving him half bald and scowling.

"Hi, Merrick. Good to see you made it," Samantha told him in a cheerful voice.

The demon mumbled something, lost behind the mask.

"Any idea what happened?" she asked.

Merrick nodded. They'd bandaged burns on his hands, which made his fingers clumsy as he fumbled with his suit jacket. "In the pocket," he said under the plastic mask.

Samantha pulled on a pair of plastic gloves and dipped her fingers into the ruined silk of Merrick's coat. She pulled out a piece of paper, which she unfolded.

Tain read over her shoulder. In the same kind of cutout letters as the others, the message read THY DOOM IS HERE.

Merrick slid the mask up. "It came in this morning's mail. I didn't know what the hell it meant, but I guess I do now."

Samantha folded the paper and put it in a bag to give to forensics. "I'll have it checked for prints or anything else that can help us, but I'm not hopeful. Do you know how the fire started?"

"Explosion of some kind, I think in the room right under my bedroom. It spread fast—I didn't know fire could move that fast."

"It can. Especially if it was helped along by fuel or magic. Or both."

"No kidding. Please tell me you're going after the bastards."

Samantha nodded, looking competent and confident, another thing she was good at. "You'll be happy to know that Kemmerer is in jail. He sold Nadia and her sister to their captors."

"I heard." Merrick oozed satisfaction in spite of his club

in ruins around him. "Did he tell you who the captors were?"

"He didn't know. They took good care to keep from being seen. We had a telepath do lie detection on him, and he's telling the truth—he doesn't know. And lo and behold, he's been getting the same kind of 'doom' letters you are. I have the feeling these captors and letter senders are one in the same."

"Good work, Detective," Merrick said in an ironic voice.

"Don't push it. The fire is a pretty good way to hide traces of Mindglow we might find if we searched your club."

"Oh, please. I'm not blithering stupid enough to burn down my own club to get rid of evidence."

"I know." Samantha patted his shoulder. "I was just teasing you. I will get whoever's doing this, I promise you that."

Tain believed her. Samantha's eyes had a determined look, and Tain had the feeling she'd do any kind of cocky thing she could think of to bring down the perpetrators. Which meant Tain needed to stick with her to keep her alive through it all. Samantha had saved his life once. Maybe if he got her alive through this, it would make things even.

He knew things between them would never be even, but the idea was one he could grasp amid the smoke and madness, a tiny lifeline that he clung to.

When Fulton said Samantha had to dress formally to meet the clan matriarch, he meant it. No slinky dresses, no spike-heeled shoes, no bare legs, no bare shoulders.

Samantha had to rent a gown, a shimmering blue silk with elbow-length sleeves, a collar that hugged the base of her neck, and a long skirt. The bodice itched and she had to kick the skirt out of the way to walk, but Fulton said it was modest enough for the matriarch. "I feel like I'm being presented to the queen," she muttered as she studied herself in the mirror. But, in the demon way of thinking, she pretty much was.

Tain met her at her father's house, from which Fulton would take them to the matriarch's. Fulton had made clear that the matriarch had agreed to see her only after a long debate, and Fulton speculated that the reason she'd granted the audience was her curiosity about Tain.

Tain's idea of formal was a Scottish dress kilt. Samantha stopped in heart-pounding astonishment when she saw him.

Whatever the Celtic man of fashion had been wearing eighteen centuries ago Samantha didn't know, but Tain had chosen a formal black coat and red and black plaid kilt. He was a big man, but the coat fit him perfectly. The kilt's hem brushed his knees, and his muscular calves were encased in supple black boots.

He'd cut his hair close, shaving off the hanks that had singed in the fire. Samantha had loved his long, sleek red hair, but she had to admit he looked pretty good in a buzz cut, too. The cut emphasized the sharp lines of his face, his high cheekbones and square jaw, the pentacle tattoo black against his skin.

She wet her lips. "We don't match. I would have worn black or something."

"It doesn't matter."

Of course not; it wasn't as though they were going as a couple.

"Never mind. My father is ready to go."

Samantha kissed her mother good-bye and climbed into Fulton's SUV. Her mother wasn't allowed to go, being human, a fact that Fulton didn't like, although it was clear he could do nothing about it.

Samantha sat in the front with him, and Tain took the

seat behind her. As Fulton made for the freeway, he gave them plenty of other instructions.

"When we get there, don't talk to anyone, and don't ask any questions. Don't look around the house, and don't let on if you're curious about anything you see. Don't talk to the matriarch before she talks to you, and then only if she asks you a direct question. If she decides when we get there that she doesn't want to speak to us at all, we leave. No questions, no arguments."

Samantha listened with a qualm. "I'm starting to think this is a bad idea."

Fulton scowled. "It *is* a bad idea."

"It's her way of protecting herself," Tain said from the backseat. "Matriarchs live in constant fear of being overthrown either by a rival clan or from within."

"I suppose that's true," Samantha conceded. "I'm surprised she agreed to see Tain at all."

"She knows who he is and what he did to the Old One last year," Fulton said. "She admitted to being curious."

Fulton drove them through Beverly Hills, winding up manicured streets and past gated mansions. At the end of one particularly long, twisting road was a huge iron gate that looked almost delicate, but Samantha could see it was thick and strong.

Fulton pulled to a stop in front of a gatehouse, where two guards, both demons, sauntered out to ask them their business and then to search the car. Tain had to relinquish his short swords and Samantha the gun in her purse, though Tain made sure the guards locked everything in a cabinet in their gatehouse instead of tossing them on their desk.

After talking via radio to the main house, the guards told Fulton to park in a designated lot halfway up the drive. Two more guards came in an electric cart and drove them the rest of the way to the house. Samantha realized that the parking area was located so that if they'd managed to smuggle explosives in their car, it lay too far from both gate and house to do immediate damage to either one.

"It's easier to get onto a military base," Samantha remarked as Tain helped her from the cart at the front door.

"The matriarch can't afford to take chances," Fulton answered in clipped tones.

He was nervous, which showed in his walk and the rigid way he held his gaze. Tain kept his hand lightly on Samantha's back as they walked up the shallow steps bathed in security lights. His warmth behind her contrasted to the death magic she felt blanketing the house, and she wondered how he could stand it.

More guards met them inside the front door. The mansion was as opulent as any movie mogul's, with glittering, empty reception rooms on either side of a wide hall. A wrought-iron staircase wound up through the middle of the house, but it, like all the rooms, was utterly empty.

The setting sun slanted through western windows, and trees outside cast thick shadows. The guards took them to the very back of the house to a small elevator.

The elevator took them down, not up. Off balance, Samantha reached for the nearest thing to steady herself, which happened to be Tain. Her hand locked on his wrist, and when she would have pulled away, he put his hand on hers, keeping her there.

The underground floor was as opulent as upstairs, the rooms that opened off the square hall lit with warm artificial light instead of sunlight. The rooms were also just as empty.

The guard tapped on a closed double door at the end of the hallway, and a tall, thin woman with a short haircut and dressed in a business suit opened the door.

She was a demon but reminded Samantha of a severe maitre d' in a posh restaurant that catered to CEOs and movie executives. The woman regarded the three of them with cold dark eyes, told them she was the matriarch's majordomo, and announced that the matriarch would see them now.

"Samantha, what will you drink?" came a voice from across the room. Another woman turned from a gilded, wheeled drink cart clustered with crystal glasses, decanters, and bottles. She lifted an ice cube from the bucket with silver tongs and regarded Samantha quizzically.

The matriarch was as tall and thin as her majordomo, her salt-and-pepper hair cut short in a severe, no-nonsense style. Her gray silk suit screamed *expense* as did the stately, high-heeled shoes, and she wore gold rings with small precious stones on every finger. Her entire look said *powerful businesswoman*, one who'd been around long enough to become a force to be reckoned with. Demons could make themselves look any human age they liked, and the matriarch's deliberate choice of late fifties was likely designed to command respect.

Fulton sent Samantha a look that said she'd better hurry up and choose what to drink. Samantha said quickly, "Whatever you'd like is fine with me."

The matriarch gave her a look of disappointment. "Scotch and soda, then."

"All right."

The matriarch mixed the drink herself and pointedly did not offer anything to Tain or Fulton. "I heard what you did last year against Kehksut," she said conversationally to Tain. "I was pleased at his death—he disrupted the balance of power among demonkind, especially here in Los Angeles."

"I was pleased at his death, too," Tain said, his blue eyes quiet.

"Yes, you would be," the matriarch said with a knowing look. She lifted her dark gaze to Samantha. "You, Samantha, work to protect humans against your own kind."

"Not just humans," Samantha answered, taking the

heavy crystal glass the majordomo brought her. "Against any paranormal criminal, demon, vampire, or otherwise. I also protect our kind against humans or other paranormals who would harm them."

"All the races living together in our vast city," the matriarch said, her tone acid. "Celebrating diversity."

"It's the only way to survive in Los Angeles."

"Your human blood taints your perspective. Demons don't want to live with other races. We are for ourselves. The vampires can't come out into the sunlight, which gives us great advantage. The humans fear the night, which gives us another great advantage. When the lesser races kill each other off, the demons will be left standing. Where will you be?"

Samantha felt Tain at her back, saying nothing, his obvious strength a comfort. The matriarch, she saw, was a demon for demons. She might seduce humans to imbibe their life essence, but she would regard them only as foolish victims. She'd give human beings as much respect as a human might give the slice of chicken on his plate. A demon with human blood likely got still less respect.

"I asked my father to bring me here to tell you about demons that are being targeted in the city," Samantha said, deciding to get down to business instead of fence with her. "Merrick, a Lamiah demon who owned a club in Venice, received threats and then his club burned down. A Djowlan club owner was threatened, and two young women from the Lamiah clan were kidnapped and tortured, one of them killed."

"I heard about the one called Nadia and her sister," the matriarch said, her voice frosty. "No vengeance will be taken. They are no longer clan Lamiah. They weren't even before the incident."

Samantha blinked. "They weren't? Why not?"

"Their family shunned them, as should be. A demon woman who walks the streets enticing humans for pay is a disgusting creature. Working in clubs is barely acceptable, but when they become nothing more than prostitutes, they shame their family and their clan."

"Oh." For some reason Samantha had it in her head that whatever a demon did to a human would be fine with every other demon. The idea that demons would frown upon feeding on humans who paid for the experience hadn't occurred to her.

"You think me harsh?" the matriarch asked.

"Yes."

"It is necessary. Women rule the clans for good reason—because if men were allowed to rule, there would be chaos and destruction, and we'd have died out long ago. For women to let themselves be slaves to men is an abomination. Those who don't obey the rules shall be clanless."

Samantha wondered if the matriarch directed the last barb to Samantha personally. "Still, someone is targeting demon clubs and the people associated with them, either past or present. The fact that two different clans have received similar threatening letters worries me."

"Vampires," the matriarch said dismissively.

"Not vampires," Samantha said. "When vamps want to kill demons, they just kill them."

"Maybe."

"If I'm to stop these people, I need to ask if you've seen or heard anything that might help. Have you received threatening letters?"

The matriarch snorted. "Of course I have. I receive threatening letters every day. I am the matriarch, and there are always those in the clan who want more power than they should have."

"But I think this is more than clan politics," Samantha said. "It started with the clubs, but it might spread to include all demons."

The matriarch gave her a cold look. "No being can

topple the most powerful clan of demons on earth. Except him." She gave Tain a pointed look. "You overestimate the danger."

"Merrick's club burned to the ground, and he nearly died," Samantha said angrily. "Nadia's sister *did* die, in a most brutal way. Are you saying all this has nothing to do with you?"

"Yes. And if you were true demon, you'd know that." The matriarch's gaze turned cool. "What is it you really want, Samantha? You are a half demon, neither one thing nor the other. Is it power? Over demons? Is that why you work for the human-controlled police department?"

"I told you, I try to help people—both human and non-human."

"It eats at you, doesn't it, being split down the middle? Your demon instincts tell you to do one thing, your human instincts, something else."

Fulton moved closer to Samantha, uneasy.

"I'm used to it," Samantha said.

"For instance, would you arrest me?" The matriarch smiled coldly.

"If you were committing a crime, yes."

"You sound so sure of yourself." Her aura began to darken, her death magic filling the air around her. "How would you arrest me if I didn't permit it?"

"I usually work with a partner." Samantha kept her voice steady, determined not to let the woman intimidate her—or at least not to show that she did. "For really tough cases, the department has powerful witches, or vampires, even demons."

"But if you came across me alone? Or if I tried to kill your father, right here and now, what would you do?"

The field of death magic around the matriarch strengthened, and she raised her hand. Samantha stepped protectively in front of her father, painfully aware that her pistol was locked far away in the gatehouse. She had cuffs with her that had a subduing magical field, and she could control even strong vampires with them, but she'd have to get close to the matriarch to use them.

"Show me," the matriarch said. "Show me what you'd do if you had to arrest me right now."

Samantha sensed her father's rising anger, and she touched him, signaling him to keep quiet. The majordomo watched the drama with cold, glittering eyes, a hint of a smile on her face.

And Tain—Tain did nothing. He stood a little apart from Samantha and her father, looking utterly devastating in his kilt, his legs braced apart, his arms folded across his chest.

"I'd call for backup," Samantha said, opening her purse. "Then I'd try to subdue you."

"How?" The matriarch watched her with almost fanatic intensity. "I want to see."

Samantha drew a breath, and then let her anger take over. Fine—if the matriarch wanted to know what would really happen, Samantha was happy to give her a demonstration. The woman obviously wasn't going to help or accept Samantha into the clan, so she had nothing to lose.

She handed the majordomo her untouched drink and yanked her cuffs from her purse. "I'd call for backup," she repeated, tossing aside her purse and advancing with a swift stride. "And then I'd get you cuffed and read you your rights."

Samantha knew that physically she could spin the slender woman around, pin her to a wall, and cuff her quickly and efficiently. She'd done it to men twice her size, having them shackled and subdued before they knew what hit them.

She couldn't best the woman magically, however, and she suspected that magic was what this was all about. The matriarch was testing her resolve, and Samantha determined not to back down, no matter what.

The matriarch let her get within two feet. Then she let fly her death magic, both at Samantha and Fulton. It was nasty magic, designed to kill.

It never reached them. As soon as the snake of darkness lashed out, Tain's magic knocked it aside in a blinding flash and crushed it into nothingness.

It happened so fast that Samantha barely had time to blink at the light before the air cleared and all was quiet. A smell of sulfur mixed with the acrid scent of burned wire trickled through the room, then dispersed.

Tain hadn't even moved. His blue gaze met Samantha's, and the power in it made her flinch. She'd let this man in her car, in her apartment, had been ready to take him to her bed. She remembered how gentle he'd been when he kissed her, a complete turnaround from the dangerous brutality he exuded now.

He really could wipe out a room by twitching his pinky. She shivered.

The matriarch shook out her hand as though she'd been stung, but she smiled. "I wondered what you'd do," she said to Tain. "What is she to you?"

Tain switched his gaze to the matriarch, and Samantha had the satisfaction of seeing her flinch. "She saved my life," Tain said. "I owe her my protection."

"Even though she's demon?" the matriarch asked. "After a demon enslaved you for seven hundred years?"

"Even so," Tain said quietly.

"That's what I thought," the matriarch said, sounding smug. "Thank you, Samantha, for a most enlightening display."

Samantha followed the guards out of the matriarch's house, her heart thudding. Tain strode behind her, his footfalls loud in the silence.

Fulton had remained behind, at the matriarch's insistence. Samantha hadn't wanted to leave him, but the matriarch smiled and said she was finished with intimidation today and needed to speak to him on clan business.

Fulton had given Samantha a brief hug. "Tell your mother I'll be late."

The same guards met them outside and led Tain and Samantha back to the elevator, up through the house again, and out.

It had grown fully dark while they were underground, and the floodlights now lit the mansion and gardens. Guards escorted them past Fulton's car to the gate, Tain's hand on the small of Samantha's back. One of the gate guards called for a taxi.

"She owes me cab fare," Samantha muttered as they left the grounds to wait for it.

Samantha's pistol and Tain's swords had been returned to them, the guards handling the life-magic-infused swords gingerly, and now the iron gate rolled closed behind them.

"She likes to manipulate," Tain agreed. "It's part of her power."

"I didn't notice you saying much." Samantha folded her arms over her shining blue gown. "I rented this damned dress for nothing."

"I wouldn't say for nothing."

Tain raked his gaze down her body, and her skin warmed as though he'd brushed his hand all the way down the silk.

"Why do you think she brought us here then?" Samantha asked in a subdued voice.

"To learn about you. And me. So I let her learn what she could."

"Keeping yourself to yourself, are you?"

"To her. For now."

"Not only to her," Samantha said.

He stared down at her, his eyes deep blue in the glare of the floodlights. Damn, he looked good. The black coat only emphasized his broad shoulders and trim waist, the strap that held the sheathed swords in place crisscrossed over the white shirt beneath. With the swords and his kilt, he looked like a Scottish warrior of old, one that every maiden would want fighting for her. The goddesses had certainly done good work with him.

"It's better that I keep myself to myself," he said.

"Better for who?"

"Everyone. You've seen me come close to losing control again—I know you noticed. The gods only know what I will do if that happens. Better to hold myself away, don't you think?"

He spoke in his usual hard voice, but something flashed through his eyes, a loneliness so deep and wrenching that her heart tore. He'd been alone for seven hundred years, ripped from everything he knew and loved, and now that he was free, he didn't know how to find what he loved again. Everything had changed, everything was gone.

She hurt for him, and it hurt even more to know that he didn't want her sympathy or affection. "What about that Ravenscroft place?" she asked. "Isn't that supposed to be some kind of Valhalla where nothing can hurt you?"

"I was there for a time, and it helped. But I can't hide forever while I lick my wounds and whine. I'd rather face my pain and try to make up for what I've done."

"I suppose that's a point."

"Would you hide from yourself? I think you wouldn't." He touched her cheek, a brief touch, like he had at the fire at Merrick's.

"I want to help you."

"You are demon." His finger drifted to her lips. "That calls to me. I should back away from you most of all."

"I told you, I don't cast a glam. Half demons don't—why don't you know that?"

"I didn't know any half demons in my old life. Most were killed at birth."

"Oh, that's pleasant."

"The world is different now."

"And I say, thank the goddesses for that. It's not a glam, Tain. I don't have a tenth of the magic that the matriarch in there has, or even my own father."

"It doesn't matter. You're twisting me around inside so all I dream of at night is you."

She was sure every woman in the world wanted a man with a great body in a kilt to tell her he dreamed about her. "You do?"

"I fall asleep, and there you are next to me."

"Looking like the demon I am?" she asked.

"Looking like you do now, with your eyes drawing me in and your hair like silk on my shoulder."

His voice went soft, his lilt pronounced, hot breath brushing her cheek. "I'm not wearing this awful dress, I take it?"

"You're bare for me. And I want you. I want you so much I'm burning from the inside out."

"I hope this dream has a happy ending."

"I take you. And I take you again. I take you all night, coming alive inside you like I haven't been alive in centuries."

She couldn't breathe. Her veins were on fire, the hot space between her legs growing wet and needy. She remembered his kiss, how smooth and seductive his lips were, and she wanted to burn up and melt right there.

"But then I wake up and you're gone," Tain said. "You were never there."

His bleak tone made her heart ache, and also gave her a spark of hope. "I made a fool out of myself the other night asking you to stay," she began.

"If I'd have stayed I wouldn't have gone slow. I might have hurt you. In the dream I can do whatever I want, but in reality . . ."

Her heart beat faster. "I'm not a delicate flower. I'm a cop. I went through some pretty hard training and then extra because I'm a paranormal cop. Arresting a vampire in a blood frenzy isn't exactly the same as bringing in a jaywalker—unless it's a jaywalking vampire in a blood frenzy. I survived."

"You've never survived me."

"I did. In Seattle, remember?"

"In Seattle I decided to let you go. You never fought me in truth."

"If I asked you to stay the night again, what would you say?"

"I should say no."

Samantha slid her fingers up the side of his neck. "Please say yes."

He looked at her with his fathomless blue eyes, and she saw the spark of pain and darkness deep within them. She knew he would never kiss her, especially here on the sidewalk next to the matriarch's mansion. He'd never let go of the tight hold on himself to do it. So she stood on her tiptoes and kissed him instead.

He jumped but didn't move away. For the first instant, he let her lightly kiss his lips. Then he made a low noise in his throat and furrowed her hair with hard fingers. He slanted his mouth over hers, opening her lips with a bruising, punishing kiss.

He tasted like fire, one Samantha would be happy to burn up in. She touched the back of his neck, loving the strength she found there, then smoothed her hand to the short silk of his hair.

Her opening squeezed, her body imagining him inside her, his thick stem parting her and taking what he wanted. She would readily let him because she wanted it, too. She daringly stepped closer to him, indulging in the feel of his hard body through the thin gown. Stupid dress had to be good for something.

Headlights swept over them, the taxi arriving. *Damn the driver's great timing.*

The guards at the gate started shouting. The headlights swerved sharply, and Tain wrenched Samantha away from him just as a large pickup truck slammed itself into the gates.

The iron structure was sturdy enough to take the force, and it held. Without waiting for the guards to react, two demons leapt out of the truck and started running at Tain and Samantha.

Tain shoved Samantha behind him, his hands on his swords, but the demons parted around them, sprinting up the street away from the mansion.

Samantha yanked her badge out of her evening bag. "Oh perfect end to a perfect day. Hey! Stop, I'm a police officer. . . ."

Tain grabbed her with rough hands and threw her around the corner of the high block wall just as the truck exploded. White-hot fire lit up the night and the roar of the blast rang to the stars.

CHAPTER EIGHT

Tain stood up, staying protectively in front of Samantha, the light from the burning truck hot and red. The iron gate lay on the ground inside the wall, and the gatehouse was in ruins, the guards running for the house.

Three vans screeched to a halt in the middle of the road. Demons leapt out of them to run past the burning truck into the complex, completely ignoring Tain and Samantha. Samantha struggled to her feet, her blue dress torn and mud stained, fury in her eyes.

She tore her cell phone out of her purse and punched a number. "Lieutenant," she yelled into the phone. "We have a situation."

More demons attacked through the gates as Samantha finished the conversation and snapped the phone closed. She drew her pistol and started for the compound, but Tain grabbed her and held her back.

"My father's in there," she shouted, trying to wrench away.

"He's a demon, he knows how to fight," Tain said in a hard voice. "And if he's with the matriarch, he's more protected than we are out here."

Her eyes were anguished, but she held her pistol ready. "What are we going to do then? Watch and hope they can't break in?"

"No," Tain said grimly.

He drew one sword and pulled Samantha around the burning truck and into the compound. Demons were everywhere, some still in human form, in combat gear, some having changed into their overly muscular, mottled-skin form. The demons didn't all look the same—some were large and fearsome, some were smaller and had wings, others looked nearly human except for hideous faces and horns.

Tain wasn't expert enough to tell the Lamiah clan defenders from whatever clan was attacking. He knew the difference between Old Ones and lesser demons, but after that nothing was clear. Lesser demons had politicized themselves into complex clans with complex loyalties while he'd spent seven hundred years in captivity, and the world was no longer simple.

Tain knew he could kill all the demons—he had that power. The matriarch had known it, too, and had indicated, by the little test in her lair, that she was trusting him not to. She had metaphorically stretched out her neck and waited to see what he'd do, and he'd showed her that he wouldn't practice indiscriminate slaughter.

The problem was, Tain didn't know whether he could stick with that resolve. The temptation to raise his hand and obliterate every demon in the place was strong, and he gulped breaths of night air trying to fight it.

Samantha was watching him, waiting for him to perform a miracle. Tain drew his second sword, brought the blades together, and pointed them toward the house. Life magic flowed from the sword tips to cover the mansion, and as it did, he willed it to change from destructive magic to protective. A glow of flickering blue light encased the house, throwing back the attackers who'd reached it.

The defenders inside didn't much like it, either. He heard screams, shouts of "we're trapped," and "it's life magic—I'm going to be sick." Tain turned away without sympathy. Better they suffer a little nausea than let Samantha's people be chopped into pieces.

Samantha watched in awe, her face grimy in the glow of the compound's lights and the still-burning truck. "Wish I could do that," she said.

She smiled at him, a warm smile that reminded him of how good she'd tasted when he'd kissed her. He wanted to draw her up to him, lean down, and kiss her smiling lips, savoring every bit of her.

The attacking demons looked around for the source of the magic and quickly homed in on Tain and Samantha. A demon in human form, his face fine boned and almost delicate, pointed an automatic rifle at them. "Who are you?" he demanded.

"I protect them," Tain answered calmly.

"This is our fight," he snarled. "Get out of it."

Tain lowered his swords in silence, but the blue light remained intact around the house. It would stay until he decided to remove it.

The demon gaped in mindless fury, then brought his rifle up again and opened fire. Samantha dove for the ground, but Tain held up one hand, and the barrage of bullets parted around them.

The demon stared, his dirty face white. "What the fuck kind of thing are you?"

"A protector," Tain said.

"Since when?"

"Since always."

The demon let loose another string of profanity and screamed at his followers to surround Tain and Samantha.

You could so easily kill them all, the voice inside Tain whispered.

He knew exactly how to do it, how to lift his hand and send a wave of pure death to pour over them. They'd drop, lifeless, and all would be silence.

Then Samantha would look at him with horror in her coffee-brown eyes, and she'd slip away from him. He'd lose everything she'd given to him since that day in Seattle she'd faced him down. She'd been terrified and convinced she would die, and she'd stood her ground and told him what she thought of him.

The darkness in his mind kept screaming at him, willing him to forget Samantha and sweep out with his magic. *These are demonkind, and they should die.*

Samantha struggled to her feet. "You are such a diplomat," she growled. "Now what?"

Tain hooked his arm around her waist and pulled her up beside him. He pushed the voice into a corner, concentrating on the smells of the night and Samantha tight against him. "Why don't you arrest them?"

"Very funny. How are you going to get us out of here?"

Tain turned to the delicate-faced male demon. "Who are you?" he asked. "What is your quarrel with the Lamiah clan?"

The demon's eyes widened. "What do you mean, what is my quarrel? My quarrel is that Lamiah trash stole my daughter and sent back her corpse. They'll die for that."

"They didn't," Samantha said.

"What?" The demon pointed his weapon at her. Samantha flinched but didn't back down. "Of course they did it," the demon snarled. "It had Lamiah clan all over it, along with those damned letters."

"Printed in cutouts?" Samantha asked quickly.

"That's them. Did you send them?"

"Lamiah clan has been getting them, too," Samantha answered. "And they've been losing daughters as well."

"They'd kill their own kind to cover up a murder. Take the magic off the house and let us in there. I'm cutting the heart out of that matriarch bitch."

A demon next to him, this one in slavering monster form, jerked his chin at Tain. "He was at Kemmerer's."

The first demon's attention snapped back to Tain.

"He was there, yes," Samantha broke in. "Talking to

the demon who sold a Lamiah clan woman to her captors—likely the same captors who killed your daughter."

The second demon sneered. "This bitch was there, too. Demon tainted with human blood. And the one in the kilt killed our boys at Merrick's."

"Tain," Samantha said nervously.

Demons were closing in from behind.

"Once more chance," the lead demon said. "Stop defending Lamiah and we'll let you live."

"No," Tain answered.

The lead demon snarled in fury and shouted a command. All the demons attacked at once.

Samantha swung around to be back to back with Tain, firing her pistol and telling him at the top of her voice what she thought of his powers of persuasion. Tain sent streams of white magic from his swords to hold the demons back, but he was running out of options. He was powerful, but he had to keep the magic over the house, beat back the demons without killing them, and keep them from hurting Samantha.

Killing them all would be easier, the voice reminded him.

At one time he'd thought that was for him to decide. Kehksut had killed and tortured arbitrarily to prove that his power was great, but Tain knew, had always known, that power didn't mean wielding death. Kehksut had never been able to take that understanding away from him, which was one reason Tain was now free. The woman fighting like mad at his back was the other reason.

A smaller demon with wings sailed out of his reach and swooped behind them, letting out a stream of gelatinous acid that splashed all over Samantha and up and down Tain's back.

Samantha screamed. Tain swung around and swept

the demon aside, but Samantha was already writhing on the ground, covered in acid. Tain threw a final burst of magic at the demons and dropped to his hands and knees beside her, desperately gathering his healing magic to pour into her.

The acid was a thick gluelike substance that clung stubbornly to Samantha's skin and would eat her flesh to her bones in minutes. The thin silk dress couldn't keep it out, and already her face was red with blood, her screams dying to hoarse sobs.

The battle around them receded and grew dim. Tain saw nothing but Samantha, the interconnected fibers of her skin and muscle, felt nothing but her torment. Sweat dripped from him as he willed all of his magic into her, swearing as the acid opened the skin he'd just closed. He had to get it off her or she'd die.

Beyond the gate, blue and red lights flashed, and a helicopter cut overhead, training its spotlight on the compound. More bullets flew, this time between demons and the police that came through to put them down.

Tain lifted Samantha and made for the gate. Police meant police cars, and one could get her to safety.

Logan stepped in front of him, his handgun ready. "Holy shit. What the hell happened?"

"She got acid-burned," Tain said shortly. "I need to get it off her. Do you have a car?"

"Sure—"

"No," Samantha rasped. "Get one of the uniforms to take me. McKay will have your hide if you leave the scene."

"Paramedics can deal with acid burns," Logan began.

"Not fast enough," Tain snapped. "Get me a car—*now*."

Logan swung away, galvanized into obeying. He signaled to a passing uniformed policeman and gave him instructions, and in a few minutes, Tain held Samantha in the back of a police car, its lights flashing as they sped out of Beverly Hills to the grittier parts of town.

Tain cradled Samantha in his arms, the black grill between them and the driver throwing spangled lights over her face, whispering words of healing as he sank his magic into her, trying to slow the corrosion.

The uniform dropped them off inside Samantha's complex, and Tain was out of the backseat and halfway up the stairs before the officer could offer to help take her inside. He followed them partway, then when Tain told him to go, went back to the car and peeled off in a hurry to get back to the matriarch's house.

Pickles sensed something wrong and meowed and danced frantically as Tain banged in. Tain slammed the door behind him, strode down the tiny hall to the bathroom, and cranked on the shower. He stood Samantha under the spray, dress and all, and began scrubbing the slime from her face with his fingers and the water.

Heal her. Cerridwen, help me.

He was wet himself, his ruined clothes heavy with water. He pulled them off and dropped them on the floor, then began peeling the sodden clumps of silk from Samantha's body.

He ran his hands over her, willing her muscles to meld, her skin to knit. He poured every bit of magic he had into her, trying to make her whole again. He knew exactly what it was like to have his flesh stripped from his bones, the excruciating agony, the fear, the hope for death that would make the pain stop.

He'd felt it every three days for seven hundred years, until his entire existence revolved around pain. He never, ever wanted Samantha to know what that had been like. He didn't want her to look in the mirror and see scars from this ordeal, didn't want her to loathe herself like he loathed the mess of his own body.

Samantha's head lolled, weak moans escaping her lips.

The acid had burned him as well, eating through his coat, but he'd barely felt it.

It took a long time. The shower water and soap began to soften the goo and help him scrape it from her skin, allowing his magic to fully ease the burns, close the abraded flesh, make her skin whole and new.

Samantha began to awaken from her stupor, the healing filling her body and making her respond. She opened her eyes, which were whole and unburned, thank the goddesses.

She looked wearily at the ruined clumps of silk in the bathtub and on the wet floor and tried to smile. "I hated that dress anyway," she said, her voice weak. "How do I tell the formalwear place their gown got slimed by a demon?"

Tain didn't answer. He slid his touch down her breasts, fingers searching her skin for more acid. He moved across her belly to her hips and round to her buttocks, touching, washing, healing.

She looked at him through half-closed eyes, the gleam of black-brown soft, her body aroused from the healing. He knew exactly what kind of fire it poured through her, because the same fire poured through him. They were connecting, soul to soul, body to body.

He was fully erect and aching for her. Her breasts were full and slick under his hands, and her body came against his as it sought his magic.

Their mouths met, lips and tongues tangling, delving, seeking. Her hand stole down to his stem, fingers fumbling a little as they slid against soap. He pulled her to him as she closed her hand solidly around him and began to stroke.

His magic flowed through himself and her until her skin glowed with it. Her mouth moved in a frenzy against his, lips suckling his tongue, teeth scraping his lip. He wasn't sure she was even aware she squeezed him, pulling at his arousal, until he was rocking his hips against her, seeking the sensation.

She was sweet and salty and vibrant, a warm-blooded woman responding to his touch. He needed her, he wanted her, and he couldn't stay away from her. He thrust his fingers between her legs, seeking the hot folds that let him into her. She was wet with desire, her body clean now, and he slid two fingers inside her without resistance.

She rocked her head back, her hips rising, her cleft squeezing his fingers. She twisted her hand around his staff, stroking and kneading, building the fire high.

Tain hadn't been touched like this since his freedom, and it was so different from the disgusting perversions of Kehksut in her female form. Samantha touched him because she couldn't help herself, because she wanted to feel him and love what he did to her.

She was small against his large frame, so mortal, so vulnerable, and so incredibly gentle. Sex to him had become the same as pain, until he thought himself unable to have one without the other.

Samantha was teaching him differently. She rocked her thighs against his, slick with soap, her sheath pulsing around his fingers so damn tight. What would it feel like to slide inside her, to feel her clamping down on his cock?

At that moment she squeezed his staff hard, and climax swamped him. He shouted as he pumped through her fist, and he rubbed her folds, screwing her with his fingers.

Her climax was silent, and she squeezed her eyes shut as she let it take her. Her sweet cream poured over his fingers, scalding hot, to fall to the swirling water at their feet.

It went on and on, both of them holding on tight, both of them shuddering with release. Tain captured her mouth again, their kiss mutually bruising and brutal.

He lost all sense of time and place, much as he did

when he retreated into the darkness that always waited for him. But this time when he opened his eyes, he was on the floor of the bathtub, Samantha lying against him amid the ruins of her sodden silk gown.

Samantha looked up at him as the water cooled. "Thank you," she whispered. She smiled at him in gratitude, and the smile broke his heart.

The blanket was prickly on Samantha's wet back as Tain laid her on the bed, then stood back and looked at her.

He was breathtaking. She'd feared his body would be a mass of horrifying scars, but only faint white lines crisscrossed his arms and thighs and abdomen. His hardness rose, unscathed, from a thatch of dark red hair. He must have been incredible before his ordeal, and he still was, but now he wore the weathered, weary look of a man whose innocence had been beaten out of him long ago.

Samantha again wanted to beg him to stay, but she hesitated to bring up the subject. It was likely he'd turn and go, now that she was healed and safe at home. She needed to contact Logan and find out what was happening at the matriarch's, if the battle was over, if her father was all right. Real life went on.

Her skin was pink where the acid had burned it, but she'd been in such incredible pain that a little pinkness was a small price to pay. She'd known she was dying until his healing magic had wrapped itself around her and pulled her back to life.

No way could she have stopped herself grabbing him and holding on, her aroused body wanting to pleasure his in return for the healing. Now he gazed at her in silence, taking in her body from her toes to her spread legs to her breasts to her face.

To her joy, he put one knee on the bed and stretched himself out beside her, not speaking, not smiling. He kissed her, taking her mouth in slow strokes, sliding his tongue between her lips.

She rubbed herself against him, needy, and traced the pentacle tattoo on his cheekbone. Tain's obvious wanting pressed hard against her abdomen, his thick shaft warm with his pulse.

He stilled, something dark flickering in his eyes, as her fingertips brushed up each point of the pentacle and around the circle.

"It doesn't hurt you to touch it?" he asked.

"No. Should it?"

"It's the mark of the mother goddess. Cerridwen put it on me when she first came to take me to Ravenscroft."

"And I shouldn't be able to touch it because I'm death magic?" Samantha drew her palm over the tattoo, then showed him her hand. "See? No burning, no screaming."

"Kehksut could never touch it."

"Good," she said softly. "Then he couldn't steal all of you."

Tain took her hand and pressed it again to his tattoo. She felt his pulse beneath her fingertips, the swift beating of his heart as he let her touch what one of the most powerful beings in the world couldn't.

He slid on top of her while he kissed her, heavenly warm, his skin still damp. He parted her legs with a strong hand—no sexy talk, no play, just *need.*

Samantha felt plenty needy herself. She lifted her knees and drew the sole of one foot up the back of his leg.

"You make me want to go slow," he whispered. He kissed her chin, then worked his way down her neck. "Just to make you more desperate."

She gasped as his lips reached her navel, and he licked stray water from it. "That would be cruel," she managed to say.

"I'm a cruel man." He kissed his way to the black swirl of hair between her legs, his breath hot. "Not nice at all."

The tension in his muscles as he worked back up to her breasts told her he was holding himself back, tempering his strength. Even in the shower, she'd sensed that he was trying to contain himself. She wondered, with a shiver of delight, what it would be like if he didn't hold back. She was strong, her demon blood making her tougher than she looked, but he could do what he wanted with her, and she wouldn't be able to stop him.

He drew his tongue firmly around each areola, then sucked one between his teeth. He closed his eyes as he plied his mouth, his dark red lashes resting on his cheekbones. Yet his teeth and tongue were gentle, scraping her a little, but only enough to make her shiver for more.

When he looked up at her again, his eyes were so heartbreakingly blue she wanted to hold on to him and never let him go. *I could love this man,* she thought. *If he let me, I could love him.*

His hand went to the spread of her thighs again, fingers making her wetter. Slowly he eased himself up to her, his gaze meeting and holding hers.

"Please," she whispered. She rubbed her foot on him again, her body open and aching for him.

He said nothing, but his eyes went wide and dark as he slid the tip of his hardness inside her.

Samantha went hot, then cold, then hot again. He pushed in a little farther, then lay still, watching her with his intense blue eyes.

The feeling of him in her hand was nothing compared to what he felt like inside her. He was huge and spread her and touched something basic and carnal in her.

He waited until she adjusted to him, and then very slowly he moved. She gasped, and he started kissing her, his mouth mastering hers and muffling her cries. Samantha gripped his buttocks, rocking her hips wantonly as he built up the rhythm they shared. It felt wicked and wild, this big man *screwing* her after he'd rescued her from demons, cleaned her off in the shower, and healed her.

His fists bunched in the bedding next to her, his arms as tight and as hard as his penis inside her. He closed his eyes as though fighting his release and fighting himself. He filled her so full, and she pulled him into her and begged for more.

"Samantha," he whispered.

"I'm right here."

Tain looked at her. His eyes were almost glowing, blue and powerful, filled with his life essence. She put her fingers to his face, over the pentacle, wishing she could touch what burned white hot inside him.

And then she *was* touching it. Samantha was demon, and her kind had the capacity to draw the life essence—that integral *something* that made a person alive and aware—out of others. She'd never done it. She didn't know how, and she'd never wanted to explore that part of her demon self.

But Tain's life essence exploded in through her fingers before she could stop it. She cried out with the weight of it, a sheer force that nearly lifted her off the bed.

A wave of climax swamped her body, and she screamed. She saw Tain's face, eyes wide in concern, and then an amorphous blackness rose in front of her and blotted out her world.

CHAPTER NINE

"Samantha."

Someone sounded very worried, shook her, even. Samantha turned a groggy face away and tried to burrow back into the warmth of the pillows.

"Samantha, look at me."

A strong hand pinched her chin and forced her head from the comforter. She groaned.

"Wake up, love."

She liked the voice, deep and musical and full of sinful promise. She wished he would keep talking, keep calling her *love*.

Warmth tingled where his fingers contacted her, magic that pulsed against her skin. She remembered the incredible heat that had jolted through her when she'd touched Tain's pentacle tattoo, and she awakened with a gasp.

Tain lay next to her on the bed, long and strong and naked. He propped himself on his elbow, his hand softening on her face, his blue eyes watchful. Pickles perched on the pillow above his head, staring down at her with as much intensity.

"What happened?" Samantha tried to sit up and then gave it up for a lost cause. "Whatever kind of orgasm that was, I'd like to do it again. I think. Or maybe never again, I'm not sure."

"You took my life essence."

She pushed her hair from her eyes. "Is *that* what that was? I thought you were trying to kill me—with ecstasy."

He gave her an odd look. "How does it normally feel when you feed on life essence?"

"I don't know. I mean, I never have. If I did just now, it was an accident." She blew out her breath. "Believe me, if I wanted a diet of life essences, I certainly wouldn't start with yours."

She knew by the look on his face that what she'd done could have hurt her, maybe killed her. "Really, I had no idea what I was doing," she repeated.

"The demon part of you needs to feed. You couldn't have stopped it."

"No, I vowed I'd never do that to anyone. I've seen humans who let themselves get addicted to demons and the pleasure demons give during life-essence draining, and it's not pretty."

"All demons need it to survive," Tain said. "Lesser demons, Old Ones, demons of mixed blood. Your touch is practiced."

Samantha tried to sit up, but her body was limp and warm and so comfortable. "I know you want me to be an evil, life-sucking, death-magic demon, but that's not how I was raised. My mother treated me like a human child, and that's what I became."

"You must have taken life essence before, many times," he said, his eyes holding something she didn't understand. "By instinct, maybe without realizing you were doing it."

"Nope, not once. If I took from someone, they'd feel it, and tell me. Who would let me do that without saying anything?"

Tain looked at her for a long time. "Your mother, perhaps."

"No." She sat up abruptly. "I'd never do that."

Tain remained stretched out beside her, a tall godlike being who'd just given her the greatest sex of her life.

"When you were a baby and a child," he said, "you wouldn't have known or understood. You probably didn't need much, being only half demon, but the fact that your mother let you do it speaks much of her."

Samantha clenched her hands, panic welling in her throat. "You have to be wrong. I never did that."

"But I'm not wrong, am I?"

"You must be." A thought gave her hope. "I haven't lived at home for five years—where would I have gotten life essence since then if I need it so much?"

Tain shrugged, a slow rippling of muscle. "You see your mother often. And for the last year, you've had a very strong life-magic werewolf for a partner."

"Logan?" Samantha rolled off the bed and onto her feet, angry and agitated. "I couldn't have done that to him—he'd have noticed. Wouldn't he?"

"Maybe not if you didn't take much. He has strength to spare—he's a very powerful werewolf, maybe even a pack leader or close to being one."

"You're wrong," she said, her breath hurting. "About me—and about Logan. Why would a pack leader hang out in Los Angeles as a low-ranking detective? Logan's strong, but he wouldn't let me feed off him."

"He might if he knew you needed it. He must have known the risks of working with a demon before he took the job."

"*Half demon.*"

"You aren't used to taking much," Tain said, his voice low. "My life essence overwhelmed you because you got too strong a dose of it. I should have muted it for you."

"I don't want to take *any* dose of it."

He came off the bed, dominating her small bedroom. The sleek little gewgaws she collected from the various craft fairs around Los Angeles and the curtains she'd made from scrap upholstery seemed dull next to him.

"It is what you are, Samantha," he said. "It's the hardest thing in the world, to be what you truly are."

"Are you trying to hurt me because I'm demon? I'm not the one who kept you prisoner all those years—it wasn't *me*."

"I know." He caught her elbows and pulled her against his warm body. He smelled of warmth and sleep and their lovemaking, and his fingers in her hair tingled with healing magic.

She dimly heard him through her clenching confusion. She didn't want to believe him, but something deep down inside told her he spoke the truth. That something was relieved that her secret had finally been revealed, but she wanted to scream and deny it.

She wasn't like Merrick or his demons or the girls who sold themselves to take life essence. She wasn't like the matriarch, cold and businesslike, or her equally cold majordomo. She wasn't even like her father, who'd met her mother in secret while waiting for Samantha to grow up enough to accept him.

She'd lived her life as a human, with human ambitions and needs. Being demon was just an inconvenience or something that gave her insight into catching demon criminals.

"I don't want this." She balled her hands against his chest.

"I know."

She felt his magic slide through her, trying to soothe her, but she fought it, needing to feel grief and guilt. "Please go away."

"No."

The one-word answer was typical of Tain, taciturn and indicating he'd do whatever he damn well pleased. She knew he'd decided to stay with her tonight because it was *his* agenda, not hers.

"I have to get some sleep," she said, hardening her voice. "I have to go to work in the morning."

"Sleep then." Magic trickled through her, too strong to fight, numbing her grief. He had to be wrong, and in the morning, after she slept, she'd prove it.

She felt his lips in her hair again, his warm hands on her back. He lifted her and laid her on the bed, then got in beside her and pulled the covers over them. She saw Pickles decide that all was well and curl once more into a nose-to-tail ball at the bottom of the bed before she slid into hazy sleep.

Tain stirred the charred bits in the frying pan as he heard Samantha's bedroom door open. Without turning, he felt her gaze on his bare back and the kilt he'd pulled on over his hips. The rest of his clothes had been ruined by the demon's acid, the kilt the only thing salvageable.

He also felt the weight of her beauty, her dark eyes and straight black hair, the memory of her body under his. He remembered those lovely eyes widening in shock and horror when he told her what he'd assumed she already knew.

What had he expected? That she'd smile and gloat about her death-magic power, about how she'd just drunk an Immortal? The astonished look in her eyes and the tears that followed had turned his ideas upside down.

"What are you burning?" she asked.

He warmed with pleasure at her voice, the sultry one that haunted his dreams. But her tone was sharp, the prickly, don't-touch-me Samantha returning.

"It was eggs and bacon."

Samantha came to him, took the pan off the burner, and peered at the ruined contents. "I'll grab something on the way."

She'd dressed in conservative black slacks, blouse, and blazer, Samantha in her professional garb. It made him want to kiss her while he peeled back the jacket and parted the buttons of her rather virginal blouse. He settled for skimming his hand through her hair, liking that she let it hang loose and free. Her face had healed completely, only a few pink lines remaining from the attack.

She stepped away. "Can I drop you somewhere?" She'd become all business and no nonsense, putting what had happened between them behind her.

"My brother is bringing me some clothes," Tain answered.

"Then you'll be gone when I get back."

It wasn't a question. Tain lifted a brow at her and put the pan back on to the burner. He liked burned eggs and bacon.

"The attacking demons were Djowlan," Tain said. "Each clan is assuming the other is responsible."

She blinked, and he saw her shift through gears back to the demon problem. "How did you know that?"

"Logan called on your cell phone."

"It survived demon acid?"

He shrugged. "Guess so."

She grabbed the phone from the counter, checked its readout, then clipped it onto her belt. "Why didn't you wake me?"

"You needed to sleep."

He'd gone back into the bedroom after speaking to Logan early this morning to find Samantha curled on her side, her head resting on her bent arm. Her black hair had fanned out on the pillow, her even darker lashes tight against her cheek. He'd stood still and let her beauty soothe his heart.

"I don't even know if my father's all right," she said, angry. "We left him with the matriarch. . . ."

"He called while you were showering. The matriarch had him driven home, but he'd heard you were hurt. I told him I'd healed the burns and you'd be fine."

Samantha flushed. "I'm sure he wondered why you were answering my phone at six in the morning while I was in the shower."

Fulton hadn't sounded very surprised; instead, Tain had sensed relief that Samantha hadn't been left alone and unprotected. "I don't think he wondered at all."

"Terrific." She swung away from his touch and grabbed her purse from the sofa. "I have to go. Don't give any of that burned stuff to the cat."

He came to her, greasy spatula and all, and touched her face, subtly and quietly sliding a protection spell around her. It wouldn't stop a bullet, but it would keep her from ordinary kind of harm.

"Cerridwen's blessing on you," he said, then kissed her forehead.

Samantha jerked away and started for the door. On the threshold she turned back. "Thank you," she said awkwardly. "For the healing, I mean. I wouldn't have survived that attack."

He didn't answer. In his mind, he thanked the goddesses for giving him the healing gift so he was able to save her life. He knew that if she'd died last night, he would have drifted back into his madness and not come out.

Samantha gave him another self-conscious look, then turned and left him.

Tain watched her go from the kitchen window, enjoying the way her backside swayed under the blazer as she hurried down the stairs. Pickles jumped to the counter to sit next to him, and Tain absently slipped him pieces of blackened bacon as they both watched Samantha climb into her car and roar off to join Los Angeles traffic.

"You look pretty good for a woman who got slimed," Logan observed, leaning back in his chair. "You all right?"

Samantha's attempt to slip in quietly and bury herself in paperwork on last night's incident had failed. Everyone had heard about her injury—the uniform who'd driven her home had made sure the story whizzed around the department at the speed of light. She'd had at least twenty congratulations and commiserations before she even reached her desk.

"I got lucky," she told Logan. She couldn't make herself look him in the eye, still trying to sort out what she believed. Now that Tain had introduced the possibility that she'd taken Logan's life essence, and that he'd let her, the knowledge rose like a wall between them. She could plunge herself into denial and invent all kinds of reasons why Tain had told her what he had, but something in her heart knew the truth.

She distracted herself with the question of Logan's real identity. If a wolf high in his pack had left it to come out to Los Angeles and work a mundane job, that spoke of big problems in the pack. Werewolves weren't Samantha's specialty, but she did know that much.

"It wasn't luck, it was an Immortal," Logan said, cutting into her thoughts. "One good at healing, I think you told me."

She looked up at him, still avoiding his tawny eyes. "What are you implying?"

"Implying? Me? I think you'll make a great couple."

"We're not going to make any kind of couple," Samantha said sharply. "He kept the acid from burning me, that's all."

"Sure thing, partner. The Lamiah matriarch is calling for blood, but the Djowlan matriarch is claiming no responsibility for the attack. She says the attackers were rogues who acted without her approval."

"I see that." Samantha glanced at his report, thankful

to focus on something other than Tain. "One of the demons who led it said his daughter was kidnapped and killed. Was he brought in?"

Logan looked surprised. "I hadn't heard this. We arrested a lot of demons last night, but haven't had time to question them."

"Can I talk to him? Damn, I knew I should have called in."

"You were down, Samantha," Logan said, the teasing leaving his voice. "You needed to recover—I'm surprised you're even here this morning."

Samantha was, too, but Tain's healing magic amazed her. The acid should have killed her—painfully—but here she was walking around with barely any scars. Besides, she also couldn't have stayed home after Tain's revelations, no matter how delicious he'd looked in that kilt. When she'd walked in and seen him in the kitchen this morning, she'd wanted to get down on her knees, lift up the plaid, and enjoy what was beneath.

She hadn't wanted to talk about her feelings or her inner demon or his past. She'd just wanted to make love to him again and again until she forgot her own name.

Logan took her down to the cells where last night's arrests waited. Demon cells contained strong witch wards that kept demons from breaking down the doors with their immense strength, but the demons from last night looked defeated and subdued, not about to attempt a breakout.

The leader of the demons who had attacked them looked up in anger as Samantha entered the interview room and sat down across the table from him.

"You," he spat. Then he looked past her to Logan. "Who's he? What happened to your Lamiah-protecting lover?"

Samantha slid a paper encased in a plastic sheet across

the table to him. "Is that like the letters you've been getting?"

The demon glanced at it, the last letter Merrick had received before his club burned down.

"Like that, except the one they sent back with my daughter's body and her ripped-out heart was more specific."

"What did it say?" Samantha asked, keeping to her no-nonsense interview voice.

"Two lines." He shoved the letter back at her and folded his arms. *"Another down. The rest of you to go."*

Hunter brought Tain clothes, then lounged on Samantha's sofa flipping channels with the remote while Tain showered and changed.

"Did you bring the other things I wanted?" Tain asked when he emerged again.

Hunter lifted a duffel bag from the sofa beside him. "I raided your apartment. You didn't have much to raid."

"I like to travel light."

"A man after my own heart. Leda likes to buy mysterious gadgets for the kitchen and learning toys for the baby every time she leaves the house. I tell her we can't take any of it to Ravenscroft, but she doesn't care."

Hunter growled but Tain noted the gleam of pride in his eyes. "She's enjoying herself."

"She is." Hunter looked around the apartment with its soft chairs and the kitchen's matching towels and curtains. "This is pretty cozy. Better than the dump you live in."

"Where I live is cheap."

"There's always an extra bedroom at Adrian's house," Hunter offered. He brought it up every time they spoke.

"I don't want Samantha to be alone right now." Not with demons spitting venom at her and clans at war. Tain didn't want her out in the city without him, but he acknowledged that most of the time she'd be with Logan or inside the well-warded police headquarters.

"You and she can share Adrian's extra bedroom," Hunter said.

"She won't."

"She's proud and independent, like someone else in this room. You two should get along famously."

Famously was not how Tain would put it. The look in Samantha's eyes when he'd told her she'd always taken life essence, like the demon she was, had been anguished. Tain hadn't realized she didn't know. Demons loved to suck life essence, and Samantha's orgasm had been intense. But instead of triumphing that she'd tasted the life essence of an Immortal, she'd been scared to death.

Hunter watched him, his green eyes narrowing. "Are you telling me Samantha hasn't fallen for you yet? You can't be trying hard enough."

Tain sat down next to him and snatched the remote from his hand. "The last thing I need is advice about women from you."

"No, the last thing you need is for Leda to come down here and try to shove you two together. Seduce Samantha until she can't live without you—end of problem, and Leda and I can go off to Ravenscroft."

"Leaving me with someone to look after me?"

Hunter looked slightly embarrassed. "Something like that."

"I'm glad you care." He was, in truth. Having his brothers cluck around like mother hens was preferable to not having his brothers around at all.

"But leave you alone?" Hunter finished. "Sorry, we left you alone for too long. You're stuck with us now."

Tain sat back on the sofa, flicking through channels full of curious activities people thought of as entertainment. He and Hunter had spent many days like this whenever

Tain had visited during the past year, sitting side by side in companionable silence in front of the television. Staying still too long made Tain restless, but he realized the importance of it, the bond strengthening between himself and his brothers.

Samantha needed life essence, and Tain had it to spare. The solution was simple. Samantha could take life essence from Tain and never hurt him, and that way she wouldn't have to worry about harming her mother or Logan or any other friend.

Is this my redemption? he silently asked Cerridwen. *To give this woman my life essence so she won't hurt the people she loves?*

He didn't think that this was quite what the universe had in mind for his atonement, but at the moment he didn't care. Samantha could have all she wanted of his white-hot life essence, and he'd assuage his own inner pain by letting her take it.

"Don't let me lose track of time," Hunter said abruptly. "Leda's giving a lecture at six to some group about using protective witch magic. She'll kill me if I miss it."

Tain glanced at him, feeling interest stir. "Mind if I tag along?"

Hunter shrugged. "If you want, sure."

Tain looked back at the television, where two wrestlers were enjoying themselves slamming each other to the floor. For one brief moment memories of himself and Hunter and Darius slid through the turmoil in his mind—sparring and then arguing about who'd won, and then going off to get drunk. Or he and Adrian fishing on the bank of some flowing river, neither speaking, just watching the water go by and the silver flip of fish that always seemed to avoid their poles.

He let the memories of past contentment come. He didn't have to wonder what had opened the dam to let them in—he knew it had happened when he'd dragged a half-demon woman back from death and made love without pain for the first time in centuries.

Samantha reached home that evening feeling drained. She'd been tense all day, keeping Logan at a distance and avoiding any phone calls from her mother or father. Logan knew something was wrong—apart from her being nearly killed by demon acid—but hadn't asked, and she hadn't said a word to him.

How do you ask your best friend if you've been sucking out his life essence?

She wearily climbed the stairs and entered her apartment. It was dark, Tain gone, Pickles meowing like a cat who hadn't eaten in three days. She flicked on the lights, noting that Tain had done the dishes.

"What a dream man," she murmured as she closed the door. "A one-night stand who cleans the house before leaving."

She dumped her purse and briefcase on the sofa and went into the bathroom. She didn't notice until she was at the sink splashing water on her face that an unfamiliar toothbrush rested in the holder next to her own.

She stared in surprise, then reasoned that Hunter had probably brought it with Tain's clothes and Tain forgot to take it with him. Same with the razor hanging from the shower caddy.

Samantha snapped on the light in the bedroom and opened a drawer to grab one of the oversized T-shirts in which she liked to lounge around the apartment. Half the drawer was filled with men's T-shirts. Her underwear drawer above that shared space with a handful of folded boxer shorts and rolled socks.

Samantha slammed the drawer and yanked open the closet. Tain hadn't brought many clothes—shirts and jeans and another duster coat—but they were all hanging next to hers. Above them on the shelf was an empty duffel bag.

She shoved the closet door closed and stormed out to glare accusingly at Pickles. "He's moved in."

She couldn't help thinking her cat looked a bit smug. Samantha grabbed the phone and called Leda, needing in her panic to talk to someone used to Immortals, but no one answered.

Samantha hung up, fed Pickles, then started pacing. She hated waiting to see if and when Tain would return, but that's what she would have to do.

She stared at the phone a little bit longer, then slowly picked it up again and called her mother.

Tain stood in the back of the small auditorium with Hunter, listening to Leda answer questions.

"Ms. Stowe," said the interviewer, a slender woman who'd introduced herself as Ms. Townsend. She wore a business jacket and skirt, had blond hair wound in a careful knot, and wore minimal makeup. "How do you feel about the city of Los Angeles allowing demonkind and vampires to go on living here after they nearly destroyed all of us last year?"

Hunter leaned to Tain. "I don't like her."

Tain looked at the woman's aura, which was fiery red orange next to Leda's blue and green hue. "She doesn't have death magic," he murmured. "She's just an angry woman."

The group called themselves No More Nightmares, and were very interested in how normal human beings could protect themselves against demons and vampires. They'd asked Leda how she and the Coven of Light had destroyed the demon Kehksut the year before and what she'd gleaned from it.

Leda answered serenely enough. "As a member of the Coven of Light, I learned that death magic and life magic must balance in order to maintain the status quo of the universe. Last year, there was an unhealthy dose of death magic, which resulted in the chaos that we had to live through. Once life magic was allowed to return to its normal level, harmony was restored. But we need death magic to keep the world on an even keel."

"You have a son," Ms. Townsend cut in, glancing toward the back of the room. A carrier rested at Hunter's feet, his sleeping child in it. "As a mother, don't you worry for him? Do you want him playing outside, exposed to any demon who might happen along? Or any vampire?"

"Of course I worry," Leda answered. She laughed a little. "Being a new mother, I'm paranoid. But we have guarded our house with the strongest wards, and I'm confident that my husband and I can keep him safe until he learns to protect himself." She looked out at the audience, her smile reassuring. "Demons keep to themselves, mostly. Their clans are close-knit, and few venture outside them, except in the clubs. Humans seek out vampires and demons for the thrill of it, not the other way around. Last year was unusual."

"Not all of us have the benefit of possessing witch magic," Ms. Townsend snapped. "What of us mundane human beings?"

"There are plenty of witches around who are happy to ward your house, your car, whatever you like."

"For a fee."

The audience murmured angry agreement.

"For a modest fee," Leda corrected. "Witches have bills to pay, and supplies cost money. If a witch wants to charge you an exorbitant price, of course, you should seek another."

"Do you do these wardings?"

"I don't have time to do much, but I can refer anyone to witches who do."

"Witches who practice death magic, like yourself?"

The crowd started their murmuring again, and Hunter stirred uneasily.

Leda flushed. "I admit that I have twice used death magic to perform a ritual. I didn't want to, and I didn't like it, but both times it was absolutely necessary."

"Necessary?" Ms. Townsend asked coldly. "Or the easiest way to get what you wanted?"

"Necessary," Leda repeated. "The first time, it saved a life. The second time, it helped kill an ancient demon that was threatening the world."

"So you advocate using death magic if *you* feel it's justified."

"No, I don't advocate using it at all, unless—"

"And in fact, I believe your coven asked you to leave after you performed this death magic."

"I left of my own accord," Leda said with a hint of frost.

"I've spoken to other witches of this so-called Coven of Light—some of them tried to cover up for you, others openly left because of the coven members who condoned what you did."

Leda started to answer, but Hunter thrust the baby carrier at Tain and strode up the aisle. White-hot magic surrounded him, making people cringe out of his way.

Hunter grabbed Leda by the hand and glared at Ms. Townsend. "What happened in Los Angeles was nothing to what would have happened if Leda hadn't done what she did," he said. "She doesn't deserve to stand here and be berated by people like you."

"Hunter," Leda hissed.

Ms. Townsend regarded him down her long nose. "I am pointing out that even those whose motives are pure can be seduced by death magic."

"Well, point it out without us."

He pulled Leda down the steps and up the aisle, Ms. Townsend watching with glee.

Hunter took the carrier with the waking baby as he passed Tain. "You coming?" he asked when Tain didn't move.

"No. I want to listen awhile."

"You're kidding. What for?"

"It might be important."

Hunter growled, but didn't argue.

"Be careful," Leda said to Tain.

Tain gave her a reassuring nod. The two of them left, and Tain stepped into the shadows beside the door.

Ms. Townsend regarded her audience with a chill smile. "Wasn't *that* interesting? Aren't you glad I asked her to come?"

Her followers applauded. Ms. Townsend waited for the admiration to die down before she spoke in clear, strident tones. "Death magic is insidious. It comes at us when we least expect it, seducing us as the demons seduce their victims in their so-called clubs. We must work to eradicate the darkness any chance we can."

She waited for the next round of applause, then launched into a speech about demons and what they did, much of it inaccurate. She brought in vampires, too, talking about the laws that barely held them back from slaughtering the population.

"We need to take back the night, ladies and gentlemen. Our children need to be protected from these evil beings that our laws favor, before it's too late."

Her audience, ordinary-looking men and women, cheered. The trouble was, Ms. Townsend wasn't completely wrong. The network of laws that kept demons and vampires in line worked only as long as the demons and vampires respected them.

Septimus was strong enough to keep the vamps in L.A. under his thumb, and his power extended to other cities up and down the coast. Demons harbored so much resentment between clans that an overall leader would not likely emerge. But if the balance of power ever shifted, humans would be sitting ducks, and these people knew it.

Tain had the feeling, as the meeting went on, that they weren't about to combat the problem with bake sales and sticking fliers on car windows. His hunch was confirmed when Ms. Townsend began describing the exact methods for subduing and killing a demon, including how to cut out its still-beating heart.

CHAPTER TEN

Samantha's apartment windows were completely dark when Tain reached it at eight that night, after he'd done what he'd needed to do. Her small truck sat in the parking lot, and Tain made his way quickly up the stairs, worried about why she hadn't turned on any lights.

When he opened the door, he saw Samantha sitting motionlessly on the sofa in the glare of the outside lights, her feet on the coffee table and a lump of cat curled up on her thighs. Tain exhaled in relief and closed the door, making his way to sit next to her in the dark.

"You were right," she said after a while, so low he barely caught the words. "About my mother."

Tain said nothing, sensing she didn't want comfort from him right now.

"I talked to her tonight," she continued in a bleak voice. "I asked her point-blank if she'd let me take her life essence, and she said yes. I asked her why, and she said she knew I needed it, and she didn't mind."

"She loves you," Tain said.

"That makes it worse."

He smoothed his hand down her bare arm, finding her cold. "I wouldn't have told you so abruptly, but I thought you knew already."

"Because I'm demon, and that's what demons do?"

"Something like that."

"And you believed I'd do that to my own mother." She bit off a laugh. "Well, you were right."

Tain sat in silence, trying to find words to help her. It seemed strange that he wanted to comfort a demon, but this was Samantha. This was different.

"When I was a lad," he began, "I used to hurry through tedious chores using my magic. My father used to shout at me about it."

She looked at him as though wondering why he was bringing this up right now. "Your Roman soldier father?"

"He valued hard work and honor above all else. He considered using magic as a shortcut to be shirking."

"Not on the same scale as sucking out life essence," she pointed out.

He went on doggedly. "I couldn't control this vast power inside me, and I nearly killed him with it. I collapsed a stone shed on top of him, because I was trying to cheat while helping him repair the roof. That was the day I discovered my healing ability."

"Thank goodness you had it."

"What I'd done terrified me for a long time, and I was afraid to use my magic again. My father understood, but he never chastised me, just made me work very hard." He paused. "He's dead and gone now, centuries ago."

"It sounds like you loved him."

"You didn't say it in those days—respect and honor were what you gave your father. But I did."

Samantha rubbed his arm. "I'm sorry you lost him."

"He was a mortal human, and grew old and died." He tried to sound stoic, but the day his father died had left a hole in his life that had never quite been filled. "I would have lost him sooner or later."

"That doesn't make it easier."

"No," he agreed.

The day Cerridwen had come for Tain, his father had gruffly told him to go and not to shame him. Tain had seen tears on his father's face, but the man had turned around, stiff shouldered, and walked off into the woods.

Tain slid his arm around Samantha, unable to keep from touching her, and pressed a kiss to her fragrant hair. "Let me warm you," he said softly.

She looked up at him, her eyes holding both anguish and need. "I think I'd like that."

Tain carefully set the sleeping Pickles aside and carried Samantha to her bedroom. He undressed her, and by the time she was bare, she'd recovered herself enough to help undress him.

Their lovemaking was slow this time. He licked her mouth, tasting the salt-tang of her sweat, then ran his tongue down her throat and breasts. He worked his way down to press his lips to the swelling bud between her legs, teasing her there until she moaned. Then he rolled off her, lifted her onto his body, hands parting her legs, and slid into her.

He made a low noise of ecstasy as her sheath closed over him. He *belonged* here.

Samantha rested her hands on his chest, her knees against his sides, moving gently as he rocked up into her. In the light that leaked through the slats of the window blind, he saw the glitter of her dark eyes, the faint hue of her aura like sunshine on midnight velvet. Her head lolled back, her sleek hair falling across her shoulders. The movement thrust her breasts out, and he cupped them, teasing the nipples with his thumbs as she rode him.

When she started to come, he took her hand and laid it over the tattoo on his cheek, feeling the tingle as his life essence trickled into her.

"No," she whispered.

"Take it. Take all you need. You won't hurt me."

Her mouth twisted. He knew she wanted to argue, but her climax was on her, and she moaned and ground herself against him. At the same time she drew his life essence into her through her fingertips on his tattoo.

The high of that was like nothing he'd ever experienced. Kehksut had tried to make sex with his female form the ultimate in erotic satisfaction, but Tain had loathed every minute of it. He'd been trapped in pain and madness and the demon's magic, the tiny, sane part of him screaming while his body obeyed the demon's wishes.

With Samantha, the whole world was different. His body wound up tight with wanting, and he lost control in the best way, finding his hands digging into the mattress as he thrust up and up into her. The white essence of him swirled over her fingers and into her body, making her eyes glow with it.

"Take me," he said hoarsely. "Take every bit of me. I want you to have me."

Samantha gasped as he pushed upward, all the way inside her, farther than he'd dared go their first time. Her eyes widened with the shock of it, and then a second orgasm overtook her.

Tain moaned his release at the same time his seed shot deep inside her. He rocked into her a little longer, still tight, until the climax wound its way down to sweet languor.

Heart thudding, he drew her down on top of him, kissing her face and throat and lips. "Thank you," he whispered.

She slid her arms around him, breaking contact with his tattoo but folding him into her warmth. He could stay here forever in silence and darkness that was peaceful, not terrifying. Being with her was a haven, not a prison. He closed his eyes and let himself relax for the first time in centuries.

Samantha sat up, with him still inside her, and touched his cheek again, but the connection between them had gone.

"I didn't mean to do that," she said.

"I hope you did."

Her eyes were pools of darkness but held warmth, not triumph. "I didn't want it to happen again, but I couldn't stop it."

"You shouldn't stop it. You crave it like your body craves food. You have to have life essence to survive."

"You know so much about it."

He gave her a half smile and nuzzled the line of her hair. "I became the demon expert."

"Is that what Kehksut did to you? Stole your life essence? Over and over again?"

Tain shook his head. "He couldn't stand my life essence—it was too much. That's why he had to break me."

Samantha's eyes glittered with sudden tears, and she traced the scar ridges on his chest. "I'm sorry. I'm so sorry." She was crying now, and he pulled her down to him again so he could hold her.

Samantha laid her head on his chest, hot tears wetting his skin. "I don't want to forgive your brothers for not finding you, for letting you suffer so long."

Tain had come to terms with this a while ago, knowing his brothers weren't to blame. "They tried for a long time, but they couldn't. When Adrian did find me, I was so far gone in madness that I refused to go with him. It took my brothers' collective power to get me out. And you."

It had taken a long time after that for Tain to realize that he was truly free, that Kehksut was dead and had no more hold on him. His brothers had expected him to dance around rejoicing, but the scars inside him were so deep that they might never heal. He could only withdraw into himself and wander the world, waiting for the darkness to go away.

Samantha was frowning down at him, her brown eyes wary. "You moved your stuff in," she said. "Without asking me."

"I moved in because there are people out there teaching other people how to kill demons." There was more to it than that, but it was a good excuse. "In fact, I met one of them today."

Samantha listened with trepidation as Tain described the meeting of No More Nightmares and their treatment of Leda. He twined his hands behind his head, which made his muscles move beneath her in all kinds of nice ways, as he talked.

"The woman in charge, this Ms. Townsend, she had details about how to incapacitate a demon long enough to cut out its heart," he finished.

Samantha propped herself on her elbows and regarded him thoughtfully. "That's not new. I've been hearing complaints from the demon and vamp communities about such organizations as long as I've been a cop. Someone is always passing out pamphlets on the best way to stake a vampire. Occasionally the fanatics go on a rampage, human customers get hurt, someone gets sued, and the group dies down awhile."

She traced a scar on his hard chest as she spoke, hating the pain it represented but liking the strong, even beat of his heart beneath her fingers. "But Logan and I can check out what all the groups have been up to, lately. Maybe one of them has gotten out of hand."

"Maybe." He didn't sound convinced.

"I'll interview this Ms. Townsend, though. She sounds interesting."

His gaze flicked to her. "*Bloodthirsty* is the word I'd use."

"I can't really blame these people, you know. Last year was horrible. The police stopped responding—my mother disappeared and a demon gang took over the neighborhood, and the only one helping was Septimus. This Ms. Townsend and her followers are frightened it will happen again."

"But it won't." Tain's eyes were still. "I won't let it."

"You're only one man—I mean, one Immortal."

"I am enough. I won't let demons kill humans."

"You've reassured *me*," Samantha said. "But how will you make the other millions of people in L.A. believe it?"

"You'll convince them."

"You're confident."

"You have more power than you know, Samantha. You even saved my ass, as you like to say."

"That's different. That was easy."

He gave her a faint smile. "That is what you call *easy?*"

"It was easy because I wanted to save you."

"Why did you want to?" He sounded like he truly wanted to know, as though he didn't consider himself worth the trouble.

"You needed saving." She let a teasing note enter her voice. "You were the best-looking Immortal there, and I wanted one of my own."

"I was a long way gone in madness by that time. None of it seemed quite real. But you did."

She remembered how blue his eyes had been when he'd looked at her through darkness, and then the horrible grief and sorrow in them when he'd healed her later. "If I was so wonderful," she asked softly, "why did you leave Seattle without saying good-bye?"

"Because I didn't trust myself near you."

"You're near me now."

"I need to be here."

For how long? she wondered. Until she adjusted or he did? When he felt better, and things were safe for demons, would he move on?

The peal of her phone cut through her thoughts, and she groaned. "What now?"

It was Logan, her caller ID told her. "Can't I have a night off?" she bleated into the phone.

"You need to get down here, Samantha," he said, sounding

more serious than she'd ever heard him. "There's been another murder."

Her thoughts flew to her demon father and her mother, and her heart leapt to her throat. "What murder? Who?"

"The matriarch of the Lamiah clan. She was found in her own bedroom with her heart cut out."

"How the hell did this happen?" Samantha shouted to Logan outside the matriarch's Beverly Hills mansion.

Tain strode behind her as she entered the house, resting his hands on the reassuring bulk of his swords under his duster. He'd accompanied her without arguing about it—he'd simply dressed and waited for her in her truck, giving her no choice.

The glittering opulence of the mansion was infested with plastic-garbed policemen roaming through it as uniforms interviewed the residents of the house. The remains of the protection spell Tain had cast over the mansion the previous night tingled in the air, but he saw plenty of death-magic wards pulsating around the doorsills and windows. The wards had been removed from the front door so they could walk in, but he still felt the weight of them.

Logan had met them at the remains of the gate, grim, not questioning that Tain was there. He explained what happened as they walked through the house. "The majordomo left the matriarch in her bedroom alone at seven to get ready for dinner, as usual. The matriarch apparently always had an hour or so to herself after the business of the day and before dining, often with guests, though tonight she was to eat alone. When the majordomo knocked on the door at eight, the matriarch didn't answer. Majordomo grew alarmed, used her key to open the door, and found the matriarch dead on the floor. Heart cut out, same as the others."

"And where is it?" Samantha asked. "The heart, I mean."

"No one's found it yet. Chest cavity open, heart gone. Not that I could tell with all the blood, but that's what the medical examiner said."

"Is her body still here?"

"In the bedroom," Logan answered. "But it's nothing you'd want to see."

"I should look anyway."

"I can't stop you." Logan gestured for her to follow, and Tain fell into step behind them.

Death magic pressed around him, mitigated somewhat by the presence of the police, most of them human. Whoever had killed her had not disturbed the mansion's wards at all. Interesting.

Samantha continued her questions to Logan as they rode down the elevator to the matriarch's underground quarters. "Have you started a list of who went in and out all day?"

"Yes," Logan said, "but security has apparently been a nightmare since the Djowlan demons blew up the gates. The guards patrolled, but it's not the same as having a huge gate and electronic surveillance of every nook and cranny. Plus they've been cleaning up from the attack, having repairmen coming in from outside, that kind of thing."

"Does the majordomo have a list of them?"

"Yes. She's a frosty bitch but highly organized." Logan shook his head. "I imagine she has to be with this job."

They reached the matriarch's bedroom and walked in. The body lay where it had fallen, the stench of it terrible. The matriarch had been dressed in a white linen suit and low-heeled ivory pumps. The crisp suit made the blood all the more stark, every splash sharp edged against the white.

Samantha glanced once at the chest cavity that had been ripped open, then quickly looked away. Tain roved his gaze around the body, noting that the matriarch was wearing a necklace of pearls and that her face registered shock and amazement.

"She didn't try to assume her demon form," Samantha mused.

"Unless she was drugged first, like Nadia," Logan suggested.

"It's possible. Forensics can let us know after a tox screen."

Samantha turned away from the gruesome body. The entire room was neat and tidy, an empty glass sitting in the middle of a doily next to a chair that faced a television set.

"Television on or off when she was found?" Samantha asked.

Logan scanned his notes. "Off, the majordomo said. Glass was empty except for a few ice cubes, and yes, the dregs have been taken for testing. Before you ask, the door was locked and not forced. The majordomo easily opened it with her key."

"So she finished her drink, stood up, and met her killer in the middle of the floor," Samantha concluded. "Either the killer had a key and walked in, or the matriarch let them in herself." She rubbed the bridge of her nose in frustration. "Just great. I love a locked-room mystery."

Tain had remained looking down at the body, noting absently that the forensics team working in the room gave him a wide berth. "No rival demon should have been able to enter the house," he said. "The windows and doors are strongly warded. Plus the remains of my own protective magic are still around it."

"So it was someone in the Lamiah clan?" Samantha asked. "Better and better."

"Or a human," Tain answered. "One of those repairmen or whatever other people came in and out of here today."

Samantha sighed, hands on hips. Tain liked the way she looked in her square-cut blazer, her sleek hair falling straight to her shoulders. When she'd gotten dressed, she'd started to scrape her mussed hair into a quick bun, until he'd pointed out the love bite he'd left on her neck. She'd flushed and left her hair down.

"I want to interview the majordomo," she told Logan. "And anyone else who admits being on this floor today, plus anyone who was *seen* on this floor. Double-check the majordomo's list of who came in and out with the guards. And find a Ms. Townsend of a group called No More Nightmares, one of those antidemon petition organizations. It's a long shot, but I'd love to know what she was doing tonight."

"Easy enough," Logan said, jotting notes. "There's something else I'd better tell you," he added, glancing at the forensics team nearby.

"What's that?"

Logan stepped to her and Tain, out of earshot of the others.

"A few of the demons here are saying you did this, or at least had it done."

Samantha stared at him in shock. "What? Why in the names of all the gods would I want to kill the matriarch?"

"Because, partner," Logan said, "the majordomo told me shortly before you arrived that the matriarch was toying with the idea of having you take her place when she retired. Groom you for the position. The inhabitants of the house are saying that perhaps you wanted to get a jump on things."

CHAPTER ELEVEN

Samantha took a startled step backward to find Tain's strong bulk behind her. "Someone's feeding you a wad of bull," she said, trying to laugh. "You weren't here when I met the matriarch. She hated me on sight."

"New blood, is what they're saying," Logan went on, watching her carefully with his wolf's eyes. "The matriarch thought you'd bring a dose of common sense and a sense of the outside world into an inbred culture. Her very words. Well, her very words as told to me by the majordomo."

"Shit." Samantha's head started to throb, and she rubbed her temples. "I need to talk to that majordomo. What's her name?"

"She calls herself Ariadne."

"Fine. I'll interview her in one of the reception rooms upstairs." She looked at Tain. "I suppose you're coming with me?"

"In a minute. There's something I want to look at first."

Samantha didn't like that she felt bereft when he turned and walked away without explanation. He'd resumed wearing jeans, shirt, and coat, no more delectable kilt, but he looked plenty good even so. Strong, too. She'd felt so close to him tonight, so connected, and this murder had ripped her out into the real world again.

She sighed and took the notes Logan gave her, then marched upstairs alone. She wished she could send Logan home—the wolf in him must be having a hard time with all this blood and all these demons.

One of the ornate reception rooms had a desk, a polished antique with serpentine legs standing in the exact center of the room. Samantha plopped her notebook on it and lowered herself to the chair, wishing the whole house didn't intimidate her. The careful décor reminded her of the matriarch, her every hair in place, every finger decorated with tasteful rings.

The rings were still on her body, as was her circlet of pearls. Whoever did this was out to kill, in a very specific way, not rob her.

Samantha rubbed her temples again. Logan had listed the names of the two companies who'd come out to repair the security system and start rebuilding the gate and gatehouse, but it was an even bet that if the culprit had come in with them, he or she was long gone now.

Ariadne the majordomo, whom Samantha remembered being as stiff and cool as the matriarch, entered the room. She refused to sit down, so Samantha stood as well.

Ariadne repeated her story of knocking on the matriarch's door and unlocking it to find her dead. She went on to relate what had happened during the day, giving the details on who had entered and exited the house and when. The repair people had stayed outside, except for those who'd gone to the basement to look at the wiring, and they'd entered the basement through an outside door in the back.

Samantha nodded when appropriate or jotted notes. Then she laid her pen down and gave Ariadne an even stare. "Someone is trying to tell me that the matriarch talked about grooming me to be her replacement."

Ariadne's thin mouth pinched. "She did."

"Why? She didn't like me."

"No, she didn't." Ariadne looked as though she agreed

with the matriarch's assessment. "She thought you were disrespectful, full of yourself, and far too modern in your thinking. But she also believed those were the characteristics of a good matriarch. She'd been thinking of retiring for some time."

"How would that work, exactly? She wasn't even going to admit me into the clan."

Ariadne folded her hands across her stomach. "A matriarch can choose who she wants to replace her, but that choice must be approved by the heads of the most powerful families in the clan. If there is no candidate when a matriarch dies, the families can each put forward someone they feel is best."

"And it's voted on?"

"Sometimes voted. Sometimes it's a fight to the death."

Samantha blanched. "Oh."

"The matriarch has to be strong enough to defend her clan," Ariadne said primly.

"This matriarch died without the chance to revert to her demon form."

Ariadne nodded. "Which is highly suspicious, don't you think?"

Of course it was highly suspicious—that was why they were investigating. Samantha hid her irritation and asked the majordomo if anything out of the ordinary had happened that day.

"Apart from the repairs to the gate and security, no."

"Why did the matriarch ask my father to remain behind the night of the attack?" Samantha asked her.

"I really have no idea." Ariadne looked annoyed. "You'd better ask him."

Samantha didn't respond, though she ground her teeth. She asked a few more questions about where everyone was and what they were doing for the hour the matriarch was alone in her room. As far as Ariadne knew, most of the staff was in the kitchen or dining room preparing for dinner, or out if it was their night off. Ariadne herself had finished up some phone calls in her office, then gone downstairs to fetch the matriarch.

Which had left Ariadne alone during the time in question. Samantha would have to know whom she'd called and how long those conversations had been.

"Does the matriarch have a . . ." She broke off, trying to think of the appropriate word. The matriarch was a widow, according to Logan's notes, but the word *boyfriend* didn't seem quite up to par for a woman like her.

"Lover?" Ariadne supplied. "Of course she did."

Samantha picked up her pen. "Does he live here? What's his name?"

"*She* is attending a conference in San Diego."

Samantha suppressed her surprise and wrote down the name. "She'll have to be contacted."

"I have already seen to it."

Of course you have. Ariadne was one of the coldest women Samantha had ever encountered, and that included the matriarch. Ariadne was her second in command, and now the woman would be out of a job.

Samantha dismissed her, which Ariadne took with poor grace. Once she'd gone, Samantha sank to the gilded chair with a sigh.

Tain walked in and closed the door. It dismayed her how much better she felt now that he was back with her. She was used to being independent, and now she found herself watching for him. That was probably because she'd tasted his life essence, she reasoned, and wanted more. She feared the wanting would turn into an insatiable craving, and she wasn't certain she could handle that.

Not that Tain had an average life essence. He was the son of the goddess Cerridwen and a hardworking Roman soldier, and his life essence was amazing, heady, fulfilling.

She sighed and laid down her pen. "The repercussions of this are going to be bad."

Tain remained on the other side of the room, not coming to her. "When people realize that the most powerful demons in the clans can be killed?"

Samantha nodded. "The other clan demons will feel eager to take over Lamiah territory and at the same time be vulnerable to attack. Plus ordinary humans will believe that if one matriarch can be killed, they all can, thus destroying the power of the demon clans. I really need to talk to that Townsend woman."

"Only if I'm with you."

"Fine." She sighed again. "What is going on here? One day I'm doing a routine stakeout looking for Mindglow, and the next I'm chasing a demon serial killer capable of murdering a matriarch." She looked up at Tain. "Funny how all this started the day you showed up in my life again."

"I'm not doing these killings."

That hadn't been what she'd meant, but she had to admit he did look like a killer, with his bulging muscles, swords at his sides, his hair buzzed short, and the pentacle tattoo on his face. Any demon would run screaming from him, and Samantha knew she should, too.

"You took down the demons attacking Merrick's easily enough," she said.

"They were on a killing rampage. I'm a warrior, but I fight to protect."

"Is that why you came to Los Angeles? To protect us against rampaging demons?"

"Partly."

His one-word answers drove her crazy. "What was the other part?"

"To see you."

She stopped, her heart speeding. How nice if he'd come for her because he liked her, not for some strange, cryptic, Immortal reason—to make up for the past or something like that.

"You know that when a demon feeds on your life essence, it gives you a high," she said softly. "After a while it grows addicting."

"So I've heard."

"I've seen it happen again and again throughout my career. That's why Mindglow is illegal—it takes away the last vestiges of a person's ability to resist a demon. Someone can get over the addiction by staying away from demons, but Mindglow always turns the *no* into a *yes*."

Tain folded his arms, dominating the room without moving. "You fear that I'm giving you my life essence because I'm addicted to the feeling."

"What else can I think?"

His look said that she didn't understand, and he didn't have time to explain it to her. He walked to her slowly, stopping a foot away from her. "You should think that I am a healer who needs to be healed."

"And me taking your life essence heals you?"

"For now."

Samantha considered herself a stolid person, able to take in horrific crime scenes and help the victims without breaking down. She channeled her compassion for the victims and her anger at the perps by making sure she did everything in her power to find the ones responsible, bring them in, and get a conviction.

But with Tain, her emotions were all over the place. She sensed she shouldn't trust him; then she'd turn around and trust him implicitly. Doubt and surety went back and forth in her mind, and it didn't help that she was falling in love with him.

Falling? A cynical voice laughed at her. *You fell in love with him the day you saw him, and it's only gotten worse since.*

Like now—she was on duty, this was a crime scene, he shouldn't be here. But she couldn't stop herself leaning into him. He slid his hands to her hips, and she rested against the solid strength of his body.

He always smelled so good, like male musk and the outdoors scents of wind and rain. She'd made love to this god-man, had him inside her and entwined with her.

His breath was warm as he kissed her lips. She could drink him in all day, taste the sharp spice of his mouth, suckle his tongue as he darted it into her. She slid her hand to his cheek, fitting her palm over his tattoo.

His life essence came to her, less powerfully than when they made love, but still intense. Samantha didn't want to want it, but she didn't stop herself pulling it inside herself, letting it fill her empty spaces.

He deepened the kiss, bunching her hair in his hands as he opened her mouth with his. Being with him had made her understand why demons wanted life essence. They were creatures of the dark who craved the light; they were strong yet needed human beings who were physically weaker than themselves to fulfill a part of them they couldn't.

Tain was ten times stronger than a normal human, ten times as magical as the most powerful life-magic creature. He could crush her like he could a fly, yet he was healing her and making her whole.

"We have to stop," she whispered, forcing her hand from his face. "If we don't, I'll pull you down on this desk, and I know we'll break it. It looks delicate."

His smile was positively sinful. "I don't care about the desk."

At the moment, Samantha didn't care much about it, either. "I'd get fired."

"Then I'll keep you with me and safe."

"That sounds nice." She rubbed her cheek on his shoulder. "Maybe after this case is done I'll take some vacation. We can go—I don't know—anywhere. A tropical island in the middle of the Pacific where I can sip Mai Tais and watch you walk the beach. You won't be wearing anything, of course."

"Neither will you."

"But then if I spilled my Mai Tai, I'd be cold."

"Not with me there," Tain rumbled.

She imagined him licking the droplets of liquor from her skin, and her head spun. "This is a very nice fantasy."

"I can make it reality in the blink of an eye."

She looked up at him. "How? Can you transport us, or something?"

He touched two fingers to her forehead. "I can put it in your head, make you see it. It will be real, and it won't be."

"You're tempting me." She dreamily traced the points of his pentacle tattoo. "I'm supposed to be the demon."

He only smiled again. Damn, he looked good when he did that. He made her want to forget all about the matriarch and the Lamiah clan and her career and dead demons.

She swore she felt a tropical breeze touch her skin, smelled coconut oil and the pungent odor of a tropical drink and the salt of the sea. If she closed her eyes, maybe she'd see Tain with bright sunshine on his bare backside as he walked away down the beach.

The door to the reception room banged open, and Samantha jumped away from Tain, flushing. Tain looked in no way guilty or ashamed to have been caught holding her, only slightly annoyed at the interruption.

Logan shut the door quickly behind him, his raised brows indicating surprise but not censure. "McKay wants you off the investigation," he said.

Samantha blinked. "What? Why? I've barely started."

"Because you're clan Lamiah and demon and because of the majordomo's claim that the matriarch wanted you to take over when she retired. Serious conflict of interest, my friend."

Samantha stared at him in dismay. "No one really believes that, do they?"

"The press might," Logan said. "She's here, by the way. McKay. Taking over the investigation herself."

"Terrific. Making it look like she doesn't trust me."

"Making it look like she's protecting her favorite detective. If you are nowhere near this crime, no one can accuse you of jiggering the results."

Samantha suppressed her wave of anger, knowing that there wasn't much she could do about it at this point. "Fine," she said, her jaw tight. "I'll walk away if it's that big a deal. You can have my notes, although the majordomo didn't tell me much more than she told you."

She handed Logan her notebook, and he looked grateful that she wasn't making a fuss. He tried to make it lighthearted. "Go home and kiss your new boyfriend."

"Very funny."

Tain said nothing. When Logan left again, Samantha twined her fingers through his. "Will you come with me to talk to this Ms. Townsend? I want to know how a woman with diagrams on killing demons fits into all this."

Tain leaned down and whispered into her ear, "For a price?"

Her body heated. "Possibly."

"I'll make sure I think of a good one, then."

CHAPTER TWELVE

Septimus the vampire was an Old One, one of the original vampires made by a forgotten dark goddess at the dawn of civilization. He'd stayed alive all these centuries by being smarter than his fellows as well as stronger.

Once upon a time, he'd controlled vast lands and people who bowed down to him as lord and master. Now he lived in a glittering, modern city and controlled an empire of vampires—lesser vamps, because almost all the Old Ones were gone. He enjoyed his power, mostly because he liked to know things. He liked to keep his finger on the pulse, so to speak, of everything that went on in this city.

He had a partner of sorts, a vamp from Manhattan called Ricco, who had been visiting to discuss their mutual interests in other cities around the country.

His lover, the beautiful Kelly O'Byrne, had made him happier lately than he'd been in a long time. He was toying with the idea of making her immortal, so she could stay with him until the goddesses decided to send him back to dust.

At the moment, he was in his cushy private office listening to one of his employees tell him about Tain.

"Are you sure about this?" Septimus asked him.

"I saw him," the vampire said.

"I need to be very certain, or his brothers will back me

into a corner and stake me." Septimus leaned back in his leather armchair. "Slowly. And there's no telling what they will do to you."

The other vamp swallowed. "I'm sure. Tonight he went to a meeting of those No More Nightmares lunatics. Then he followed them back to their headquarters, which isn't far from here. He slipped into the building and back out again. I lost him after that, but one of my men found him again back up near Wilshire getting on a bus." The vampire fastidiously adjusted his tie. "All that magical power, and he takes the bus."

"The ways of Immortals are strange to us," Septimus said. "What else?"

"He ends up at that half-demon cop's house. He goes inside and stays awhile, probably shags her, but I didn't have a chance to see."

"I'm not interested in his sex life. What else did he do?"

The vampire consulted his notes. "He and the cop come barreling out about nine tonight and head up to the matriarch's house in Beverly Hills. The Lamiah clan bitch got her heart cut out—I'm sorry I missed that."

"I know about the death," Septimus said, placing his fingertips together. "I'm only interested in Tain and what he did the afternoon before the matriarch's death."

"You think he killed her?"

"I don't know whether he killed her. That is why I'm asking for your report."

His vampire smiled, letting his fangs show. "Your pet Immortal went to the matriarch's house this afternoon while his girlfriend was at work. The human I have watching him during the day says he went back to the matriarch's place and got inside."

Interesting. "And you have no idea what he did there or who he spoke to?"

"No. My man said he didn't stay long, maybe twenty

minutes. Then he slips back out—no one seeing him—and walks away."

"What time was this, about?"

The vampire flipped through his notebook. "Four fifteen. He walks all the way down to Santa Monica Boulevard, hops a bus again. My man lost him, but I intercepted a cell call between his brother and the brother's wife talking about meeting Tain at that No More Nightmares rally. Those people really are crazy, women getting all excited about killing demons. If they start going after vampires, I'm moving to Idaho."

"Their meetings make people feel empowered," Septimus said. "They don't want their safe, middle-class lives threatened."

"Well, they're not threatened by me," the vampire scoffed. "I only do humans who come to the club and ask for it." He smiled, his dark eyes glowing. "They beg for it."

Septimus restrained himself from rolling his eyes. He supposed that once upon a time he'd enjoyed having people fall all over themselves to offer their bodies for the night and their blood for his thirst, but lack of control always irritated him. Septimus liked control, lots of it.

He made a dismissive gesture. "Thank you, that's all I need."

"You want me to keep following your Immortal?"

"No." Septimus leaned back again. "I'm satisfied. Your bonus will be attached to your end-of-month check."

The vamp smiled. "I'll give up the bonus if you let me have one night with the half-demon cop. I bet her blood is *fine*."

"No," Septimus said. "She's off-limits."

"She's *demon*. Who the hell cares if I drain her?"

"I said no. Touch her, and you're dust."

The vamp looked disappointed but agreed. Septimus had no doubt he'd obey, because all Septimus's vampires knew the consequence of disobedience.

Septimus sat for a long time after the vampire left, thinking over what he'd been told. Once or twice, he touched the phone on his desk, then lifted his hand away.

Adrian had said, *keep an eye on him*, when Tain left Seattle for Los Angeles, but Septimus knew he hadn't meant *put a twenty-four-hour watch on Tain with detailed notes*. Then again, if Adrian asked for a report, Septimus would have it.

Of all the Immortals, Tain worried Septimus the most. Even Hunter had some sort of honor, and he and Septimus in the last year had become friends—as far as an Old One and an Immortal warrior could be friends. Hunter wouldn't kill Septimus unless Septimus either went on a mass rampage through the city or in some way hurt Hunter's wife or child.

Tain, on the other hand, was a walking time bomb. Septimus had been present when the brothers had found Tain, who'd been a crazed killing machine. The ensuing fight between Tain, his brothers, and Kehksut had been the most desperate Septimus had witnessed in his vampire life. He'd been surprised to survive it intact.

Tain had been instrumental in ending the battle, and then he'd disappeared into the blue to nurse his hurts. A year later, the man still had darkness swimming behind his eyes.

What would it take to push Tain over the edge? Or had Tain already been pushed and was taking his revenge, one demon at a time?

And was Samantha Taylor just another piece in his vengeance game? Or did he have something else in mind for her? Septimus hated not understanding exactly what was going on. It made his fingers twitch.

The door opened and Kelly entered unannounced. She was the only one allowed to come and go from his club office as she pleased, and the other vamps understood that she was completely untouchable.

Kelly had been filming most of the day for an independent studio on a movie that might propel her to superstar status. Septimus had read the script, watched some of the filming, and knew that Kelly was poised to take the world by storm.

Her smile warmed him as she took his outstretched hand. "You look so serious, my love," she said. "What's wrong?"

Septimus took in her breathtaking smile, his blood warming. "I find myself on the horns of a dilemma."

Kelly stroked one finger across his lips, then leaned and kissed them. "You'll figure it out. You always do. I believe in you."

"That's why I love you so much, my dear." Septimus pulled her to his lap, his needs stirring. "Are you ready for me?"

Her voice went low. "Aren't I always?"

Septimus's body thrummed. He loved the way she smelled, the way she touched him, the beauty of her. She let him savor her any way he liked, and she only smiled at him and loved him back.

Septimus kissed her lips again. Then he tilted her head to one side and tenderly bit her throat.

Early the next morning Samantha drove with Tain to a high-rise in the downtown financial district not many blocks from Septimus's vampire club. The directory inside the lobby boldly said that No More Nightmares had a suite on the twelfth floor. Samantha had looked up No More Nightmares and discovered that they had a main office here and branch offices throughout the state.

On the twelfth floor they walked out of the elevator to find a line of glass-fronted offices, most of them still dark.

The office with NO MORE NIGHTMARES, A CALIFORNIA NON-PROFIT ORGANIZATION on the door was lit, but the door locked.

Samantha knocked on the locked door, showing her ID through the glass to the startled woman who came out of the back.

The woman opened the door and peered around it. "Yes?"

"I'd like to speak to Ms. Townsend, please."

"She isn't in. I'm her personal assistant. Is this about our petition?"

Samantha didn't know what petition she meant, but it was a good enough opening. "I have a few questions for you."

The woman let her in. Samantha noted that the office didn't seem to have any witch wards on the doors, nothing to keep out the death-magic creatures they purported to loathe. But perhaps they couldn't do anything so obvious in a large building in downtown L.A., where many death-magic and life-magic creatures had to work side by side.

Tain walked in behind Samantha, and the assistant stared at him. "You again?" Her eyes narrowed. "I didn't know you were with the police."

"I'm not."

The woman flushed and looked uncomfortable, but she gestured for Samantha to sit in a square, hard chair in front of the desk. She introduced herself as Melanie. "What is it you need to know?"

Samantha began with innocuous questions—how long had the group been active, what were their objectives, who was Ms. Townsend?

"Ms. Townsend is an amazing woman," Melanie gushed. "She gives us hope for a better world."

"I heard that at a meeting yesterday Ms. Townsend insulted her guest speaker, who then walked out."

Melanie looked prim. "That was unfortunate. I'm afraid Ms. Leda Stowe took some of the remarks the wrong way. Has she complained to the police?"

"Not as far as I know," Samantha answered. "Ms. Townsend then gave a lecture on how to kill demons?"

Melanie's flush deepened. "In self-defense, of course. Demonkind is so much stronger than we are that we need all the knowledge about them we can get."

"Killing demons is just as illegal as them killing humans," Samantha pointed out.

"Yes, but so often demons get away with it. Look what happened last year."

"Last year was a different story." So far Melanie had given her little more about the organization than Tain had told her—this was all probably on the brochure. "I'd really like to see Ms. Townsend. Can I set up an appointment?"

Was it Samantha's imagination or did the woman's nervousness shoot sky-high? "She's out of town."

"Really?" Samantha let the word fall. "She left quickly."

"No, she didn't. She'd planned this. A little vacation."

"Fine, then I'll talk to her when she returns."

Melanie gave her a look of suspicion. "Why do you want to see her at all? She's done nothing wrong."

"I never said she had." Samantha stood. "Last night, the matriarch of one of the demon clans was murdered, her heart cut out, in the exact method Ms. Townsend described at her rally. I'd like to know where Ms. Townsend was between the hours of seven and eight last night."

"On a plane to Pennsylvania," Melanie said without hesitating.

"Do you mind if I look at her itinerary?"

Melanie stood up, covering her agitation with a brisk manner. "Yes, I do mind. You can't march in here and make accusations. You have to have a warrant."

She'd certainly watched her television. "If I can assure

myself that she was on a plane or in another state during the murder, then I don't have to bother her."

"*Murder*, you keep calling it. The woman was a demon, as you are."

Samantha tensed, and behind her Tain went still. "Why do you say that?"

"You're not full demon, but you have demon blood. I can tell."

"Really? How?"

"I have some magical ability," Melanie said, sounding proud. "I can see it in your aura."

"I'm half demon," Samantha said sharply. "It doesn't make me any less able to do my job."

"Of course it does. You'll side with them."

Melanie yanked open the desk drawer and took out a piece of crystal with thin wire twisted around it. She began tracing runes in the air with it, and Samantha suddenly felt weak.

Tain stepped forward and yanked the talisman from Melanie's grasp. The woman shrieked and shrank back against the wall.

"We're going," Tain said.

Samantha didn't argue. Tain put his hand under her elbow and steered her quickly out of the office, tossing the talisman into the nearest trash can in the hall. Out of the corner of her eye Samantha saw Melanie scuttle for it, but Tain had Samantha down the hall and in the elevator before she reached it.

The doors closed with a thump, and the elevator slid smoothly downward. "I think I can consider that attempting to assault a police officer," Samantha panted, leaning against the wall. "Thank you."

Tain said nothing until they'd scooted past security and made it to the parking garage on the other side of the street. Tain opened the truck's door for Samantha after she unlocked it, then rested his arm on the roof and looked in at her.

"I want you to move to the Malibu house with Hunter and Leda. You'll be protected there."

Samantha looked up at his grim face, his shadowed blue eyes. "What? Why?"

"Because I have to go. There's something I need to take care of."

Her heart sped. "What something? I'll go with you."

Tain touched her cheek. "Do you trust me, Samantha?"

A difficult question. She wanted to trust him. Her initial attraction to him had deepened into something intense, and she couldn't decide whether to embrace the feeling or run away from it. She wanted to embrace *him*, then fall asleep in his arms after making fantastic love. In the back of her mind was the worried question—if he went, would he ever come back?

She reached up and touched the tattoo on his cheek, letting a spark of his life essence arc into her fingers. "I don't want you to go."

He kissed the palm of her hand. "It's necessary."

Tears pricked her eyes, and she blinked them away. "Can't you give me a hint?"

Instead of answering, he said, "Stay with Leda and Hunter while I'm gone. It's the only place you can be protected. Go there now."

There was nothing wrong with his arrogance. "I can't leave Pickles alone."

"I'll have Hunter come get him. He's good with animals."

"Tain . . ."

Tain leaned into the car and kissed her with firm lips, holding her chin in a viselike grip. "Go."

He straightened up and stepped back. Samantha thought

of a dozen arguments, suppressed them, put the car in gear, and drove away.

Trust him. The thought swam through her head even though worry twisted through her gut. *He needs someone to trust him.*

As she drove out of the garage, she looked into the rearview mirror at the stretch of concrete she'd just left, but Tain was gone.

"He went where, exactly?" Hunter demanded.

Samantha sat on a voluminous sofa in Hunter's living room with Pickles on her lap later that morning, facing the inquiry of Hunter and Leda. Leda at least didn't interrogate her, just made her strong coffee and looked worried. "I don't know. He wasn't about to tell me."

Her demon senses shuddered at all the life magic in the house, even though Hunter had dampened the wards to let her in. Hunter's aura was almost as strong as Tain's, and Leda was a powerful air-magic witch. The house belonged to Adrian, the oldest of the Immortals, and his magic permeated it. The combination of all three was formidable.

Hunter sank down on a chair, his green eyes troubled. "Adrian told me to look after him while he was down here, and I go and let him disappear."

"You can't keep him on a leash," Samantha returned. "He'll never be fully healed if you don't let him go when he needs to go."

Hunter scrubbed his hand through his tawny hair. "We love him, Samantha. We lost him for such a long time that all of us are constantly scared we'll lose him again. Even Kalen calls about him."

"I know that. But if you love him, you have to show him that by letting him go."

Hunter's eyes narrowed. Pickles looked over Samantha's shoulder with interest at Mukasa the lion pacing down on the beach.

"You love him, too," Hunter said to Samantha.

"'Fraid so." She tried a smile. "Even if he never loves me back, I can't help it. I'm trusting him, whatever it is he's up to, because I need to."

"I understand," Leda said, setting down another mug of coffee. "Believe me."

Samantha saw in her eyes the brave love of another woman caught by an Immortal. *They are hard to love,* the look said, *but worth every second of it.*

Tain investigated what he needed to in the building, using a little misdirection magic to keep people from noticing him. He'd become very good at that while a captive, some part of him becoming expert at hiding his true self from Kehksut.

That tiny hidden part of him had been his salvation. Samantha had reached it, allowing his brothers to then bond with him and pull it out. He remembered the anguishing pain when his true self had emerged at last, the reluctance with which he was dragged back into the light.

Returning to the light meant acknowledging his torment and loneliness, facing them head-on instead of hiding in madness. His brothers had ripped the scab from his very deep wound, and he'd bled inside a long, long time.

Tain found out what he wanted and departed the building. He didn't have much cash left, so he traveled the way he'd learned in the last year—he walked along the side of the highway and stuck out his thumb.

CHAPTER THIRTEEN

Samantha went back down to the department, assuaging Hunter's and Leda's concerns by having Logan pick her up. Logan emerged from the car in front of the house when she came out, laughing when he saw Pickles touch noses with the lion Mukasa before the two cats strolled away together.

"At least someone's enjoying his captivity," Logan remarked as he pulled out and drove down the hill. "It must be hell for you having to stay in all this luxury near the beach with better security than Fort Knox."

"The view is nice," Samantha said. "Though all the life magic in there makes me nauseous."

"How are you holding up?"

"All right. They're trying to keep it down without jeopardizing the protection."

"Any word from Tain?"

"No."

Logan drove for a few minutes without speaking. He turned onto Sunset, making for the freeway, traffic quickly hemming them in.

"You know," he said, "I'm not the kind of guy who interferes in my friends' personal lives. And one of the things I like best about you is you don't pry into mine."

Samantha studied the cars outside the window. "I figure if it's important for me to know something, you'll tell me."

"And I appreciate that."

"But . . . ?" She turned to him. "I hear a big *but* coming."

"Something's on your mind. You look at me, then look away—like you need to tell me something and you're not sure how. You can give it to me straight, Sam. Does McKay want to fire me?"

Samantha looked at him in surprise. "Good Lord, no. You're one of the best detectives in the division. Why would you think that?"

"I don't know—you've seemed jumpy around me the last couple of days."

"Well, I'm sorry if I worried you."

"What is it then? I wouldn't push you, but I'm feeling the tension. What's up? Or is it the whole matriarch dying thing?"

They inched onto the clogged freeway, and Samantha turned to face him, deciding to stop being a coward. "Tain told me I need to imbibe life essence in order to survive. That the demon in me does it instinctively."

Logan didn't look at her. "Really?"

"He said I must have taken some from you without knowing I was doing it."

Logan said nothing, and Samantha's heart gave a painful throb. "He was right, wasn't he?"

Logan moved his shoulders in a shrug. "I didn't mind so much."

"Are you insane? You let me do that to you without asking me about it? Without saying *anything*?"

"I thought maybe you did it to all your partners."

"This isn't funny. I had no idea . . . *When* did I? It's not like we ever had sex."

He started to smile. "Just little tiny bits, when you touched my shoulder or shook my hand or whatever. Maybe the demon part of you couldn't resist the life essence of a strong werewolf. It wasn't enough to hurt me."

"Why didn't you say anything?"

Another shrug. "What was there to say?"

"Let me get this straight—say I was a vampire and bit your neck every time I saw you—you wouldn't mention it?"

"That's different."

"It's exactly the same," she said, exasperated. "Maybe the life essence imbibing isn't as obvious, but it's just as bad. How did you feel when you found out you'd been partnered with a monster?"

His smile died. "Compared to some of the wolves in my pack, it was an absolute picnic." He glanced at her, the bleak anger in his eyes surprising her. "You've never hurt me, and I was grateful I could do something for you. You were patient with me as a newbie detective."

"Things were so bad in the pack that having a demon suck your life essence was better?"

"You have no idea." He stopped talking as he navigated some tricky traffic on the freeway. "Let's just say I was happy to start over again in L.A."

"You're a good cop, Logan."

"Thank you."

She looked away again. "It's handy to have a partner who can turn into a sniffer dog."

His tone turned dry. "Thanks."

"I'm still not sure how I feel about you not telling me I took your life essence. When I figure it out, I'll let you know."

"Any time you need it. Although I have the feeling you don't need it these days."

Samantha thought about the wild, white-hot sensations she experienced when she joined with Tain. "Remember when we didn't talk about our personal lives? I liked that."

Logan relapsed into his usual chuckle. "You got it, partner."

They turned to discussing the matriarch's murder and

what Logan had discovered, which wasn't much more than he'd noted before. He and McKay were still going over the statements and tracking down whatever maintenance and repair workers had come to the estate. Forensics would tell them what they found on their end when they were finished.

Samantha listened, trying to bury herself in the facts of the case, but she couldn't quite shut out the new tension between herself and Logan plus the worry about where Tain was and what he was up to.

Tain braced himself on the hard bench backseat of a pickup bouncing along on bad shocks down the I-15. He'd found rides all the way out to Barstow, then walked along the freeway as the sun set until the two friends in their truck picked him up. Tain found himself squeezed in the back between a large cooler and a larger sleeping dog.

"So, where you headed, bud?" the driver asked as the sun sank behind them. He had a grizzled beard and a head of wiry, graying hair. His friend looked much the same.

"I'm not sure yet." The information Tain had found at No More Nightmares mentioned a hideaway out in the desert on the California-Nevada border but wasn't specific where.

The man burst out laughing. "Anywhere but here?"

"Something like that."

"I'm Ed. This is my buddy Mike."

"Tain," he responded.

Ed laughed again, a roar that drowned out the screeching engine. "What kind of name is that?"

"Celtic." When Ed looked baffled, he said, "Welsh."

"You're not American, then."

"I am now." Adrian had obtained all kinds of documents for Tain that said he was an American resident of

Seattle, even though Tain stayed with Adrian only a few weeks at a time. The pieces of paper didn't mean much to a man who'd gone where he'd pleased before his capture, but people these days liked documents, and Adrian said it would save a mountain of trouble. "From Seattle," he added.

"Well, at least you're not . . . Shit!" Ed broke off as the truck bucked and coughed before drifting to the side of the road in silence.

Traffic was sparse, and Ed pulled over without impediment. Mike hopped out as Ed popped the hood, and Tain joined Mike on the gravel.

The land here was empty and soothing. The desert stretched out to either side of the freeway, white dust broken by green-black creosote, nothing man-made except for a lit billboard advertising a twenty-four-hour casino in Las Vegas.

L.A.'s smell of constant exhaust had vanished to be replaced by the clean smell of dust and the night. It was pleasantly cool, though the temperature warned that during the day, even in September, the heat would soar.

Mike had his head under the hood, shining a flashlight over various bits of the engine. He wiggled things, and then Ed tried to start it, but nothing much happened but clunks and screeches and Ed's string of obscenities.

"Let me try," Tain said.

Silent Mike gave him a look that said, *sure, if you want*, and stepped out of the way.

Tain knew nothing about the mechanics of vehicles of this century, though he knew men enjoyed tinkering with them whether they needed to be tinkered with or not. But he could feel the engine's core, see the power snaking from it, and understood where that power was blocked.

He jiggled bits as Mike had done as he sank a tiny trickle of magic through the engine, unclogging the lines, fixing the gearshaft that had been slipping, and smoothing over the frayed belts and various cracks in the metal.

He withdrew from the machine's belly and said, "Try it now."

Ed cranked, and the engine started up, smooth and quiet. Ed's eyes widened over the steering wheel, and Mike gaped at him.

"How the hell did you do that?" Ed bellowed out of the truck window.

Tain shrugged. Mike clapped him on the shoulder and gestured him back into the truck.

Ed told him to sit in the front this time, Mike scooting over to the middle so Tain could sit by the door. The dog, who'd never awakened, began to snore.

Ed pulled out after a lone car had shot by, grinning as the truck moved smoothly down the freeway. He pressed the accelerator and easily caught up to and overtook the other car.

"Woo-hoo!" Ed screamed. "Hey, Tain, we're heading to a place out by Vegas. Want to come? The girls there like to party."

Mike spoke for the first time. "One of them is a vampire."

"But nice," Ed said. "She won't kill you or anything."

"She can bite my neck anytime," Mike said softly, and Ed bellowed with laughter.

Tain smiled along with them. A vampire might know what he was looking for, if only because she'd want to avoid it.

"Sure," he said.

Ed whooped. "Hot damn. Hang on, here we go!"

McKay had taken Samantha off the investigation of the matriarch's murder but hadn't banned her from looking into the destruction of Merrick's club, Nadia's abduction, and the threatening letters. Samantha spread the files over her desk that evening and went through them again a piece at a time, adding what she'd learned from her visit to No More Nightmares.

She wished she'd found a suspiciously cut-up newspaper and a bottle of glue on Melanie's desk, but there hadn't been anything in the innocuous office to justify Samantha asking for a search warrant. Ms. Townsend's preoccupation with methods of killing demons and her assistant's fanatic protection of her weren't criminal per se. She had to be content with putting a watch on the office and trying to track down Ms. Townsend.

She also wanted to interview Nadia again, and Merrick, to find out how someone put a firebomb in his club without him knowing it. Logan had sniffed around the morning after the club burned down and found traces of a spell—crystals and wire and small bones. A witch in the forensics department identified them as accoutrements for a spell that could remotely trigger a fire. Samantha also wanted to talk again to the Djowlan demon who'd attacked the matriarch's house, and Kemmerer, who'd sold Nadia to her captors. All these threads had to go somewhere.

Plus it kept her from thinking about Tain. *Trust me,* he'd said.

Did that mean he'd come back with the culprit in tow and give him to Samantha along with all the evidence she needed?

Or did he mean, *don't bother me*?

Her harried thoughts were interrupted by a call on her cell phone. Her hopes leapt, as she thought it was Tain, then plummeted again when she saw that the number belonged to Septimus's vampire club.

"Yes?" she said.

"Don't sound so happy to hear from me," the vampire's dark voice rolled from the other end. "I need to talk to you."

"I'm listening."

"Not on a phone that half the world can tap. Can you meet me? At my club would be best."

"Your club full of demon-hating vampires? I don't think so. How about the Malibu house, instead?"

"I want to talk to *you*, not Hunter and his charming wife. How about a late-night restaurant? I'll set it up—I know a good place."

"No vampires," she warned.

"No vampires. Just humans catering to an exclusive clientele. You'll like it."

"Can you give me a hint what this is about?"

"It concerns a mutual friend, and that's all I will say on a cell phone. I'll send the limo to pick you up at ten."

"No, I'll have someone drop me off."

Septimus sighed. "I'd rather you didn't involve anyone else until I know whether I'm right. I'll send the limo. Kelly will be there, if it makes you feel better."

"A date with a boss vamp and a famous actress? How can it get better than this?"

"Your sarcasm stuns me. Be ready at ten." He clicked off without saying good-bye.

Samantha returned to her files, scowling. A vampire who had secrets about Tain he didn't want to tell her in front of anyone, and her having to wait until ten tonight to find them out, did not put her into a good mood.

She stared in irritation at Logan's and her notes until the phone on her desk rang. "Samantha?"

"Hello . . . Dad. What's up?"

"I need to talk to you, privately, not on the phone."

"Doesn't everyone?" Samantha said. "Sorry, I mean, sure. Want to meet me for a quick dinner?"

She heard him consult with her mother, then replied that he'd drive down and meet her at La Casa Bonita, her favorite downtown Mexican place. She got to spend the rest of the evening wondering about that conversation as well.

She reached the restaurant before her father did, being too restless to wait. The staff knew her because she came in so often, and they let her take a booth away from the most crowded areas. When Fulton came in, she stood up and hugged him.

"What was that for?"

"Can't I be glad to see my father?"

Fulton looked pleased but slightly worried. "Anything wrong?"

"You're the one who wanted to talk to me."

Fulton waited until they'd both ordered, then looked around the crowded restaurant. "Not my idea of private."

"It's the best I can do. I'm on evening shift and all the interrogation rooms at my office have two-way mirrors and microphones. This place gets so noisy no one will hear a word we say."

Fulton looked skeptical, but once the waitress had deposited a basket of tortilla chips and four kinds of salsa, he leaned toward her across the table. "Do you know why the matriarch asked me to stay and talk the day you met her?"

"I needed to ask you about that." Samantha smothered her chips in pungent tomatillo salsa and took a bite. "What I recall mostly from that day is that demons attacked, and I got acid all over me."

He wore a worried-father look. "You're all right from that, aren't you?"

"Sorry, yes, I'm fine. Tell me why she asked you to stay."

"To talk about you. She asked me all about your upbringing, what you did now, why you joined the police, and about your mother and what you were taught about demonkind."

"I wasn't taught anything about demonkind. I thought I was a normal human child for a long time."

"I know. That was my fault—your mother wanted you

to know, but I begged her not to tell you until you were old enough to understand. I wanted you to be raised human, because . . . well, many reasons."

"I heard an insane rumor that the matriarch wanted to groom me to take her place. That's what Ariadne, her majordomo, seems to think."

"That's another thing the matriarch wanted to talk to me about. She asked me to put you forward as a candidate at the next clan muster."

Samantha sat back, stunned to hear him confirm it. "Muster?"

"A gathering of heads of demon households. We call it a *muster*, an old-fashioned term, because we used to only do it when we geared up to fight. These days it's more like a board meeting."

Samantha reached for more chips. Stress always made her hungry. "I thought the matriarch put forth a candidate and the heads of the families voted on it."

"Heads of families can name a candidate as well."

"So, when are you going to tell the head of our family? Or did you? What did he say?"

Fulton looked puzzled. "We never told you that, either, did we?" He touched his chest. "I am the head of our family, one of the most powerful in the clan."

Samantha's chips dropped from her fingers, and she grabbed a napkin to wipe her hands. "You always told me you were a lesser demon, not very strong."

"Magically, I'm not. But politically, I am. When my father died ten years ago, I took his place—I was his oldest son and his heir, and you are my only child." His dark eyes softened. "We were going to introduce you to all this gradually, but the matriarch jumped the gun by wanting you as a candidate. She was right, in retrospect. You need to know."

"But I'm only half demon." Samantha remembered the majordomo's words, *Sometimes it's a fight to the death.* "Why would your family, or the clan, accept me as matriarch? Not that I have any intention of taking the position."

"Because our family has that kind of clout. The matriarch is also from our family—she was my grandmother." He paused, his eyes darker than ever. "I hope you will consider it."

Samantha started to raise her voice, then remembered they were in a crowded restaurant and lowered it to a hiss. "I can't be clan matriarch. The idea is insane. I can barely work magic."

"Yet you know the activities of every demon club and gang in Los Angeles, not to mention everything the vampires do. You defeated an Old One alongside a powerful Immortal warrior, and you have friends who can do amazing things. Plus you don't take shit from anyone. I remember all the things you did to try to find your mother last year."

Fulton finished his statement as the waitress brought enchiladas and empanadas to the table. "I hope you will consider it," he repeated.

Samantha sat back again, the steam from her enchiladas and rice rising to caress her face. Of all the things she'd speculated her father would say to her today, it wasn't this. She'd thought he'd shake his head in wonder at the matriarch's declaration, maybe agree that the woman had come unhinged.

Now he was sitting here calmly eating empanadas and telling Samantha he thought she should become the next matriarch of their clan.

"What does Mom have to say about all this?"

Fulton swallowed and spoke. "She always knew this was a possibility. She doesn't really understand why it must be, but she'd support you."

"That makes two of us," Samantha said. "Not understanding, I mean." She looked her father in the eye. "I can't possibly become the matriarch. That's all I can say."

"Please think about it."

Samantha blew out her breath. "Why do you want me to so much? You said you wanted Mom to raise me as human—why do you all of a sudden want me to be queen of the demons?"

Fulton laid down his fork, the look in his eyes serious. "Because as matriarch, you will have power and you will be protected. Samantha, I married your mother because I loved her, but I defied convention to do it. In the old days, a half-blood offspring would have been hunted down and killed. Even these days, demons have been known to murder half demons and feel justified. But if you are matriarch, endorsed by the previous matriarch and from one of the most powerful demon families in the country, you would be safe. And respected."

Samantha looked at him for a long time, and he picked up his fork again and stabbed it around his rice.

"This is my life," she said in a soft voice. "All I've ever wanted to do was be a cop. When I found out I was half demon I worried I'd never be let on the force, but then I learned I could be a detective in the paranormal division. It's all I ever wanted—it's who I am. I don't know anything about the demon clans, and I certainly don't want to be head demon." She stopped. "I can't."

Fulton reached over and clasped her hand, his demon touch warm and vibrant.

"Please, child, don't dismiss it so quickly. If another matriarch is chosen, and she takes against you, you might forfeit your life."

CHAPTER FOURTEEN

"Is this a great party, or what?"

Tain had more or less been embraced by Ed and Mike and their circle of friends. They'd driven through the dark desert to end up in a bar inside the Nevada border, too far from Las Vegas to be anything but seedy. The air-conditioning was faulty, the interior dark, the door permanently open.

But for the slot machines blinking in one corner, Tain was reminded of the taverns he used to frequent with Adrian in the old days, which held the same disreputable characters, barmaids who were either smiling or untrusting, and patrons who either wanted to be best friends or want you out.

Ed insisted he stay and meet "the girls," who had a "ranch" a little way up Highway 95. The vampire woman was easy to spot. She came in at about ten in a belly-dancing costume, and swayed and twirled to tunes in her portable CD player.

The girls laughed with the regulars, which included Ed and Mike, and sized up Tain with calculating eyes. Two of the young women were demons.

The vampire finished her dance and came over to where Ed enthusiastically beckoned her. "How you doing, sugar? This is our new friend, Tain. Tain, this is Vonda."

She slid her sultry gaze from Ed to Tain, then hissed, lips rolling back from her fangs. "What are you?"

Ed looked surprised. "He's a hell of a good mechanic, that's what he is. We picked him up outside of Barstow."

Tain snaked a small bit of his magic out to touch her. She tried to counter with death magic, then looked terrified as Tain easily brushed it aside. "He's a witch," she said. "He must be."

Tain let the tendril of magic become soothing, healing. "I'll not harm you."

She stared at him, mouth open, trying to decide what to do. Then she closed her mouth and flicked her gaze from him, a submissive stance for a vampire.

Tain made an *I want to talk to you* gesture with his chin to Vonda and led her into the corner near the slot machines. Ed grinned and gave him a thumbs-up as he went, obviously thinking that Tain and Vonda had connected.

Vonda was still wary of him but finally conceded to answer his questions. "Sure, the No More Nightmares people come around here sometimes. The guys don't let on that Amy and Sandy are demons, and the No More Nightmares people don't seem to care that I'm vampire."

"They can't sense that the other two girls are demon?"

"Don't seem to. I mean, they whine about demons being a menace and how they want them all gone, but they can't even tell when one walks by them."

And yet Melanie at the No More Nightmares office had known that Samantha was half demon. "But they leave you alone?" Tain asked.

"Yes. Sometimes I think I should go to one of their stupid meetings and tear out the throats of half of them, but it's not worth getting staked for. But I could do it."

Tain knew she could. The petite young woman in the belly-dance veils and jingling sash could take out this entire room if she wanted to. "Where do they have their meetings?"

She wrinkled her nose. "You aren't thinking of joining, are you?"

He shook his head. "I'm just curious."

"I don't know. Seriously, I don't."

"Could you find out?"

Vonda gave him a wheedling look. "What would I get if I do?"

Tain thought of his empty pockets, but he knew this vampire girl wouldn't be tempted by his money. "What do you want?"

Her eyes darkened. "A sip of whatever kind of blood is riding through your veins."

"My blood wouldn't be good for you—too much life magic can kill you."

"I've done life-magic creatures before. Werewolves are especially good—they *say* they hate vampires, but when they really want one . . ."

"I'm not a werewolf."

Vonda looked him up and down. "What are you, then? A chameleon?" Chameleons were similar to were-creatures, except they were humans who could take the form of any living being. They didn't become that creature in the same way a shape-shifter like Logan became his animal self; they were still human no matter what animal they resembled.

"A guardian," he said. "Have any demon or vampire girls disappeared lately?"

"I don't know about disappeared, but a few have moved on. That happens. Girls come and go, and they don't always want to leave a forwarding address."

"Is there a place around here that's different somehow? Someplace vampires and demons are afraid to go?"

Vonda gazed at him in sudden suspicion. "Why do you want to know?"

"Because I don't like people who deal in fear. I want to know why they're doing it. Is there such a place?"

Vonda thought for a moment, then gave a grudging shrug. "All right, I have heard weird stories about a canyon not far from here. But if I take you there, you really do need to give me something in return."

She drew a finger across his left cheek, the one unmarked by his tattoo.

"I have a lover," he said.

"Sweetie, that doesn't stop anyone here."

"It stops me." His firm tone put a disappointed look on her face. "What I will do . . ." He lifted her hand from his face and sent a trickle of healing magic through her.

When she'd touched him he'd felt the taint of a weakening spell, one she strove to hide. A witch could have put it on her or a rival vampire or a customer—it was hard to say, but he easily broke and removed it.

She stared at him in shock, then smiled. "Thank you. Are you sure you don't want a little extra fun?"

She sashayed toward him again but Tain shook his head. "I'm sure. Now, how do I get to this place?"

Samantha rode in Septimus's ultraluxurious limousine to a five-star restaurant where corporate presidents made international deals and big-name producers wined and dined investors. Samantha had conceded to the limo because Septimus refused to tell her the name of the restaurant, and she'd have no idea where to go. Logan couldn't come with her because he wasn't on duty tonight, and when she called him, he wasn't home.

In the limo, Samantha checked her cell phone for missed messages and found none. She clicked to where she'd saved Tain's cell phone number and let her thumb hover over the button. She wanted to push it, to hear his Welsh-accented voice answering on the other end. She wanted to say, even if she had to leave a message, *I miss you.*

She sighed, flipped the phone closed, and dropped it back into her purse.

The waitstaff at the restaurant knew Septimus, who'd booked a small private room for himself, Kelly, and Samantha. The maitre d' guided Samantha through the dining room to the back as though she were making a royal visit.

Septimus stood up when she entered. Samantha was relieved to see Kelly O'Byrne with him as promised, looking as stunning as ever. Kelly never seemed to make extra effort on her makeup or clothes, but she was always poised and lovely in her understated and hideously expensive wardrobe, ready for whatever camera might flash at her.

Kelly greeted Samantha warmly. She owned the house next door to Leda and Hunter in Malibu, and Samantha had come to know her somewhat over the past year. As usual, Kelly wore a scarf around her neck to hide the bites of her vampire lover. It had become a signature look, imitated by her fans.

"Do you mind if I stay?" Kelly asked. "If you'd rather talk to Septimus alone, I can go."

Samantha squeezed her hand. "No, please."

"Ms. Taylor doesn't trust me," Septimus said.

Samantha slanted him a weary glance. "It's more that I don't want to explain to my lieutenant why one of her detectives was treated to dinner at a chichi restaurant by a vampire boss. If I'm here with my friend Kelly, things get much easier."

"Of course." Septimus gestured her to sit, and then flicked his fingers for a waiter to come in and pour wine. Then he ordered for the three of them, which annoyed Samantha, but since he was footing the bill, she decided to say nothing.

Septimus waited until the first course was served, then bade the waiter shut the door behind him and not return until called. He reached into a briefcase and pulled out a file, which he laid beside Samantha's plate.

"What's this?" she asked, opening it. She expected something about the demon disappearances and deaths but instead found herself looking at a photo of Tain. He was walking away from the camera, sunshine on his duster coat and thick red hair.

The next picture was of him entering the building where No More Nightmares had an office, his hair shorn off as it was now. Next was one of him strolling by the gate of the matriarch's compound in T-shirt and jeans. After the pictures came pages of notes in cramped handwriting, dates and times and notations.

"What is this?" Samantha repeated in a hard voice.

"A record of Tain's movements since he first arrived in Los Angeles."

She looked up at him in angry surprise. "Why? Who asked you to do this?"

Septimus took a casual sip of wine. "Adrian asked me, although I don't believe he meant for me to be so detailed. That, I took upon myself."

"Why?" she asked again.

"Because Tain is a wild card. I wanted to make sure I knew what he was up to while he was in my city."

Samantha slammed the folder closed. "He's been helping me on this demon case."

"Which he brought to your attention in the first place. I'm showing this to you for a reason, Samantha. I think he's more involved than he's let on."

Samantha's heart beat faster. "Explain."

Septimus set his glass down and toyed with the stem. Kelly listened but with the blank expression of someone trying to be discreet. "Tain has been seen in the vicinity of every incident that you have been investigating. He was recorded near the location where each demon prostitute disappeared. He knew unerringly how to find the demon girl who was returned. He was seen near the matriarch's mansion before she was found dead, and seen breaking into the offices of that No More Nightmares place yesterday evening."

"You've done a thorough job." Samantha felt brittle. "If you know so much about him, where is he now? What is he up to? Do you have satellite photos?"

Septimus took her outburst calmly. "He was last seen heading north out of San Bernardino, and after that, I considered him out of my jurisdiction."

"If you're that worried about him, why did you stop tracking him?"

"I wasn't 'tracking' him, as you say. I was making sure he wasn't getting himself into trouble down here while his big brother worried in Seattle. If Tain goes around the bend again, Adrian will hold me partly responsible."

"So you were covering your ass, is that it?"

"I don't like what I found any more than you do—"

Samantha cut him off. "Have you sent this report to Adrian? Told him Tain's committed the crime of walking the streets of Los Angeles?"

Septimus looked pained. "I haven't said a word to Adrian. I wanted to show you first."

"Why?"

"Because if it means nothing, I won't have pissed off five Immortal warriors who have very large swords. If it *is* something, you're paranormal police—it's your job to take care of problems like Tain."

"If Tain has gone insane again—and I'm not saying he has—why do you assume I could take care of him? I'm nowhere near as strong as his brothers, or you for that matter."

"Because you helped him before," Septimus answered. "His mind was completely gone up there in Seattle, and yet he looked at you, talked to you, even flirted with you. I was there—I remember all of it. I don't think it was a coincidence that his brothers were able to restore him shortly after he met you. Or that Cerridwen chose you as the witch whose body she'd enter during the battle."

"I think you're optimistic about my influence over him."

"I think he's right," Kelly said softly.

Samantha stopped, her heart sinking. She didn't want these pictures to be anything but coincidence, or a mistake. She didn't want to face the fact that if Tain went insane again, if she lost him, it would devastate her.

She thought of his phone number saved on her cell phone—if she'd called him when she'd been tempted to in the limo, would he have answered? Her hand had stilled because of his last question to her—*Do you trust me?*

I have to trust him. Otherwise my love for him is nothing.

She wet her dry mouth. "What do you want me to do, follow him and drag him back to L.A.?"

"I wanted you to be aware what he was doing," Septimus answered. "You can have the file. Use it as you wish."

Samantha gazed at the brown folder in loathing, then nodded. She couldn't help suspecting that Septimus was handing over the information freely because he'd already made copies.

The waiters entered with perfectly prepared plates of food, but the odor of it turned Samantha's stomach. "I'm sorry, but I don't have much appetite. I already had dinner."

"I quite understand."

She stood up. "I have to go."

Again Septimus gave her an imperceptible nod, and Kelly looked at her in sympathy and concern. Septimus snapped his fingers for a waiter. "Have my driver take Ms. Taylor home."

Samantha would have much preferred to take a taxi, not in the mood for another muffled ride in Septimus's dark limousine. But the maitre d' ushered her out again before she could gather her thoughts, leading her all the way to the open door of the waiting limo.

Samantha didn't want to return to the Malibu house and a curious Hunter and Leda, so she told Septimus's driver to take her to the paranormal police division. There she could sit in isolation at her desk, look at the information, and decide what to do before returning to the house. The last thing she wanted was Hunter calling Adrian and his brothers to go round up crazy Tain.

No, the last thing she wanted was for what she'd seen in the file to be true—that Tain was taking his revenge on demons one at a time, starting with the most helpless and working his way up to the matriarch. She remembered how easy it had been for him to kill demons at Merrick's club the first night she'd seen him—two blasts of his lightning magic, and they were dead. No butchering necessary.

But she realized when she reached her desk and spread Septimus's notes and photos over it that Tain was closely involved in all of this. The time stamp on one of the photos put him outside the matriarch's mansion just before her death.

Samantha stared at the photo and put her head in her hands, wondering where the hell Tain was now.

Ed dropped Tain off about midnight on the dirt road Vonda had named, but neither Vonda nor Ed would get out of his truck.

"You sure?" Ed said, leaning on his arm out the window. "It's spooky out here."

"I'll be fine."

"Well, all right. Give me a call if you want another ride. See you."

Vonda nodded at Tain, glancing nervously across the empty desert. Tain raised his hand in farewell, and Ed's truck screeched around and rolled away, bathing Tain in exhaust and dust.

This stretch of road was deserted, an unpaved washboard that rolled with the contours of the land. A mountain ridgeline rose high and sharp to the east, the moon filming the landscape with silver. The white desert floor showed the black outlines of creosote and stunted Joshua trees.

At the end of this road, Vonda had said, was the bad place, but she wouldn't be more specific than that. She'd never seen it, but she'd heard stories of people going there and never coming out.

By "people" Vonda had meant death-magic creatures. Tain, boiling over with life magic, walked down the road with a little more confidence.

His boots stirred puffs of white dust but nothing else moved in the stillness. It was a fine night, pleasantly cool but not sharply cold, and the moon lit everything well. But he heard no noises of night creature—coyotes, owls, bats, snakes—only silence and the crunch of his boots on rock.

The road ended at the entrance to a box canyon, its walls rising sharply from the desert floor. Hardy thistle bushes clung to minute ledges all the way to the top. An obvious path led inside the canyon, and Tain followed it.

The canyon wound with the wash that had formed it, the very bottom still damp with runoff from the last rain. As the walls closed off the open desert behind him, Tain felt a faint diminishing of his magic that he at first thought was imagination. But as he went on, the sensation grew stronger, a definite suppression of the power inside him.

Perhaps this was what Vonda meant—that the strong natural magic of vampires and demons was negated here. If so, whatever field or spell hung over this place squelched *all* magic, both life and death, which was unusual.

Tain drew one of his swords and kept walking. The interior of the canyon was even more silent than the open desert—not an insect moved across the rocks. The moon, high overhead now, showed him the blank end of the canyon, a wall pockmarked with man-made openings.

He cranked his head back to study the sides of the canyon, finding the telltale evenness of cliff dwellings, houses that had been built hundreds of years ago, high out of the reach of coyotes and wolves and wildcats. He wondered if the ancient Americans had chosen this place precisely because its natural field kept them safe from magical creatures.

He sensed another taint over the place that was more recent, as though someone had taken the repressing properties of the canyon and twisted it for his own purposes.

Tain scanned the cliffs, magically searching for any living thing. He felt as though he was trying to swim through deep water, the effort to send out even a small thread taking much strength.

His thin tendril of magic touched something only about ten feet above him, a life, single, alone, powerful. He sensed that many others had been here, felt their gloating, their glee.

He thought about what Nadia had said, that when she'd been held captive she couldn't shift into her demon form or gain her demon strength. Samantha had thought drugs had done that, but in a place like this, where all magic, including powerful demon magic, was suppressed, ordinary human beings would have the advantage.

Tain pulled out his cell phone and flipped it open. The picture he'd asked Leda to put as his wallpaper was one of Samantha—Leda had taken it at a family gathering this summer and had sent it to Tain's phone. Samantha's face was slightly turned to the left, but her dark eyes had fixed on the photographer. Sunshine gleamed on her black hair, and she smiled a subtle half smile like she knew a secret she wasn't about to share.

Tain touched the image, feeling empty spaces inside him, before he tapped the button that would bring up his list of phone numbers.

The phone blipped, the readout saying *No Service.*

He thoughtfully closed the device and shoved it in his pocket. Another advantage to having a meeting place out in the middle of nowhere, he supposed, was that no one could secretly call the police.

He scanned the ruins again and asked clearly, "Who are you?"

His voice echoed around the canyon and up to the slit of open sky. After a long five minutes, a few pebbles dribbled from a shelf above, and someone stepped out onto the ledge.

"You were followed."

Tain looked behind him, trying to probe for an aura, but he still felt as if he were pushing through molasses. "I know that, Ms. Townsend."

The woman drew herself up, no longer wearing the smart suit she'd had on at the lecture, but a flowing black robe.

"Who are you?" she asked.

"A traveler. Who are you?"

Ms. Townsend laughed. "I am the voice of vengeance, the hand of justice. Through me, the world will be rid of darkness, and life will shine once again."

"Will it, now?" Tain answered. "That's interesting."

Ms. Townsend looked down at him with icy hauteur. "It will be done. I have been chosen."

"Who chose you?" Tain asked.

She didn't answer. "This barren world will be green again, when all the death creatures are gone."

"This part of the world is supposed to be barren," Tain pointed out. "And death magic has to balance life magic, or there's chaos."

"There is chaos now."

"Not really."

As Tain spoke he thought through ways he could ascend the walls and snatch her, truss her up, and drag her back to Samantha for interrogation.

"You feel weak, don't you?" Ms. Townsend went on. "Your magic is gone. It's not beings like you who will heal the world, it is us. Through me."

Her eyes were like windows of darkness as she looked down at him. Tain wondered if someone channeled magic through her, if it was possible in this place. It confirmed something he'd found when he poked around the matriarch's house by himself after her death, a few things he wasn't yet ready to tell Samantha.

"I've seen what the imbalance can do," Tain said. "Now I seek to maintain the balance."

"The balance of life and death magic," she said, sneering. "Propaganda from the death realms so that right-thinking people don't swoop down and eradicate the demons. Demons have invaded our world, running 'businesses' and 'clubs.' They've oozed their poison into our lives, and it will cease."

Tain drew his second sword and crossed both blades in front of him, pouring every bit of magic he had into them. Despite the dampening field, he might be strong enough to at least knock her off the ledge, and once she was on the ground he had the physical strength to subdue her.

"No," she shouted down at him. "I am chosen!"

Sudden darkness surged behind her, and she floated out over the canyon like an enormous bat. Tain reached up with a snake of white magic, but it dissipated before it could reach her.

Ms. Townsend continued to float across the rocks, untouched, until she disappeared into the shadows on the other side of the canyon. Tain started climbing toward the ledge on which she'd stood, rocks and pebbles sliding wildly under his feet. About halfway up, the cliff became sheer with no handholds—he'd need rope to go any farther.

He scooted back down in time to see glowing eyes vanish into the shadows of the cliff face. Tain straightened up and brushed off his coat.

"Come out," he said. "I heard you."

CHAPTER FIFTEEN

A gray timber wolf walked out into the moonlight, a huge male with a powerful body and thick coat of fur. It stopped a few feet from Tain and lowered itself to its haunches without fear.

Tain spoke in a low voice, aware of how sound carried in the still air. "Did you come on your motorcycle?"

The wolf made no indication that he understood, but rose and slowly walked toward the entrance of the canyon. Tain followed.

The night was quiet again, no sounds of pursuit from behind, and none of Ms. Townsend. As they walked, Tain felt the restraining field lessen and his magical strength return, and then the cliffs receded and a chill breeze from the open desert washed over him.

The wolf padded on back down the wash to the unpaved, rutted road where Ed and Vonda had left Tain. He turned aside and led Tain over a slight rise to another wash, which was nothing more than a narrow slice in the desert floor. A motorcycle had been shoved behind a thick stand of brush, the Harley-Davidson logo gleaming when Tain pulled it out.

The wolf's body elongated as it rose on its hind legs, his features contorting and twisting until they resolved into those of a man. Tain turned away so Logan could grab his clothes, though Logan, like most shifters when they changed, didn't seem bothered by his nudity.

"I got your call," Logan said as he pulled on his T-shirt. "Why didn't you want me to tell Samantha?"

"Because she would have insisted on coming."

Logan grinned. "True. She's one tough woman. But when it comes to strong magic, I like to go in first, and she doesn't always appreciate that."

"No." Tain smiled slightly, imagining her outrage when she learned that they had come to investigate without her. "You're protective of her."

Logan shrugged. "I'm a wolf. I like to take care of my friends."

There was more to it than that, Tain suspected. He didn't pursue it, but Logan's answer confirmed his idea that Logan was high in his pack—the closer to alpha the wolf was, the stronger his need to protect.

"Once you disappeared into the canyon, I became the wolf to follow you by scent," Logan was saying. "Then the vortex hit me and I couldn't change back."

"Is that what it is?" Tain glanced at the ridge in which the canyon hid.

"You get a lot of vortexes out here in the desert—places where energy and magic collect. Some of them enhance magic, some cancel it out. I've never felt a dampening one as strong as this, though."

"You know a lot about what's out here."

"I'm a biker. I explore roads that other people don't."

"The Townsend woman is possessed by something, and the vortex didn't seem to suppress that."

"Well, there's definitely something weird about these No More Nightmares people."

Tain leaned against the bike while Logan put on his jeans and boots. "Something unusual about you, too."

Logan looked up sharply. "Look who's talking."

"There can't be much you don't know about me by now," Tain said. "Whatever Samantha hasn't told you, I'm sure my brother has. But no one knows much about you. I'd guess you were Packmaster."

Logan glared. "What would make you think that?"

"An alpha wouldn't walk away from his pack. He'd fight to the death rather than choose exile. But a second-in-command might leave—in fact, if shunned by the pack, he'd have to."

Logan turned his face to the moon, his tawny eyes glittering in the white light. "The pack is no longer part of my life. I made my decision."

"Did they force the decision on you?"

Logan sighed, his expression bleak. "It's something I'd rather not talk about, if you don't mind."

Tain was curious, but more than anyone he recognized the need to leave the past in the past. "If you promise me the reason won't hurt Samantha, I won't ask you."

"Now who's being protective?"

"She's worth protecting."

Logan's eyes narrowed. "She's becoming pretty wrapped up in you. Do me a favor and don't break her heart. If I have to punch you I will, even though I don't think the odds are in my favor in a fair fight."

"It won't come to that." Tain had no intention of leaving Samantha until he stopped whoever was cutting out demon hearts. After that it would be her decision whether he went or stayed. If either of them ended up brokenhearted, it would likely be Tain. He was so twined in Samantha now, it would be very difficult to let her go.

Logan picked up his helmet. "It will take us about six hours to get back to Los Angeles. We'll be there by morning."

He climbed on the bike and slid forward enough to accommodate Tain, clearly finished talking about his past.

Tain settled his swords out of the way and climbed on behind.

Logan fired up the bike, and they took off into the night, the sound of the motorcycle ringing back up the still, silent canyon.

Logan walked in late the next day, reaching his desk as Samantha was eating lunch at hers.

"Where have you been?" Samantha demanded.

"The Nevada desert." Logan yawned, very much like a wolf stretching after a long night. "Ran into construction on the freeway, which slowed us down more than I thought. Then I had to take a shower or you wouldn't have liked me sitting next to you."

"The Nevada desert?" Samantha repeated. "Us?"

"Tain came back with me." Logan rubbed his eyes with the heel of his hand and logged in to his computer. "He said he'd crash at his own place and meet up with you later."

"Oh." The explanation felt anticlimactic and at the same time awakened more worries. "What were you doing in Nevada?"

"Looking for the No More Nightmares compound." Logan then told her an incredible tale of a narrow canyon with a magic-dampening field and Ms. Townsend floating across the sky.

"Am I supposed to understand any of this?" Samantha asked. "Is this evidence that No More Nightmares is doing the killings?"

"You tell me." Logan yawned again. "My brain is fried."

Samantha regarded him without sympathy. She'd stayed up far into the night at the Malibu house looking over the file Septimus had given her on Tain, then tucked it into her briefcase and brought it in with her this morning, not wanting to chance Leda or Hunter stumbling across it.

The evidence Septimus had gathered was pretty damning. The photos and surveillance notes showed Tain in places where he shouldn't have been, meeting with people like the fine-boned demon who'd led the attack on the matriarch's house. She couldn't recall whether that demon had acted like he'd known Tain, but of course he could have hidden the fact.

And now Logan talked about Tain hitching across the desert to track the No More Nightmares group to a bizarre canyon in Nevada.

"We can contact the county sheriff out there," she suggested. "See what he knows about it."

"Sheriff in that county's a she. I called her already, and she said she'd send a couple of deputies to check it out. Humans only, I said, because of the magic-killing vortex. She laughed at me and said they weren't much for paranormal police in Jackson County anyway."

"If that's the case, they might be sympathetic to No More Nightmares. Another thing to be careful of."

"Yep."

Logan turned to his computer, looking ready to bury himself in work. Samantha left him to it. She told McKay she'd be out following up her investigation of No More Nightmares, and left without Logan. She took the file on Tain with her and made her way to the apartments in east L.A. where Septimus's vamp's notes said Tain lived.

The apartments were as worn out as any she'd expect from this neighborhood, with a staircase leading to a railed balcony that ran along the front doors. She climbed the stairs and walked briskly along until she reached number 210.

She found the door ajar, but when she listened she heard nothing from within. She reached into her blazer and closed her hand around her pistol before she ducked inside.

The apartment was small, with a tiny living room beside an equally tiny kitchen and a door leading to a bedroom in the back. The bedroom door stood open, but still she heard no sound.

The bedroom was so small it could contain only the bed and the man in it, who lay facedown in a pool of sunshine. A sheet bunched around his lower body, revealing his sun-kissed back and arms, a tan from wind and weather that some red-haired men could achieve. He'd scrunched the pillow beneath his head, fists clenched as though he'd been fighting it. His tattoo was stark black on his cheek, his lashes curled against it.

A powerful urge welled up inside her to touch the tattoo. His life essence called to her, a need that swirled through her in red-hot waves. She didn't want the need, had been fighting it, not wanting to let loose the dark demon she'd suppressed all her life.

She closed her fingers over her palm and backed a step, sweating. The demon in her snarled at her. *Take it—it is what you are.*

This was a mistake. She turned to go.

"Samantha."

His deep, accented voice slid over her, forcing her to look back at him.

He rolled over onto his back and tucked his hands behind his head, regarding her with his sky-blue eyes. His torso was hard with muscle, red-brown hair dusting his chest and hiding the thin scar lines there. The sheet dipped to his hips, revealing a swirl of darker hair south of his navel.

Samantha wet her lips. "The front door was open. I thought I'd better check if everything was all right."

"I must have forgotten to close it right. It drifts open."

"This is a bad neighborhood for doors that drift open."

Tain flicked his fingers and sent a wave of magic swirling past her. The front door slammed and the lock clicked into place.

Samantha jumped. "You don't set wards," she said, a little breathlessly. "I walked right in without feeling anything." If he had warded the apartment, the strength of his life magic would have prevented her from even poking her head in the open door.

"I didn't in case you happened by," he said.

"You were expecting me?"

His blue gaze raked up and down her. "I hoped."

"Logan told me what you'd found out in the desert."

"Is that why you came?"

"Partly." She stopped.

He doesn't need to trap me with magic, she thought. *All he has to do is reach out his hand.*

He reached for her now, his strong, scarred fingers stretched out to her, wordlessly inviting her. She went to him and let him pull her down to the warm goodness of him.

He slid her on top of him, then cradled the nape of her neck and kissed her. His mouth was all kinds of delicious, his skilled tongue roaming. His lips tasted of sleep and need, warmth and smoothness.

He suckled her lower lip, fingers furrowing her hair. Beneath her thighs she felt the solid hardness of his arousal through the sheets.

She broke the kiss, pushing at his chest, but it was like trying to move a brick wall. "I can't. I'm on duty."

His heated breath brushed her face. "Then why did you come?"

"To talk about what you were doing last night."

"Logan told you. I'm sure he left nothing out."

Samantha licked her bottom lip, tender from his kiss. "A good cop always follows up." Following up, checking to see if Septimus had been right was just an excuse to see him, and she knew it.

He traced her cheek. "You want me to tell you the part when I wasn't with him."

"That would be nice."

He only looked at her. She could drown in his heated gaze, the one that probably had made hundreds of generations of women wilt. She traced his lips with her fingertip, liking that right now she was his sole focus.

"You need more life essence," he said.

That was part of why she'd come, but only a small part. "I'm trying to cut back," she said, trying to sound lighthearted.

"You can take it from me whenever you need it."

"Funny, most people have to be seduced or given Mindglow before they'll let demons anywhere near their essence. The first time anyway. After that, they're addicted."

"I'm not human, and I'm not giving it to demons. I'm giving it to you."

"Why?"

His touch drifted to her lips. "It's what I'm meant to do."

"I never understand you."

"There's nothing to understand." He took her hand and started to move it to his cheek, but she pulled away.

"I can't right now. Whenever I get a taste of it, I want to have sex with you."

His rare smile flashed. "Is that a bad thing?"

"It is right now. I'm supposed to be working."

He kissed her fingertips. "Samantha, you need this. I see the hunger in your eyes, and if you deny it for too long, it will kill you."

"I'd like to think I'm stronger than that."

"You're not." His seductive smile vanished. "All demons need a dose of life essence if they're going to exist, especially outside the death realms."

"Another thing I don't know about demons. I've never been to the death realms."

"Good. I don't ever want you to go—it's dangerous if you're not full demon. It's dangerous even if you are. It can kill anyone with life magic if you're not under a demon's protection."

"I might not have a choice. My father wants to put my name forward to take the matriarch's place."

"It's gone that far already?"

She shrugged. "Apparently the matriarch was my great-grandmother, and my father has enough power to tell our family who to back as the next one."

He went silent a moment. "I think it's a good idea."

"Are you kidding? Me, the clan matriarch? I'm not even full demon, as you just pointed out."

"But you know this world very well, and your police training has honed your fighting skills. You are stronger than most humans, but you understand people and don't despise them."

"You're as bad as my father. I'm twenty-seven—the matriarch was about a thousand. Much more experienced than me, wouldn't you say?"

"She didn't start when she was a thousand. I think you could be very good at it."

Samantha flopped beside him on the bed, landing against the comfort of his body. "If I become the matriarch I'll be absorbed into the clan, married to it and its politics. I'll wear business suits and have a majordomo and attend meetings. Anything left of *me* will be gone. Hell, if the last matriarch even had a name, I didn't know it."

"It was Naoma."

"How did you know that?" she asked, remembering the record Septimus's vamp had made of him at the matriarch's house.

"I saw it on the majordomo's desk when you were interviewing her."

"You went through her desk?"

He shrugged, his strong shoulder brushing hers. "Perhaps I did."

"What else did you find?"

"That the matriarch had many appointments, but with the same people or businesses over and over again. No one new or different for that day, no appointments at the time she died."

Samantha raked her hair back from her face. His eyes had gone enigmatic again, and she had the feeling he wasn't telling her everything. One more mystery to worry about. "This case is driving me crazy," she said. "It's all about powerful women—the matriarch on one hand, Ms. Townsend of No More Nightmares on the other. Plus their staunch defenders, Ariadne the majordomo, and Melanie the guard-dog assistant."

"Against Samantha and her Immortal guardian."

She didn't smile. "I'm hardly a player. Those women know what's going on, and I'm swimming around trying to figure everything out."

"You are better than you know. I think there are some things they don't know much about, either—they're trying to figure things out as well."

She sighed. "I suppose if I did become the matriarch I could find out who's killing demons just because they'd come after me. Of course, I probably wouldn't know until too late whether it was demon hunters, rival clan members, or demons from my own clan—I bet all three would try."

"I'll not let you use yourself as bait," Tain said.

"I'm used to it. I've done more than one assignment where I put on a strapless dress and stilt heels and waited to be hit on, offered drugs, or killed. Like at Merrick's club."

"You looked beautiful." Tain's purr slid over her. "I had trouble concentrating on what I'd come to do. That's why I told you to stay away from me. I didn't want to want you."

"Because I'm demon?"

"I thought maybe my attraction to you was a perverse

need to be with a demon, that my madness hadn't truly gone away."

"What changed your mind?"

"It wasn't a demon in my dreams, it was you." He kissed her hair.

"I'm still technically at work." Her voice receded, her words not as adamant as she'd have liked. "See, I have my gun."

"I carry swords." He indicated the naked blades resting against the nightstand. "I like weapons."

"For defense."

"For defense. Another reason you will make a good matriarch. You think of defense rather than attack, like a protector."

His low, velvetlike tones were wearing down her defenses. "The word *matriarch* also sounds so old."

"It's a term of respect. But you can be a modern matriarch—call yourself a clan leader if that makes you feel better."

"It doesn't."

He lifted her hand and kissed her palm. "Take from me now. You need to."

"Because I won't be so crabby if I do?"

"I want you to." He kissed her palm again and then pressed it to his cheek.

The flow of his life essence seared her stronger than before, or perhaps she was simply more needy. He pulled the sheet out from between them, and her fingers found his warm skin, taut over muscle. She slid her arm around him and stroked down his spine, lingering on the hollow at the small of his back.

He dipped his head and licked her neck as lovingly as a vampire might his victim. Only she was the vampirelike one, drinking in the ecstasy of his life essence.

The demon in her rejoiced. Half-human Samantha was

still wary of the process, but the beast inside her hungered for what Tain was giving her.

"Mine," she whispered. "You're mine."

She understood why demons like Merrick wanted to possess their marks—they wanted to have *this* at their beck and call any time they needed it. Samantha brushed her hand through the silky ends of Tain's short hair and traced her way back down to his buttocks.

This gloriously strong and naked male belonged to her and her alone. She laughed with the joy of it, tilting her head back so he could nibble on her throat.

His erection pressed into her thigh through her slacks, moving as though he enjoyed the friction of the cloth. She nudged him to lie flat on his back, and he obeyed, his blue eyes half-closed, his smile sinful.

She knelt on her heels next to him, her hand still firmly connected with his cheek. With the other she traced patterns on his chest, brushing the hard points of his nipples, traveling along the ridges of his abdomen.

The indentation of his navel greeted her questing fingers. She found the warm hair above his penis, then the thick heat of the shaft itself.

Tain groaned softly as she clasped him, his smile changing. His hips pressed subtly upward, Samantha's hand closing all the way around him.

"Beautiful woman," he murmured.

The feelings rushing through her were too heady for words, so she only smiled and stroked him, while he lifted against her hand. He touched her fingers where they rested on his cheek, his eyes warming as though her taking his essence gave him even more pleasure than her stroking him.

He belonged to her, this elusive, taciturn warrior who came and went as he pleased. His body was laid out for her pleasure, his skin damp with sweat from the pleasure she gave him.

She continued stroking him, his shaft slick with sweat from her palm. She loved the heaviness of it, the satin-soft tip and the thick velvet of the staff itself. He was so large she could barely fit her hand all the way around him, the wide knob sliding between her fingers.

He closed his eyes and laid his head back, a half smile on his face, his hand resting on her wrist. He was letting her play, letting her enjoy herself. He rocked his hips, but gently, as though he was holding himself back.

His body tightened as she went on, his breath coming faster, muscles tensing. She liked that he contained his strength for her, liked imagining what it would be like if he didn't.

She kneaded and stroked him, twisting her hand around him until he moaned with pleasure. She felt the buildup in him, his buttocks tightening as he pumped up through her hand. He suddenly dragged her down to him in rock-hard arms and kissed her deeply, his body moving against hers in the joy of the moment.

"Keep taking me, love," he breathed. "That's it."

His essence flowed into her. She kissed his throat, her body limp and warm, her hand still moving on his staff. She wondered if he'd wait for her while she went back to work, if she would return to find him stretched out naked on the bed, smiling his sultry smile for her. A sudden vision flashed through her head of his thick wrists enclosed in manacles, arms over his head and fastened to the headboard. Her captive, smiling when she came in, his arousal rising swiftly when he saw her.

Command him, the demon in her whispered. *He will obey.*

The need rushed up in her so hard that she gasped and tried to yank her hand away from his tattoo. Tain clamped his hand around her wrist, keeping her palm on his cheek, his overwhelming life essence pouring into her. Her palm burned with it, the tattoo searing her flesh.

"Stop," she said. "You have to stop."

Tain's eyes were closed, his mouth twisted in ecstasy. She lost hold of his shaft, the blunt knob knocking her fingers. She tried to pry his hand from hers, but he was ten times stronger than she was, and she couldn't get free.

His essence was white light burning her from the inside out. The demon in her snarled and hissed, and the human part of her cried out in pain.

"Tain, please stop. I can't take it."

He didn't respond.

She sobbed. "Please."

Tain's eyes snapped open. He looked at her as though he just remembered she was there. He yanked her hand from his cheek and shoved her away.

She sat up, wincing when her palm contacted the sheets. Her skin bore a bright red burn of his pentacle tattoo.

"Samantha." Tain's eyes were wide with concern. He reached for her.

Samantha rolled off the bed to her feet, cradling her hurt hand. "I have to go."

He stood up, seven feet of naked male in front of her. "Let me see."

Samantha slowly held out her hand. He took it and kissed her palm, lips caressing. His healing magic sank into her, taking away the pain, and when he released her, the mark was gone.

"I have to go," she repeated.

The remorse in his eyes cut her to the heart. "Goddess, Samantha, I never meant to hurt you."

"I shouldn't have come here. I should have just . . ." *Trusted him*, her cynical side finished.

Tain scraped his hand through his short hair. "I told you in the beginning you should stay away from me. This is why."

Samantha's heart burned, tears streaking silently down her cheeks. "It's too late for that now, don't you think?"

He was still mostly erect, his body tight with need. "I thought I could go slow. I thought I could teach you—I thought I could control it. Gods damn my arrogance."

The dark horror in his eyes unnerved her. She pointed a shaking finger at him. "Don't you dare disappear because you think it's better for me. Don't you dare leave me to get through this alone."

Emotions flicked through his eyes, none of them easy to read. He stood looking down at her, stricken, making no move to touch her or to stop her.

"I'll come back," Samantha said. "After work, I'll come back, and we'll talk. You'll be here, right?"

"I don't want you to come back here. You need to go to the Malibu house."

"Wherever it is, we need to talk—privately."

Tain swallowed, his body tense, and he nodded.

Samantha let out her breath and made herself turn away. She wiped her eyes with the heel of her hand, squared her shoulders, and walked out of the bedroom.

At the front door, she felt him behind her, his large hands on her shoulders. He leaned down and kissed her hair, his lips warm and gentle. She sensed the power in his hands, the shaking as he deliberately held himself in check.

Without looking at him she walked out of the apartment. Behind her she heard Tain's door very faintly close, the lock click into place.

CHAPTER SIXTEEN

After Samantha had gone, Tain dressed, placed his votive candles in a circle, lit them with a tiny brush of magic, lay down, and tried to meditate. But his heart was beating too hard, his thoughts too jumbled for any kind of peace.

He was a fool thinking he could have something real with Samantha. She'd been right that letting her drink of his life essence would become too heady for him to resist—today when she'd naturally slowed the taking he'd sped it up, unable to stop himself, wanting her to take from him.

He'd lost all perspective on how to be human and gentle. Kehksut had been hideously strong, liking to receive pain as much as give it. Tain had grown used to not holding back his strength—in fact, he'd nearly forgotten how. Since he'd come to Los Angeles this time, he'd run into situation after situation where he'd had to stop himself from hurting others.

Giving to Samantha was supposed to mitigate the terrible things he'd done in the past, and now he'd hurt her, too.

Cerridwen, help her, he sent silently.

She needs you, came the whispered answer, and suddenly he slid into dreams.

He dreamed of a faraway land long ago that smelled of peat fires and damp and cold. He was seventeen years old, strong, and skilled, and he wanted to be a soldier like his father. All his life he'd wanted only to wear Roman armor and march with the soldiers back to the greatest city in the world, conquering territories as they went.

Rome was a fabulous city, so the legionnaires from the nearby garrison had told him, full of riches from places far across desert sands. In Rome you could find olives from Spain, fish from the Mediterranean, silks and spices from the East, gold from Egypt. Tain had spent his childhood dreaming of the day he could leave the farm he tended with his father in Britain to seek the warm climes of Rome and the blue, blue waters of the southern seas.

His father trained him with swords himself, having retired from the army to a farm in the northern colony where he raised his son. Tain's father saved for years to have the local armorer make two bronze blades for him, and then Tain had taken lessons from his father in how to use them. As a boy, he'd run off every chance he could get to the woods to fight battles with soldiers who weren't there and ghosts of his imagination, and as a young man he still retreated there to practice.

The night in his seventeenth year that he'd come across a real vampire had changed his life.

The woman had recently come to the soldiers as a camp follower, and killed several men before escaping, weeks before, into the wilds. The vampire had smelled Tain's blood and waited for him in the woods, where Tain took his swords to practice as soon as his chores were done.

He knew the woman was evil as soon as he saw her. She'd dressed in an exotic silk gown, her dark hair braided and twisted with jewels, and was breathlessly beautiful. But Tain sensed her aura like black ooze tainting her, canceling out her beauty.

"Thanks be to Minerva," the woman said in a throaty voice. "You have come to save me."

Tain rested the blade of his drawn sword across his shoulder. "Have I?"

"You're a clever young man and can get me back to camp. I'm the wife of one of the officers."

"No, you aren't," Tain said. "You are the woman who has killed some of my friends."

She dropped the pretense. "My, you are intelligent, aren't you? I thought you a mere pig farmer, but I see I was wrong."

She came closer, the stench of darkness sharp. The vampire was beautiful—no dirt or mud marred her lovely skin, her hair was gleaming and soft, and her jewels glinted. Tain had no doubt the jewels were real, nor any doubt that she could instantly kill any man who tried to take them from her.

"You want my blood," Tain said. He held out a muscular arm. "Why don't you take it?"

The woman's eyes flickered, uncertain. She stopped in front of him, then hissed and recoiled. "You stink of life magic. Why would you let me drink from you?"

"Because you're hungry. How long has it been?"

Her sultry look vanished. "Ten days."

"I can let you drink if you don't drain me. Do you promise?"

She stared at him in astonishment. "You would make this bargain with me?"

She'd killed soldiers, and she was strong, but Tain saw the illness in her, her aura torn and tainted. Ever since he'd accidentally hurt his father and discovered his healing ability, the instinct to use it was strong. There was something wrong with this vampire, and the young Tain thought if he could help her, he could train her to spare others.

"How long ago were you turned?" he asked.

She gave him a startled look, then whispered, "Six months."

"Against your will."

"Yes." Tears flowed from her red-rimmed eyes, and he saw her horror at what she'd become.

"You can take blood without killing if you do it a little at a time. I will show you, but you cannot kill any more soldiers."

"You would protect me?"

"Only if you promise."

The vampire closed her mouth, her face contrite. "I promise."

"Very well then." Tain held out his arm.

She came to him, sinking to her knees in the mud and decayed leaves on the forest floor. She lowered her head to Tain's outstretched arm, her eyes wide with need.

The bite hurt, but not as much as Tain had thought it would. He felt the blood flow into her mouth, a sensation much like when he had intercourse, but not quite. He understood now why the soldiers had died while lying in bed with this woman—the sensations of sex and her taking their blood on top of it must have been too wonderful to stop.

Suddenly she hissed and raised her head. Her eyes glowed, and his blood stained her fangs red. "What are you?"

"A pig farmer, like you said," Tain answered calmly.

She brought up clawed hands. "You're magic is too strong—you think to kill me with it. Are you Sidhe?"

"No." Tain had glimpsed the beautiful race of Sidhe when he'd journeyed to the far north with his father, seen the white-hot heat of their life-magic auras shimmering in the cold. When he'd told his father what he saw, his father had snapped that it was his imagination, that the Sidhe didn't exist.

Tain knew better. He knew that the stories of Sidhe and demons and vampires were real—he had living proof in front of him.

The vampire hesitated, her hands uncurling. "You don't know what you are, do you?"

"I'm Tain, son of a Roman centurion."

"You are not human, boy." The vampire straightened up. "You are filled to the brim with life magic, the strongest I've ever felt, even more than a Sidhe." She held out her hand. "Come with me. I'll take you to my master, and he will tell you what you are."

"I'm no one special," Tain answered with conviction.

"You're wrong." The vampire moved closer to him, brushed her hand across his unmarred face. "You're very, very special. My master will want to meet you."

"Who is your master?"

"A demon. A great one, an Old One, from the mists of time. He is powerful. He can make you great, too."

Tain thought about his life—the backbreaking work clearing and plowing fields, the sword lessons, the quiet nights spent listening to his father's stories of his days as a soldier. Leaving his father to have adventures in Rome was one thing; disappearing into the night without a word was something else.

"I don't want to meet him," Tain said. "Drink and sustain yourself, or go."

"You will come with me."

He felt her death magic sliding into him, trying to twist his thoughts to obedience. He saw flashes of the pleasure she could give him, her body, her blood, her power. He shrugged off the visions, easily seeing her as she was, a starving vampire, weak and pathetic.

"No," Tain said. He felt strange compassion for this woman, who hadn't chosen to become a killer. She couldn't help what she was, any more than a wolf could help stalking and killing a deer. He held out his arm again, the bloody holes she'd left already closing. "Drink."

She attacked. Tain sidestepped and brought up his sword, scoring her across her shoulders. She screamed and whirled for another attack, lunging for his neck, claws poised to tear out his throat.

He had his second sword out, crossing it with the first, and her momentum propelled her right into them. One jerk, and her head fell severed from her body. She tumbled down onto the carpet of leaves.

Her body decomposed before Tain's eyes, becoming the dead thing she truly was, the stink turning his stomach. In a few minutes she'd dissolved into dust. By the time Tain reached home, the bite on his arm had completely healed, and the vampire's blood on his blades had dried to dust and disappeared.

"I killed a vampire in the woods," he told his father. "The one that had been stalking the soldiers. She's dead now, so they'll be safe."

His father looked at him sharply, then turned away, but not before Tain had seen the tears in his eyes.

Tain's dream shifted. Three months after he'd slain the vampire, his father told him to dress in his best tunic and follow him. The year was the ninth in the reign of Emperor Domitian, and Tain assumed they were going to the Saturnalia celebration at the nearby camp.

Instead his father led him to a clearing encircled with standing stones, odd upright boulders that sang of magic in the moonlight. The older man regarded Tain sadly and sank to his knees in the middle of the stones, lifting his sword high, hilt-first. "Cerridwen, hear me."

Tain watched in surprise. His father had never shown an inclination to worship the strange gods native to Britain—like a good soldier, his father sacrificed to the warrior god Mars, to Minerva for wisdom, and to Zeus for strength.

Wind blew through the circle, sending leaves and twigs swirling through the standing stones. Tain sensed a stab of intense magic, brighter and hotter than anything he'd ever felt.

When the light died, a woman stood in the clearing. She had wild hair as red as Tain's own and wore a glimmering cloth that encircled her hips and covered her breasts. Tain darted forward, fear in his veins, as the woman reached down and touched his father.

Her father was crying. Tears streaked his weathered face, and he gazed at the woman with a combination of adoration and sorrow.

"I did what you asked," he said in a broken voice. "I raised him the best I could. My love, why did you never come back to me?"

"Because he couldn't know me until it was time." Her voice was rich and full, with a musical accent.

"Time for what?" Tain strode forward, his heart pounding. "Who are you?"

"Tain, she is your mother," his father whispered.

"My mother was a Gaul, a slave."

"No. She is a goddess."

Tain looked at the red-haired woman, and the life magic that flowed from her hit him with a hard impact. He remembered the vampire hissing when she'd tasted Tain's blood, declaring that Tain had more life magic than even a Sidhe.

"Why did you never tell me?" Tain demanded.

The woman, Cerridwen, turned to him. Her eyes were like fire, yellow orbs that made him both want to run away and stand gazing at her forever. "I wanted you to have a simple life, my son. Simple happiness before you must face what is to come."

"What is to come?" he asked, his voice hard.

"Danger," Cerridwen said. "Darkness. Things from which I cannot protect you. You are a warrior, Tain, one of the greatest warriors in the world. But you must be trained."

"My father trains me."

"To fight with swords, yes. But you need to learn so much more, how to defend the world from the darkness that walks it, how to use your gift of healing and your powers of destruction."

"I'm to go to Rome and join the army. I am already past old enough, but I didn't want to leave Father until I found someone to help him."

His father shook his head. "No, son. You must go with her now."

"If I choose not to?"

"You will come," Cerridwen said. She stretched out her hand, and Tain found himself walking toward her, though every muscle in his body screamed for him to stop.

His father watched, eyes wet, as Cerridwen reached out and pressed her palm to Tain's unmarred cheek. A sudden, sharp pain seared through him, but he couldn't pull away. His father cried out, but Tain held his ground, looking into Cerridwen's beautiful and powerful eyes.

When she took her hand away, he saw a black outline on her palm, a five-pointed star within a circle. He knew in that instant who he was—not the son of a slave woman and a Roman soldier, but a demigod who'd been raised as a human. His father was still his father, the chosen lover of a goddess.

Mist shimmered between two of the standing stones and when it cleared, four tall men stood there.

"Your brothers," Cerridwen said. "They've come to take you home."

Tain hated them on sight. They were all big men, as tall as Tain but a little older, their bodies heavier and more muscular. One had dark hair and an armband in the shape of a snake. The second had tattoos covering almost every inch of his bare, muscular arms. The third had intense gray eyes and a look of arrogance; the last had tawny hair, green eyes, a wide grin, and a large sword strapped to his back.

"Hey, baby brother," the fourth one said in flawless soldier Roman. "I'm Hunter. Nice to meet you."

"How can they be my brothers?" Tain turned an accusing stare on Cerridwen. "Are they your sons?"

"They are your half brothers, of a sort. They were all born of a human father with an aspect of the mother goddess of the world as their mothers."

"We'll take you to Ravenscroft," the one called Hunter said. "And teach you to be as much of a shit-head as Adrian is."

"Leave him be," the one with the snake armband said.

"Big brother's pet," Hunter growled, but with a smile.

The smile made Tain feel a little better. The four of them reminded him of the garrison soldiers: rough, foul-mouthed, and close-knit, although that didn't mean he wanted to get to know them any better.

"Go with them, Tain," his father said.

Tain turned to the only person he'd ever loved, the only person he knew how to love. "I can't leave you, Father."

"You have to. The Roman soldiers would never leave you in peace if they knew how magical you truly are. Go and be who you need to be."

Tain was an inch taller than his father, and he bent his head to look into his eyes. "There's more than that, isn't there? More than going with these people to train. What aren't you telling me?"

He saw fear flicker in his father's eyes and sorrow beyond measure. At the time, he'd only thought his father sad that his son had to leave him. With distance and knowledge and time, even in the dream, he knew that his father had been told of the pain and darkness Tain would have to bear. And still he hadn't stopped Cerridwen taking Tain away.

"Father, why?"

"I'm sorry."

His father wept openly, his body crumpling in on itself as he looked upon his son for the last time.

Two mortal years after Tain left for Ravenscroft, his father had died of a cancer. Tain had returned to find him dying, his body wasted. Tain had flooded him with healing magic, but it was far too late, and all he could do was soothe the pain and let his father die in peace.

Tears rained down Tain's face as he looked at his father's still and lifeless body. He'd realized then what being Immortal meant—that he would lose every person important to him. He'd go on, and they'd die. Like Samantha.

The chirp of his cell phone jerked him out of sleep, and he jumped awake with a cry of *No!*

He found himself on his back on the floor of his shabby apartment, breathing hard, his face wet, the candles guttering. He wiped his eyes as he sat up and plucked the phone from the nightstand with a shaking hand.

It was Samantha. She sounded strained and awkward, and she started speaking before he could say a word.

"Hello, Tain. Remember when I said I didn't have enough for a search warrant for the No More Nightmare's office? Well, I do now. Melanie, the super-assistant to Ms. Townsend, has been murdered. Heart cut out, just like the others."

Tain started to answer, but Samantha hurriedly said that she just thought he ought to know, and she clicked off. Tain remained sitting on the floor, staring at the phone, lost in thought for a while. Then he rose, took up his swords, and left the apartment, heading for the matriarch's mansion.

What he'd seen there and in the desert canyon connected with his dream of the vampire, and he thought he knew now the secret the dead matriarch had been hiding from her clan.

The previously quiet office of No More Nightmares now teemed with police. Samantha ducked under police tape to join Logan and Lieutenant McKay in the front office where Tain and Samantha had interviewed Melanie. Logan told her as soon as she entered that Melanie had been found in a large supply closet in the back.

"A walk-in closet with a copier and shelves on every wall," Logan explained. "She's stretched out on the floor, very dead, heart cut out."

"I never sensed she was demon," Samantha said. "Was she?"

"Possibly part demon," Logan said. "The scent was very faint, and I never would have smelled it if her body wasn't wide open—she might have had one grandparent demon."

"Yet she worked for No More Nightmares," Samantha mused. "Interesting."

"Maybe she didn't like her demon blood," McKay suggested. "Thought railing against demons would make her more accepted by humankind, maybe?"

Samantha shook her head. "If the humans in No More Nightmares knew, they'd be even angrier at her betrayal. It's hell being half blood."

"Tell me about it," McKay said. "I'm a short part-Sidhe. Don't think that doesn't get me into trouble."

Logan laughed, but with strain.

"Do I need to take a look?" Samantha glanced toward the knot of police in plastic gear in the back.

"Logan and I have, but suit yourself," McKay answered. "Three heads are better than one."

The body was much like the matriarch's, untouched but for the bloody, gaping hole in Melanie's chest. A woman knelt next to the body, taking swabs from it and placing them carefully into tubes.

"Logan said you didn't find the heart," Samantha said to her. "Like with the Lamiah matriarch."

"No." The woman looked up. "Maybe they use it for rituals."

"Not if they claim they're against death magic. But who knows?"

"Who knows?" the examiner repeated, wiping another swab through the dead woman's mouth. "These people are nuts."

Samantha turned away without answering and sought Logan again. "I hate that this happened," she said. "But it's a good excuse to go over these offices with a fine-tooth comb. Starting in the file room."

Officers had already started to box up files and the few PCs in the back as evidence. Samantha looked around at the mountain of folders and grimaced.

"Finding Ms. Townsend and questioning her might be easier," Logan suggested.

"Oh, you never know what interesting details files hold. I assume you're already looking for Ms. Townsend?"

"McKay is on it," Logan answered. "That Jackson County sheriff might be more willing to cooperate now that Ms. Townsend is a murder suspect."

"Yes, if she discovered that her faithful assistant was part demon, she might have lost it and taken out the knife." Samantha flicked her gaze around the room and the crowded office outside. She'd thought Tain might come down, interested in a connected death, but she didn't see his tall body among the crowd of police.

"There's another similarity between the two women's deaths," Logan said. "Neither of them struggled."

Samantha pushed aside her worry about Tain with effort. "No, you're right."

Both women had been on their backs, but they hadn't fallen that way. The expressions on their unbruised faces had been ones of surprise.

"Melanie probably didn't have enough demon in her to be able to change," she said slowly. "But the matriarch certainly did. It was almost as if they let themselves be killed."

"Drugged?" Logan suggested.

"Maybe, with something like Mindglow. You take that, you smile and let others do anything they want to you."

"Does it work on demons?"

"I think so, but I'm not sure. On the other hand, I know someone who would know."

"Our friend Merrick," Logan said.

"Exactly. Want to pay him a visit with me?"

Logan gave her an ironic look. "Oh, I'd like nothing better."

Samantha led the way back out, told McKay what they meant to do, and got the nod to leave. As they rode down to the ground floor, Samantha folded her arms across her chest.

"Tain not showing up doesn't mean anything," Logan said.

"Did I say anything?"

"You don't have to. I know you called him about this, but Tain doesn't work for the department—he can do what he wants. I'm happy he's interested in the case and giving us information, but I don't expect anything beyond that."

"I'm worried about him, that's all. We had a fight." She broke off, knowing that wasn't quite true.

Not a fight. A revelation. We can pretend all we want, but what we have isn't normal, and it isn't what either of us needs.

That thought triggered another: *What do I need?*

The answer was *Tain*, but they couldn't go on like they had been.

The elevator doors rolled open, and she and Logan walked through the lobby and out of the building. Police cars and vans lined the streets, attracting the curious. They had attracted more than the curious, Samantha saw, spying a long black limousine across the street.

She told Logan she'd catch up with him, crossed to the limo, and tapped on the back window. It slid down to reveal Septimus sitting in deep shadow, well out of the way of any stray sunbeam.

"Did you come to watch the police in action?" she began.

"No, I was following your Immortal. One of my underlings alerted me that he'd gone back to the Lamiah matriarch's mansion."

A qualm stole through her. "So why aren't you at the matriarch's mansion?"

"Because he spotted me and commandeered my limousine to drive him down here."

Samantha looked back at the building. "He went inside? I didn't see him."

"He's up there." Septimus pointed upward. "On the roof."

Samantha turned and stared up at the skyscraper, shielding her eyes against the afternoon sun. "What is he doing on the roof?"

"I couldn't say," Septimus answered. "You may look through my driver's binoculars if you like."

"No." She turned away, hearing the limo's window glide up behind her, and ran back across the street and into the building. She impatiently waited for an elevator, then dove inside and pushed the button for the roof.

The elevator let her off in a maintenance room. She could see an open door on the far side leading to the roof and blue sky. Samantha went out cautiously, hand on her weapon.

Tain grabbed her and pulled her out and around the corner of the little maintenance building. He had a sword in his hand and a look of fury in his eyes.

"What are you doing here?" he demanded.

"It's a crime scene. Why are you here? And why did you go to the matriarch's?"

"To stop up a portal to one of the deeper death realms."

She stared at him in shock. "The matriarch has a portal?"

"Not anymore, but there's another one and it comes out here."

"At No More Nightmares? They're supposed to be demon haters."

"Demon sacrificers," Tain said.

"What?" She stopped, her mind whirling. "Is that what they're doing with the hearts—some kind of sacrifice?"

"Yes," he answered grimly.

"What about Nadia's sister? Her heart was sent back."

"I don't know." His eyes gleamed with rage, and with his shaved hair, black tattoo, swords, and scarred body he looked more frightening than the scariest gang lord she'd ever come up against. "Maybe it was found wanting."

"I'd swear the No More Nightmare's office has no death magic in it. You didn't feel any, either. They aren't sacrificing there."

"The office is a front for the people who truly believe they're suppressing demons. But the temple is here on the roof."

He gestured with his sword. Beyond the building, Los Angeles spread out around them, a gleaming, glittering sprawl of city under the hot sky.

On the other side of the roof was a low shed that looked like a shelter for electronics or plumbing. For a moment Samantha felt nothing from it, and then a wave of death magic blasted out of it, strong enough to knock her over.

Tain caught her with a strong hand and shoved her back into the maintenance room as life magic boiled out of him to counteract the threat.

"So, these demons," Samantha shouted, "are they pissed at you?"

"Oh yes," Tain said.

CHAPTER SEVENTEEN

Demons, dozens of them, poured out of the portal into the late afternoon sunshine.

"Call Hunter," Tain yelled, drawing his second sword and turning to face the horde. "Tell him to get his ass down here."

Inside the maintenance room, Samantha flipped her phone open and punched keys with her thumb, her pistol in her other hand. "Why didn't you call him when you got here?"

Tain flashed her an annoyed look. "The damn thing stopped working."

"Did you charge it?"

He didn't answer, but she thought she heard him mutter something like "Fucking technology."

"Hunter?" she yelled into the phone, then stopped as a terrible noise sounded behind the elevator doors.

The phone went dead. She shoved it back in her pocket just as the elevator exploded open and belched demons through a hole of complete darkness.

She sprinted outside, adrenaline pumping, one step ahead of the demons, and made for Tain.

"Change of plan," she panted.

There were so many of them. Even the attack on the matriarch's house had only been a dozen or so demons of one clan; this was an all-out assault by an entire death realm.

She'd seen demons insane with bloodlust, attacking and ripping apart anything they could get their hands on. Whatever Tain had done at the matriarch's mansion, they were now intent on ripping *him* apart, and probably wouldn't mind if they killed Samantha along the way.

She knew her pistol would be almost useless, but the bullets would at least slow them. Tain, however, wasn't fighting. He had his swords crossed and all the lightning energy within him directed at the shed.

Sealing the portal, she realized, but it still left about a hundred demons on this side, and most of them could fly. Thinking of the horrific pain the acid-spitting demon had caused, she planted herself hard against Tain's back, staying within his protective magic.

"Do you think you could start fighting them off any time soon?" she shouted at him.

"There are thousands more behind them, and they'll come after us if I don't plug the hole."

"Damn it, Tain, what did you do to make them so mad?"

"Cut off their main portal and desecrated a shrine to their master."

"Oh, is *that* all?"

Tain swept a last blast of life magic at the shed, which folded in on itself and crumpled slowly to dust. He swung around and directed another waft at the elevator inside the maintenance room. Demons screamed and dove at them, talons and fangs bared, but any demon caught in the lightning from his swords died instantly.

"Wait a minute," Samantha shouted over the noise. "A shrine to what?"

"An Old One. The matriarch was trying to increase her power by sacrificing to him."

"But someone killed *her.* That doesn't make any sense."

Tain didn't answer. He grunted with effort and the light from his swords grew brighter still. The black portal began to shrink, swirling in on itself. Demons dove for it, a few making it back inside before the portal shuddered, then exploded into shards.

The maintenance room shook with the impact of the colliding magics. Cement blocks burst into gray chips, pipes screeched and broke, sending up geysers of steam and water. The walls of the room groaned. Then like the shed, the whole thing slowly collapsed into a pile of stone and metal and dust.

The remaining demons screamed and streamed toward them, their rage shaking the air.

"You know that was our only way out, right?" Samantha yelled at Tain, coughing.

"Do you trust me?" he asked.

"Oh, gods. Why?"

"It's a yes-or-no question, not a why."

"Are you saying you have a clever plan for getting away, and I have to go along with it?"

"Yes."

"You can fight them, can't you?" Her voice was sharp with worry. "You're strong and Immortal. This is what you do."

"Put away your gun and trust me."

"You're crazy."

"I know," he said, sending her a feral smile. "Put it away."

Her heart thumping with fear, she clicked the safety on her gun and slid it into the holster.

He continued in a reasonable tone. "You hang on to

me, and hang on tight. Do you understand? Wrap your whole body around me if you have to. Promise?"

He held his sword warily, judging the distance between the hundreds of demons, himself, and the edge of the roof. Samantha followed his gaze, and her eyes widened in horror. "Tain, you can't fly."

"No," Tain agreed.

He sheathed his swords in one smooth motion, then grabbed Samantha and sprinted past the demons who swooped after them in glee.

"I know I'm going to regret this," Samantha muttered, but she let him lift her into his arms. At the last minute she wrapped her legs and arms firmly around him before he jumped off the roof and into the empty air.

Tain expected Samantha to scream, but she didn't make a sound. *Cerridwen, give me strength,* he prayed. Then he shot all the magic he had in him straight at the ground several hundred feet below.

The demons that could fly launched themselves after him. Tain could only hope they didn't catch up, because he couldn't spare any magic from slowing their descent.

They fell and fell, wind rushing past at a sickening rate. The magic splintered and sprayed, as if he were scraping his hands along concrete at high speed. Below them traffic dove out of the way of his shaft of white-hot magic. He saw Logan bound onto the street in his wolf form and look up.

Tain felt the death-magic pull of another portal opening, and looked up to see it form high over the building. The demons whooshed into it as if they were being dragged by a giant vacuum.

Before the portal snicked shut, he felt it—the aura of an Old One, gloating, angry, powerful. The seductive pull touched him, and to his horror, his first instinct was to follow the demon home.

"Tain," Samantha said in his ear, her breath warm against the wind. "I love you."

The pull lessened. Over the adrenaline of the tumbling fall, Tain's body tingled as if it were breaking into dust.

He redoubled his efforts to get them down safely, his arms aching, his skin roiling with the life magic that streaked through him. Samantha burrowed into him, her warmth giving him a point of focus, his need for her canceling out the demon's siren call.

Finally, gradually, he felt their descent slow, the downshaft of magic acting as a cushion and a break. It gathered on the street and sent a resounding shock wave back to meet them. Fifty or so feet from the bottom the wave flowed around them, cushioning them in a bubble, which slowed until Tain's feet gently bumped the pavement.

Samantha raised her head and looked at him, her eyes black pools in her colorless face. "Are we down?"

"Yes."

Samantha made no move to let go of him, locked around him like a python. "You bastard," she said. "Don't you ever do that to me again." Then she hugged him hard and kissed him on the lips.

Septimus's limousine squealed up to where they stood, Samantha shaking and terrified and sick. Septimus's driver hopped out and opened the back door, and the vampire's voice rumbled out.

"Looks like you need another ride." He was squeezed into the far corner while the door was open and didn't lean forward until his chauffeur had safely closed it again.

Samantha collapsed into the seat that Tain had more or less lifted her into and leaned against Tain when he climbed in beside her.

Tain lay back against the leather and closed his eyes, his face gray and gaunt. He'd drained himself, she realized, the magic used to both close the portals and get them down safely taking everything he had. At the moment, he was as vulnerable as she was, and Septimus, the most powerful vamp in the country, sat across from them.

"Can you take us to the Malibu house?" Samantha asked tiredly.

Septimus instructed his driver through an intercom, and Samantha relaxed a little. Her panic was wearing off, and she wanted desperately to sleep.

With Tain out cold, Septimus's death magic filled the car, pressing against her senses. His lips had pulled back, his fangs elongating.

"I drank an Immortal once," he said softly.

"I heard." Septimus had once bitten Adrian and given him over to Kehksut, a part of a careful plan Septimus and Adrian had concocted, or so Adrian claimed later.

"It was like nothing I ever experienced, before or since." Septimus's voice was smooth as silk, the powerful vampire at his most seductive. Samantha's body tried to respond against her better judgment, as though her blood wanted to be caressed by his mouth.

Tain didn't react at all, unconscious in the gently swaying car. The vampire's gaze lingered on Tain's exposed throat, stark hunger in his eyes.

Samantha tensed. Septimus was an Old One, one of the most powerful vampires in the world. She slid her hand inside her blazer to rest on her gun. Bullets wouldn't stop a vampire, but they could hurt him or at least make the driver pull over.

"Leave him alone," she said sternly.

Septimus laughed. "I could snap you like a twig, Ms. Taylor. What would you do against me?"

"Anything I could," Samantha said.

Septimus laughed again, and then his fangs receded. "Where do these Immortals find such ferociously protective women? It's delightful."

"I'm not delighted."

"I was testing you, Ms. Taylor. You certainly are devoted to him."

Samantha eased back into the seat, but she didn't relax. "I'm armed, you know."

Septimus chuckled. "I could take your gun or shatter a stake before you could get anywhere near me."

"Possibly."

"Just so we know where we stand. You're an uncommon woman, Ms. Taylor."

"Glad you noticed."

"You're not glad at all. You only have eyes for the Immortal. What *is* it about them?"

"I don't honestly know," Samantha said in a low voice. "I'm a demon. I shouldn't love him, but I do."

"Ah, love. It makes fools of us all, doesn't it? Is that Shakespeare?"

Samantha closed her eyes, her adrenaline draining and leaving her exhausted. "I don't remember," she said.

Once Logan assured himself that Septimus had gotten Tain and Samantha safely to the house in Malibu, he took on the task of questioning Merrick.

The demon attack baffled him and McKay and everyone else present. But the demons had dispersed, vanishing into whatever death realm they'd sprung from. He hadn't even been able to catch one for questioning.

He'd almost shit himself watching Samantha and Tain fall off the roof, sure he'd witness the very messy death of his friend and partner. But Tain had pulled it off, and Samantha was all right—or at least whole. Logan continued the investigation, knowing Samantha was expecting him to come up with something the two of them could present to McKay in this crazy case.

He drove to Bel Air, where Merrick owned a luxurious house. The demon wore a crisp black business suit and received Logan in a cavernous living room.

"I'm in the process of screening construction companies to rebuild my club," he said to Logan, waving him to sit in a leather armchair. "I can open again in a year if I'm lucky."

"Excellent news," Logan said dryly. As usual he felt uneasy in a demon's domain, Merrick's death magic permeating every inch of space.

"You don't give a rat's ass about my club," Merrick said, while a butler served them coffee. "What do you want from me this time?"

"Samantha had a question. She'd ask herself, but she's a bit indisposed at the moment."

"I heard the story. Very impressive display of magic from your Immortal friend."

"Not something I want to watch again."

"I'm sorry I missed it," Merrick said. "But I'm pleased to hear our dear Sam will be harassing me, an innocent businessman, for a long time to come." He grinned. "Tell her that if she ever gets tired of arrogant Immortals, she can give me a call."

"I'll let her know," Logan said abruptly. He looked at the notes he'd taken from his short phone conversation with her. "Her question is about Mindglow and its effects. If, for instance, you were to give it to a demon, what would happen?"

"Hypothetically?" Merrick asked. "Off the record?"

"I'm here in a purely friendly capacity."

"*Friendly*, you call it. I suppose you mean you're not using hot lights and thumbscrews. Very well, hypothetically, Mindglow would do much the same thing it purportedly does to humans. Make them compliant, easily suggestible, that sort of thing."

"Anything else? For instance, would it weaken them to the point that they couldn't revert to their demon form?"

"Possibly. That's not information I'd like to see made public."

"I'm not a reporter," Logan said.

"True, but you feed things to reporters that you want the public to know. I'm not sure what it would do for certain, but I believe it would keep a demon subdued enough to not be able to change at will." He gave Logan a sharp look. "Is that what you think happened to Nadia and the Lamiah matriarch?"

"And possibly the assistant to the leader of No More Nightmares."

As expected, Merrick didn't look surprised by the news. The demon seemed to know everything that went on in L.A. thirty seconds after it happened. "An interesting problem for your police division. No doubt dear Sam will have her teeth in it as soon as she recovers. That is, if she takes her teeth out of her Immortal long enough. I'll have to wait until he leaves her in the dust before I ask her out myself. I'm a snappy dresser, but I can't compete with muscles and gleaming swords."

Logan let this speech run out without reacting. "What do you know about the demon attack today?"

Merrick raised his brows. "Absolutely nothing. I admit that when I found out Samantha had only come into my club as a honey trap I was hurt, quite hurt. But I respect her and, like I said, wouldn't mind a little something with her. How you can work side by side with her every day without jumping her bones, I don't know."

"The attack," Logan prompted.

"I'd never do anything so crude as that," Merrick said. "If I wanted Samantha dead—which I don't—I'd be much more subtle. In fact, I'd want to do it myself, make it personal. I assure you, wolf, I have no idea who instigated the attack, though I could find out, if you like."

For a price, Logan was certain. He kept his expression noncommittal and looked down at his notebook. "I came to ask you something else."

Merrick smiled. "You amaze me."

Logan met his gaze. "I'll be blunt. Who's supplying Mindglow to the demon clubs? To be fair, I don't think it's you."

Merrick made the slightest of shrugs. "I don't know why you'd think I know anything about that."

"You offered it to Samantha when you thought she was a demonwhore."

"I did no such thing, my lad. I offered her herbal tea, to calm her down. Any Mindglow found in my club was planted there by those who attacked, you know that."

Logan kept his temper in check. He knew he was lucky Merrick had agreed to talk to him without his cold demon lawyer present, but he'd hoped he could get the man to give him *something.*

"Hypothetically, then," Logan said. "*If* you wanted to get Mindglow in this town, and *if* you found it at a demon club, who would be supplying the club?"

"It would depend on what clan the club owner belonged to. Dealers like to deal within their own clans—they don't always trust outsiders."

"All right, say it was a demon club in the Djowlan clan. Who, in theory, would supply them?"

"I'm not familiar with the goings-on of the Djowlan clan, at least with regard to Mindglow. Apparently I don't even know when they're gearing up to attack me."

"The Lamiah clan, then," Logan said, clenching his teeth. "If you happened to know who supplied clubs in the Lamiah clan, who—in theory—would that be?"

Logan didn't really expect Merrick to answer. The man loved to dance around and not say anything—he was a careful criminal. He knew Merrick couldn't afford to be seen assisting the police, though he could be seen *pretending* to assist them. But whether he would tell Logan anything helpful was anyone's guess.

Merrick laughed suddenly, a deep throaty laugh of true mirth. "You're so much more diplomatic than your partner, Detective. She'd have been threatening me with bodily harm by now, or arresting me to show me that she could."

"I'm not above a little arresting myself," Logan said. "I enjoy it."

Merrick held up his hand. "Peace, wolf. I know you're dying to turn into your beast within and tear up the place. Shape-shifters are so predictable. But I'll be fair to you, since you've been fair to me. I'm only surprised you haven't figured it out yourself."

Logan said nothing, not wanting to indicate one way or another what the information meant to him.

The demon laughed again, softly, shaking his head. "Since she's dead and the route will dry up for obvious reasons, I think it no harm to tell you." He leaned forward. "The supplier of Lamiah clan clubs was the Lamiah matriarch."

Tain slept. He had no idea where he was, his body an immobile blank.

He dreamed again, of darkness swirling through standing stones. At first he thought this a continuation of his earlier dream, but in this one he was older, his body thick and strong and covered with linked mail. He was far to the north of where he'd grown up, in a crease of tall mountains surrounding a dark blue loch, with a square stone castle on the other side. He recognized the setting and tried to twist away from the dream, knowing what was coming.

His shoulder rocked from where his brother Hunter had just clapped him on it, the man walking away down the hill and the waiting menace they'd been summoned to kill. Unseelies, ugly, nasty beasties, had broken into the world and the brothers had been called to seal them again in their own bubble of hell.

Easy work for five Immortals with swords and powerful magic. They'd finish the job, retire to the castle for ale and women, and return home to Ravenscroft. This was their life.

Except Tain left for the castle before his brothers at the end of the battle. He rowed himself over in a coracle, his sheathed swords crossed in the bottom of the boat. He climbed the hill to the castle, knowing she waited for him.

She had dark hair and liquid dark eyes, and Tain enjoyed her. Unlike Hunter, with his fanatic hatred of demons, Tain let himself take what they offered. He knew how to taste without letting their death magic entwine him, knew how to enjoy giving his incredible life essence without becoming addicted.

He liked to walk in the danger, knowing he could easily walk out again. Kehksut was different, a little more powerful, much more beautiful, although she never wanted his life essence. Now she opened her mouth for Tain's kiss, and he gave it gladly.

He took her on the stone floor of the castle's empty hall, with nothing but furs beneath them. When he was finished, he noted how silent the place was. He dressed and left her, climbed up to the solar, and there found the inhabitants of the castle dead or dying.

He tried to heal them but he was too late. As anguish took him, Kehksut became who she truly was, an Old One, one of the most powerful of them. Tain's magic was depleted from helping his brothers conquer the Unseelies and from pouring his healing power into the dying. He had nothing left for the unexpected wall of death magic, more than he'd ever felt in his life, that surrounded and crushed him. He awoke imprisoned in pain and darkness, terrified and alone.

"Cerridwen, help me!"

The was no answer, only the sigh of darkness.

He called over and over again, begging the goddess to at least soothe his pain, begging his brothers to find him, to release him. No one answered, and no one came, except Kehksut.

"They can't hear you," she whispered, her red lips against his skin. "They gave up looking for you. They despise you for taking a demon as a lover."

Tain didn't believe her. His brothers would never desert him, no matter what—they'd made that clear time and again, Adrian especially.

Kehksut healed him, made love to him, and then she became a powerful male demon and tortured him, leaving him in a pool of blood and pain once more.

Over and over again, Kehksut healed him and then tortured him again, every three days, until Tain lost all track of time and memory of any life before this. He kept waiting for Adrian to find him, kept calling out, pushing his magic to enter his brother's dreams, but Adrian never came.

As time passed, he knew that what Kehksut told him was true—they'd stopped looking for him. They couldn't find him and they'd given up and gone on with their lives.

He hated them for that. The memories of them tasted of ash, his love for them depleted by rage and pain.

The only way to survive was to make himself like the torture, to embrace it, to lower himself into complete madness. As the years rolled by and Kehksut's sadistic ritual went on, Tain grew stronger. The madness grew greater as well, until the remaining tiny, hot spark of his true self got lost in the whirling vortex.

"You are mine, my love," she would say to him, caressing him with her exquisite touch. "I made you. You were born of me."

And Tain would believe her.

He saw her now, her black hair like watered silk, her eyes voids of black, her red-tipped fingers raking his skin. She never touched the tattoo on his face, the mark that meant something he no longer remembered.

"Tain," Kehksut whispered. She touched a kiss to his lips, and he felt the madness swirl around to suck him down yet again.

He screamed and fought, waking in time to see her catch his arm in a competent hand. She had the same demon-black hair, the same dark eyes, but these eyes held concern.

"Samantha."

The world stopped spinning. Samantha knelt on a wide bed beside him, wearing nothing but a long T-shirt. He realized with a sickening jolt that he'd flailed out at her, and she'd caught his wrist just in time.

"Samantha," he repeated. Saying the name helped him swim back to reality, to know that the darkness was over, and this white bed and Samantha was the truth.

He peeled her hand from his wrist, letting healing magic flow into her.

"Are you all right?" she asked.

"No," he said hoarsely.

"You were dreaming." She touched his cheek. "Everything's all right now."

"No, it isn't." Tain swung out of the bed, standing with his fists clenched. His body was cold with sweat, his head pounding. "Just because Kehksut is dead doesn't mean I'm healed. I was in unrelenting pain for seven hundred years, and my mind won't let me get over it so easily. It's only been a year."

"I know," she said, her eyes wide and soft. "That's why you're here with your family and your friends. So we can help you."

He shook his head. "Friends and family I can hurt. Look what I did to you because I loved having you take my life essence. I was so far gone in pleasure I didn't even know I was hurting you. Is that what you want?"

She swallowed, her face white. "I'm willing to try. We can slow down. That's what I wanted to talk to you about."

Tain reached for his jeans and pulled them on over his bare body. "You said that if you wanted a diet of life essence, you wouldn't start with me. But I pushed you into it, showing you how to take it, letting you get addicted to me. What if I can't stop next time? What if my insanity comes back because I'm out of control?"

He leaned his fists on the bed, putting his face close to hers. "Even here, you're not safe from me. Kehksut made me stronger than all my brothers. Hunter can't stop me, and Leda can't stop me. What if I become the killing madman I used to be and hurt Ryan?"

"You wouldn't hurt the baby," Samantha whispered. "You're a healer—you've proved it time and again even in the short while we've been together."

"You know nothing about me, Samantha. You know nothing of what I am and what I endured, and I can only thank the goddesses you'll never really understand. Kehksut tried to make me a force of destruction, but I refuse to destroy you."

She stared at him in anguish, tears beading on her lashes, but he couldn't stop to comfort her. Comfort might lead to sex, which would lead to her taking him again, and who knew what might happen after that?

He'd indulged himself believing that he was exactly what she needed, that he healed her while she healed him. His own wishful thinking.

He turned around and walked away, out through the dark living room to the back door. Samantha didn't follow, and he was grateful. Not that he intended to let her—he could wall her in the room with a shield of life magic if he needed to.

Pickles leapt off the sofa as he opened the door to the

terrace, happy to be let out of the stuffy house. Tain made his way down the stairs to the beach, the cat at his heels, the cool sand on his feet welcoming.

While Mukasa lumbered out to greet Pickles, Tain strode into the water, embracing the way the waves pulled at him. He kept on walking, his jeans soaking and heavy, water spilling into his waistband.

Behind him in the house, the light went on in the room he'd shared with Samantha, but Tain kept walking forward until the dark, cold ocean closed over his head.

CHAPTER EIGHTEEN

"Can't it wait?" Samantha asked her father four days later.

She'd been working almost nonstop on the death of Melanie Atkins, knowing she threw herself into her work to forget that she hadn't seen Tain since the night he'd woken from his dreams and left her.

At first she worried that he truly had gone insane again, but Hunter didn't seem concerned at all, which told Samantha that Hunter knew where he was. Leda also looked anxious, but she wouldn't talk about it with Samantha, which meant Leda knew where Tain was, too, or at least knew that Hunter knew. Neither of them would share the information with Samantha, which was enough to drive her crazy.

In addition, she was feeling sick and weak, and she knew it was because she'd stopped taking life essence. Now that she was aware she'd taken it from others, Samantha deliberately tried not to. As a result, she was cranky, tired, and had a four-day headache. *Like permanent PMS*, she thought irritably.

Her father had gone ahead with plans to declare Samantha as a candidate for matriarch. Samantha grudgingly let him, remembering the cryptic things Tain had told her during the demon attack—that the matriarch had set up a shrine to an Old One and that the prostitutes' deaths and No More Nightmares were somehow connected with it.

Melanie Atkins had been part demon, as Logan had discovered. She hadn't been either Lamiah or Djowlan, but of a clan from the heart of Nebraska. It turned out that her clan rejected all those not of pure blood, so Melanie had been raised human with no contact with her clan at all.

Logan speculated that Melanie had joined demon haters because of her clan's rejection, but that brought Samantha no closer to finding the killer.

Ms. Townsend had returned to the No More Nightmares office the morning after Melanie's murder, seemingly upset at the death of her assistant and surprised to learn that Melanie had been part demon. She behaved as though her encounter with Tain out in the desert had never happened, and she had an alibi for the time of Melanie's death. She'd been at a conference in Phoenix, six hours away by road or one hour and however long it took to navigate airports by air. The medical examiner said that Melanie had died at two in the afternoon, and precisely at two, Ms. Townsend had been speaking to a room of five hundred people.

Searches of the No More Nightmares offices had turned up no evidence that they'd been sending the threatening letters. McKay had agreed to send Logan out to Nevada to meet with local authorities there and investigate the canyon, but the locals hadn't been very cooperative, and Logan found nothing.

Merrick's revelation that the matriarch of Samantha's clan had been supplying Mindglow to the clubs bothered Samantha, and she wondered how it tied in with the matriarch's shrine. She wondered, too, if anyone else in the clan knew about it, or if the matriarch's fixation on the ancient demon had been private. Tain hadn't told Samantha which Old One was involved. Was it because he didn't know, or because he didn't want *her* to know?

The afternoon after the matriarch's funeral, which Samantha had not been invited to, her father called her and asked her to come over to their house to talk.

Samantha arrived and hugged her mother, Joanne, who'd also not gone to the funeral, then her father. She was still getting used to hugging Fulton, and he was, too.

They sat in the kitchen sipping coffee her mother had provided, while Fulton told Samantha of his plans to put her forward as matriarch. "The decision must be made soon, or we'll lose the chance of keeping the rise of the next matriarch civilized. A battle within the clan right now could mean the destruction of it. The Djowlans would take the opportunity to move into our territories while we're busy fighting and either kill every Lamiah or drive us back to the death realms."

"It's a lot to ask," Samantha said.

Fulton gave her a quiet look. "Samantha, this is important. You don't know how important."

She thought she did understand. If the matriarch had been dealing Mindglow and sacrificing demon hearts to an Old One, or at least using No More Nightmares to sacrifice them, the Lamiah clan was in trouble. She wished Tain would have left a fully detailed outline about his findings before he disappeared, maybe a nice file folder with all the evidence neatly laid out.

Becoming the Lamiah matriarch would give her a prime opportunity to investigate—she'd be privilege to info even the police wouldn't be able to find out. She could possibly crack this case and stop the killings. But then, once she'd closed the investigation, she couldn't simply quit and go home. She would be matriarch for life, giving up all she knew to do it.

"I can't believe there isn't a venerable full-demon woman in our clan who wouldn't leap at the chance to become matriarch," she said to her father. "You don't need *me*."

"We do need you." Fulton took her hand in a firm grip. "The matriarch wanted you, and I am head of the most powerful family in the clan. If I put you forward now, we can do this. And, no, the other families don't have good candidates. We need a leader, and we need her now."

Samantha disengaged his grasp and stood up. "I'm not special, and I barely inherited any magical ability from Mother. I'm not even full demon."

Fulton's eyes burned with an adamant light. "Samantha, as matriarch you can have far more power than you ever could as a police officer, even if you made captain. If you want to keep demons from hurting people you certainly can do that as matriarch. They'll listen to you."

"And you can have a family," her mother chimed in. "You can marry and have children. I always hear that a police career is hard on a family. I know I'm always worried sick when you're out chasing criminals."

Joanne's eyes and Fulton's both held worry, hope, and the need to see their only child happy.

"You want this for me," Samantha said in surprise. "Not for you, for me. Why?"

"Because we made so many mistakes," Joanne answered softly. "We wanted to raise you apart from your true heritage because we weren't sure the clan would accept you, and that proved to be a mistake. I never meant for you to despise your father and hate what you were. We were trying to protect you, and sometimes parents get so protective that they make fools of themselves."

Samantha sat down again. "You're trying to get me elected matriarch to make up for my childhood? Isn't that a bit extreme? Just take me out to dinner or something."

"There's more to it than that," Fulton said. "Samantha,

I want you to be happy, in any way you can, but this goes beyond our own needs."

"How can I lead a clan I know nothing about?"

"The majordomo will help you. She's ready to retire, but I got her to stay awhile until you can find a good assistant of your own."

Samantha gave a sharp laugh. "Telling me I have to work with that ice queen is not a good way to convince me."

"She's smart, she's wise, and she knows the clan," Fulton said. "She'd be the best assistance you can have at first."

"Why doesn't she become matriarch?" A good question—how much did the majordomo know about the matriarch's interesting activities and how deeply was she involved?

Fulton looked surprised. "She can't. Ariadne's from one of the lowest families, one step above the untouchables. Their line only serves, although they can become very powerful in their own way. They like being the powers behind the throne. But you don't have to worry about that with the majordomo, because she really does want to retire."

"There are untouchable demons?"

"Yes," Fulton said in a matter-of-fact voice. "They mostly keep to themselves and don't interact with the others."

"Isn't that a bit cruel?"

"Everyone in the clan has a part to play," Fulton said. "You'll learn all about it."

"I still think you're crazy," Samantha told him. "You want me, a human-raised, half-demon cop, becoming the matriarch of a clan I know nothing about."

"I am prepared to give you my full support," Fulton said.

"*You* will, but will other demons?" She broke off. "Wait a minute, let me try something."

She unhooked her cell phone from her belt and tapped a number. "Merrick, please," she said when a smooth-voiced demon answered.

After a moment, Merrick's voice boomed out. "Ah, it's my favorite policewoman. How did I know I couldn't get through a week without being harassed by you?"

"Merrick, if I became the Lamiah matriarch, would you support me?"

Dead silence came from the other end.

"Are you still there? Did you hear me?"

"I heard you." Merrick sounded subdued. "Are you in the running?"

"I haven't decided yet. But would you?"

Another silence, then Merrick said thoughtfully, "You know, I think I would. Once I got over the utter shock, that is."

"Why?"

"Because you're an annoying bitch but you can think for yourself, which are good qualities in a matriarch. You wouldn't take shit from someone like that majordomo, Ariadne."

"Would you work for me?"

Merrick's reply cut off with a squawk. "Me? For you?" He started to laugh, then quieted. "I might consider it. Why, would your sword-toting boyfriend cut off my head if I didn't?"

"Maybe. I'm just putting out feelers for now, nothing definite."

"You really are a piece of work, Samantha. I sensed it the moment you walked into my club."

"I love you, too, Merrick. I'll be in touch."

She clicked off the phone before he could say good-bye.

Fulton raised a brow. "Drumming up favors already?"

"I agree with the matriarch that Merrick's a thug,"

Samantha said thoughtfully. "But he'd be a handy person to have on my side."

"The gap must be filled soon," her father said. "Our family will meet on Saturday, on the last quarter of the waning moon. I ask you to please come with me and declare your candidacy." He smiled a little. "Who knows? You might lose."

"Will that involve me fighting someone to the death?"

"I shouldn't think so," Fulton said, his smile widening. "That hasn't happened in at least two hundred years."

Tain gazed out across the flat white of the dry lake bed, a sharp contrast to his vantage point inside a cool, green garden on the hill above. He leaned against the low wall that separated the monastery from the sloping desert mountain and contemplated the lake bed, empty, stark, and beautiful.

Adrian leaned next to him, sun glinting on his black hair that he'd drawn back into a ponytail. At their feet a cobra lolled in the cultivated flower bed, basking in the cool dirt.

The two of them—three, counting the snake—had sat here in silence most of the morning. Now Adrian stretched, his big frame pulling at his T-shirt, and asked, "So, are you going to tell me what happened to your hair?"

"Fire," Tain said laconically. "Rescuing a demon."

"Trying to impress a girl?"

"Something like that. Once I actually thought it through, I realized the demon probably had a contingency plan. Merrick isn't the type to calmly wait for death."

"Look at it this way—you got to be a hero. Was she impressed?"

"She seemed to be. But I might have done more harm than good." He scrubbed his hands over his face. "It's not going away, Adrian."

Adrian studied him a long time, his dark eyes quiet. "I didn't think it was."

"All of it was meant to happen—I get that. I suffered, you rescued me, we saved the world. But it won't stop. I still have the dreams."

"Go back to Ravenscroft. Stay there, stay safe." Adrian's look was tense, the guilt his eyes sharp.

Tain shook his head. "Not with Samantha facing what's out there. I can't be with her, but I can't leave her unprotected. I can't go to Ravenscroft and let it all flow past. She'll live and change—and I don't want to miss any moment of her life."

Such a dilemma, the snake's voice hissed in his head. *Snakes never have these problems.*

"Ferrin," Adrian growled.

We fertilize the eggs and we're done.

Adrian picked up one of Tain's bronze swords. "Small snake, large sword," he said.

I speak the truth.

"He's a wise reptile," Tain said, squinting against the glare on the dry lake, white against blue. "But there's more to it than wanting her, or even wanting her to take my life essence. I felt the presence of an Old One." He paused, letting the desert breeze tug at him a moment. "I wanted to go to him, Adrian. It was a powerful reflex."

"One you successfully fought. Obviously. You're here."

"It was very, very close." He felt a tinge of fear, not of the ancient demon, but of himself. "What if I succumb, and he uses what I become?"

"Then Kalen, Darius, Hunter, and I will drag you back out," Adrian said softly. "I'm not losing you again."

Tain didn't answer. Unlike his brothers, he knew the rescue had been his own choice. He had so much power, he didn't need Kehksut anymore. That, and the demon had threatened Samantha.

"There's more," he said. "I found the portal to his death realm under the Lamiah matriarch's mansion. I sealed it, but if Samantha becomes the matriarch, she'll have to deal with him."

Adrian leaned down and stretched out his arm, and the snake curled itself around it, blinking sleepily. Ferrin twisted all the way around Adrian's biceps, then shimmered and became a silver, snake-shaped armband. "You should be there with her then."

Tain's eyes narrowed, his blood warming. "Oh, I intend to be."

For the meeting with her demon family, Samantha got another dress, a black satin sheath with a mandarin collar that skimmed her body to the floor. She hoped, as Leda helped her dress, that this one wouldn't get acid slimed. But Fulton had said that they were simply going to a family dinner, no attacks anticipated. Samantha still bought a matching purse large enough to carry her gun and police ID.

She'd also bought a pair of very high heels to go with the dress, the straps decorated with rhinestones. The shoes would kill her feet, but looking at herself in the mirror, she thought it might be worth it.

She wanted to look good when she met her father's family—*her* family. But she wanted to look modest good, not the demonwhore she'd dressed as when she'd staked out Merrick's club or the virginal look she'd gone for when meeting the matriarch. She wanted to be Samantha, equal to any of them.

"You're gorgeous," Leda said, hugging her. "You'll knock 'em dead."

"Don't say that about a demon gathering," Samantha warned. "It could happen."

Fulton picked her up in his SUV and drove down out of Malibu, heading north and west along the mountains that hugged the coast. Eventually they pulled off the highway into Santa Barbara. Fulton drove through the small city, then up a winding road into the hills, until he halted at a wide iron gate. The electronic gate slowly rolled back, and Fulton drove on under arching trees.

The house he stopped in front of was less opulent than the matriarch's mansion but twice as big. It spread gracefully across the grounds in old California style, with arches and tile roofs and little balconies popping out here and there. Eucalyptus and tall palm trees surrounded it, leaving a space for a wide gravel drive.

A man in white gloves opened the doors of the SUV for them, then got into the driver's seat and drove the vehicle to an open garage.

"He's human," Samantha observed.

"Most of the people who work for us are," Fulton said. "Not many demons live up this way, and our family . . . well, you'll see."

The interior of the house was also old California, with vast saltillo tile floors, arched corridors, and colorful tiled staircases twisting intriguingly out of sight. The way was lit with candles flickering in wrought-iron wall sconces instead of electric light.

Fulton led her along twisting halls to a cavernous dining room. A heavy Spanish-style table stretched the length of it, encircled by heavily carved chairs. Well-dressed people wandered about drinking from crystal glasses or warming themselves in front of the arched fireplace.

Conversation ceased as Fulton ushered Samantha in, twenty pairs of dark eyes regarding them with interest. The matriarch's mansion had been intimidating enough, but that house had been built and staffed to serve the needs of one woman. This was a family house, where these people lived or visited as they pleased. There was no atmosphere of a business office; this was their home, and Samantha had come to claim that it was her home, too.

Her blood was cold, her skin prickled with goose bumps. Even the stoked fire couldn't warm her.

A darkly handsome demon in a suit held up a glass. "Drink, Fulton? Parker brought a bottle of single malt." Fulton nodded, and the demon went on. "Samantha, for you?"

Samantha swallowed. She'd love to drown her nerves in alcohol, but she shook her head.

"So this is Samantha," another man said. "We've heard so much about you." His keen look made her wonder what they'd heard.

"My reprobate brother Parker," Fulton said. "Your uncle."

"And who is *he?*" Parker demanded, looking past them. "He reeks. Who let him in here?"

Samantha swung around, her mouth opening in shock as Tain came through the dining room door. He wore a modern suit, black jacket and pants with a tie knotted at his throat, with the hilts of his twin swords showing underneath the coat.

The demon in her throbbed, suddenly hungry for the life essence he exuded like crazy. It was all she could do not to run at him, grab him, and drink him down. Her cleft tightened and her previously cold blood suddenly flowed hot. She hoped her nipples weren't poking against the thin silk of her dress for all to see.

The human half of her wanted to ask him where the hell he'd been and why he'd left her to *worry* about him like that. As a result, she could only stand numbly, her mouth dry while Tain took in the crowd of demons that stared back at him.

The woman next to her uncle Parker coolly took a sip of her drink. "Maybe he's a gift? His essence is heady." She wet her lips, her demon eyes darkening.

Samantha sensed others in the room looking him over

as though he were the first course at dinner. Tain gazed back at them steadily, standing out like a biker in the royal enclosure at Ascot. His buzzed red hair and twin swords were at odds with the roomful of people who'd glammed themselves to have dark hair and eyes and elegant young bodies that showed off their graceful clothes. Tain was dressed well enough, but he still had the look of a thug, one who wasn't worried about a roomful of demons.

"He's with me," Samantha said in a strangled voice. "He's . . . helping me out." In reality she had no idea what he was doing, and Tain didn't enlighten her.

"I see," Parker said, dark brows rising. "That's not going to sit well with Tristan."

"I don't give a damn what sits well with Tristan," Fulton rumbled.

"Who's Tristan?" Samantha asked.

"Our unfortunate nephew," Parker said. "An orphaned brat who's gotten full of himself."

"He's a little more than that," his wife added, but her gaze was still fixed on Tain.

Samantha couldn't look away from him, either. He'd sprung out of nowhere, looking as devastating as ever, but he bore a half-healed gash high on his cheekbone.

He would choose this moment to walk back into her life, when she couldn't take him aside and ask what had happened to him. Or take him aside to hold on to him and reassure herself he was truly back—if he was, and this wasn't some quick visit between disappearances.

Human servants began trucking in carts of food, and the family dispersed to take seats for dinner. Everyone seemed to know where to sit, with Fulton at the head of the table. A place to Fulton's right had been left clear for Samantha.

Tain made a little gesture for Samantha to sit next to

her father, then silently took up a stance behind Samantha's chair. Questions about what he'd been up to and why he'd suddenly reappeared would have to wait. She looked nervously at her family, who had started eating the first course.

It didn't help that what the servant carefully laid on her plate was long, gray, and unidentifiable. It was also very gently pulsing.

Tain leaned down and murmured in her ear, "Haggert,"

"What?"

"It's haggert," Fulton said, his dark eyes unsurprised. "It's a beast found only in certain death realms, hard to bring down. A delicacy."

"Why is it moving?"

Her uncle answered. "It takes a long time for them to die. Often, their pulse is still going even when they're sliced and roasted. Better that way—full of life essence."

Samantha sat back, letting her fork drop. Parker's wife leaned forward. "You mean you've never had haggert? It's wonderful. Although I suppose you'd rather stick to dead cow?"

"Maybe a salad," Samantha said hastily.

"Salads are good," her aunt continued. "Especially with mushroom grubs and vampire blood wine."

Parker snickered. "I have the feeling the new matriarch will be ordering out Chinese."

"Oh, I love Chinese," his wife said. "Koreans are quite good, too. . . ."

The doors banged open, breaking off her words. The demon who entered wore a well-tailored suit, but Samantha sensed he could burst out of it and shift into a snarling monster at any moment.

"Tristan," her father murmured. "Your cousin."

"So, this is Samantha," Tristan said. "Our half blood."

In the course of Samantha's career she'd faced down plenty of hotheaded, belligerent, out-of-control perps, and Tristan reminded her of every single one. He looked into her eyes, unapologetic, angry, unremorseful.

"Sit down, Tristan," Fulton said.

"Who is *that?*" Tristan demanded, glaring at Tain. "What have you brought into our house, Fulton?"

Fulton squeezed Samantha's hand and gazed calmly down the table at him. "If Samantha becomes our matriarch, it is her choice whether to bring in Tain to guard her. Considering what happened to our last matriarch, I welcome his help. Are we still agreed?"

Samantha expected reluctance and resentment, but to her surprise the family, except Tristan, nodded, her aunt with the strange food preferences smiling across the table.

"I can see Fulton has brainwashed you, as usual," Tristan sneered. He moved to the foot of the table where his seat waited but would not sit down. "You would put a half demon and her pet *thing* over us, instead of my candidate?"

"Candidate?" Samantha asked her father. "This is the first I've heard about another candidate."

Fulton's gaze flickered and slid away.

"Her name is Ariel," Tristan answered in a loud voice. "A pure demon who knows how to stop the harassment of demons that's going on in Los Angeles."

"Oh, really?" Samantha said.

"Demons are stronger than humans. There was a time when humans were nothing but food for demons, and Ariel will bring those days of glory back to us."

Samantha's aunt nudged Parker. "With him on top . . . of her." Parker guffawed, and Tristan glared at them.

Fulton observed calmly, "Ariel is from a rival family and is a protégé of the matriarch's majordomo."

Samantha saw distrust of Tristan and dislike of this Ariel on every face at the table, and pieces fell into place.

"I see," Samantha said to Fulton, her anger rising. "Better the demon you know . . ."

Fulton nodded without shame. "Exactly. Although there's much more to it than that."

No doubt there was. Samantha, young and inexperienced, could be told to put the needs of her family over the others. Anger flowed through Samantha's body, clean, strengthening anger that chased away the last vestiges of doubt.

She knew now what she had to do. She glanced at Tain and saw the same grim realization reflected in his eyes.

Tristan was rambling on. "We demons have stayed hidden too long, assimilating, adapting, letting humans rule us."

"They don't rule us," Fulton said.

Tristan stretched a long finger toward Samantha. "*She* works for those who arrest us, imprison us, humiliate us."

"Only when you're stupid," Samantha said in a hard voice.

"Half-breed females are only good for one thing. You should serve us whatever we want—on your back, on your knees, however we please."

Tain moved, and Samantha suddenly understood that he'd been holding in the full extent of his power ever since she'd seen him at Merrick's.

His white-hot life magic crackled abruptly through the room in a blinding flash of light. It found and destroyed every warding and death-magic spell that had been placed on the room, then flowed through the house to find more. Tain replaced the demon's magic with his own, strong, protective, deadly. She heard groans of dismay and fright from her family. Even Fulton, who had seen what Immortals could do, paled.

Tristan tried to launch a stream of death magic at Tain, but the small trickle faltered in the face of Tain's overwhelming force.

Tain reined in his magic without even breathing hard,

the light vanishing. The guests at the table sighed with relief.

"Well," Parker's wife said. "That was a display. Do you lend him around, Samantha?"

Down the table Tristan declared in a loud voice, "You had no right to bring that life-magic being here, Fulton. He killed the matriarch."

CHAPTER NINETEEN

The guests either gasped or looked disbelieving, but all swiveled their gazes to Samantha and Tain behind her.

"You were misinformed," Tain said calmly.

"Was I? That's not what the vampire said."

"What vampire?" Samantha demanded. If Septimus had leaked the information about Tain, he would see the sharp end of a stake, Old One or not.

"A vampire who works for the one called Septimus," Tristan said. "He followed your boyfriend all over town and sold me the information—I have it here."

"The little rat made copies," Samantha cried, her fury mounting.

Tain's gaze snapped to Samantha, the cold in his eyes chilling. "Show me," he said.

With a smile of glee, Tristan reached into his coat and pulled out a large manila envelope, which he tossed to the middle of the table. No one seemed to want to touch it, recoiling from it like Samantha had recoiled from the haggert.

Fulton at last retrieved it, then pulled it open and unfolded papers and photocopies of pictures. He laid them on the table in front of Samantha, and Tain leaned down to look.

Tain was clearly visible in the photos, which were

time- and date-stamped. Tristan had placed the ones of Tain at the matriarch's mansion on top.

"Behold the killer of our clan matriarch and family leader," Tristan announced. "Why he did it, I don't know. Maybe he just likes to kill demons, or maybe Fulton put him up to it to promote his own daughter?"

No one answered. Tain said to Samantha, "You knew about these."

The noise of the room receded, and for the moment none of this mattered, not the matriarch's death or her case or her family, or the fact that Tain had popped back into her life as suddenly as he'd vanished from it.

"Septimus gave them to me."

"And if I told you I was not in those places in those times, would you believe me?"

Do you trust me?

Samantha looked over the photos spread before her, the evidence of a camera's eye. It was possible that Septimus's vampire had faked the whole thing, but she didn't think Septimus would have used him if he weren't reliable. She suspected the vamp's decision to sell the information to Tristan came after the fact—an opportunity seized, not a planned event.

She looked up at Tain again to see the darkness in his eyes. Something had changed about him, but she couldn't put her finger on what. His shaved hair was still in that silky red buzz she found incredibly sexy. She kept envisioning running her hands through it while he slowly slid his coat and shirt from his body.

"Your hair," she whispered.

"What about it?"

Samantha grabbed the photo of him taken inside the matriarch's grounds twenty minutes before she was found dead. "I knew something bugged me about this. Look at your hair."

The photo was black and white, but it clearly showed Tain's thick hair rolling back from his forehead to his shoulders.

"The matriarch died *after* the fire at Merrick's," Samantha said. "Your hair had burned, and you'd shaved it off. This can't be you, or else the date stamp is wrong."

She wanted to dance around the table and wave the photo under Tristan's nose, but she retained her dignity.

Tain examined the picture. "It looks like me."

"Maybe it's a chameleon," Samantha suggested.

"Or a demon casting a glam," Fulton said. His gaze went to Tristan, and Tristan's eyes widened.

"Don't look at me. I bought all that from a vampire, I swear it."

"I believe him," Samantha said. "I think Tristan bought these in good faith, happy he had something to incriminate Tain and me with."

"I don't think I need to ask why," Fulton said.

Samantha heaved a resigned sigh. "Dad, if I don't let you put me forward as matriarch, what happens?"

"Tristan and the majordomo back Ariel, the only other candidate."

Samantha's head began to ache. "I'm thinking the majordomo was horrified when the matriarch talked about grooming me to take her place. I wonder if *she* faked the photos to make it look like Tain and I had something to do with the matriarch's death."

"She could have. She's a 'demons should dominate' type. She's not happy with us trying to work well with others."

"But didn't you tell me the majordomo is from one of the lowest classes of our clan? No matter who is matriarch she doesn't really get any of that power."

"The underclasses are amazingly conservative," Fulton answered. "And the majordomo enjoys being the power behind the throne. The matriarch only let her get away with so much, but with a matriarch that the majordomo herself has mentored . . . the possibilities are endless."

"And that is why you want me to do this?"

"One of the many reasons."

Samantha saw her life abruptly split into two roads. One led back to her job as a police detective, where she'd arrest vampires accused of turning more people than allotted or she'd do stakeouts on demon bars suspected of dealing Mindglow. Her father's family and clan would remain under the thumb of the majordomo and her trained matriarch, the consequences of which, if the new matriarch gained enough power, would be felt in the world.

Or Samantha could take the other path, fully embrace her demon family and their world, and keep the clan from becoming nothing but a gathering of evil. She could figure out what the old matriarch had been up to and why she died, and prevent demon sacrifices in the future. She could come to terms with her need for life essence and figure out a way to get it without hurting others. But the possibility for Samantha to have any kind of normal life would be gone.

She glanced up to find Tain's gaze still on her. If she became matriarch, she'd be swallowed by her clan and their problems, by the people who were Tain's enemies. She could not predict what he would do once she was the matriarch, but she knew that she'd fallen in love with him, and these past few days without him had been unbearable.

He said nothing, only watched with his enigmatic blue eyes as she made the most difficult choice of her life.

Samantha swallowed the lump in her throat. She anchored herself with Tain's gaze, which was the most steady and solid thing in the room. She slowly got to her feet. "All right," she said to Fulton, who watched her anxiously. "I'll be your matriarch."

Tain thought he'd never seen anything more beautiful than Samantha standing in front of her father, her black dress as sleek as water, quietly declaring she'd change her life for the good of her clan.

He'd missed her more in the last couple of days than he ever imagined he would. He'd needed to leave town and didn't regret going, but when he'd ridden back into Los Angeles with Adrian, his heart had lightened, knowing he was on his way to see her again. It was the first time since his escape from Kehksut that he'd looked forward to entering a town.

He'd learned from Logan that today Samantha was meeting her family at a formal dinner in Santa Barbara, and Tain knew he needed to be there at her back. So Adrian loaned him a suit, and Hunter drove him up and dropped him off.

At Samantha's declaration, the entire table of her aunts, uncles, and cousins cheered, except for Tristan. Samantha looked down and away, but not before Tain saw the tears in her eyes. The decision had been difficult for her, and he understood hard choices.

"What happens now?" she asked her father in a low voice.

"We have a muster," Fulton answered. "And the clan decides whether to accept you."

"And if they don't?"

"You go home, and we seek another."

"As easy as that?"

Fulton looked uncomfortable. "Not really."

"I see. Will Mother be able to come to this muster?"

He shook his head. "The clan isn't yet that open-minded. No nondemons allowed in our realm beneath."

"So when will this muster be? I'll have to resign, and there's a process . . ."

"The muster is right now," Fulton said. He put his hands on her shoulders, kissed her cheek, then moved to the richly paneled wall opposite the fireplace.

"Right now?" Samantha's voice went sharp. "Can't I have time to prepare, or at least fix my makeup?"

"Candidates are not allowed to prepare," Fulton said, facing the wall. "Matriarchs have supreme power over clans when they take up the mantle, but before that, the clan has supreme power over them."

"I wish you'd have mentioned that. I'd have worn better shoes."

Fulton didn't answer. Tain saw in his stance worry that his daughter wouldn't be accepted warring with the need to do everything the right way.

The wall in front of him dissolved to reveal a darkness beyond and a waft of death magic. Tain tensed. He hated the death realms, the lands of demons where mortals could go, but only with a death-magic creature. The realms beyond those were only for the dead, true hell realms where Old Ones ruled. Tain had been to those as well, and survived. He knew the matriarch had, too.

He drew a breath, forcing himself to take in the air of the tainted place, willing the blackness in his mind to dissolve.

Beyond the wall Fulton had cleared lay a hall of carved stone, pillars of white marble flowing in arches down the cavernous room. The pillars seemed to glow from within, bathing the place in a luminous white light.

Fulton walked by himself to the middle of the room, where a small table waited. He picked up a small mallet and struck a chime, and a sweet note wafted through the stone hall.

Fulton turned back and held out his hand to Samantha. "It is time."

Samantha, hands clenched at her sides, stepped into the room, and Tain moved to follow.

Her uncle Parker tried to put himself between Tain and the opening. "No nondemons at a muster," he said sternly.

Tain gazed down at Parker, immobile. "I go, or she does not."

"Tain—" Samantha began.

"I won't let you step into a death realm without me at your side. They manipulated you to get you this far—what else might they have in mind?"

The spark of anger in Samantha's eyes flared, not at him, but at the truth of his words. "He has a point, Father."

Fulton looked back from the table. "Let him pass, Parker. They're coming."

Tain walked into the room, the frosty chill of death magic threatening to drag him to his knees. He refused to let it, holding himself rigid against the madness in his mind that whispered to him. He had to stay alert, to discover if the portal the matriarch had made was connected to this death realm.

Demons flowed toward them from every quarter, in demon form or as well-dressed humans. All the demons of the Lamiah clan, Tain assumed, entering from each of their families' strongholds.

They grouped themselves around the room, gathering in disparate clumps, as though each family knew exactly where to stand in the hall. Tain recognized some of the demons—Merrick stood near one pillar in his human form, wearing his customary well-tailored suit and a sly smile. Near Merrick was Nadia, her shorn hair neatened, her look defiant. Tain remembered the matriarch claiming that Nadia was no longer of the clan, but perhaps the matriarch's death gave Nadia a chance to claim her part of it again.

Notably absent was Tristan, who had disappeared as soon as Fulton opened the way to the death realm. Also absent was the matriarch's majordomo.

Six men joined Fulton in the middle of the cold room—heads of households, Tain surmised. Fulton greeted them all solemnly, their breaths fogging in the cold air.

They looked at Samantha like they might eye a racehorse, wondering if it would bring in the biggest prize for them.

The meeting was simple. Fulton spoke to the six men, formally presenting Samantha as both his daughter and the candidate for matriarch. The household heads went back to their collective groups and murmured among themselves while Samantha and Fulton and Tain waited.

Tain silently urged them to hurry. The chill of death was like ice in his blood, and he wasn't sure how long he could stand it. The pentacle tattoo on his cheek burned, and voices seemed to whisper in his ear.

You are a hundred times more powerful than they are. Even in this death realm, you can crush them. You can take Samantha far away and have her as your own, make her your slave.

He clenched his teeth against the thoughts. Kehksut had thought that way—*destroy everyone and take what you want.* Lesser beings should bow down to the more powerful or be destroyed.

Now Tain, the being who'd been strong enough to kill Kehksut himself, fought the urge to do as the demon had taught him. He closed his eyes, willing himself to calm, calling words of soothing meditation.

Samantha touched his hand. He opened his eyes to find her at his side, her cool hand in his.

She trusted him. She looked up at him with her soft, dark gaze, believing that he'd come here to protect her, believing he'd support her. She'd even found a way to prove that damning evidence against him was false.

The six men detached themselves from their families again and returned to Fulton.

"We have decided," one of them said. "Samantha, daughter of Fulton, will become our matriarch."

Fulton nodded solemnly, and Tain saw Samantha grow

still more rigid. She was uncomfortable here, too, but he saw her trying to make herself believe that she *did* belong here.

She jumped when Fulton and the six other heads of households drew short-bladed, black knives. Tain stepped closer to Samantha, but the men drew the blades across their palms, scoring a line of deep red blood. Each man stepped in front of Samantha, dipped his finger in his own blood, and traced it across her face.

"I pledge my blood, my loyalty, and my house to you, our matriarch," they intoned in turn.

Each one provided a line that created a seven-sided pattern, Fulton tracing in the last piece. "I pledge my blood, my loyalty, and my house to you, our matriarch," he said in a warm voice.

He whispered something into Samantha's ear, and when he stepped away, she said, "I accept and will protect my clan against its enemies, come what may."

The clan gave a rousing cheer and someone shouted for champagne. Fulton gave Samantha a handkerchief with which to wipe off her face, then kissed her cheek. "Thank you, daughter. You've made me very proud."

The clan came to congratulate her. Samantha was surrounded first by her own family and then those that made up the rest of the clan. For the most part they were friendly and smiling, though Tain detected a few speculative and unhappy glances.

Merrick was one of the last who came to pay his respects. He held a champagne flute negligently in one hand and looked her up and down.

"So you made good on your threat. I bow to you, my matriarch." Merrick made a mock salaam. "Perhaps I can make an appointment with you to talk business?"

"You'll have to speak to my assistant," Samantha said, meeting his gaze with a cool one of her own. "Which I don't have yet, so you'll have to wait until I appoint one.

But no more Mindglow, Merrick. This matriarch is not going to assist in your illegal activities."

Merrick's smile widened. "What activities would those be? I don't think I ever actually *said* the last matriarch supplied me with Mindglow. That would be so wrong of her."

"I'm glad you agree. I don't get to be a cop anymore, but then again, I imagine there's a file on you in the matriarch's office this thick." She indicated a substantial size with her thumb and forefinger.

Merrick only let his smile widen. "I look forward to fencing with you, dear matriarch. Here's to the start of an interesting friendship."

He moved off, whistling to himself, and Samantha's defiant stance faded. The face she turned to Tain was wan and lined with exhaustion. "Are you all right?" he murmured.

"I will be," she said. "I have to be. But don't let them give me any more champagne. My headache is monumental."

He plucked the half-empty glass from her hand and transferred his grip to her elbow. "I won't let you fall," he said.

Her dark eyes were full when she looked up at him. "Thank you," she said. "Tain, what did I just do?"

"Chose your life."

Her eyes shone with fear. "What if it was the wrong choice?"

"There are no right and wrong choices—there is only what we do with the choices we make."

She frowned. "Of all the Immortals, I had to get stuck with the philosopher."

"It's what happens when you're a prisoner for seven hundred years."

Samantha laughed, then shivered. "Let's get out of this hellhole. Isn't it making you sick?"

"Yes. Serves me right for showing off for your cousin Tristan."

"He needed to be slapped, the little monster. I'll deal with him." Her humor faded, and she put her warm hand in Tain's. "This is what I am now."

"I know," he said, and led her back to Fulton's dining room.

"You're the what?" Hunter growled, then turned an accusing green glare on Tain. "She's the *what?*"

"The matriarch of the Lamiah clan," Tain said. "Pay attention."

Samantha stood in the middle of what used to be the matriarch's study. Fulton had sent her here after the champagne ran out, explaining that she'd take over that very night. The majordomo had been terse when Samantha arrived, but seemed to accept the decision of the clan as final. She'd stated that she still wanted to retire, but she'd help transition Samantha's new assistant, whoever that might be.

Samantha thought the woman's acceptance too quick and resolved to keep an eye on her. She'd immediately called Leda and Hunter and invited them down to Beverly Hills, wanting to tell them in person why she wouldn't be returning to their house tonight.

"So you're the leader of the demons now?" Hunter repeated.

"Just of this clan," Samantha corrected.

Hunter's gaze flicked to Tain. "Are you going to be all right? The death magic is pretty heavy in here."

Tain gave him a brief nod. "I'm used to it."

"I know, but I had the idea you wanted nothing more to do with it—ever."

Tain merely shrugged. He'd been quiet since the muster, staying close while they rode to the matriarch's mansion. He didn't touch Samantha in the car one of the human drivers had chauffeured, but sat thigh to thigh with her, his bulk reassuring. He hadn't offered an explanation of where he'd been for the last four days, but then again, they hadn't been alone for a solitary moment.

He'd been very protective of her tonight, but she knew Hunter was right—Tain didn't belong with demons. He might stay long enough to reassure himself that Samantha would be all right, maybe until they figured out who was cutting out demon hearts. But then he'd be gone, off to protect the next person who needed an Immortal. It was difficult to think about, but she'd have to face that sooner or later he'd go.

Hunter and Leda departed, Leda giving Samantha a tight hug.

Shortly after this, the compound came on alert as a limousine delivering Septimus pulled to the front of the house. Samantha received him in one of the ground-floor rooms whose tasteful opulence matched his own.

"This is a first," Septimus said smoothly when they were seated. "And a last. A vampire lord visiting a demon matriarch. Quite unprecedented."

"We can note that for the record," Samantha said. She'd decided on one of her female cousins as her secretary, a smart-looking young woman called Flavia. Tain had left her office when Septimus arrived, saying he wanted to look around. She'd thought he'd want to confront Septimus about the vampire having him followed and photographed, but he didn't seem interested—or maybe he had some idea up his sleeve that he wouldn't share with Samantha.

"So you're not with the police anymore?" Septimus asked once they were settled.

"I'll go in and resign tomorrow. But that doesn't mean I won't be in touch with my best friend, Logan, and keeping an eye on excessive vampire activity."

"I'm sure you'll keep an even better eye on it now," Septimus said. "And I'll be keeping my eye on you. I have the vampire interests in this town under my thumb, but you . . ." He leaned forward, his smooth, handsome face showing concern. "Samantha, the other clans will challenge you. You'll have to work hard for their respect, because respect is much more important than fear. They'll want to rule you, if they don't simply try to wipe you out."

"I'm aware of that." Fulton had already briefed her on the other clans and what they could do, and on the strength of the Lamiah clan. The Lamiahs might have let themselves become civilized and citified, but they still had a private army.

"I can help you," Septimus offered. "You can have my strength behind you in an instant. All you have to do is ask."

Samantha lapsed into a smile. "As smooth as ever, Septimus. Me having vampire backing would ostracize me from all the clans, leaving me completely dependent on you. I know what much."

Septimus smiled, his dark eyes showing the shrewdness of centuries. This was a vampire who'd advised Julius Caesar on how to take Rome, if Septimus's stories were to be believed. "I had to try." He rose, holding out his hand.

Samantha clasped it, knowing that their friendship, such as it was, would be distant and diplomatic now.

"I wish you the best of luck."

"Thank you," Samantha said. "And I'll keep your offer in mind. You never know."

"That's true, you don't." Septimus swept her a bow, then turned and walked out.

Samantha couldn't stand the thought of sleeping in the bedroom in which the previous matriarch had been killed, so she chose a generic guest room on the second floor. One of the staff startled her by going through the room and disabling about a dozen hidden cameras and bugs before letting her in. The matriarch had liked to spy on her guests. Samantha went through the room again herself once the woman left, to satisfy for herself that they'd *all* been removed.

Samantha told Flavia good night and retreated to the bedroom, dismissing every member of staff who wanted to accompany her, all the way up to tucking her into bed. She very much wanted, and needed, to be alone.

She'd snapped off all the lights and stripped down to her underwear when she heard the locked door open. In a moment she felt a warmth behind her, and then strong hands over her abdomen, warm through her camisole.

"I hope that's you, Tain," she whispered in the darkness.

"Is that your idea of security, asking the intruder if it's who you think he is?"

She leaned back against his hard body, feeling the tension in him. "No one else in this place has life magic crackling like yours."

She felt his lips graze her neck. She responded instantly, as tired as she was, warmth pooling between her thighs, her breasts aching. She craved him, and not just for his life essence.

"Are we going to talk now?" she whispered. "You'll tell me about your adventures for the last four days?"

"Not yet."

Part of her chafed with impatience, wanting to know where he'd been and what he'd done, and the other half thought maybe it was better if he didn't tell her.

"No asking about my feelings," he said. "No discussing demons, no worrying about tomorrow."

"No?" She closed her eyes, letting the fire of his touch slide through her in spite of herself. "What are we going to talk about?"

"You and me."

She tensed a little, waiting for him to reiterate how he couldn't stay with her. "What about you and me?"

"How I want you until I'm crazy with it."

He skimmed the spaghetti straps of her camisole from her shoulders and followed them down. His lips brushed her neck, the stubble on his jaw like sandpaper on her skin.

"You have to tell me what happened, where you went. I'm going insane not knowing."

Tain stilled. She saw him in the full-length cheval mirror across the room, his red head bent to her, his suit coat and tie gone, his shirt a pale smudge in the gloom.

"I thought it would be a relief for you to be without me for a while," he rumbled.

"I was afraid."

"Hunter would have protected you from any danger. So would Leda and their pet lion."

"I meant I was afraid for you. I was afraid you'd gone crazy again—and that you'd never come back."

He kissed the side of her neck. "I came very close."

"Please tell me what happened."

"I was with Adrian."

"Your oldest brother? The scary one with the snake?"

"That's him."

"You went to Seattle?" Samantha hated to sound like an interrogator, but if she'd learned one thing about Tain it was that she had to pry information from him piece by piece.

"We met out in the desert east of here. There's a monastery, very quiet and protected, no death magic. Adrian told me that if I ever thought I was losing it, I should go there."

Samantha had heard of the monastery way out at the foot of a desert mountain range, located at the end of a winding, unpaved road. It had been there since the eighteenth century, with white arches, cool tiled floors, quiet bells, and silent monks.

"Did Adrian sense you were in trouble and come to find you?"

Tain smiled. "No, I called him on my cell and told him, and he flew down. We talked about a lot of things."

"Good," she said. A tightness in her released. "I'm glad you weren't alone."

"We talked about Old Ones and this case. And you."

"I'm not sure I want to know what the two of you said about me."

"I will tell you, but not right now." His voice went softer, his lilt pronounced, his breath on her neck burning. "You've taken no life essence since I left, have you?"

"Does it show that much?"

"You need to take, Samantha. A human being can't go without water and sleep, a vampire can't survive without blood, and a demon can't live without life essence. You'll kill yourself if you go without it for too long."

"I'm coming to that conclusion." It dismayed her to give in to her baser needs, and her instinct was to fight that. But she'd felt so awful the past few days, exhausted and sick with no relief.

Tain ceased speaking, and her camisole crumpled to the floor at her feet. Tain's lips traveled down her spine until his hot breath touched the small of her back. She shifted her feet, loving the sensation of his mouth.

"Why do I crave it all the time?" she whispered. "I used to not even notice."

Tain pressed a kiss to the silk over each of her panty-clad buttocks and moved down to her thighs. His short hair brushed the insides of her legs in passing.

"You need to let it come naturally," he said.

He was kissing the backs of her ankles now. He knelt on his hands and knees, but he was hardly submissive.

"I don't know how," she said.

"I'll teach you."

"You're guarding me, not to mention you're an enemy

of demons. How is that going to look?" At the moment, she didn't much care.

"I don't plan on letting anyone watch. I'm not a—what do you call it now?—an exhibitionist."

"What was it called in the old days?"

His kisses moved to her calves. "In the old days we called it not enough rooms with doors."

"I suppose I'm lucky to have privacy," she whispered. "I always need somewhere I can retreat and figure out how to get through another day."

"We all need a place to lick our wounds."

Right now he was licking the inside of her thighs. He hooked his fingers in the waistband of her panties and slid them down her legs.

"Do you?" she asked. "Need a place to lick your wounds?"

He kissed his way up her back as he rose to his feet, then slid his strong hands around her waist again. "Yes, but I don't want to retreat anymore. I don't want to wallow. I want it all back."

"All what back?"

"My strength. My sanity." He kissed the corner of her mouth, enveloping her in his body. "My ability to love a woman without fear."

"Not an unreasonable thing to want."

"Everything I ever knew or loved was taken from me."

"I know." Samantha turned around in his arms, wishing she could give it all back to him. She reached up and undid buttons on his shirt. "Someone wanted me to think you'd killed the matriarch."

Tain put a finger under her chin to turn her face to his. "I didn't. Do you believe me?"

"You asked me to trust you," Samantha said softly. "And I do."

He kissed her shoulder, then back up to her mouth. She started to tell him she'd believed in him no matter what anyone tried to prove, but he kissed her until she couldn't breathe, then lifted her in his arms.

She licked the bare curve of his neck, his skin hot and salty, while he carried her across the room. She expected him to lay her on the wide bed, but he stood her up in front of the mirror instead.

The mirror reflected not a dignified, powerful clan matriarch, but Samantha, her hair disheveled, her body naked and pale with Tain's strong brown arm across her abdomen. He looked delectable, his shirt parted and sliding off one shoulder.

She reached back to smooth her hand over his hip, at the same time he slid his fingers down to the space between her legs.

"Gods, you're beautiful," he murmured. She felt his teeth on the shell of her ear. He knew how to touch her, rubbing the nub that was swelling for him, then the opening that was hot and wet.

"I used to dream only of darkness," he said, watching her intently in the mirror. "Now I dream of you."

Samantha's mouth was too dry for speech. She dreamed about him, too, him coming to her hard and naked and making love to her until she forgot the world.

He lifted her hand to his cheek. "Take it," he whispered. "Please. I won't hurt you this time."

She hated how quickly her hand rose to touch his face. She swallowed, nervous, fearing the bright hot pain that had flashed through her body when she'd drunk his life essence in his apartment.

"Don't be afraid," he said. "*Trust me.*"

It had been too long. Her heart thumped as she pressed her palm to his tattoo, and his life essence spilled quickly through her veins. In the mirror she watched the tips of her breasts peak, her eyes grow heavy with pleasure.

"That's it, love," he said, lips in her hair. "You need me. Let it happen."

With a groan, she surrendered. His hand went to his waistband as she pressed herself to him, and he kicked out of his pants and underwear.

He knelt in front of her, her hand still firmly on his cheek. With gentle fingers, he moved her legs apart, then leaned forward and closed his mouth over her swollen nub.

She gasped, and rocked her head back. He started to lick and suckle, using his teeth and tongue, and she wriggled against him, wanting more and more. His mouth was talented, her skin burning under it as though he branded her.

She'd never talked dirty to a man before, but she heard all kinds of wicked things come out of her mouth—what he made her feel like, what she wanted him to do to her. The half smile on his face told her he heard her, and liked it.

All the while he pleasured her, his life essence seared into her. He filled her with what she'd denied herself, as though she'd been dying of thirst and was at last drinking cool spring water.

Just as ecstasy spiraled through her, he wrenched his mouth away and stood. Her opening was burning and wet and throbbing for him, and she whimpered.

He lifted her in his strong arms and wrapped her legs around his hips, his mouth finding hers. She was so slick and ready for him that when he positioned his tip against her, he slid right in.

She leaned back in his arms, gasping as he filled her, huge and hard. Time seemed to stand still as he held her, arms around her back. His life essence still flowed into her, soothing her hurts as her psyche absorbed it.

Samantha surrendered to the feeling of him stretching her wide, the hot beating of her heart. His fingers bit into her buttocks, and he slid in even farther, filling her with every inch.

"I can't," she moaned. "I can't take you. You're too big."

"Yes, you can." He opened his eyes, which were nearly black, lights flickering inside them. "You can take all of me. You're so strong, my Samantha."

She ached where they joined, her sheath so full and hot that he moved easily, his arousal slick and stiff. She twisted her hips on him, feeling him drive deeper. She wanted it to go on forever.

He moved them to the bed, and she was panting and gasping when he slowly lifted her off him. She cried out, not wanting to lose him, as he deposited her on her hands and knees on the blankets.

She lost contact with his life essence, but it didn't matter, because her skin was sparkling with it. It tingled through her and only got better when he knelt behind her and thrust himself into her.

She dimly hoped the room was soundproof because she began to scream, long, glorious screams of ecstasy. Tain's hands were heavy on her back as he drove into her over and over. She came in an exquisite orgasm that went on and on, and still he rode her, building her back up into another peak.

Samantha wasn't clear how long it went on, because she lost all sense of time and place. After the incredible feeling ground on forever, she found herself breathless and hoarse on the bed, Tain's large hot body on top of hers. She started to cry because it was all over, but Tain wrapped his strong arms around her and held her close.

CHAPTER TWENTY

The next day Samantha resigned her position with the paranormal police. Lieutenant McKay tried to get her to stay on as a consultant, but Samantha declined, explaining that the rival demon clans wouldn't take well to having the Lamiah matriarch hand-in-glove with the police.

Logan better understood, werewolf pack politics sharing similarities with demon clans.

"You're one of the good ones, Samantha," he said to her regretfully as he walked her out. "I never thought I'd give a demon the time of day, but you proved me wrong. Are you sure you want to do this?"

"I need to," Samantha said.

Logan nodded. "I hope you make time for the occasional werewolf visit."

"Always."

Samantha hugged him, wiping tears from her eyes. Logan held her hard. "Take care of yourself," he growled.

Samantha rode back to the Beverly Hills mansion in the matriarch's limousine. The house was still being repaired from the Djowlan attack, workers fixing the security equipment and parts of the house that had been smashed before Tain had raised his protective shield.

Tain had returned to the Malibu house to pack his things and hers and fetch Pickles, while she'd gone downtown. Samantha had been surprised he'd let her go alone, but he'd heavily warded the matriarch's limousine until there were more protective spells on it than on any house in Los Angeles. He'd been there to greet her on her return, Pickles grooming himself happily on the windowsill in her new office.

Tain kissed her with a hint of the heat they'd shared last night, then said he was going to poke around in the basement where he'd found the shrine to the Old One and the portal to a death realm. Samantha was happy to let him. Portals leading to pissed-off demons or an Old One were not what she needed to deal with right now.

Flavia brought Samantha a cup of coffee in the office Samantha had moved to an upstairs room. Samantha sipped it as she continued going through a mountain of files, much of it not computerized, that the last matriarch had left.

Samantha reflected darkly that she'd thought being a police detective required a lot of paperwork, but it was nothing compared to the accumulation of knowledge in the matriarch's offices. The majordomo was a surprising help, though she worked with tight lips and an expression of one hoping to get something painful over with soon.

Much of the information in the files concerned other members of the clan, their backgrounds and expertise and when and if they could be called on to help in times of need. The information went back a thousand years, but Samantha realized that many of the demons mentioned were still around.

There were also files on other clans—bios of their matriarchs, the locations of demon clans throughout the world and their activities. And then there was information on Los Angeles since Los Angeles had existed—who was in power in human society as well as vampire, werewolf, chameleon, and other shifters—the shamans and skinwalkers native to California.

There was enough information to pinpoint exactly who was doing what to whom at any given time, which, Samantha realized, was the point. The matriarch's power was not so much demon strength but knowledge and negotiation, much like being a cop.

She didn't find anything on Mindglow, which was suspicious. Merrick had nothing to lose hinting that the matriarch had supplied it, and she believed him. If the majordomo had known about the drug trafficking, she'd likely gotten rid of the records the night the matriarch died. Samantha said nothing to her now, but she wasn't going to let Ariadne quit before the woman answered some hard questions.

She sipped coffee and read the fat file on Septimus, which offered few surprises. As an Old One, the vampire could afford to be open about his activities, but he was also very diplomatic. He was a good ally to have, but Samantha knew that if he ever turned against them, she'd be in trouble.

She yawned as the majordomo set another stack of files on her desk, thinking that if she stayed awake all night having sex with Tain, she should expect to be tired. Pulling all-night stakeouts with Logan had never wiped her out as much as a night full of sex with Tain, not to mention he'd made her take his life essence again.

The life essence should have given her energy. It had jolted through her last night, filling the emptiness inside her. She'd awakened alone but feeling refreshed.

Now her limbs were heavy and tired, her thoughts straying too often to Tain kissing her swollen lips as he made love to her. That had been the best sex of her life—maybe they could try to top it tonight.

She found herself leaning back in her chair, her body glowing warm with need. "Has Tain come back upstairs yet?" she asked the majordomo, who picked up a file off her desk.

"No," she said with crisp disapproval. "I have made an

appointment for you with the Djowlan matriarch for three o'clock tomorrow. Tea in fine china, I think, in the front reception room."

"Yes, sounds terrific." Samantha stretched, running her fingers through her hair. She loved how it felt against her hands, silken soft, almost erotic. She let it fall against her neck, making a humming noise as it tickled her skin.

"Matriarch?" the majordomo asked, mouth flattening.

"What is the matter with me?" Samantha murmured. "I was fine when I woke up." Sudden worry worked its way through her strange happiness, and she shot a glance at the cup of coffee she'd drained. "Oh gods."

"What?" The majordomo leaned over, her sharp face uglier than ever. "What has happened?"

"Mindglow," Samantha whispered. Then she laughed. "There was Mindglow in the coffee. Merrick was right—this is wonderful stuff."

Ariadne snatched up the coffee cup and sniffed it. "I don't smell anything."

"You can't smell it. But it makes you . . . oh, so compliant."

Ariadne glared at the cup, glared at the closed office door. Her eyes widened in horror. "This is the coffee Flavia brought. I drank it, too."

Samantha laughed, her eyes drifting closed as a pleasant heaviness took over her body. "Well, crap, then we're both screwed." Another wave of contentment swamped her, and through her blurred vision she saw the majordomo put her hand to her head and sit down hard on her office chair. Pickles broke off his grooming and eyed her in concern.

"Find Tain," Samantha whispered, and then her lips wouldn't work anymore.

Tain easily found the hidden door in the mansion's basement he'd discovered before and descended the narrow stone staircase spiraling downward.

The first time he'd descended it, he'd found a shrine set up at the portal to a death realm, erected to pay tribute to an ancient demon called Bahkat. Tain had never met this Bahkat, though Kehksut had talked of him, another Old One of great power.

Tain had destroyed the shrine, smashing the offering bowl and breaking the altar. The portal had opened, demons who guarded Bahkat attacking him. He'd quickly killed the few demons who made it out before he sealed the portal, then traveled downtown to the No More Nightmares building to seal the portals there.

Now everything was back—the altar, the bowl with demon runes for Bahkat on it, the map on the wall that showed the locations of portals throughout the city.

The bowl held a heart, black and shriveled and stinking. Tain covered his mouth to keep from retching and burned the heart away with a short burst of magic.

He'd at first thought the matriarch had set up the shrine, offering Bahkat hearts of demons she didn't like in return for favors from the Old One. But then, the matriarch had died by the same method as the demon prostitutes, and someone in the house had clearly re-erected the shrine this long after the matriarch's death. That someone was asking an Old One for power, and that spelled grave danger for Samantha.

Tain studied the map pinned above the shrine. To anyone unfamiliar with demons, it would look like concentric rings radiating from a central point with cryptic runes around each. The demon script read now that the portals at the No More Nightmares building had been destroyed—"by the Enemy." Tain smiled.

He stopped smiling when he saw another portal had been marked on it. Whether it was new or had been secret before, there was no way to tell, but Tain's blood went cold.

The portal came out in the canyon in the Nevada

desert, high up in the cliff dwellings. Because of the magic drain of the vortex, it would be hard to detect from the desert side and be plenty protected. It also explained the waft of death magic he'd sensed that propelled Ms. Townsend of No More Nightmares across the cliffs—likely someone had opened the portal, and it had sucked her inside.

Tain drew one of his swords. It took death magic to open the way into the death realms, and Tain hummed with life magic. But Tain had also spent seven hundred years in thrall to the most ferocious Old One of them all, and he'd learned to draw on death magic and channel it when he needed to.

He didn't like how easy it was for him to tap the dark magic from both the shrine and the mansion full of demons above him, how painlessly it flowed through him and down the sword.

The sword sliced open the portal to the death realm like a hot knife through butter, and Tain stepped inside.

Logan piled what he'd found on a long table in front of McKay. "It's all here," he said. "Tons of clippings of newspaper headlines, paper, glue, scissors, lists of demons all over Los Angeles—names, addresses, family connections, where they work, what they do on their days off—the FBI couldn't put info like this together."

"And you arrested this Tristan?"

"He's in the cells," Logan said. "He wasn't hard to find, and he seemed plenty proud that he'd sent the threatening letters."

McKay beamed up at him, her half-Sidhe beauty shining. "Please tell me he confessed to the kidnappings and the murders, and he named all his accomplices, and then signed the confession."

"Sorry, boss," Logan said, and McKay gave a resigned sigh. "He insists he didn't do the killings or kidnappings, and he wants his lawyer. But we pretty much got him on the terrorizing letters."

"Oh well, I didn't really think it would be nice and neat."

"But he must know who's doing it," Logan said. "Lawyer or no lawyer, if we can get him to give away his buddies or whoever employed him, we'll be finished."

"He said nothing about the compound in Nevada?"

"No. I'd swear he had no clue what I was talking about when I mentioned it."

"What has the sheriff there told you?"

"Not a damn thing. She said neither she nor her deputies could find anything out of the ordinary, just another canyon that woo-woo people liked to call a vortex. A collection of energies that she thinks is bullshit."

McKay grimaced. "Unfortunately, we need their cooperation if it really is something, or we have to make it a federal case, which I'm not in a hurry to do. On the other hand . . ." She gave Logan a look. "I can't stop you hiking into a canyon in Nevada on your day off."

Logan nodded. "I planned to check it out."

"Not that I know this," McKay said.

"Know what?" Logan grinned.

As he started to turn away, his cell phone vibrated in his pocket. He pulled out the phone and smiled when he saw Samantha's number on the display. He already missed talking to her.

But it wasn't Samantha that shouted at him as soon as he lifted the phone to his ear. "They're gone!" a woman screamed at him.

"What? Who's gone? Who is this?"

"Samantha is gone," she panted. "I'm Flavia, her cousin. Someone put Mindglow in the coffee. When I went into her office, she was gone, she and the majordomo both."

"Slow down a minute," Logan said, his heart pumping hard. "What about Tain? Where is he?"

"I don't know. I can't find him anywhere. There was one of those letters in cutouts left on Samantha's chair." Flavia faltered, crying. "It said 'The Final Sacrifice.'"

Samantha awoke in pitch-dark. Her head pounded and made her sick, not helped by the fact that she lay face-down on something hard, her ankles and wrists tightly bound with what felt like duct tape. She was happy to find she hadn't been gagged, but her mouth was so dry it didn't much matter.

"Damn it," she croaked. "Is this what Mindglow does to you?"

"I hope not," a male voice rumbled. "Or I've been getting ripped off."

"Merrick?" Samantha groaned. "Hell, I'd decided you were innocent of all this."

"I am innocent, sweetheart. I'm lying here trussed up hand and foot, and I have the feeling the next heart in a box will be mine."

Not good. "You can't become your bad demon self and break your way out?" she asked hopefully.

"Oh, gee, I never thought of that. The answer is no, I can't. I've never felt this weak and sick in my life. All I can do is lie here and spout feeble sarcasm."

"If I can find you, do you think you we can get each other untaped?"

"Worth a try. Not that I expect it to do any good. I imagine that if there *was* any way out of this pit, they'd have chained us to the walls."

"Who's they?" she asked.

"Hell if I know. I never saw their faces."

Samantha spent the next few minutes tying to roll in the dark, hearing Merrick doing the same. It took a long time, but eventually she landed on her side and felt the warmth of his suit coat behind her. She groped for his wrists and found the slick tape around them. His fingers connected with the tape on her wrists and started picking at it.

"Demon claws would be handy about now," Samantha muttered.

"Your warrior boyfriend and his big swords would be handy about now, too, even if he did almost cut my head off once. I'll forgive him if he gets me out of here."

"You hit me."

"Pardon?"

"In your club, you hit me," Samantha said. "That's why Tain tried to cut off your head. He didn't do it all the way, because a headless man can't learn a lesson."

"Very, very funny, and anyway, you'd just shoved a gun in my face."

"Making an arrest for possession of Mindglow."

"*Hypothetical* possession of Mindglow. My club has burned to the foundations now so it's a moot point. Funny how my life has gotten so exciting since I met you."

"Pure coincidence," Samantha said.

"Really? I wonder. Ah, I think I might have found an edge to the tape. I've always hated this stuff."

For silent moments, Merrick tugged and pulled at the bonds on Samantha's wrist until she heard a hiss of tape being ripped from tape. After an infuriatingly long time, the tape was loose enough for Samantha to pull it free. She lay still, her aching arms at her sides, wincing as circulation returned to her fingers.

"Will you be returning the favor any time soon?" Merrick asked.

"Give me a second to get the feeling back. It's not like we're going anywhere."

"True."

When Samantha felt well enough to roll to her knees, she groped for Merrick's wrists.

"Once we get out of here," Merrick said as she started

working, "how about we ditch your sword-toting boyfriend and spend a wild weekend in Vegas?"

Samantha snorted. "I don't think so."

"You think the matriarch doesn't fool around with her underlings? The previous one certainly did."

"Really?" she asked in surprise.

"Oh my, yes. When she was younger, especially. She'd host orgies and join right in. She liked sex, with men or women, she didn't care."

Samantha patiently picked at the tape. "She seemed so straitlaced when I met her."

"In her later years she calmed down, but she certainly got a lot out of her system until a couple hundred years ago. She did humans, demons, vampires, shifters—used her position to find the best-looking of the bunch, and sucked down life essences like there was no tomorrow."

"And yet she was so snotty about Nadia. No sympathy whatsoever."

"Ah, but the matriarch didn't sell her services or exchange anything for life essence. She wasn't a prostitute. Stayed home like a good girl and used the power of her rank to get whatever she wanted."

"Maybe that's why she was murdered," Samantha mused.

"Could be. Or it could be that the killer knew you were likely to be the next matriarch and wanted you in power."

Her fingers stilled as she thought of that possibility. "Why?"

"Who knows? Maybe whoever it was wants to control you, like the majordomo controlled the matriarch and planned to control her protégé, Ariel."

"How did you know about that?"

"Everyone knew, my dear, except you. You know, this tape isn't coming off by itself."

Samantha resumed the task. "You're an asshole, Merrick."

"Yes, but a very shrewd one, don't forget that."

"What am I doing here?" Samantha muttered as the tape started to give. "A few weeks ago I wasn't doing anything more difficult than stakeouts of demon clubs. All of a sudden I'm hunting people who cut out demon hearts and becoming matriarch."

"And screwing an Immortal warrior."

She gritted her teeth. "That's none of your business."

"Poor Samantha. You're a good cop, and you'll make a damn good matriarch, but you are so innocent about sex. Tain isn't the kind of man you settle down with."

"Neither are you."

He laughed. "I never claimed to be, but I can make that weekend in Vegas the best of your life."

"Save it." Samantha peeled the tape from his wrists, and he sat up and rubbed them. Samantha worked on the tape around her ankles and after a while, got herself free.

"Now what?" she asked, trying to looking around. It was so dark she could see nothing, not even shapes in the gloom. The air smelled close and dank and more chilled than the September weather should make it. "I think we're underground," she concluded.

"You have amazing powers of deduction, Sam, my love. I know we're underground, but there must be air coming in or we'd be dead by now, or at least very sleepy."

Samantha got shakily to her feet and instantly regretted it. She held her stomach, gasping, until her head stopped spinning.

"I wasn't hard to capture, was I?" she said, angry at herself. "They carried me off without a struggle."

"I struggled," Merrick said. "Until they shot me with a tranquilizer."

"Who?"

"I don't know. Obviously someone crazy. They abducted me as I was leaving the muster."

"In Santa Barbara?"

"No, I have a portal into the Lamiah clan realm around my old club. One minute I'm walking out of my portal, minding my own business, the next, I'm waking up here, sick as a dog. I bet there are snakes down here."

"They hibernate when it's cold," Samantha told him. "I wonder who else they plan to take." Her heart squeezed in fear as she thought of her father, head of the most prominent household in the clan, whose daughter had just become matriarch.

"There might not be snakes down here," Merrick said as he moved around their prison, his coat rustling in the dark. "But there are scorpions. The little buggers are all over the walls."

"You're a big, bad demon, Merrick. Are you afraid of a few insects?"

"Ones that sting? Yes." He turned around, his shoes scraping on rock. "So, what's your great plan, oh my matriarch?"

"Getting out of here?"

"Now, why didn't I think of that? Any ideas how, brilliant one?"

"No," Samantha snapped. She found a wall, smooth and seamless, and felt her way along it. "Just help me look for a way out."

"You know," Merrick said as he joined her, "in movies, when the hero or heroine gets captured, the helpful secondary character dies during the rescue or escape. To give that touch of grief."

"This isn't a movie," Samantha said shortly.

"The question is, whose movie is this? Yours or mine?"

"Merrick." Samantha rested her hands against the wall. "We're both getting out of here, no sacrifices. That's my job, not just to uphold and enforce the law, but to protect."

"Ah, but you're not a police officer anymore, my dear."

"No, but I'm the matriarch, for better or worse. It's my job now to keep the clan from falling apart, which means I protect those in it. At the moment that means you."

"Hmm." Merrick continued to tap on the wall, shuffling next to Samantha. "Then I know what kind of movie this is."

He wouldn't say what he meant by that, and they worked their way around the room in silence.

CHAPTER TWENTY-ONE

The chill of the death realm filmed Tain's skin like sweat. Unlike the marble-pillared chamber Fulton had taken them to for the muster, this vast room had crumbling square columns carved with strange square designs, as though someone mocked the clean lines of the Native American petroglyphs etched into the canyon walls outside.

A demon stood in the middle of it, as sensual and lush as Kehksut in her female form had ever been. He sensed evil in the darkness behind her, and evil so vast it made his stomach churn.

"Who are you?" he asked.

"Haven't you guessed yet?" She slid her hands around Tain's waist and pressed her body along his. "I am the matriarch of the Lamiah clan."

"The matriarch died. I saw her body—what was left of it."

"No, simpleton. She was my majordomo, playing the part I assigned her."

Tain stilled as he digested this information. The woman they'd met as the matriarch and the woman who'd been murdered had definitely been the same. "How long had she been playing this part?"

"Nearly six hundred years. She put on pearls and met with heads of clans while I did as I pleased and went where

I wanted, discovering oh so many things. It was wonderful—having all that power and no one knowing it."

"Then why start calling to the Old One?"

She smiled, the black in her eyes spreading to fill the whites. "I've always preferred the company of Old Ones. They know what it is to have all bow before them."

"In ancient times, maybe," Tain said. "Now they hide in demon realms and don't like to walk the surface of the earth."

"No thanks to you and your Immortal brothers." She backed up and spat, the spittle landing hot on his forearm. "You drove my master underground, and you killed Kehksut, the most beautiful of them all."

"It's what I was made to do," Tain said. "Sort of my job description."

She made a noise of disgust. "You were a demon's slave. You killed your own master. For that, you will be punished."

"You've sacrificed demons of your own clan. The new matriarch is pretty pissed about it."

She laughed, as he'd suspected she would. "The new matriarch has no power. Precisely as I planned. And the Lamiah clan is weak—more interested in buying stocks and shopping on Rodeo Drive than acquiring human slaves. They've been *yuppified*."

"So they deserve death?" Tain asked in a mild voice.

"They deserve to be utterly destroyed," the matriarch said. "And I have found the means to do it."

"Not all the demons killed were Lamiah."

She snorted. "I can't help it if the Townsend woman is too stupid to distinguish one clan from the other. But they were good kills and helped blind the pathetic paranormal police to my true purpose."

"You used Tristan to send the letters for the same reason," Tain said, wanting to keep her talking while he tried to figure out what the Old One was doing.

"Tristan was easy to manipulate, silly little fool. I look forward to ripping his heart out and tasting his blood."

"And Samantha? Why did you want Samantha to become the matriarch?"

"Because of you, of course." She laughed a silky laugh and sauntered to him again. "Did you really think I'd want a half blood to take over the clan? She'll not last past the first challenge to her authority. I told the young fool Tristan that I'd back his girlfriend because I knew damn well that the rest of the clan would balk and beg Samantha to save them from such a fate. Fulton was easy to flatter into putting Samantha forward, and he convinced her she had to become matriarch for the good of the clan."

"He wasn't wrong," Tain said softly.

She ignored him. "But the real reason I chose Samantha in particular was because of you. The Immortal warrior who killed Kehksut would be a wonderful gift to bring to my master."

Tain looked down at her from his height, letting his voice grow cold. "What makes you think I will let you make me your gift?"

"Because Samantha will be the next to die if you don't. You hate demons, but you're addicted to them—why else would you be sniffing at the skirts of that half blood? I know exactly how to make you obey."

Tain said nothing. He knew that his love for Samantha had nothing to do with addiction and everything to do with *her*. Kehksut was dead, the ancient, powerful demon master dissolved into dust. Kehksut had broken Tain with pain and loneliness, despair and madness, and Samantha had slowly but surely pulled him back into the light.

He knew he could best the matriarch, who was a lesser demon, no matter that she'd live a thousand years, but he wasn't so sure about the Old One that waited behind the cloak of darkness. Tain's power was diminished in the death realms, not to mention the magic-draining vortex outside the portal. This could get tricky.

The matriarch's body shimmered and took on the features of Kehksut in his lush, female form. Tain knew it was a glam, but she had down to the last detail what Kehksut had looked like in Tain's eyes.

"He was one of my lovers," the matriarch said in Kehksut's seductive tones. "He told me all about you."

"He was one of my lovers, too." The Old One's voice rolled out of the darkness as he walked slowly toward them. "I have brought you here for *my* vengeance."

Tain held his swords ready, but here they were only so much metal. He could imagine his brother Hunter pointing out, *Yes, but metal with an edge.*

The matriarch smiled, her red mouth curving in delight. "Have I pleased you, master?"

The demon Bahkat chuckled, a chill sound. "You have pleased me well. Enjoy him as you wish."

He waved his hand. Darkness rolled over Tain, and when his vision cleared again, time had passed and things had changed. He'd had been stripped to the waist, his hands chained behind him around a square pillar.

"This is what you're used to, isn't it?" the matriarch purred. She came close to Tain and drew her fingernails lightly down his bare chest. "Kehksut told me all about what you liked and what you craved, and how he did it to you." She pressed her palm flat between his pectorals. "Your heart is racing now. Is it fear? Or anticipation?"

Tain tensed his muscles, but the chains that held him were extra thick and spelled with death magic, and the weight of Bahkat's death magic made him sick and spent.

"A little of both, I think," Bahkat said.

The matriarch reached behind Tain, then showed him a long, hooked knife. "I think I'll enjoy this. Feel free to scream when it hurts."

She touched the point of the knife to Tain's neck, and he closed his eyes, comforting blackness swirling in to coat his brain.

Samantha made a complete circuit of the smooth-walled prison she and Merrick were in without finding so much as a crack in the rock. The walls were natural, not man-made, but the stone was polished by weather and time.

"You see?" Merrick said when she stopped, frustrated. "They knew it didn't matter if we unbound ourselves. There's no way out if you don't have climbing gear or a lot of magic."

"Don't sell me short," Samantha said, irritated. "I'm pretty resourceful—I was trained to be."

"Ah yes, at the police academy, where you were taught how to bring down demons and hungry vamps."

"Exactly."

"Did you learn orienteering? Like figuring out where the hell we are? This doesn't feel like a death realm, but it doesn't feel like the sewers of Los Angeles, either."

"I think we're in the place Tain told me about," Samantha said. "A canyon in Nevada, in the middle of the desert."

"Wonderful. That means if we do manage to get out, we'll be miles from anywhere with no water."

"One thing at a time," Samantha muttered.

"If your boyfriend knows about this place, shouldn't he have rescued you by now?" He rubbed his arms. "It's getting damn cold down here. Even demons can get hypothermia."

"Shh," Samantha said sharply.

"I'm merely pointing out that if we don't die of thirst we will certainly freeze to death—"

"Quiet, I'm trying to listen."

Merrick snapped his mouth shut, and the darkness went silent. Samantha strained for the sound that had come from far above, but she heard only Merrick breathing next to her and the skitter of an insect as it fled across the rock face.

"Not hearing anything," Merrick said softly.

"Wait."

The sound came again, faint and far away, but she knew it because it was familiar. Far off in the desert, a wolf was howling.

Her heart beat faster in relief, adrenaline rushing through her body. "That's Logan."

"How do you know? There's probably another werewolf pack out here somewhere. I know there's one in Las Vegas."

"Because every wolf has a unique cry, and that's Logan's. I worked with him for more than a year—I got to know what he sounds like. It was useful when we had to split up while investigating."

"All right, I'll believe you, but how do you know he's come to help and not bury you?"

She stared at him, trying to see him in the dark. "Why would he do that? I know him—he'll help."

"You only believe you know him. Why do you think he's in Los Angeles playing lone wolf? He was forced out of his pack, that's why."

Samantha stopped. "How the hell do you know that?"

"My dear, when you and your partner busted up my club, I made sure I found out everything I could about each of you. For leverage, of course. A few phone calls to an old friend in St. Paul, and voilà."

She wanted to know more, but she didn't want to hear it from Merrick. "It's none of my business."

"It is entirely your business. As matriarch, you need to learn that any anomaly is potential danger and to keep your eye on it."

She knew he was right, and she knew with a sinking heart that being matriarch gave her the potential of becoming just like Merrick, or Septimus with his network of vampire spies. As a police officer and detective, Samantha had always believed herself to be helpful to those who needed it, one of the good guys.

As matriarch, she had the potential to become vastly powerful, to make her world one where good and evil blurred. That was how Merrick lived his life and Septimus lived his. She also realized that Tain walked that line every day, deciding whether to help and heal or use his power to destroy.

The howl came again, closer. Samantha beat her hands on the wall. "I'll never have the chance to be matriarch if I don't get out of here. Logan!" she shouted.

Merrick winced and covered his ears. "Warn me next time you do that."

"Help me, then. It's your butt on the line, too."

"Good point."

They both began shouting Logan's name over and over again.

Far above her, something moved, rock on rock, and then pebbles trickled down on them. Merrick cursed and jumped aside, but Samantha peered upward. Was it her imagination, or could she see a faint smudge of stars?

What she didn't imagine was the solid *click* of a shotgun being cocked, and then she saw starlight gleam on a very long barrel.

Tain's skin healed rapidly, as it always did, but blood ran in rivulets down his chest and pooled in the waistband of his pants. The matriarch didn't carefully flay him as Kehksut had—she simply cut his flesh over and over again.

The excessive power he'd spent a year and a half getting

used to had drained away, leaving him spent, but he no longer cared. He'd realized in the last few weeks that magical strength meant little unless you knew exactly how and why to wield it. Samantha always thought she had very little power, but she was wrong.

Samantha had an inner strength that could quiet the entire city of Los Angeles. She'd come to a crazed, out-of-control Immortal who was ready to destroy the world to heal his pain, and snapped at him to stop being selfish. Then she'd taken in that same Immortal warrior, beaten and bewildered and terrified he'd slide back into the dark place, and she'd trusted him.

She kept giving and giving of herself, and that giving was far more powerful than Tain was or ever could be. He had to face that she meant more to him than anyone or anything, and if he lost her, he'd have to face the grief. This was sane, human hurt, and the fact that he could feel it was the gift she'd given him.

The matriarch wasn't finished hurting him. After she cut his chest and sides and arms in crisscross patterns, she whipped him, laughing as the lash came down. She knew exactly where to aim each stroke to sting the hardest, how to find the welts of his cuts and open them again.

Bahkat said nothing, neither gloating nor laughing. He just stood with his arms folded over his bare chest and watched. He'd taken the guise of a man, handsome of course, with smooth skin over a well-muscled body. He wore blue jeans only, and his naked arms were covered in tattoos, demon runes that contained spells of power.

"Kehksut's killer," he said in a matter-of-fact voice. "You don't seem up to much now. I wonder why you killed him. You loved him."

"You're wrong," Tain rasped. "I hated him."

"I don't believe you. He let me watch sometimes, did

you know that? How he flayed every bit of skin off you, then fucked you. You used to beg him for it."

Tain forced his mind to go blank, trying not to remember, but the scenes welled up before his eyes. Kehksut smiling much like the matriarch was now, the horrible agony as his skin was peeled from his body, the strange ecstasy of sex as he began to heal. Over and over again, until he couldn't tell pain from joy.

The fact that this demon had watched for entertainment made his rage rise. Tain might be without magical power in this place of death, but he was still a warrior, trained long ago by soldiers of Rome, some of the best fighting men who ever lived.

He twisted his body and jammed his knee at the matriarch. She lost hold of the whip and stumbled back. "You son of a bitch," she shrieked.

Bahkat shoved her aside and stood directly in front of Tain. "You don't understand how to make him pay," he said to the matriarch. "You play at torture. We will make him so mad with pain that he will do anything for us, and the first thing he will do is kill the pretty half demon he's been banging like a lovesick rabbit."

Tain's heart constricted. He wasn't certain what he feared more—the two of them hurting Samantha or being pushed into madness and hurting her himself.

Never, he thought. *She is my salvation and I will never let her be touched. This I vow by all the gods.*

Bahkat picked up one of Tain's swords, the bronze that had been forged nearly two thousand years ago by a master Roman sword maker in faraway Britain. The demon examined the weapon, tracing the Roman runes of protection on it, then tested the blade on his thumb.

"Excellent workmanship," the demon said. He drew the sword back, his muscles rippling, and drove its point straight through Tain's eye.

Tain's scream rang throughout the vast cavern, and hollow echoes overlapped each other on the way back.

"Keep your hands where I can see them," a slow male voice came down to Samantha.

"You can't see anything down here, it's pitch-black," Merrick returned. "Are you with the wolf? If not, I'm not coming anywhere near where you can see me."

There was a little silence as though the man with the gun was working through this. "Just don't move."

"Is Logan with you?" Samantha shouted up. "Logan?"

"He's here," the man said shortly. "He can't answer, being a wolf right now and all. You Samantha? Tain's girl?"

"Yes, that's me," Samantha answered.

"And her friend," Merrick called. "Her best friend."

"Good thing I brought a rope," the man said. "Looks like that's the only way you're going to get out. I'm Ed."

"Hi, Ed," Samantha said in a weak voice.

"You sit tight, we'll get you outta there."

Samantha backed away from the opening as a rope came hurtling down. When she looked up again, she saw a wolf shape outlined against the stars.

"Thanks, partner," she said in relief.

Samantha knew how to tie a rope around a person so he could be pulled out without hurting him or cutting off his breath. She insisted Merrick be hauled up first, and he didn't protest too hard. As his clan leader now, she felt responsible for him.

Merrick got out with some cursing on his part, mostly about his clothes. Then Samantha fixed the rope around herself and let Ed pull her up.

She lay on solid rock and gratefully breathed the fresh, dry air. Stars stretched above her thick and bright, unmarred by pollution or clouds.

Logan bent over her, his lupine nose touching her face.

She used his shoulder to brace herself while she sat up, still feeling the effects of the Mindglow or whatever drug had been slipped in her coffee. Two men stood next to Logan, both with graying hair and stubbled chins. The one with the gun was Ed and he introduced the other as his buddy Mike.

"Is Tain with you?" she asked them.

Ed shouldered his shotgun. "Nope. Logan here calls us and says he's Tain's friend and can we meet him outside this canyon? He said Tain disappeared, and he thought maybe you were together. Then Logan changed into a wolf—that was a sight, I tell you—and he hasn't changed back since we walked into the canyon. He said he might not be able to, because of this vortex thing."

"So we are in the place Tain thought was being used by No More Nightmares."

"Looks like. That's what Logan said, anyway. Tain's not with you, then?"

"No." She felt sick. "Do you have a phone? I can try to call him."

Ed shook his head. "Logan's already tried to find him, and he said some woman at your place says he'd been nabbed, too. Girl was hysterical, he said."

"Flavia?" Samantha felt both worried and a little relieved. She'd liked and trusted Flavia, and she hoped her cousin had nothing to do with this abduction. "Now what?"

"We go up to the cliff dwellings," Ed said. "That's what Logan told me, anyway. He also said to give you this. Mike?"

Mike stepped forward, unbuckled a shoulder holster with Samantha's Glock, and handed it to her. She found it loaded and in working order, and slid it back into the holster.

"Looks like everyone's armed but me," Merrick said, sitting down on a rock. "And I'm here with diminished powers. Anyone mind if I wait in the car? If you brought a car—and if you'll tell me where it is."

"That might be a good idea," Samantha said. Merrick couldn't help them in his weakened state, and it would be the best way to keep the civilians safe. "Ed, can you and Mike show him where your car is? Logan will lead me back once we check this place out."

Mike immediately nodded, but Ed needed to be persuaded. He'd taken to Tain and wanted to help find him, but Samantha managed to convince him to go. Either that or it was Logan blocking his way and snarling. A giant snarling timberwolf a few feet away was an intimidating sight.

Samantha shouldered the ropes and a pack of gear they had brought while she got her bearings. She and Logan stood near the end of a box canyon strewn with enormous boulders and rock slabs, looking as though giants had spilled them out of a cup. Above them cliff dwellings were tucked on a shelf under an overhang, protected from above and below.

Samantha began to climb, going carefully over the loose gravel sliding under her shoes. She was wearing slacks and nice loafers, clothes for an office, not clambering around canyons. Everything would be in shreds by the time she found Tain—if he was even here.

Logan kept up with her, his huge paws finding purchase that Samantha missed. Logan could also leap from ledge to ledge when Samantha couldn't, and gain ground faster that way.

Using the ropes and handholds that Logan dug with his claws, Samantha made it to the bottom tier of the cliff dwellings. She sat down to rest and look around, while Logan rose from his haunches and explored.

The cliff dwellings were crumbling and not well preserved. Starlight flashed on a faded sign that said an archeology team from the University of Nevada was examining it. The sign looked so old it would soon be an archeological treasure itself.

Logan sniffed around the bottom of the cliff dwellings. There were no entrances here—most cliff dwellings were entered from the top, the ladders or ropes leading to the roofs drawn up for defense when needed.

Logan growled softly and reared onto his hind feet, his front feet scrabbling on one corner of the rock wall. Samantha joined him, shining a flashlight from the pack into a dark hole. The faint light showed that the hole led to a deeper cave that was small, dusty, and empty. On the cave wall opposite them was a precisely drawn ring of circles within circles, and runes inscribed all around it.

"I'm willing to bet that symbol isn't Native American," Samantha said, ducking into the cave. "It's demon, but I can't read it." She examined it while Logan pressed his wolf nose to the wall beneath it, sniffing hard.

"Do you think they're behind there somewhere?" she asked.

Logan looked up at her, frustration in his tawny eyes.

"I know—you can't tell me. I feel like I'm in an episode of *Lassie*."

Logan growled, his eyes narrowing.

"Sorry," she said quickly. She pressed her palms to the rock, being careful not to touch the symbol. She sensed the chill behind it, similar to what she'd felt when Fulton had opened the way to the Lamiah's death realm.

"If there's something behind this, I have no clue how to get to it."

Logan sat on his haunches and stared at the wall as though he could dissolve it by gazing at it hard enough. Samantha was tempted to ruffle his fur but knew Logan wasn't the "ruffle the fur" kind of werewolf.

"I'm not demon enough to know how to enter the death

realms," she said. "But we have a demon handy who might."

She looked back down over the cliffs all the way to the canyon floor. She didn't relish the climb down and back up again, but she'd endure a little sweat and sore muscles if it would help her find Tain.

"Be right back," she said to Logan, and began the arduous descent.

"They are coming," the matriarch said.

Tain barely heard her through the pain. His eye socket pounded in agony, blood clotting on his face. Bahkat had taken Tain's eye, held it in his hand, and destroyed it with a single dart of fiery magic.

"All you have to do is kill the half demon," Bahkat said. "Sacrifice her to me, and I will raise you again, help you heal, set you at my right hand. You may have this female as your prize." He gestured at the matriarch in contempt.

The matriarch didn't seem to mind. "Together we will raise demons to their former glory. No more white picket fences in the suburbs."

Tain said nothing. Even through the pain, he felt a grim gladness. Kehksut had never touched Tain's face, wanting it whole and handsome. Now Tain would be scarred forever—even if he healed from this, his face would bear deep lines and creases. He would no longer be the prize Kehksut had sought to keep beautiful.

Tain would survive, kill Bahkat and the matriarch, and be finally free. He smiled, the drying blood on his face cracking.

"You forget," he said softly, "what I am."

"An Immortal," Bahkat scoffed. "That means I can keep you alive while I torture you slowly."

Tain laughed, a grating sound. "I'm a madman," he said. "And you never know what madmen will do."

He enjoyed the looks on their faces before he let his

good eye roll back in his head, reaching for darkness and the incredible strength it gave him.

Merrick collapsed on top of the cliff dwellings, panting and swearing. "I take it back," he gasped. "Your Immortal can have you. You're one sadistic bitch, Samantha. To think, I used to say you were cute."

"Save it, Merrick." Samantha put her hands on her hips. "I wouldn't have dragged you back here, but I can't open the portal to the death realm—I don't know how."

"You need magic to do it," Merrick snapped. "If you haven't noticed, this vortex thing sucks magic out of us."

A shotgun landed on top of the rocks, and a grubby pair of hands followed it. Samantha hurried over and helped Ed the rest of the way up, until he lay on his stomach like Merrick, gasping for breath. Mike followed more slowly, then sat down cross-legged, his shotgun across his lap.

"I'm not the most powerful demon in the world, you know," Merrick said. "Good thing, or your Immortal boyfriend would have killed me by now."

Ed sat up, carefully picked up his shotgun, and aimed it at Merrick. "Why don't you do what the little lady says?"

"Oh, perfect," Merrick muttered. "Samantha and her redneck defender."

He growled a little more but heaved himself to his feet, swearing again while he examined the ruined remains of his suit.

"Today, Merrick," Samantha said. Her heart beat fast with impatience as she removed her gun from her holster.

Merrick eyed it in trepidation, though she didn't point it at him. "I still haven't decided whether I love you or hate you, Sam, my dear. All right, let me take a look."

Merrick dusted off his hands and stepped to the back of the cave. He pressed his palms to the smooth black rock, as Samantha had, closing his eyes to concentrate.

"It's an entrance to a death realm, all right, but I don't

know if I can open the way." He leaned his cheek to the wall, dark brows drawing together in concentration. Disturbed pebbles trickled from his fingertips, and he frowned harder before sighing and stepping back.

"Sorry, sweetheart, this place has drained me. You need a much stronger demon—"

He broke off as the wall in front of him dissolved, and the chill of death magic poured out from the cavernous room beyond. Merrick took a wide-eyed step back, at the same time Tain stepped out, his face and bare torso covered in blackened blood. He twirled his bronze swords in his hands and brought them to rest, crossed, on Merrick's neck.

CHAPTER TWENTY-TWO

Samantha went rigid in shock. Tain was naked to the waist and barefoot, his skin slashed and covered with blood. His handsome face was ruined, a mass of blood over his left eye, his right eye wide and dark with madness. His black tattoo stood out amid the blood, almost glowing. Manacles encircled his wrists, the remains of chains dangling from them.

"Tain."

He wouldn't look at her. The muscles in his forearms bunched as he squeezed the swords into Merrick's neck.

"Tain, no." Samantha grasped his arm, fingers sliding on his blood. Her heart beat hard in hurt and desperation as she saw herself losing him again.

She felt a wash of death magic stronger than any since Kehksut, and a demon stepped out behind Tain—a tall man with an impossibly beautiful face and eyes that were pools of black. She knew immediately he was an Old One, like Kehksut, and his death magic coupled with that of the death realm behind him blanketed the ledge.

The bubble of death magic would lend strength to the demon woman with him, but Samantha and Logan were sitting ducks. The Old One's strength might also help Merrick, but whose side Merrick was on was still up in the air. Merrick was an opportunist, not a hero, and right now his neck was in danger of being severed.

"Start with that one," the demon woman said, pointing at Merrick. "I will give his heart in sacrifice. Then the humans and the werewolf. We'll save dear Samantha for you."

Logan snarled, lips curling back from his fangs, his hackles rising. Ed and Mike stood against the wall, white-faced, guns cradled in their big hands.

The Old One swept his dark gaze over them all. "Tain serves me now," he said.

"Who the hell are you?" Samantha demanded.

"My name is Bahkat, and this is my realm."

"I meant her," Samantha said, using her Glock to gesture to the demon woman. "Are you Ms. Townsend or the majordomo?"

"Neither one, dear. And you call yourself a detective. I am the matriarch of the Lamiah clan."

"The matriarch is dead."

"Funny, that's what your boyfriend said. It was so easy to drug your coffee, pretend to be drugged myself, and transport you here for safekeeping."

"Why?"

The matriarch sighed. "They always want to know why. They can't simply obey." She made a slashing gesture, and suddenly Samantha was on her knees, rock cutting her skin. "Because having you is the best way of enslaving Tain. I want vengeance for my beloved Kehksut. Bahkat will provide that and then take me for his own."

"Merrick was telling me what a demonwhore you were," Samantha said.

"Excuse me," Merrick broke in. "Could you *not* piss them off? See the swords in my neck? The blood?"

"Tain is life magic," Samantha said. "His magic can't work both this vortex and amid so much death magic. You can't use him to do anything right now." She hoped.

"Tain doesn't need his magic to cut off heads," the matriarch said. "He just needs all that gleaming muscle."

"He has plenty of magic," Bahkat interrupted. "He has given himself to me, and I make him strong."

Bahkat stepped to Tain and licked him across the lips. Tain did nothing, only remained rock-steady, his swords crossed over Merrick's throat.

Logan suddenly leapt, a streak of snarling wolf fury, and latched on to the matriarch. She screamed and went down, blood spurting from her throat. Bahkat gestured contemptuously and Logan flew through the air, slamming hard against the rock wall, then skittering to the edge of the cliff. He made no noise, paws scrabbling in a desperate attempt to save himself. Then he went over.

"You bastard," Samantha spat.

Ed cut off her words by bringing up his shotgun and firing straight at Bahkat. Bahkat twitched his fingers again and the gun swung wide. Ed was lifted off his feet and slammed into the cave wall. He groaned as he slid to the floor, the shotgun falling uselessly aside. Mike hurried to him and crouched next to him, looking terrified.

The matriarch laughed and climbed to her feet, but Samantha had her Glock in hand, the familiar weight reassuring. She sighted and fired one, two, three rounds into the demon woman's body, bracing herself for the gun's kick.

Samantha didn't think the bullets would kill her, but they did make her stumble. Samantha ducked into the chilly stone room, caught the woman around the waist, and threw her outside onto the ledge.

The matriarch scrambled to her feet. Her demon glam fell away, and Samantha found herself looking at the grim, lined face of the matriarch's majordomo.

"What the hell?" Samantha asked, bewildered.

"Don't cross me," the woman rasped. "I am your matriarch, and I command you."

Bahkat watched with emotionless dark eyes. "She *was*

your matriarch," he said, his voice chill and dark. "She was a good disciple and lover. Now that I have the Immortal I have no more need of her."

He held out his hand as though reaching for the matriarch, then closed his fist. The matriarch morphed back into the beautiful woman, staring at him with wide eyes. Then she screamed.

Her body began to compress, as though a hidden force crushed it all over. Her cries turned to ones of unbearable anguish. Blood burst from her body, and her screams died to gurgles. After an excruciatingly long time she fell in a broken pile of bones and flesh that dissolved slowly to dust.

Samantha stared at the gently swirling dust, her hand still locked around her gun.

Tain finally moved. He lifted his swords from Merrick and sent the demon flying with a wave of magic that bore the stink of death. Merrick crashed into the wall beside Ed and Mike, blood gushing from the wound on his neck.

Samantha had lost Tain, and she knew it. His good eye was blank, the blue swallowed by black, and he looked at Samantha with no recognition.

She loved him, had always loved him, and knew it was a futile, impossible love. He was an Immortal and half crazy at the best of times. His brothers had healed him and helped kill his enemy, but his mind had been taken long ago.

"Tain," she whispered. "I love you."

Bahkat swung his full attention to Samantha. "That's very sweet," he said. "It really is. She'll make a wonderful slave if she already loves you, Tain."

Samantha knew she had no magic at all, no power to best him, and her bullets would have no effect on him. She figured she could either throw herself over the ledge and try to run for it—if she survived—or stay here and brave it out.

"Why don't you suck him off, my dear?" the demon taunted. "I'd enjoy watching that."

Samantha looked at him in loathing. "Screw you," she said. Then she fired.

The bullets stopped in front of the demon and clinked harmlessly to the floor. Samantha had known shooting him wouldn't work, but it felt good to try. Bahkat flicked his fingers and the gun flew from her hand.

Tain stepped to her. A brush of Bahkat's magic forced her to her knees again, and she looked at the waistband of Tain's jeans, the fabric spattered with blood. The jeans rode low on his hips, revealing smooth skin below his navel, a few red hairs that disappeared under the waistband. He smelled like blood and sweat and death magic, but also of him, the warmth of his skin, the strength of his body.

Tain grabbed her around the wrist and dragged her up to him. "No, my way is better," he grated. "It will hurt more."

Bahkat stepped forward, interested. Tain's fingers clamped down on Samantha's wrist, forcing her hand to open, and he guided her palm to his pentacle tattoo.

"No," Samantha cried. She already felt the enormity of his magic before her skin contacted with the mark. The tattoo seared into her palm, even hotter than it had when he'd overwhelmed her in his bedroom. He poured all his life essence into her, not slowing it, not preparing her, not stopping it from hurting.

The demon in her at first lapped it greedily, and then as the essence continued to gush in, she started to scream. She couldn't take it all at once; it would kill her. She struggled and tried to pull away, but Tain held her remorselessly.

His essence filled her with white-hot heat, stronger even then when Cerridwen had entered her at the battle with Kehksut. Samantha's real self had become entwined with the goddess and she'd felt enormous power, but it hadn't hurt.

This was unbearable pain. She felt every cut of his torture and the horrible agony when Bahkat had cut out his eye. Samantha took all of it, every pore filling with Tain's life essence and his magic. Her skin began to glow, the power of it lighting the dark cavern.

Bahkat snapped his gaze to her, suddenly alert. He flickered and elongated, death magic pouring from him to surround the life essence radiating now from Samantha.

A roar filled the air, the sound of a shotgun, and Tain's hand tore from her. Samantha stared in shock as Tain fell to the ground, his chest bloody. She whirled to see Mike standing behind her with terrified eyes, the acrid smoke from his shotgun curling around his face.

She felt Tain's grip, slick with blood on her wrist. He pressed the hilt of one of his swords into her hand. "Do it," he whispered. "You're strong enough."

Pain burned her, her head pounding so hard she was sure it would burst. Her vision was all wrong, too—white lines crisscrossed in front of her, bright points that stabbed around the cavern. Bahkat rose in front of her, huge and dark, his body morphing to his demon form.

Tain's hand closed hard around her wrist. "Help me," he whispered.

Like a veil lifting away, she understood. He'd infused her with the life essence he'd trained her to absorb, life essence that had been too powerful for an Old One like Kehksut to take. She pulsed with his power; his sword was in her hands as Bahkat rose before her, ready to crush her like he'd crushed the matriarch.

"I love you, too," Tain murmured. His grasp went slack.

Samantha roared. It was a terrible sound, ringing through the cavern and out into the night. Samantha the demon and Samantha the woman both screamed in rage, and Samantha the matriarch came in for good measure. She raised the sword, full of Tain's beautiful magic that he'd drained himself to give her, and brought it down on Bahkat.

Bahkat slid out of her reach, throwing a wave of death magic at her. It flowed around Samantha without touching her. She came at him again, sword out, laughing wildly.

"Do you know what happened when Tain suffered all those years?" she shouted at Bahkat. "He got strong—stronger than all the Immortals put together. Did you really think you could defeat *him?* He's got more power than any life-magic creature in the world, and your friend Kehksut made him that way." She stalked him as she talked, terrible strength rushing through her. "Wouldn't he love it if he knew the being he'd created was the one who killed you?"

Bahkat came at her, claws out, his body huge and horrible. Samantha drew back Tain's well-balanced bronze sword, made a quick feint, then came in up and under the demon's grasp to stab him in the neck.

Bahkat screamed. Black blood poured over her hands and he shuddered violently, but she kept the sword there, holding it hard. Tain's white-hot magic poured out of her and up the blade. Bahkat writhed and twisted, trying to get away. Samantha stayed steady, even though her arms felt like they were being wrenched from the sockets. She knew it took a long time to kill demons.

A second sword joined the first, this one driving deep into Bahkat's chest. Tain stood beside Samantha, his body shining with sweat, muscles contracting as he held his sword in rock-steady hands.

Bahkat thrashed in panic, and death magic exploded over them, crushing the air from Samantha's lungs. She lost her hold on the sword and went down, hearing the blade clank faintly on the rock next to her.

Tain landed on her, shielding her, while Bahkat's death throes went on and on. The cavern began to crumble, the death realm losing its patron, the pillars falling one by one into dust.

Tain dragged her up and over his shoulder as he hurtled out into the canyon. Ed, Mike, and Merrick were gone, having sensibly run when Samantha fought Bahkat.

Tain half jumped, half fell over the ledge with Samantha,

and they landed on a slab of boulder below, where Ed, Mike, and Merrick already cowered.

The cave above them exploded, the ancient cliff dwelling going up with it. Bahkat's screams grew faint, then faded. Boulders and pebbles rained down around them, plinking on the rocks like hail. Tain shielded Samantha with his body, wincing as the rain of gravel cut into his skin. The others huddled together, Merrick growling and cursing as the fall of rock went on and on.

It ended abruptly, the pebbles pattering out around them, and then all was silence. The wave of chill from the death realm dispersed into the vortex, and white dust spiraled into the light of the coming dawn.

What was left of the Old One Bahkat slithered through the portal he'd opened back into the matriarch's mansion. He'd fled here in blind panic, drawn to the life essences of the group of humans repairing things in the basement. He could drain them and regain strength, then lie in wait to capture Tain and his half-demon bitch. He'd kill the woman and seal the Immortal in a hell dimension. If Tain thought he'd been tortured before, it was nothing to what Bahkat would do to him there.

He crawled out, gasping and half dead, to the secret room below the house. He heard a strange whooshing sound and raised his head to see a sword with flames running up and down it in front of his face.

A green-eyed, tawny-haired man held its hilt, and behind him stood a lion, snarling softly. Beyond the beast was a man glowing with life magic, a snake in his hands that was just changing to a sword.

"Look, Adrian," the green-eyed one said. "Tain sent us an Old One. This should be fun."

"He's dying," Adrian said shortly. "Put him out of his misery."

The flaming blade swung around and swiftly and cleanly

struck Bahkat's head from his body. The last thing the demon heard was the Immortal saying, "Oh, that was too easy. Tain got to have all the fun. . . ."

Tain hobbled out of the canyon with his arm around Samantha. His magic was spent, the vortex and the battle sucking him dry, the white-hot essence he'd used to fill Samantha gone. Samantha stumbled along beside him, insisting on helping him walk, although it was clear she could barely walk herself.

On her other side was Mike, the only one of them unhurt, who silently guided her with a hand under her arm. Ed and Merrick limped behind them, Merrick uncharacteristically quiet.

They found Logan partway up the canyon, as far as he'd dragged himself before collapsing. He lay still, his fur matted with blood, a hind leg twisted and broken. He looked up with dull eyes when Samantha fell to her knees next to him.

"Mike, can you carry him?" Tain asked. "I can heal him, but we have to get out of this damn canyon first."

Mike nodded, handed Ed his shotgun, and leaned down and hoisted Logan up and over his shoulders. Logan yelped in pain and squeezed his eyes shut.

"Was that really the matriarch?" Samantha asked Tain as they moved on again. He liked her arm tight around his waist, liked her warmth against his skin.

"She said she switched places with her majordomo years ago," Tain answered, his voice like broken rock. "There aren't many demons left who remember what she looked like."

Merrick laughed hoarsely. "Little vixen. I told you she was a wild woman in her youth."

"Well, she'd dead now," Samantha said. "Just when I thought demons could be civilized, one tries to sacrifice me to an Old One."

Merrick chuckled again. "When demons age, they get a little crazy. They start hankering for the old days, which are gone forever. Live with the times, I always say."

Samantha slanted Tain a glance, not smiling. He'd hurt her deeply, he knew that, and there was a chance she wouldn't forgive him for it.

As the canyon walls receded, he felt his magic return slowly but surely. After a while they emerged onto flat ground, a chill morning breeze wafting across the desert floor. He saw the glint of rising sun glance off the roof of Ed's pickup a long way off, and a motorcycle parked next to it.

Once they reached the washerboard road Tain told Ed to lay Logan on the ground. The wolf shimmered and became Logan, lying naked and gray faced, covered with blood. He moaned, eyelids fluttering.

Samantha knelt next to him, smoothing his hair. "Merrick, give me your jacket."

Tain expected the demon to argue, but Merrick slid his suit coat from his shoulders and handed it to her. "Two thousand dollars at Armani on Rodeo. They know my size."

"Shut up, Merrick." Samantha spread the coat over Logan's body, and Tain crouched next to him.

Magic flowed to his fingertips, tingling and hurting, his own body wanting to heal first. He ignored the pain and sank his magic into Logan, taking comfort in the familiar ritual of healing. He saw Logan's injuries as a jumbled mass of torn muscle and bone, and he let himself straighten the threads one by one.

Logan groaned again, moving as his body healed. Then he gasped, normal color flooding his face. "Hell," he said, looking around weakly. "Looks like I missed all the fun."

Tain next turned to Ed, healing the man's abrasions and broken ribs. Next Merrick, whose neck became whole and smooth under his touch.

"You could sell that skill," Merrick said, fingering his throat. "Maybe when I open my club again, we could work a deal."

Tain ignored him. He turned to Samantha and cupped her face in his hands, letting magic flow into her. He healed what he'd damaged with his flood of life essence, letting the feel of her soothe his own battered soul. He sensed her growing aroused, as he always did when he healed her, and his body responded even through the pain.

But she said nothing, did nothing, and when he finished, she turned away from him without meeting his gaze.

CHAPTER TWENTY-THREE

Cleanup from a case was always a bitch, no less now that Samantha was not on the force. As the Lamiah matriarch, she had to find a way to explain that the majordomo and the real matriarch had switched places long ago, that the matriarch had called forth a nasty Old One and that she'd met her death at his hands.

Logan helped her tell the story to McKay, who listened with a tense look on her face. "And that portal is closed?" she asked. "No more demon Old One coming out to wreak havoc in my city?"

"Tain's brothers sealed it up," Samantha said. "And made sure Bahkat was dead. I don't think there will be any more Old Ones from the matriarch's house."

"Thank goodness for that. Good work, Detective." She stopped. "I mean matriarch."

Samantha smiled, always enjoying hard-won praise from her boss.

Tristan was arrested for sending the threatening letters for the matriarch, charged with being an accessory to murder. He expected Samantha to provide him with a top lawyer and get him off, and was shocked when his own cousin refused and also refused to supply the bail money. He needed to pay for knowingly causing the deaths of girls who'd done nothing to deserve being turned into a demon sacrifice. Samantha deemed it harsh but necessary.

Ms. Townsend of No More Nightmares was brought in as well, and coldly confessed to kidnapping young demon prostitutes for the matriarch. She showed no remorse at their deaths, not even at the death of her assistant, Melanie. Once Ms. Townsend realized that Melanie had demon blood, she had to die, she said, in order to cleanse the organization. It was easy to make Melanie's death look like the others.

Samantha worried that a human jury might sympathize with Ms. Townsend's antidemon point of view, but Logan said that Nadia had agreed to testify and tell the world what she and her sister had suffered. He was confident that he and Nadia could persuade a courtroom to see Ms. Townsend's cruelty.

Samantha was exhausted and happy to return home, even though Flavia had become very maternal. The young woman felt terrible that her coffee had been drugged and Samantha taken while she obliviously worked in the next room. Samantha reassured Flavia that it hadn't been her fault, but Flavia still went about looking guilt-stricken.

Samantha hadn't seen Tain in days, because he'd retreated to the Malibu house with Hunter and Adrian to heal. She longed to be there with him, but Tain insisted she remain at the matriarch's mansion to smooth things over, reassure the clan, and keep the peace.

She was surprised the clan still wanted her, now that she knew the matriarch hadn't really backed her. But Fulton said that Samantha had been chosen legitimately—put forth by a head of household and voted on at the muster—and the clan accepted her as leader. Samantha helping to kill the Old One that the matriarch had summoned only raised her in their estimation.

As for Merrick . . . Samantha learned that by demon law, he was due compensation for his ordeal, because he'd suffered as a result of helping Samantha in her role as the clan matriarch. Samantha made a generous donation to the rebuilding of his club, giving the money directly to the builders instead of Merrick himself. She even bought him a new suit from the shop on Rodeo. So all was well at the matriarch's mansion, but Samantha went to bed alone every night, her heart aching.

At the Malibu house, Tain waited for his Immortal body to close his wounds and return his strength. He realized that the eye Bahkat had cut out would not regenerate, though the socket scarred over, the flesh itself healing. Leda assured him he looked like a dashing pirate with the eye patch and his swords, but he found no humor in it.

He waited until his strength returned in full, then made his way down to the matriarch's mansion. Using spells to make himself unobtrusive, he slipped past Samantha and Flavia in the hall and waited for Samantha to return to her office.

When she entered the room and closed the door with a sigh, he kept the spells in place and let himself look at her. She wore a classic suit, the skirt revealing her long, slender legs. She lifted her hair from her neck, letting it drop slowly back. Her hair shimmered as she shook it out, and his arousal swiftly rose. He couldn't resist coming up behind her and sliding his hands over her shoulders, kissing the silken fall of her hair.

Samantha cried out and turned, eyes wide. "Tain," she gasped. "Jeez, don't do that."

The door swung open and Flavia hurried in. "I heard you call out. What's wrong?"

Samantha stepped out of Tain's grasp, flushing. "I'm fine. Tain startled me, is all."

Flavia fixed Tain a cold stare worthy of the old matriarch. "You didn't make an appointment."

"That's all right," Samantha said quickly. "I'll cut him some slack. This time."

Flavia frowned once more, then stalked out, closing the door behind her.

Samantha softly touched Tain's cheek below the eye-patch. "Are you all right?"

I am now, Tain wanted to answer.

She swallowed. "You look . . ."

"Like a pirate?"

"I was going to say normal. Human."

"Do you like me more human?"

"Yes."

His heart hammered with relief. He'd half expected her to recoil from him, to stare in horror at the mass of scars that covered the left side of his face. He'd welcomed the scars because Kehksut would have hated them, but he didn't want Samantha to hate them, too.

"I came to tell you something," he said.

"And that is?" she asked warily.

He wished she didn't look so delectable in those clothes. He wanted to lick her legs all the way up to the delight in between them.

"I'm going to Ravenscroft," he said.

Her eyes flickered. "I thought you might be."

"Did you?" he asked in some surprise.

"That's what Immortals do, isn't it? You come when someone summons you, kill the bad guys, and go back home. Problem solved, you move on. The Old One is dead—you're heading out."

"No . . ."

"But you just said you were going to Ravenscroft." Her dark eyes glittered as she moved back to her desk, as though wanting to slide back into her role as matriarch.

He couldn't do this. Adrian had told him to come here and tell her flat out what he was going to do. Hunter had advised Tain to charm Samantha first, flirt with her until she was melting and compliant.

His brothers were assholes. Tain didn't have the commanding air of Adrian or the flirtation skills of Hunter. When he wanted a woman, he smiled at her, and that did the trick. Or at least it used to. Now his face was a hideous mess, and no woman was going to respond to his smiles anymore.

"Damn it." He was across the room and had Samantha bent backward over the desk before she could speak or push him away. Pens and file folders and little ornaments clattered to the floor, and then he was kissing her, cradling her head in his hands. She tasted so good, like cinnamon, and coffee and heat.

"Did you mean it?" he whispered against her lips.

"Mean what?"

"When you told me you loved me, when you tried to save me from Bahkat. Or was it just to get me to stop?"

"I thought I was going to die," Samantha said softly. "I thought I'd better say it in case."

"Say it again now, when we're safe. I need you to. I need something I can believe in."

Her eyes filled. "I love you, Tain."

The words floated around him like fires on a frozen night. "I love you, too," he breathed. "Gods, Samantha, I love you so much."

She smiled, hope and wonder in her eyes. "I'm glad."

"You were right when you said you saved my ass back in Seattle. For too long I wandered around thinking the last thing I needed was you in my life, when you were exactly what I needed. You could have healed me a long time ago."

"Why are you going to Ravenscroft?" she murmured. "If you need me so much?"

"I want to take you with me."

Samantha stopped, her dark gaze searching. "I thought you had to be Immortal to go there, or get special permission from the goddesses."

"You have Cerridwen's permission, and you'll be with me."

"But I'm matriarch now. I can't just leave."

"If you want, the goddesses can arrange it so we arrive back here minutes after we leave."

Her brows drew together. "If you're coming right back, I don't understand why you want me to go with you."

"For a good reason." He kissed her again, long and slow this time, while he opened the portal that would take them to Ravenscroft.

The matriarch's office faded and dissolved to be replaced by a warm grassy slope down to quietly flowing water and bright sunshine. He broke the kiss, and she smiled and touched his hair before she realized what had happened.

Samantha sat up with a start. Tain stretched out next to her, enjoying the lovely view of her legs as she gaped at the meadow, the river, and the long, almost Japanese-looking building at the edge of the woods.

"Where the hell are we?"

"Ravenscroft."

She gulped a few breaths of the sweet air. "What did you mean, for a good reason?"

He gentled his voice. "When I filled you with my life essence in the cave, I hurt you. You are incredibly strong, but so am I. I healed you, but here I can make sure you heal all the way."

She sank back down beside him, sunshine on her beautiful face. "It did hurt. But it worked, and I'd do it again in a heartbeat."

"I hope to the gods you never have to." He stroked his fingers through her hair. "I'll make sure you never have to."

"How long can I stay?" she asked, gazing at the beauty around them. "It's amazing. I'm so used to city sprawl for miles and miles and barren desert beyond. I get excited when I see a tree."

"You can stay as long as you want."

"I have to go back, though," she said wistfully. "They've accepted me for whatever reason, and they're my clan, my family."

"I think it's a good decision." He kissed her hair. "I'm going back with you, as personal bodyguard to the matriarch. I don't intend to lose you again."

"Personal bodyguard?" She stared.

"To you and to the clan. You also need my life essence, and this way I can be on hand to give it to you."

"I see." She sounded uncertain.

He laid her on the grass and rolled onto her. Then he did what he'd been longing to, pushed back the lapels of her blazer and unbuttoned her blouse with gentle fingers. "Will you have me, Samantha?"

She traced the pentacle on his cheek. "As a lover? Yes."

"As a mate, my wife. Forever. The goddesses will make you immortal to be with me, if you can stand the thought."

She gaped. "Of course I can stand the thought, but you're saying you want to stay with me forever, too."

"That's usually what it means." He smiled, feeling his scars pull under the eye patch. "I love you, Samantha, and I need you. Be my life mate."

She stared at him while his heart thudded with the enormity of what he'd asked her.

"My father once told me I'd live a long time anyway," she said faintly.

"Does that mean yes?"

She smiled, her eyes beautiful and full of love. "Yes."

Relief flooded him. "Thank you." He brushed her hair back with his thumbs, palms on her cheeks. "Will you say it again, that you love me? I need to hear it."

She laughed. "I do love you," she said fervently. "I've loved you since I saw you in Seattle. I love the way you smile like the smile is only for me. I love your deep voice and your accent and your body wet in the shower. And I especially love your gorgeous, tight ass." Her smile shook as she squeezed his backside. "I love how you worried about a young demon prostitute hurt and alone in an alley. And I love how you feed my cat junk he's not supposed to eat when you think I'm not looking."

"You noticed that?"

"You're not very subtle."

"It's not my strong point." He wanted to get on with the business of screwing her right now, but he dug into his tight pocket and pulled out a box.

Samantha's eyes widened. She took the box with trembling fingers and opened it to reveal a large white diamond ring winking from a blue velvet cushion.

She gasped and almost dropped it. "Good Lord, Tain."

"Hunter had to take me to the bank and explain it all again. But he didn't mind—this time it was for a good cause."

Samantha worked the ring out of the box. "Put it on me."

Tain slid it on her fourth finger, then lifted her hand to press a kiss to her fingers. "If it doesn't fit, the jeweler said it could be resized."

"It's fine." Tears filled her eyes. "It's fine."

He lifted her hand to lay it against his tattoo, liking that she took him in, but gently. She wasn't afraid anymore.

"I used to love so easily," he said. "Teach me how to love again, Samantha."

"I'm not sure I can."

"If anyone can, it's you."

"I'll try," she said. "I promise, I'll try."

"Good." He kissed her damp cheek. "Now, no more tears, love." He parted the blouse and kissed the tops of her breasts, then slid his hand around to unhook her bra.

"I want to celebrate gaining my freedom again. Do you know how I want to celebrate?"

She kissed his throat. "I'm getting an idea."

He pressed his forehead to hers, his smile wicked. "I want to make love to you. I want to do it hard and fast, and then I want to do it loving and slow. I want to be inside you, and I want to savor you, and I want you to feel so good you never want me to stop."

"That sounds nice," she said shakily. "If this is what giving me a huge diamond does to you, you can give me one every day."

"Hunter wouldn't like that—he'd have to take me to the bank all the time."

"He can get over it."

Tain laughed. "I want to give you my world, Samantha. Because you gave mine back to me."

She twined her hands behind the nape of his neck. "Maybe you can thank me now."

His eyes went dark. "Oh, I intend to."

"You know," she murmured as he slid his hands under her skirt, finding the heat of her. "I wouldn't mind if you cut your hair again. I kind of like it short."

EPILOGUE

Days later Tain sat on a verdant field overlooking a lake, its blue like a reflection of his own eyes. A pavilion up the hill floated with pink and white streamers, and laughter echoed from his brothers—Adrian, Kalen, Darius, and Hunter, and their wives and children, Logan, and other friends they'd made last year during the fight against Kehksut, here with the blessing of the goddesses.

Samantha was in the pavilion with them, being passed around for hugs in her sleek white gown. They'd all come to see them wed, and not an hour ago, Tain had slid a plain wedding band on Samantha's finger—a human custom, but one he liked.

Now he lounged in the grass, and his mother, the goddess Cerridwen, stood near him, her red hair swirling in the wind. No longer insubstantial as when she visited him on the earth, she was tall and stately, wrapped in gossamer that glittered like starlight.

"This is your ending," she said. "No more suffering, Tain."

Tain glanced at the pavilion, feeling the soft scrape of the eye patch he was still getting used to. "She's worth it."

"Nothing is worth what happened to you. I grieved every time you hurt, my love, knowing I'd forced you to that."

Tain looked at her, but the pain and anger had gone from his heart. "It was necessary, or Kehksut never would have been defeated. I understand that now. The only thing I would have changed was you and the goddesses not giving me a choice. I would rather have made the decision myself to submit to Kehksut's torture, walked that path of my own choosing."

Cerridwen raised her fine brows. "If the choice had been yours, if you'd known you had to sacrifice yourself, would you have done it?"

Tain replied readily. "Yes. To keep my brothers from having to go through that, I would have."

"How could you, knowing what would happen to you?"

He stood up and took her hands, looking into the swirling silver blue of her eyes. "Because even if I hadn't survived, they did. That's all that really matters, isn't it?"

Her lips parted as though she were seeing and understanding her own son for the first time. "Tain . . ."

"It is no longer worth talking about," he said, his Celtic lilt pronounced. He smiled as he heard renewed laughter floating from the pavilion, Samantha's voice raised above it all. "This is my redemption, isn't it? To be a guardian of her and her people—the same kind of beings as the one that tortured me for centuries, and now I protect them." His heart warmed as he laughed. "I like the irony."

Cerridwen started to speak, but at the same time, Samantha came out of the pavilion and called down to him. "Tain, come up here and explain to your brother that I am *not* carrying a piece under my dress."

Tain waved to her, wondering which brother was teasing the life out of her this time. He softly kissed his mother on the cheek, wiped away the tear that had leaked from the corner of her eye, and turned and sprinted up the hill to Samantha's laughter and her waiting arms.